Nothing works . . .
MAG

Coming soon in hardcover

MAGIC TIME: ANGELFIRE
by Marc Scott Zicree and Maya Kaathryn Bohnhoff

MAGIC TIME

MARC SCOTT ZICREE
— & —
BARBARA HAMBLY

An Imprint of HarperCollinsPublishers

EOS
An Imprint of HarperCollins*Publishers*
10 East 53rd Street
New York, New York 10022-5299

Copyright © 2001 by Paper Route, Inc.
Excerpt from *Magic Time*: *Angelfire* copyright © 2002 by Paper Route, Inc.
ISBN: 0-06-105957-9
www.eosbooks.com

First Eos paperback printing: November 2002
First Eos hardcover printing: December 2001

Eos Trademark Reg. U.S. Pat. Off. and in Other Countries,
Marca Registrada, Hecho en U.S.A.
HarperCollins® is a trademark of HarperCollins Publishers Inc.

Printed in the U.S.A.

10 9 8 7 6 5 4 3 2 1

For Elaine, of course

Acknowledgments

MAGIC TIME has been a long time coming, and there have been many midwives and cheering sections along the way. First and foremost in making this happen was Elaine Zicree, who created the original two-hour pilot with Marc and then jumped in with total devotion throughout the writing of the novel whenever we strayed and found ourselves without a compass in the dark woods.

Early encouragement was vital and was provided by Brian Henson, Michael Robins, Les Landau, Halle Stamford, John Copeland, Bruce Sallan, Jim Botko and many others.

Our editor Diana Gill was a gift and a guiding light to us, as was Jennifer Brehl, also of HarperCollins. Special thanks to you both.

Steve Saffel, Shelly Shapiro, John Douglas and John Silbersack all provided invaluable assistance in creating this book. Chris Lotts, agent extraordinaire, was our guardian angel and got us out of numerous tight spots. Our dear friend and lawyer Susan Schaefer battled the remaining forces of darkness.

Vital research into ballet, physics, mountaineering, law, New York geography and other arcane disciplines was provided by Tiekka Schofield, Steve Zicree, Christina Zicree, Mitch Suskin, Alan Favish, Robert Ramos, Nick Roberts, Javier Grillo-Marxuach, Jesse Olsen, Robert McWilliams, Kerry Ashcroft, Ira Brady Rubin, Paul Witcover, Joe Rodriguez and the staff at the Beverly Hills library.

Those who read the manuscript, gave notes, suggestions, invaluable assistance, wise counsel, artwork or general good fellowship include Aaron Iverson, Michael Reaves, Mark Lungo, Winston Engle, Floyd Kephart, Beth Sullivan, Merlin M. Stone, Derrell Abbey, Peter Roth, Alice Hautvast, Armin Shimerman, Leonard and Alice Maltin, Brannon Braga, Rockne S. O'Bannon, J. Michael Straczynski, Kathryn Drennan, Kim Stanley Robinson, Orson Scott Card, Frank Darabont, Ray Bradbury, Theo Siegel, Bobby Israel, Joe Haldeman, Harry Turtledove, Kevin Anderson, Mel Raab, Pat Pedersen, Dave Mino, Dennis Etchison, Norman Corwin, Lisa Jackowiak, Judy and Bob Browning, Donato Giancola, Sheila Stone, Chris Lacson and John Vourlis.

Iain McCaig, designer of Darth Maul and Queen Amidala, has long been a torch bearer for this project. His magnificent concept art for *Magic Time* has inspired us and filled us with gratitude, as have his powerful ideas and good, pure self.

Maya Kaathryn Bohnhoff provided endless inventive details and backstory that added richness and texture to this book, and Robert Charles Wilson added his own special magic. Laurie Perry did the copyediting to make sure we wouldn't look like wolf-children raised in the wild.

Heartfelt thanks to all of you, for the help on this book and for the countless favors and blessings you bring to our lives.

To those we've inadvertently neglected to mention, our apologies. Drop us a line at *sliderutv@aol.com* and we'll rectify the situation.

"Our whole life is regeneration."

Vaslav Nijinsky

MAGIC TIME

PROLOGUE

Resonance

Cal Griffin dreamed chaos.

Darkness, blacker than anything he'd ever conceived of, center-of-the-earth black, no-universe-yet-made black, dead-a-thousand-years black. Voices shouting, so clear that he could distinguish not only male and female, but each separate human soul screaming. He could tell rage from pain from terror. In the darkness of the dream he could hear his own blood hammering in his ears.

The sound of blows, metal on metal—metal tearing flesh. The stink of blood and of earth soaked with blood, of smoke and of charring.

He stood at the black heart of the tumult as they cried their anguish, their despair, demanded and pleaded—

That he act.

The darkness flailed him, whipped his breath away. He should rise to their call, should help them.

But how?

A shard of light split the blackness like a razor stroke. It glanced across an immense, irregular mound that might have been the bodies of men or merely the things they had used.

An object gleamed atop it, brilliant in the light, and Cal saw that it was a sword. Not opulent and bejeweled but plain, the leather of the hilt palm-worn. This weapon had seen use.

He reached out, seized it. The grooves and creases worn into the hilt by sweaty usage fit his palm. It was his palm that had made them.

As he drew it out, the light danced liquid on the blade, flashed a Rorschach of half-glimpsed living things in its silver-gold. Around him, the cries rose and blended to a single keening of raw need and pain. Holding the sword high, he knew what he must do.

But still he hesitated.

The cry was drowned in thunder that rent the universe apart.

Cal jolted awake.

The silence was shocking after the clamor of his dream. He felt a terrible regret; guilt washed over him. Though the summer night was warm, his body was clammy and he trembled.

He looked at his hand, *hoping* that . . .

That what?

He sat up in bed, rubbing his forehead. The dream fell back into the invisible river of night and was gone.

A murmur sounded from the other room, and he thought, *Tina.* The Marvin the Martian clock she had given him on his birthday last August displayed the time. 3:10 A.M.

Cal threw back the covers, made his way to the door by the yellow glare of street lamps, the bulbs ringing the sign on Patel's Grocery, the Amoco billboard on the corner. After three years the ambient light of New York nights still impressed him. So different from Hurley, where all illumination—even the mercury vapors along Main Street—was damped by midnight and the only glow came from the cold, indifferent stars.

Barefoot, he padded across the hall to Tina's room, not so much concerned that his sister might be locked in a dream as disturbing as his—the nightmares about their mother, the endless, heightened replays of the loss of her, had long since eased back—but mainly to assure himself of the reality of this moment, this place, to jettison the last vestige of dream and accusation.

He slid open Tina's door, stood watching her. Asleep, curled on her side, her dark hair an anonymous tangle on the pillow, she looked fragile, younger than twelve, and troubled even in repose. Her textbooks—so many!—lay stacked and open about the bed, mingled with myriad dog-eared copies of *Dance Magazine* and programs from the Met, Kennedy Center, Lincoln Center, their covers ablaze with pas de deux and arabesque. The posters and clipped pictures taped to her walls gazed down, guardian angels. Anna Pavlova, Fonteyn, Makarova, Buffy. . . .

On the nightstand, he could discern the framed snapshot Luz Herrera had taken of her at the March recital (the one he'd missed thanks to the damn Iverson deposition). In toe shoes and tights, Tina hung weightless in midleap, enraptured. Beside it lay open a volume from Nijinsky's diaries. Nijinsky had slid hopelessly into madness, Tina had explained intently to Cal the other day as he'd gulped granola and coffee, and no one could save him. But he had been glorious in his moment.

Under Cal's bare toes, the shag carpet was worn to the weave: New York wasn't the place to live if you didn't have major money; it was a miracle they'd scored this barely affordable sublet as it was. But Hurley, Minnesota, wouldn't have provided them with even minor money. Not the kind of money that a good college demands, or private schooling, or the array of courses in technique and variations, character and pointe that Tina had been inhaling whole at the School of American Ballet. The kind of money that will buy chances for the future.

And he'd had to make a choice.

We're doing all right here.

Even if midnight in Manhattan meant the time he usually bid the night-shift paralegals adieu after pulling his fifteen hours of research, memoranda, and every other dreary chore that might fall to a third-year associate drub.

Even if, more often than not, Tina was asleep when he arrived home, and he'd hear of her life secondhand from nannies and hired companions and neighbors charmed and wheedled into keeping an eye on her. They would sing her praises, in awe of some new movement she had mastered, some miracle of expressiveness. Or they'd cluck in disapproval at how she pushed herself endlessly for greater perfection, as though she were pursued.

Her teachers at the SAB had spoken of her promise, that college might not be the path for her, but rather a future with one of the preeminent companies, perhaps their own New York City Ballet. Time would tell, and chance. But there were occasions when she seemed to glow with discipline and joy.

Glorious in her moment.

But, lately, he had learned from her watchers that she had withdrawn, vanishing into herself, into her drive to forge something pure and keen. It worried him, left him with a pang of culpability. And yet . . .

They had put that gray town with its gray people behind them, its derelict factory and sky that stretched forever and went nowhere. To have remained there and seen the light in her eyes die, have her old at twenty-five, working at the poultry plant. . . .

No. Whatever it cost him, no matter how he might have to compress himself to a tight core or sheathe himself in steel, because at Stern, Ledding and Bowen you did what you were bid and never, ever said no. . . .

He would keep the machine going.

Tina gave a soft moan of protest, turned in her sleep. Stilling his thoughts, Cal backed out, eased the door shut.

Turning, he caught a flash of his tense face in the large practice mirror in the living room, saw the unsettling resemblance to the father who had abandoned them so long ago. In the night-washed hallway, he looked forty rather than twenty-seven. And felt it.

He returned to bed, willed himself to drowsiness. The paperwork on the Schenk suit had to be filed by noon. He put the dream of the sword away from him, as he'd put aside other dreams in the past.

What would I do with a weapon?

His palm remembered the smooth worn leather that fit so perfectly, the way he remembered the smell of rain sweeping across the Minnesota prairies, the summer nights on the front porch listening through the open window to their mother's voice, all melody, lulling Tina to sleep.

Just before he fell into sleep, he thought: it wasn't a weapon.

It was a soul.

As he slipped over the edge into dreams again he understood whose.

1

Last and First Day

ONE

NEAR GROUND ZERO—BEFORE DAWN

Randy Waller had heard all the stories about Medicine Water Creek.

It was a load of bullshit, as far as he was concerned, dreamed up by some drunk sad-sack Sioux to make up for the fact that they'd got their asses kicked by the U.S. cavalry and hadn't done a damn thing since.

He drew rein at the top of the draw and lit up, scanning the fence line in the glimmer of first light. Fuckin' miles to cover today, and they were saying it'd rain tonight. That meant Black Hat Coulee would flood by tomorrow and he'd have to dick around with wire and fence posts and nails while standing knee-deep in muddy water, oh joy. Better to get up early and get the whole thing done today and talk the foreman into letting him take the truck into town tonight.

Under him his horse snorted, rubbed a cheek on the fence post. Randy nudged the animal forward along the fence, down into the long dip of bottomlands where the clay-colored stream appeared and disappeared among twisted hummocks of rock. The city kids who came up here in vans, with their long hair and their two-hundred-dollar hiking boots, to "find communion with the Earth"—

which, by all Randy could see, meant smoking pot and humping in the bushes—talked about old Indian legends and ate up stories about how horses would spook here in broad daylight and even the coyotes would avoid the place at night.

Of course, they didn't come here at night. Randy blew a double line of smoke from his nostrils and scouted the matte-blue shadows among the rocks, the waving thickness of grass that grew everywhere on the level ground. *They were all over at the ranch house, raiding the garbage.*

And as for "Medicine Water"—which Randy's dad had called Piss Creek . . .

It was low this time of year, midsummer. A glistening thread among the dark convolutions of eroded rock, course echoed by the pale bands that marked the water-chewed banks. Mounds and turrets of gray-black lava lifted like sleeping buffalo from the deep grass. This time of the morning, before the prairie winds started up, the place was deathly silent, filled with the hard cold of the night.

That'd wear off goddam soon. Randy stubbed the butt on his boot heel, flicked it away into the creek. "Let's go, Bean," he said and twitched the reins. Whole place'd get hot as the inside of a cow by . . .

Movement caught his eye. The horse flung up its head, reared and veered sidelong, and Randy hauled savagely on the bit. *Just a goddam cow for Chrissake.*

Only it wasn't a cow, he saw, when he'd dragged his mount around to a trembling standstill. It was a buffalo.

Shit, where'd that come from? Government herd taking up good grassland over in the national fuckin' monument . . .

The smell of blood hit him, metallic and savage. He saw it glisten darkly on the buffalo's muzzle, long strings dripping down to the grass. The buffalo shook its horns warningly and lowed; Randy saw the nasty glitter of a small black eye. More blood smell; ol' Bean jittered and tried to run again, and Randy saw there was another buffalo close to the first. *Holy shit, must be them ritual mutilators like in the newspaper!* Because this one, a huge curly-haired bull, had been hacked savagely, the whole hump cut off its back, raw meat gleaming where the skin had been pulled back.

Like the old buffalo hunters used to do, he thought suddenly, *the ones the city kids talk about—the ones that killed a hundred animals for their tongues or humps or hides and left the rest to rot.*

The world all around him seemed suddenly to breathe.

Where the hell the buffalo came from Randy couldn't imagine. Hell, he'd looked down this way not ten minutes ago from the top of the draw, and there hadn't been so much as a chipmunk, let alone six—ten—twelve—full-grown buffalo. And why hadn't he smelled the blood?

It stank to Christ now. In the thin gloom of the place he shouldn't have been able to see, but he could. Some of them had had their humps torn away, others, it seemed, only their tongues. Something came around the corner of a rock pinnacle, and Randy screamed, for this buffalo had been skinned, meat gleaming naked and pearly and rubied with dots and runnels of oozing blood—it worked its jaws, ruminatively chewing, and it looked at Randy with deep-set black eyes.

Bean reared, fighting the brutal drag of the bit, humped his back and fishtailed, throwing Randy to the ground. Randy cursed, scrambled to his feet, made a futile snatch at the reins as the horse pelted wildly away, and the buffalo—*how the fuck many of them WERE there?*—let it pass.

Bloodied mouths. Bloodied fur. The hot smell of them, like thunder in the ground. A glimmer of blue lightning crept half-seen among the rocks before sinking into the dust. The earth quivered, and voices seemed to cry out—chants, maybe—endlessly far away.

Randy screamed again and ran for the nearest hummock of rock. But something tore at his leg, what felt like huge broken tusks ripping through the leather of his boot, and looking down he saw the white bones of an old skeleton rising up through the grass and the earth. Ribs snapped shut on his leg like the bony fingers of a giant hand. He wrenched his leg free and stumbled two more feet, and then another skeleton speared through the topsoil, ribs closing around his ankle again. The ground shook a second time and there was a sound, and he looked up to see them—hundreds of them now, robbed of humps and tongues and skins—all lower their heads and charge.

THE SOURCE—BEFORE DAWN

"Dr. Wishart?"

A fast staccato at the office door, though he'd turned out the light. Opening his eyes, Fred Wishart saw the red gleam of the clock—4:58. For a moment he couldn't remember whether it was morning or evening. He was tired, tired to his bones.

"Dr. Wishart?" Whoever was in the hall—it sounded like Yeoh, one of the assistants in the particle-trace lab—tried the doorknob.

Wishart was glad he'd locked it. A day, a night, however long it had been, calculating and recalibrating the accelerators, trying to pin down, once and for all, the mathematical model for resonance alignment so it wouldn't set up a feedback loop. . . . He took off his thick black-framed glasses, closed his eyes again, shutting out the dim shapes of the monitors all around him. Hating them. Hating this place. Hating even the screen savers that played across their square flat faces now: peaceful scenes. The paradise beauty of the Allegheny Mountains in high summer. Two Sisters Rock with a day moon standing above it in an opal sky. The old shaft-head buildings on Green Mountain, robed in shaggy honeysuckle and ivy, deep grass covering the ruin man's greediness had left. Bob had taken that picture and had been tickled when Fred had scanned it and made a screen saver of it, to remember home by.

Home.

Home and the family he loved.

The home he had fled.

He was so tired. They were all tired, he knew, exhausted. Everybody on the project had been working sixteen- and twenty-hour days for weeks. He'd locked the door and turned out his light when he'd made the fourth error in his input—not good. He wondered if the others would be sensible enough to steal a little downtime as well. His hand twitched toward the nearest of the regiment of white foam coffee cups that littered the hollow square of his workspace, among the keyboards and printouts. But he gave it up. The stuff would be dead cold, and there wasn't a soul in the place, from Dr. Sanrio down to the humblest clerk or security officer, who could get decent coffee out of those godless little machines.

Yet they had to have something to show the Senate committee if there was a hearing. And Sanrio seemed to think that new woman with the cleaning crew had been asking an awful lot of questions, though her clearances seemed okay. But spies or no spies, if they continued to push this way, they'd only make more errors.

And errors were something they could not afford.

Knocking.

Go away.

A rattle of the doorknob.

I'm asleep. I'm dead. I've decided to work at home today.

"Dr. Wishart? Are you in there?"

No.

"Dr. Wishart, there's been a leak."

TWO

OUTSIDE KANSAS CITY—DAYBREAK

Tickets.

I.D.

Rental car papers—the proper rental car papers. She'd used, and abandoned, at least three vehicles between Pierre and Kansas City.

Jerri Bilmer's hands shook as she sorted the pink and yellow forms for the red Prizm she'd be driving back to the airport. She told herself to get a grip and tucked the papers concerning the blue Cherokee she'd driven in from Pierre to Omaha, the red Ford pickup that had taken her from Omaha to the outskirts of K.C., and that sorry old rent-a-wreck Chevy she'd had in Pierre itself into a manilla envelope addressed to Selena Martin at a P.O. box in East Falls Church, Virginia. The real Selena Martin had died of SIDS in 1974, and Bilmer had kept the alias—and the birth certificate—as one of the "cold" ones in her private repertoire: a just-in-case identity and rented drop box that, as far as she could tell, nobody knew about. A lot of people in the service had such identities.

She crossed to the window of the motel room, moved aside the rope of garlic hanging half-hidden by the drapes and angled her head to see into the courtyard without opening the blinds. Still cinder dark, iron dark. The street lamps in the parking lot showed curtained windows all around, shut-in stillness, silence, anonymity. Bilmer hadn't had much sleep last night, partly because of the smell of the garlic—she'd kept dreaming she was in an Italian restaurant. *Like a vampire movie*, she thought. *If only it were that simple*.

She had no idea if garlic was supposed to work against things other than vampires. It hung on both sides of the windows, knotted carefully on strings with a variety of seemingly random objects: old keys (she'd read legends that said iron was supposed to help), forks bought from a local antiques shop and warranted to be sterling silver, aconite and wild roses. Glass shards sparkled on the dresser, the carpet, in the bathroom, because she had carefully broken every mirror and anything that could serve as a mirror. She had no idea what the management of the Crystal Suite Inn was going to say when the maids reported what they found in the room.

Not that it mattered. The woman whose name was on the register didn't exist, either.

No one was in the parking lot that she could see.

Not that *that* meant anything.

Was Kansas City far enough away? Had driving rather than flying this far helped? Did it matter?

Crazy people do this, she thought, turning away from the window. She remembered the "psychological observation" at St. Elizabeth's Hospital, required of all service members. Getting to know the look of the crazies, the way their eyes moved and how the muscles of their faces differed subtly from the faces of the sane. The ones who'd come to the White House gate, who'd push through the crowds at any speech; the ones she and her colleagues would have to go check on every couple of months, sometimes in their homes but mostly at St. Elizabeth's.

The ones who wore tinfoil or collanders on their heads to keep the CIA from broadcasting voices into their brains.

Did they hang garlic and iron and wild roses on their curtains before they could sleep at night?

It was not knowing that scared her most. Not knowing what to expect, not having a plan to deal with it. How could she make a plan when she didn't know when, or in what form, or from what direction the attack might come?

A minimum of packing. Carry-on, never check-through. Jeans, hiking boots, underwear, a brush. She'd long ago ditched the T-shirts and overalls she'd worn doing maintenance, emptying trash and keeping dust out of underground rooms, had cut her hair and darkened it back toward its normal hue after bleaching it trashy blonde for the job. Bilmer fell gratefully back on routine. She dressed carefully, avoiding both the formality that screamed SECRET SERVICE and the jeans-and-flannel slobbiness that might get her pulled for a security check. A vaguely dowdy leggings-and-top set, Nikes, a big black purse. The Browning Hi-Power she'd picked up a couple of years ago at a gun-show in Texas would be trash-canned in the airport parking lot. It made her nervous to be without one, for the flight, but the chance of getting caught at the airport because of it scared her worse.

These were definitely not people you wanted to mess around with.

She had no idea what she'd say to President McKay when she saw him.

How the hell could she talk about the things she'd heard and seen?

She moved carefully so as not to step on the enormous circle she'd drawn with Magic Marker on the carpet around the room's perimeter. Plugged in the cheap hot-glue gun she'd bought in Omaha yesterday, glanced at the clock.

Just four. The motel lay close enough to the K.C. airport that she could get there easily but far enough away that it wasn't a specifically "airport" motel. The Houston–D.C. flight came in at five-thirty, took off again at six. How soon was too soon to be in the airport itself?

Her heart was pounding. *Come on, kid*! she told herself. *You got through Tehran and you got through St. Petersburg.*

But in Tehran and St. Pete you knew what to expect. You had some idea of what would be coming at you.

We don't know how far Sanrio's gotten, Stuart McKay had said, that afternoon last month beside the fountain in the White House Rose Garden. There'd been some kind of little fête going on, put on by Mrs. McKay for the uptown rich ladies as a fund-raiser, and the music was just loud enough to confuse a directional mike. McKay had signed the other members of the White House detail to keep their distance, and seeing him talking to one of their own, they had.

Not far enough to show results to a Senate committee and ask for regular funding, the President had gone on. *Not far enough to convince any of the Joint Chiefs that they should have regular military backing—thank God.*

Thank God indeed. Bilmer shivered at the recollection of things she'd seen—or thought she'd seen—in back corridors or at the bottom of those underground stairways at that installation in the Black Hills. Remembered rumors she'd picked up in small towns and badlands bars concerning creatures half-glimpsed in twilight, sounds heard on the wind or objects seen among the eroded rocks or floating in summer-dwindled streams.

We don't know what they've done so far. And we don't know what they CAN do. Literally. At all.

Stu, thought Bilmer, tucking two film disks and a sheaf of onionskin-thin notes behind the lining of her purse, *you don't know the half of it*. She'd considered taking a microdot camera and all the rest of that rig but had abandoned the idea and relied on handwritten notes instead. Would film develop or come out blank?

She didn't know.

Could they have traced her somehow along the backroads and half-deserted highways down the Missouri valley?

She didn't know.

She laced up her sneakers, pulled the baggy red sequinned top over her head. *Wear what you're wearing today when you come back*, McKay had said. *In case someone has to meet you, they'll know what to look for.*

They'll know what to look for. The very thought made Bilmer antsy, as did the idea that McKay knew she'd be coming in on the 9:20 from Houston, whichever day she came. She was already a week later than they'd planned. And every day multiplied the things that could go wrong.

Nothing will go wrong. She hot-glued the lining back into her purse, replaced the contents: compact, three lipsticks (being careful to use both powder and lipstick on her face), two checkbooks, notebook, a double handful of crumpled ATM slips and grocery receipts from towns that matched her current set of I.D., four pens, a bottle of ibuprofen, three little plastic-wrapped sanitary napkins and a package of tissues. Anything to make shadows on an x-ray and obscure the disks and the papers in the lining. If they tried to stop her at the airport, what shape would the attack take?

She didn't know.

All her life she had known or tried to know. Tried to be prepared, to be ready. Caches of weapons, food, money, identities, plane tickets. Bank accounts in other cities under other names. Long before she'd entered the service she'd planned for contingencies, never telling everyone everything, never saying where she'd been. Was that what scared her so about the Source? The wholeness of it, the uncontrollable nature of the threat?

Everything was possible. And there was nothing she could do to keep herself safe.

There has to be something, she told herself firmly. *I just don't have a handle on it yet.*

Keep your head and you'll be fine.

She unplugged the glue gun, wrapped it and its packaging in a newspaper, made sure there were no stray spots of glue anywhere. That could go in a trash-bin in the ladies room at the airport. *Tickets? I.D.? Rental papers? DO NOT DISTURB sign to hang on the door when she left?*

She checked them again, compulsively.

She realized she was afraid to go out of the room.

All the rules had changed. All the things she lived by were obsolete.

And worse to come, she thought, if she didn't get back to McKay with this proof. If they—he—didn't stop these people while they could still be stopped.

If they could be stopped.

She checked the parking lot one more time, took a deep breath. It was time to go.

NEW YORK—6:45 A.M. EDT

When he thought back on it, Cal Griffin was glad Luz Herrera's four-year-old cut his foot on a piece of glass, so she stayed home that morning. But at the time, all it brought was the frenzy of one thing too many heaped upon far too much.

"No, no, senora," he said into the phone, fumbling through his laborious Spanish, "*esta . . . esta* okay. Okay? *De nada.*"

She thanked him, promising to be there at two, to escort Tina from summer school at St. Augustine to the SAB's afternoon and evening dance classes, then home again. Cal pushed away the question of where the *pequeño* Herrera was stashed on a normal day, and Cal returned home at ten or eleven to find Luz and Tina hunkered before the TV, his sister glancing up from a bent-double stretch, expectant and pleased.

I'm not worth that kind of welcome, his guilt scolded him. But it was one of the few moments in his current life that gave him any worth at all.

He turned from hanging up to see Tina in her leotard and tights, leaning against the kitchen door. She had been up since four, doing her homework, in order to keep the rest of the day and evening clear for her obsession, her bliss.

"Sorry, kiddo," he said. "Looks like I'm your chaperon today. How quick can you get your act together, so we can get you to nun central?"

She groaned. She could get there and back alone, *en avant et en arriere*, no problem. I mean, come on, why did he and Luz keep insisting she was some kind of *infant*?

"Not a chance," Cal answered, his thoughts flashing on all the assholes, muggers, and perverts lurking in this city of wonder and infinite possibility.

He knew he could put her in a cab and send her safely on her way; that this was the sensible choice. But he rebelled, chiding himself for the many absences, the shortfalls. He would walk her there himself, the young lawyer on the rise who rarely, if ever, mentioned her existence in the professional sphere. He'd punch in the time with her today, even though he couldn't tomorrow or the next day or the next.

Tina shot him a scowl. But beneath her mock displeasure, he sensed her relief.

"Can I get us some coffee?" Without waiting for a reply, she headed for the counter. So light and fluid. Mom had been thin like that, fine-boned and graceful. Her legacy to Cal had been fair hair and deep-set hazel eyes. From their father, Cal inherited nothing. Tina had the man's coloring and precious little else, even memories. Cal's own recollections were fading fast, and just as well. In the years between Cal's birth and Tina's, he had been a hazy, inconsistent presence, an occasional and unwelcome guest.

"You know, NYCB's dancing 'Afternoon of a Faun' in October. Reuben Almeida's gonna be guest artist from the Royal." Tina was pouring coffee, adding a dollop of 2 percent milk to her own while he punched in the number for Stern, Ledding and Bowen to tell the voice-mail he'd be late. "If you wanted, you and me and Luz could, well . . ." She spoke casually but he heard the wistfulness in her voice, saw the longing in the quick glance she gave him.

He nodded, noncommital. It was absurd to make promises. Even now, his mind was dancing a frantic reel to make up the time, to reimpress on his unforgiving superiors his dedication. Through the earpiece, a canned voice intoned a litany of options. Impatiently, Cal punched buttons as it led him down its maddening labyrinth.

With a start, he realized Tina was still talking. He hadn't heard a word. *I'm not even here when I'm here.* He was a ghost in his own life.

The beep on the voice-mail sounded just as the doorbell rang. In one of those horribly elongated moments, Cal saw Tina dart across the living room, past the practice mirror and the folded-back carpet to the door. He cried a warning, was in the room seconds behind her but too late, she'd whipped off chain and deadbolt and burglar bar.

A huge shape bulked in the open doorway, blocking the dim yellow lights from the hall.

"Listen, I'm sorry," a phlegmy voice gabbled, "I know what time it is, Mr. Griffin, but I been up all night, that meeting today, I—your daughter?"

Irwin Schenk. Cal recognized the gray-stubbled basset face, the rumpled black suit. Four greasy strands were combed carefully over a shiny scalp.

Tina had fallen back, shy. Cal stepped protectively between her and the door. "Sister." Cal took a deep breath. How had Schenk found where he lived? "It's okay," he said to Tina. "He's a client. Why don't you go get dressed?" She melted into the shadows of the hall.

"Look, I shouldn't be here." Schenk ran a flabby hand over his face.

Damn right you shouldn't, Cal thought hotly, invaded. "It's all right." He heard his voice glide silkenly into lawyer mode. He gestured Schenk toward the one good chair, a recliner that had only one tear (hidden by the wall) and no wobble. As Schenk settled heavily into it, Cal stepped back into the kitchen, switched off the phone and poured out a third cup of coffee.

"So," Cal handed Schenk the steaming cup. "You're concerned about the meeting this afternoon."

"I can't sue my own nephew," Schenk said desperately. "He's all I got."

Cal barely listened, studying the blossom of veins on Schenk's nose and cheeks, the watery, scared eyes. As so often when in this guise, Cal felt curiously outside himself, observing the cunning machinations of a stranger. "Mr. Schenk, when we spoke, you said—"

"I was hurt. My brother left him the business for a good reason. I'm a fool!"

"Getting cold feet in these big suits—" Cal's voice was a scalpel, precise, calming. He glanced beyond Schenk and stopped.

Tina stood in the hall watching, barefoot. Her eyes were wide, fixed on him with an expression of pained surprise, as if seeing him newly minted and counterfeit; they held pity and accusation.

Shame burned in Cal. His sister drew her pride and conviction, he knew, not just from the purity, the perfection for which she herself strove, but from her certainty that he held himself to the same standard.

He followed her gaze as it shifted to Schenk. Like a camera twisting into focus, he suddenly saw the anguish on the old man's face, the need and fear and fatalism. Images of the dream flooded back: the sword and those who had cried their need to no avail.

Schenk was staring at him, waiting. Trying to regain balance. Cal ventured. "In these big suits, that's not unusual. Only—"

"My nephew wasn't gonna freeze me out! But my friends, then your boss, they all said, 'Idiot! Big money! More.' " He sighed, wretched. "Would I really win . . . ?"

There it was, the straight line, just waiting for him. Cal looked to his sister, but she would not meet his eyes. Rage flared in him. Schenk's gaze was locked on him, pleading.

Slowly, with deliberation, Cal shook his head.

"I knew it," Schenk said. "The will's sound, right?"

Cal shook his head again.

"Then who—?"

Cal was silent, and his night-shrouded reflection reared

up. Only the image now was not his father but Ely Stern, senior partner, gazing back with cool certainty. Cal's belly grew cold.

"We do. Your lawyers. This kind of law suit, we get the candy store."

"How do I get outta this?" Before Cal could respond, Schenk rose, closing on him. "I can't face that table full of suits, that boss of yours, with his eyes like stones. I'll fold; I know myself. What do I do?"

With his eyes like stones. "Don't go. I'll draft a letter, you fax it, that ends it."

"But I signed stuff. Your boss said penalties, something. . . ." Schenk was in panic now. "I *signed.*"

Cal fetched his briefcase, propped on the rocker—long minus its runners—his mother had bought the day he was born. He opened the case, found the contracts. He paused and felt, without turning to see, his sister's eyes upon him. He tore the sheaf of papers in two. The sound reminded him of a guillotine.

Schenk drew a vast handkerchief from a pocket, mopped his face. Pumping Cal's hand, he gushed words of gratitude and departed.

Cal stepped to the window and opened it. A wind from the west, like a hot breath, stirred his hair.

If he hadn't come here, Cal thought, *if he hadn't come and forced his way in, I'd have sat at that big conference table and let the machine shred him, and I wouldn't have said a word.*

An arm slipped around his waist, and he looked down to see his sister there, gazing with nervous admiration.

"How much trouble are you in?"

He smiled reassuringly and felt only dread.

He had no armor now, no sword.

And Stern would be waiting.

WASHINGTON D.C.—6:54 A.M. EDT

One more mile. The hill was steep, but he'd done it before.
Sweat crawled out from under the terry cloth band around
Stuart McKay's head and down unshaven cheeks. He could
feel the faint persistent tug of the old shrapnel wounds in leg
and thigh as he drove hard against the pedals. Not much pain
today, more like a reminder of an unforgettable afternoon at
Dak Kon, like initials carved into a tree: *Charlie was here*.

The steepening hill, breath coming harder: *I really have
to do this more often.*

And on the page in front of him, propped on the handlebars:

". . . a 2 percent increase on import tariffs of electronics
will offset cost increases of General Motors and Microsoft,
enabling a balance to be maintained. Mr. Sugiyama has ap-
proved this conditionally, with the stipulation that a cap be
put on increases over the next five years. . . ."

A drop of sweat fell on the page. The green line on the
readout before him, half obscured by the typed precis,
dipped as his pedaling slowed, and a small, tinny female
voice admonished, "Your heart rate has fallen below opti-
mum level, Mr. McKay."

With an inner sigh McKay cranked harder. *I'm the President of the United States,* he thought. *In two hours I'm
going to sign an agreement with Japan that will affect the
economy of the entire electronics and automotive industries,
and I'm being told to get my fat ass in gear by a microchip.*

*Would Sugiyama go for it if I suggested a rider adding a
25 percent import tariff on all electronics devices with
snippy little voices?*

The stationary bike achieved the crest of its imaginary
hill and the pressure against the pedals slacked. McKay
straightened his body—*a little paunchy,* he thought, *but not
bad for a fifty-seven-year-old who had a close encounter
with a fragmentation grenade in his youth*—and dropped his
hand to touch the phone clipped to the waistband of his

shorts. Throughout his workout he'd been listening for its ring, but he automatically glanced at the light that would have signaled that a call had come in, in case he'd been too preoccupied (*With THAT report?*) to hear it.

It was dark. *Damn.*

Damn, damn, damn.

Bilmer should have called by this time.

Something clutched, tight and cold, behind his sternum.

Checked in. Said everything was all right. Said there's going to be a delay. Said SOMETHING.

She was a week overdue already.

And now he was going to have to shower and shave and get ready to meet the Japanese, and if Bilmer's call hadn't come in by then, it might make for an extremely awkward conversation when it did. He had no idea what she'd tell him—nor any notion of what or how desperate her circumstances would be. He grinned a little at the mental picture of himself and Sugiyama, an elderly gentleman of enormous dignity, in the Oval Office, surrounded by secretaries and ministers. The President or, worse, the Japanese Trade Liaison picks up his pen to sign . . . *oh, 'scuse me a minute, I have to take this call.*

He glanced across the white-tiled basement gym, where his aide Ron Guthrie puffed stoically on a recumbent set to one notch above "coast," and Secret Service Agent Larry Shango—one of the few who could keep up with McKay on an actual road ride—peddled in his usual ebony silence, a refrigerator in a sweat suit.

Guthrie? wondered McKay, touching the phone again.

But who was to say Guthrie wasn't in on it?

Someone close to him was.

Someone was lying. Someone was covering up. His mind ticked off the men who'd been with him in his Senate years, and down the campaign trail; he felt as he'd felt in the jungles, surrounded by a wall of greenery that could conceal anything.

And responsible for everyone. Responsible for their lives.

His glance again caught Shango. It amused McKay a little, that the man would be that invisible.

Yet that very invisibility, that very quality of being utterly withdrawn from even service politics, added to McKay's sense that this was a man who could be trusted. If he'd known him longer. . . .

But he hadn't. McKay wondered if he'd known anyone long enough.

Impatient, McKay stepped from the cycle prematurely. He took the private elevator back to the third floor. Officer Shango loomed discreetly behind, then positioned himself outside the residence as McKay went in. Jan, whom McKay had left curled in a sleepy little lump in bed, was now in the Yellow Sitting Room, wrapped in her bathrobe at the cherrywood breakfast table by the curved windows that overlooked the south lawn. Early morning light made soft chaos of her short, graying blond curls, and she had on her glasses, something she never allowed the Press to see on the grounds that they made her look like an owl, which they did. Coffee perfumed the air. She, too, was perusing the printout of her itinerary for the day, though a carefully printed letter from their son—plus Polaroids of him and his cousins at Jan's brother's place in Maine—lay nearby. A treat, McKay guessed, if she was good and read the itinerary first. She looked up at once as he closed the door and asked, "Did you get your call?"

She'd noticed. Of course, he reflected ruefully, the way he'd been nursing that phone for the past twenty-four hours, she'd have to have been blind not to notice.

He poured himself coffee and set the phone on the table. Bilmer had mentioned laconically that its number was one of her own, an account taken a month ago with somebody else's name, not an NSA secured line; this needed to be outside the loop.

"Not yet. Jan, listen." He pulled up a chair, and Jimmy, the First Dog as the papers liked to call the big shepherd, moved ten inches from lying next to Jan's chair to lying next to his. Jan pushed a plate of English muffins at McKay.

"You remember Agent Bilmer." He touched the phone lightly with the backs of his fingers.

"Jerri?" Jan smiled. "Of course. I talked to her again at the fund-raiser last month, which of course was a little awkward, since I know I'm not supposed to ask her what she's been doing since the campaign. Teaching, I think she said, though goodness knows what the actual story is."

McKay remembered a dozen nights or a hundred, on the campaign trail, when Jan would come out with some astonishing piece of information about load-vs.-weight ratios of semiautomatic weapons or what Richard Nixon's Secret Service detail had called him in the duty room, courtesy of Jerri Bilmer. One night Bilmer had showed Jan how to conceal a weapon in a bikini. That had been some demo.

McKay drew a deep breath. "She's going to call sometime this morning—I hope she's going to call," he revised. "I don't have time to explain to you what's going on, partly because I don't know. Who's in on it, who can be trusted . . ."

Jan, who'd started to hand him the letter from Ricky, set it down again, and he saw the shift in her eyes as she processed what he'd said. "The CIA? Or people like Steve and Nina?" She named two of the White House aides who'd been with them longest. "Who's in on what?"

McKay thought about the small fragments of facts, the odd discrepancies in reports from the supposedly routine project that had caused him to meet with Bilmer in the Rose Garden.

At length he said, "I don't know. Bilmer is trying to find out for me. She was supposed to call a week ago."

"I see." Jan nudged her coffee cup out of the way of her elbow. "Sort of."

"And if her call comes in, I can't take it during the meeting with Sugiyama."

A small, amused crease tucked into the corner of Jan McKay's mouth. "But you figure I can say, 'Oh, excuse me, girls.' " She went into her Gracie Allen voice and fluttered her hands. And then, sobering, "What do I say?"

"Tell her I said that she can trust you. Do whatever she says, make whatever arrangements she asks for, to get her and her information here as fast as possible without being seen. And notify me the second I'm out of that damn meeting."

Jan was silent for a time, toying with the edge of the Polaroid. Dense tall pines, blue sky, a joyous nine-year-old boy and two small girls at the lake's rim with Secret Service Agent Minsky hovering behind. Early sunlight sparkled on the coffee things; it was so quiet McKay could hear the roar of the mowers out on the lawn. Among the gilt porcelain cups and bright orange day-lilies the small gray telephone stood up like a stubby tower.

"It's that bad?"

He sighed. "It could be. And it could be nothing. I'm pretty sure now that every report I've received about the Source Project has been a carefully fabricated lie, but I don't know who's doing the fabrication. Or at what level. Or why. I hope I'll find out when she gets here."

"And after that?"

McKay shook his head. Dismissals, maybe. A shakeup in the Pentagon. Maybe a scandal, at best. At worst . . .

He shivered despite the summer warmth and forced a smile. "That's another thing I don't know." He picked up his son's letter and headed for the dressing room to make himself ready for whatever the day would bring.

THREE

At the velvety, experimental touch on her cheek, Wilma Hanson opened her eyes. Paws tucked up neatly under him, Sebastian was sitting on her chest.

She sighed. "Good morning, Sebastian."

She had long suspected the big cinder-gray tom of watching for the first movement of her eyelids. Most mornings, her first awareness—even before the whistle went off at the mine on the other side of town—was of Sebastian's hefty weight walking up the length of her body and settling himself on her chest, and then, if she didn't respond, putting out a paw and tapping her nose. *Breakfast?*

The purring in her ear informed her that Dinah had returned to being a hat, sleeping on the pillow just above Wilma's head. And that soft little rumble at her right hip would be Imp. "I suppose it could be worse," she said aloud and made a move to turn over. Sebastian climbed down, offended, and leaped gracefully off the bed, followed immediately by Rhubarb, Anastasia, Eleanor of Aquitaine, Mortimer and Spartacus. "I could have St. Bernards." She put on her bathrobe and padded to the kitchen, trailed by the rest of the gang: O'Malley, Isabella, Theodora, Clinton, Fish and Tara of Helium. Dinah remained where she was, for she was old and arthritic, but she mewed to remind Wilma that she wanted breakfast, too.

The house on Applby Lane was old, the kitchen large. Back when there'd been any money in the family—or in Boone's Gap—there hadn't been such a thing as air-conditioning. Wilma had left the door onto the sun porch open last night, and the room was drenched with early sun and the scent of morning, the fresh tingle of the air still bearing the scent of mountains and the woods. When she was a girl growing up in this house—*back when dinosaurs walked the earth*—the woods had been right out the backyard, and she and her tribe of sisters sat on the steps and watched the fireflies on hot summer nights. During the coal boom of the seventies the Applby Mining Corporation had put a trailer park there for its workers, and about three-quarters of the spaces were still occupied, mostly by retirees. There was a little shopping center just beyond.

Even so, you could still smell the woods on a summer morning.

Wilma smiled, a tall, rangy, gray-haired woman in a pink chenille robe, and knelt to portion out can after can of Friskies onto fourteen plates. The eight o'clock whistle blew at the mine, a groaned *carpe diem*—summer half over, and what had she done of all she'd planned to do before kids came back to her classroom in the fall? Four sisters yet to write those long letters to—though of course Hazel was of the opinion that all of them should get computers and communicate by e-mail. Weeds luxuriated between the long rows of berry canes across the back of the enormous yard. Many, many books yet unread. She'd kept up her work at the Senior Center, that was something. But mostly she'd just walked the green Allegheny trails to this or that hidden hollow, to spend a magic afternoon listening to folks sing old songs, tell old tales. She'd worked some on her weaving, relaxing into the rhythmic thump of the huge loom Hazel had built her in the living room, the cats all watching in fascination and reaching hesitant paws out to catch the shuttle.

Time and summer, like shining gold cupped in her hands.

Her smile faded a little as she thought of her pupils. Not so happy a time for most of them, with not enough work even for their parents. The town council of Boone's Gap had been trying, since Applby had mechanized the mine ten years ago, to get a garment factory in town; there were a couple of small shops where wives could augment their husbands' welfare checks, but that was all. Despite government efforts to widen and improve roads, there still wasn't much tourism, and the one motel in town didn't boast the amenities apparently indispensable to folks from Philadelphia or Baltimore or Washington.

A pity, she thought, looking out into the green stillness of yard and sunlight and berry canes. A thousand pities, that people couldn't live in this magical beauty untroubled; that you had to weigh the sweetness of the morning and the rumpled velvet grandeur of the mountains towering over the town against the need to feed your family, the need to make a living, to make something of your life.

A thousand pities that this beauty was the only thing you had to trade. And so many traded it for a life in the cities.

She shook her head, her heart hurting for those sunny-hearted sixteen-year-olds who wouldn't be in her classroom when school convened again in the fall. At times she had a sense of standing on a stream bank, watching the flashing water leap past her: a glimpse and it's gone.

She had made a choice long ago, and, in spite of the meager pay that she augmented with weaving and quilting, she told herself she was content. Nieces and nephews, students and cats. Sitting on the bank of the stream of time. She smiled at the morning, wondering what the day would bring.

"Fred!" Bob Wishart reached out from the bed where he lay as his brother came into the room. "Fred, you came!"

"I'm sorry." Fred touched him, looked down into his face—round, fair-skinned and soft, a familiar, comforting mirror of his own—and then around at the big first-floor bedroom of their mother's house. It was the only room large enough to contain the softly beeping battery of respirators, filters, monitors. The blue-flowered curtains were open, showing the fence cloaked in honeysuckle whose smell almost drowned the faint whiffs of antiseptic; the light dimmed the green watching eyes of the surge suppressors and backup batteries that clustered around the feet of the life-support equipment. "I'm so sorry I couldn't come before, when this happened."

"Doesn't matter." Bob's smile, his joy, was like standing happily naked in summer sun. Bob had always been the twin to take life as it came. "You wrote the checks, anyway. God, what would Mom and I have done if you hadn't come through? And you're here now."

"I'm here now." Fred settled himself by the bed in the old purple plush chair that had always graced the living room. Someone must have carried it in here for Mom to sit in.

It was good to be back. Good to be home. Funny—when he'd left this place, fled to Stanford and the promise of more than the University of West Virginia could teach, it had felt like escaping prison. Even his love for Bob hadn't outweighed the sense of suffocation, of being trapped in this small town and this dusty house; held prisoner by their mother's nameless fears. He wished he could embrace his brother, but Bob lay tangled in the ghastly sterile spiderweb of tubes and monitors and stanchions bearing IV bags, as he had lain for ten weeks now since the accident. Thank God indeed for the money the Source Project paid, the money that had been ready when word reached him, to provide the care Bob needed without requiring their mother to stay at the hospital in Lexington to look after him.

She wasn't strong. She had relied on their father to deal with the world, and when he'd died, abandoning her as Fred had later abandoned her, she'd relied on her boys. Going away among strangers would have terrified her, killed her, maybe. Yet Fred knew she wouldn't have abandoned her son.

It was enough—almost—to embrace Bob in his mind, his thought. And Bob, looking up smiling from the pillow, returned the hug with his eyes and his heart.

After the nightmare of the past few years, what had been stiflingly provincial now showed its true nature: safe and familiar, the heart of his self. In the peaceful sunlight of the bedroom the guilt he'd felt—the sense that he, Fred, should have been the one in the car when that truck roared around the corner in the dark—dissolved, like dirty grease in those time-lapse dish soap commercials they'd seen as children.

He was the one who could help. Who'd save them both.

Fred reached out with his mind, his heart, his thoughts, as if to draw the whole old house around him like a comforting blanket. The sounds and scents and the way the boards of the upstairs hall creaked, the cracked glass of the sun-porch window, the huge old Populux stove in the kitchen, everything. . . . Every memory of their childhood. The taste of every cookie they'd eaten in the cluttered kitchen and the smell of the attic dust.

He could give it back to Bob. Come back to it himself.

It was good to be home.

Hank Culver put his head through the dispatcher's office door. "Anything I need to know before we go down, Candy?"

She checked the line of Post-it Notes stuck to the edges of her monitor—not that she needed to. Plump and curly-haired Candace Leary had been dispatcher at Applby Mining Corporation since long before they'd computerized, before there'd even been phones down into the mine. *I'd have to stand at the top of the hole and shout,* he'd once heard her telling Mr. Mullein's secretary—Norman Mullein was son-in-law of the original old bastard whose name was on the mine. *I thought it was heaven when they got us a couple tin cans on a string.*

The secretary had half-believed her. There wasn't a tram that left the downcast or a malfunctioning sprinkler pipe she didn't know about. "You're still developing the main panels in Twelve?"

He had been all week. "It's still looking good. The seam's about four feet thick and pretty level—maybe a little dip. Floor and ceiling look good."

"Good deal. The geology boys'll be glad to hear it." She checked the status board. "Everything clear. Hillocher's crew is starting to retreat out of Area Ten."

"Good. Thanks." As he clumped down the porch steps of the little office and crossed the dust-blackened gravel and mud that lay between it and the pithead, Hank checked his helmet light and his radio and touched the lumbar pack where he stowed the spare batteries—including an extra nick-cad for the radio, which weighed a ton. He'd paid for the extra battery himself, not trusting the one the company provided. In spite of all the union's griping, the company tended to go cheap on equipment and keep it longer than they should. Back in the mid-sixties, when he'd started working at the old Green Mountain shaft on the other side of town, he'd gotten into the habit of buying as many spare parts as he could afford and carrying them in his lunchbox.

Twice, in those days, he'd been caught in cave-ins, once seen his brother Gil half-crushed when the face collapsed. It had taken the company hours to even locate them and nearly two days to dig them out.

Though Gil had survived—he'd been back at work in six months and had worked for Applby until emphysema got him in '88—it was not something Hank planned to ever let happen again if he could help it.

Men were coming out of the locker room to crowd around the pithead elevator, gray coveralls still damp from yesterday, clumsy-footed in boots and kneepads. Sonny Grimes stubbed his Marlboro on the elevator doorjamb and with the other hand fished a pack of smokeless from his coverall pocket, chewing even as he tucked the half-smoked butt behind his ear. "The fuck you lookin' at?" he demanded, when Hank put distance between himself and the inevitable spit to come.

"My mama was frightened by a cow in the pasture," said Hank. "Gave me a complex."

"Fuck you."

A few feet away Ryan Hanson was twisting his body into a corkscrew in an effort to demonstrate Hideo Nomo's pitching style to Gordy Flue: "Kicked the Braves' ass that one year."

"Bunch of Japs," opined Grimes and spit tobacco on the cement floor. "Damn dumb game anyway. Give me football."

"You like those guys in the spandex britches, Sonny?" asked Gordy, getting a general laugh and another "Fuck you" from Grimes.

Ryan grinned, ridiculously like Wilma when she was nineteen, the year Hank had first proposed to her. Her brother—Ryan's dad, Lou—had been only fourteen then, a towheaded kid picked on by the bevy of long-legged girls that comprised the Hanson family; Hank remembered playing sandlot ball with him in a weedy field behind the old pithead. Remembered Wilma in the first miniskirt the town had ever seen (and not all that mini, compared to these days), somehow managing to make it look prim, as if she were laughing at herself. Long slim legs in what looked like a mile and a half of stocking.

"Whole National League's got Nomo's timing down now," added Gordy, as the car doors slid open and the men crowded in.

They continued to argue amicably about baseball as the elevator headed down, not really wanting to think about the endless drop in darkness, the rock whizzing past outside. Everybody talking and thinking about something else with the adeptness of long practice. Young Al Bartolo was showing pictures of his son to Tim Brackett, who was grinning his big slow brilliant gap-toothed grin with the cheerful understanding of a man who's felt the same high at seeing the little red monkey face of his own child seven times before: "Gina all right?" he asked, and Al nodded.

"She's fine. It was only a couple hours, and them Lamaze classes she took at Adult Ed work like a champ. Her mom's over there now, helping her out."

And Tim's bright brown eyes in the electric dinginess seemed to say, *Wait till his eyes track for the first time, and he looks at you. Wait till the first time he reaches out and grabs your finger. Wait till the first time he throws a baseball to you, or comes into your room at night because he's had a bad dream and he's scared. Wait till you see him graduate high school with honors. You're on the road, my friend, but you don't know what happiness is yet.*

A good man, thought Hank. Not very bright—not the way Ryan was bright—but good.

The doors opened to the yellow blear of electric bulbs, the smell of earth and rock, of coal and mud. The damp touch of cold air on the cheeks. Up close to the downcast the company had put in sprinklers to keep the dust down, and it even worked, though everyone still came out of the mine looking as if they'd been spray-painted, and Hank still spit black and blew black out of his nose for hours after he went off-shift. Still, it was far better than it had been when his father had worked for Applby before him.

There was a little electric tram, like a string of golf carts, to haul everybody out to the coal face, and that was an improvement, too. Hank recalled places in the Green Mountain diggings where the coal bed was thin, the men had had to be trundled through tunnels on a conveyor belt with their tools between their knees and the rock seven inches above their prone backs. The headlamps of the men, and the single glaring light on the front of the tram, glittered on mud and wet rock on the conveyors that bore the coal back to the downcast, flashed on the puddles dripped from the pipes. Glistened on the coal.

And beyond those feeble lights, night blacker than the coal.

By the time they got to the new main, the conveyors had started up in the areas behind them, and in the distant mazes of rooms and pillars machinery started to buzz and clank as other teams got going. No sprinklers here, just the smell of the rock dust that lay like dirty snow on the floor to keep the coal dust down. At least the seam was thick here, nearly five feet. It meant he could stretch his back, if he got down on his knees to do it.

The uneven ceiling pressed down overhead, making the steel props seem feeble and small. The darkness, too, seemed to press in close from all sides, as if the headlamps made a watery wall, a weak denial of some inevitable fact.

Hank's father had been a miner. He'd started each day with a shot of whiskey; ended it with half a dozen more.

Hank understood.

Almost more than the fear of explosions, fear of the roof falling in, or of a boulder loosening from the ceiling and squashing you. It waited for you, that darkness.

In a way it was worse that there were so few men, that so much of the work was done by machine. Not just because of all the men Hank knew who'd been laid off, whose families had been on food stamps for three or five years, who were trying to make ends meet on what their wives could earn. As Al disappeared to chart butt entries in the new section and Sonny loafed over to his loader, Hank felt an uneasiness that had nothing to do with the logistics of coal or manpower. In the sixties and seventies there'd been lots of guys down here, lots of friends. Voices to keep the silence at bay.

"C'mon, Hank," Sonny called out as Hank methodically checked over the shearer. "The fucker was all right when you left it yesterday. What you think, the fairies came and fucked with it while you were away?" Hank ignored him. Diesel—okay; hydraulic fluid—okay; oil levels—he checked everything about the big, grimy yellow world-eater before he hit the switches that woke it to deafening life.

Sliding back and forth, chewing at the coal face, the black seam between the gray. Spewing rock and mud and shining black lumps onto the greasy shale floor for Sonny's loader to pick up, to start their long journey back to the top of the ground. Tim's headlight swooping and swaying as he shoveled. Shadows dipping, reaching like monster hands.

Ryan and Roop McDonough angled the metal supports upright, wedging them with hunks of shale or working them into shallow drilled sockets in the floor, and Hank thought, *It's no good pretending. No good trying not to think about the weight, and the dark, and the silence.*

They were close to a mile down. If the world ended, they wouldn't know a thing about it until they went back up again.

FOUR

"All right, here I am. What is it?" Dr. Fred Wishart strode into the Ops Chamber, the blast doors hissing softly closed behind him. The others were already bent over the electronic schematic that tracked the flow of energy in the Resonance Chamber beyond the dark windows filling the opposite wall. Through the two-inch Plexiglas it looked like curious fleeting blue gleams among and between the narrow, mirrored walls of the maze, here and there a sort of glowing mist. On the schematic he saw half a dozen places where hot spots had glowed violently white, now cooling down to the safer hues of red-orange, dulling back to green. "What happened? What caused it?"

Marcus Sanrio sighed. "The siren song of cause and effect . . . And if causality were irrelevant, if all were mutable, what then?" His long, sensitive fingers trailed across the tracking schematic, slightly ridged and grooved to accommodate his handicap; the energies electronically mirrored from Resonance showed up on the surface as changes in temperature. Probably, reflected Fred, it was a more accurate system than the colors. "There was a sudden intensification of energy starting in the eighth sector, building up very quickly to burnthrough levels. We ran tap rods into it, and everything is fine."

"Everything is not fine," Fred said quietly, "if we don't know what caused it." Anything in the nature of a burn-through scared the hell out of him, even the ones that didn't result in bizarre manifestations like telekinetic energy flows at Sioux burial sites or the resurrection of packs of skeletal prairie wolves. Thank God they'd been able to hush that one up. For security reasons alone they were deadly—sooner or later something like that would occur under circumstances that couldn't be passed off as some poor Indian with d.t.'s—but what really scared Fred was the fact that they didn't know why such things occurred. What unknown stresses they might foreshadow. "Was it a malfunction of equipment?"

"We could tell that better," muttered Jill Pollard, "if we knew exactly how the equipment works. I don't mean how to increase or decrease the intensity of the energy at the Source, or tapping it off or directing the flow of the field. I mean what *is* it, exactly? What little electrons or neutrons are bumping into each other; what's happening at a sub-atomic level? *Why* is it happening?"

"To answer Dr. Wishart's question," said Sanrio, pointedly ignoring her, "no, there does not at this point appear to have been an equipment malfunction. Lilleburger noted the development of spontaneous hot spots in 1940 . . ."

"Which my investigations of the Russian research never found any mention of," cut in Pollard.

"Well, God forbid we should proceed without confirmation from Dr. Pollard's research," purred Sanrio. He turned back to Wishart.

"According to the schematic the leakage involved a very small area northeast of here, along . . ." he checked a Braille notecard with one insectile forefinger, "along Medicine Water Creek. At that hour of the morning it's unlikely anyone was there to see a manifestation anyway—if there *was* a manifestation."

"You are minimizing the extent of the burnthrough!" St. Ives slapped the table angrily with a sheaf of papers. "I've warned this committee before about security."

"And *I* have warned this committee about timidity!" retorted Sanrio. "Some members of this organization seem to have the two words confused. We're running a system-wide check to make sure, but there should be no reason we cannot proceed to the establishment of a limited field later this morning."

"That's nonsense," cried Sakamoto. "I'll barely have time to set up proper observation equipment."

"You can't be serious," Pollard added. "No responsible researcher could countenance . . ."

"Might I suggest that the limited-field experiment be put off until tomorrow?" Wu's soft voice cut across the general clamor of *My research, My observation, My data.*

Sanrio heaved an exaggerated sigh and made a slight gesture of turning his head, like a glance, from her to Pollard— the two women had become close friends during the months of incarceration at the project.

Unperturbed, the old woman continued, "Not for any reason of equipment failure nor even due to the fact that we still have no idea why hot spots develop. It is simply that you have not taken a rest period in the past twenty-four hours, Dr. Sanrio. It is over ninety hours since you have remained off-shift for a complete rest period. Dr. Wishart has not had a formal rest period for sixteen, and prior to that, two rest periods in eighty hours. I believe one reason that this hot spot developed to burnthrough was because the technician on duty was overtired and his reflexes slow. The human body is not designed—"

"If you need to go take a nap, Dr. Wu," Sanrio cut her off, "please feel free to do so. I apologize for taking up your time." He swung his head around, not so much like a sighted person as a machine, zeroing in on the body heat of the others in the room. "And that goes for the rest of you. Evidently none of you remember—perhaps because, as Dr.

Wu so obviously points out, of the *bonecracking* labor involved in sitting at a computer terminal in an air-
conditioned room all day—that we are working against a
deadline, a deadline that none of us know. Some fool in
Washington may even now be standing up on his hind legs
in a Senate sub-committee and yapping about cutting ex-
penditure, and tomorrow's mail may very well contain a request that we pack up our things in a little cardboard box
and get out; they're giving our money to buy crayons for
day-care centers."

His thin white hand, its long nails stained with nicotine,
bunched tight where it rested on the schematic, whose lights
had all cooled now to green. Behind him a random swirl of
white sparks blossomed from some corner of the Resonating
Maze, framing him in misty diamond fire.

"And what will we be able to say, when the imbeciles in
charge of appropriations ask us, 'What do you have to show
for five years of active research? What do you have to show
for seventy years' worth of research by some of the best
minds in prewar Germany, in Russia, in America?' I'm not
talking about next week, or next month. I may be talking
about tomorrow. I don't want to have to say—" and he transformed his light, expressive voice into an apologetic whine,
" 'Well, sir, we're working on it.' "

He gestured sharply to the black glass behind him, and
Wishart thought he saw, all along the tops and edges of the
resonator panels, a blue flicker of lightning, eerily mimick-
ing the sweep of his arm.

"I am going to put forward plans to establish a limited
field this morning," Sanrio said. "Now the rest of you have
my permission to go and take your little naps."

Fine, thought Fred. *I'll do that.* Dreaming of home—
dreaming of Bob—was more productive than wrangling
about whose research conflicted with whose and whether or
not St. Ives' theories were being proved or disproved.

While the others were still arguing, he walked quietly out
the door. He thought he heard Dr. Pollard call after him, but

he didn't turn his head, hastening back to the safety of his office.

NEW YORK—8:11 A.M. EDT

Mornings were always a bitch.

Colleen Brooks slicked back the wet hair from her face and stepped from the shower, not even glancing at the bathroom mirror, which was steamed to a silvery fog anyhow. Most people would have thought she was referring to the five-mile run, the pushups, the lat pulls, the crunches, the rest of the routine that it took to get her motor running, but that was just something she did; something that burned off the fumes of the previous day.

No, it was the gauntlet. She steeled herself as she buttoned the denim shirt, zipped up her work pants, slid thick socks into steel-toed boots. She opened the bathroom door.

"You gonna comb your hair?"

"It's combed, Rory."

"That thing washed?"

"Yeah."

He reclined, resplendent in the old BarcaLounger, the Simpsons TV tray in front of him, sucking up Frosted Flakes and knocking them back with a Bud. He was on day three of his shaving rotation—shave one of every four—which he thought gave him that cool Johnny Depp look (which was so old, anyway) but which to Colleen seemed more Jed Clampett. Mainly, he looked like a younger, taller Danny DeVito. Not that much taller, though. At five-six, he had only an inch on her. "It's got a spot."

Like his T-shirt wasn't dribbled with them.

"They don't pay me for my looks."

"That's the truth."

Colleen felt tired and looked away. It hadn't always been like this, she told herself, trying to remember the sweetness. That week in Cabo they'd had three years back; he'd filled the place with orchids and roses and irises and God knew what, an explosion of blossom, told her not to pack a thing—they'd buy it all there. He'd blown a month's pay plus commissions on that. That was before the FTC had cracked down on the toner-cartridge phone scam and his boss had flown the coop to the Caymans. Not that he'd ever bothered to mention to her what his phone sales consisted of till it hit the *Daily News*. Thank god the feds hadn't cared about the little fish . . . at least, as long as they proved co-operative.

She poked in the fridge, found last night's fried-egg sandwich and, as she gulped it down, extended the newspaper to him, folded over to one item.

"What's this?" he asked.

"Read it." He rolled his eyes, his old standard I-don't-need-this-shit look. She held his gaze, not backing down. With a martyred sigh he took it and read.

" 'Dear Abby, the man in my life is a boorish pig who drinks up my paycheck and won't get work.' " He tossed it back to her. "Who writes this crap?"

She tried not to think about breaking one of his fingers. Tried not to think about living by herself. About waking up in the darkness, in a cold bed, alone. Looking at him, she spied her reflection in the flamingo-framed mirror they'd gotten in Cabo. Maybe they didn't pay her for her looks, but she was cut and strong and not bad for twenty-six. She still had all her teeth and not that many scars. Not on the outside, anyway.

Let's not deal with that today, she told herself and pitched the paper in the trash. One day at a time, right? And what the hell would happen to him if she walked out on him now? He'd end up living in a refrigerator carton under a bridge. She wouldn't put a cat out like that. But as soon as he was more on his feet . . .

She owed it to the man he used to be and, she hoped, would be again, once he found the thing that really rang his chimes. Not that she'd ever found that thing for herself.

She reached over to the antlers where her belt hung.

Thing was a heavy sucker, especially now that she was packing that big wrench. She fastened it on, grabbed up her sack lunch and made for the door.

"Hey, babe," Rory called to her. He seemed to be melting into that ratty lounger, ever more one with it. Colleen turned, tensing for the parting shot. "Don't let the bear eat you."

Her shoulders relaxed; she even smiled. "Not a chance," she said. The bear wasn't out there. And whatever was, she knew she wouldn't break a sweat.

"This city's a sewer."

Ely Stern stood by the window, glowering down at the glinting towers of the city in the early morning sun. From behind the mahogany desk, Dr. Louis Chernsky considered the tall, lean figure: slicked-back, shining black hair, black Italian suit, handmade shoes, white linen shirt, black silk tie. White-gold Piaget on his wrist, white gold at his belt buckle. A stiletto of a man.

Sitting behind one's desk was no longer really de rigueur for a therapist; in some circles it was frowned on. But on these Monday and Thursday mornings Chernsky appreciated the added distance it provided between him and this particular client.

The mood of Stern's litany was always the same, only the specifics varying. "Water's poison; air's poison. I can't stand the art in the galleries anymore. And the women, they look at you, they're measuring you for the settlement."

Chernsky stroked his beard, aware as always of how much of a Freudian caricature it made him seem, and doing it anyway. "You're feeling isolated."

Stern gazed out the big plate window. Like Jesus on the mountain, the kingdoms of earth lay before him, jagged eruptions of steel and stone and glass. The view added fifteen hundred dollars a month to the cost of the office, but Chernsky felt his clients would have scorned a lesser locale.

Stern's eyes were dreamy. "I have this image in my mind. Going to the top of a building, emptying a flamethrower on the passing parade."

Dr. Chernsky's mind drifted to the Winnebago, and the route he and Susan had planned last night. Down to D.C., then through the Blue Ridge Mountains. Only two weeks, three days and twenty-two minutes away. His mouth said, "You're feeling discontented."

"No, I'm the guy they modeled the happy face after." Stern snapped open a case (white gold, of course), fished out a Gitanes, lit it with a high, blue flame. He drew the smoke in deep then exhaled impatiently, turned on Chernsky. "I've been paying you more than the national debt. Just when do I start to feel better?"

Never; you're a narcissist, thought Chernsky. But he said, "This isn't only about feeling better. It's about gaining insight."

"Insight?" Stern's black eyes flared. "I'll give you an insight. I wake up every morning of my life angry. I wake up, and I feel like—"

A timer on Chernsky desk chimed. "We have to stop now."

"We do," Stern said, eyes hooded. Chernsky shrugged and let the silence settle. Stern blew out a cloud of smoke.

"Well," he said. "Guess I'll just go to the office and spread a little insight."

WEST VIRGINIA—8:13 A.M. EDT

Fred retreated from the side of the bed when the door opened. He doubted their mother even saw him as she made her way across to where Bob lay. "Good morning, son." Her voice was the soft archaic lilt that people who weren't from Appalachia made jokes about: *hick* and *redneck* and *hillbilly*. At Stanford, Fred had worked very hard to eradicate it from his speech, but now the very intonations were like a gentle song.

She adjusted the pillows, checked all the tubes and bags and readouts. She'd nursed at Kanawha General before her agoraphobia got so bad, and from her letters and phone calls Fred knew that the nurse who looked after Bob in the daytime had filled her in on what to check and what to do.

"Mom," said Bob, but of course she didn't hear. She fussed gently with the catheter bag, changing it as neatly as a nurse would have, talking all the while.

"Now, let's get rid of this old nasty bag and get you a nice new clean one. How you feeling this morning, honey? I had a tolerable night myself, but you know what I dreamed? I dreamed I was having dinner at Winterdon's, you know that pretty restaurant they got on *Hope for Tomorrow*? Well, I was at the next table from Steve and Christine—you remember me telling you how Christine lied to Steve about being pregnant with Lester's baby and broke into the hospital and switched the blood tests. . . ."

She talked on, a soft babble like a brook, and from his corner Fred watched her with concern, pity and an agony of guilt. She looked worse than she had the last time he'd seen her, unbathed, her hair uncombed, clothed in a pastel warmup suit with food stains on the bosom and thighs. *Damn it*, Fred thought, *she used to get out a little. Doesn't Wilma Hanson still come over Saturdays and make sure she gets out to a store or something?* He realized he hadn't phoned Wilma in weeks.

Nor his mother, he thought. Had he called at all last week? He must have. He couldn't remember.

He was so tired.

". . . locked in a dungeon under her house. But when Shelley went in to talk to Veronica, Owen accidentally threw the switch that sealed the door, so they were imprisoned together. . . ." She wrung out a washcloth in a little basin of water, carefully cleaned Bob's face, what she could reach of it around the tubes and the tape. Fred felt, across the room, his brother's gratitude for the touch, for the knowledge that she cared, that she would perform these services for him and not leave him to the care of a paid nurse.

In the onyx dark of the screens, green and orange lines ran their jagged little courses, like a background whisper, *All is well. All is well.*

Mrs. Sanders, the day nurse, had told Fred three weeks ago that the doctors regarded Bob as hopeless, one of those heartbreaking, financially backbreaking cases in which the patient is stable but cannot be revived: *A miracle*, was what she had said. *It will take a miracle.*

But if the Source Project succeeded, a miracle was exactly what would become available.

Oh, Bob, whispered Fred, going to the side of the bed, gently reaching out to touch his brother's still shoulder. *Hang on. Hang on.*

FIVE

Glancing through the ground-floor window, half-screened by the honeysuckles that seemed sometimes as if they would devour the big white house on Applby Lane, Wilma watched Arleta Wishart sponge her son's face and thought, *I'll give her a call as soon as I'm back from the Piggly-Wiggly.*

Since the collision that had broken her son's neck, Arleta, who had never dealt particularly well with the world, had barely been out of the house. Even as a child, Wilma had been aware that Mrs. Wishart Next Door didn't like to be outside. Playing in the yard, she'd see the small, sloppily stout young woman in her white uniform hurrying to the bus stop to go to her job, then hurrying home again in the evenings as if she didn't dare pause. As if there were snipers in the trees, ready to shoot her if she didn't get to a safe place quickly.

Later, as a teenager, Wilma made it a point to drop by in the afternoons, or ask her to go shopping or to a movie on those frequent Saturdays when the twins would be at Little League and her husband, Dr. Wishart Sr., was working at the hospital. Like the boys—who were seven years her junior—Wilma had come to accept that this was the way Mrs. Wishart was. Her husband always answered the telephone or the door, always took her shopping. When she wasn't with him, she looked confused.

The summer Wilma graduated from high school, a movie house opened in Beckly that had deliciously icy air-conditioning and fifty-cent matinees. She and Mrs. Wishart—whom she was calling Arleta by that time—would spend at least one afternoon a week there and hit Farrell's for ice cream afterward. But at three o'clock Arleta would always say, "I have to get home now."

If asked, she'd come up with a good reason concerning the boys or her husband. But from the way she said it, Wilma understood that Arleta was afraid.

Call Arleta, she made a mental note to herself, *as soon as the nurse gets there.* In the hurly-burly of graduation and the closing-down of the school year, followed immediately by the family uproar surrounding her sister Siobhan's third divorce, it had been weeks since Wilma had been able to make sure her friend got out of the house. Arleta had never been a churchgoer, and, with no brothers in the mine, she'd never made friends in the Women's Club that went hand in hand with the union. Wilma knew there was no one else in town with whom Arleta went anywhere.

An odd family, she reflected, without judgment. The twins wrapped up in one another almost to the exclusion of anyone else, the mother wrapped up in the boys, particularly after Dr. Wishart's death. One of the other young teachers at Allegheny High School had dated Bob for a while—past Arleta's shoulder, through the open windows, Wilma could see the beautiful photo Bob had taken of the woman. But talking to her later, Wilma gathered that Bob's story was pretty much the same as his mother's. The mind always just slightly elsewhere, and at ten o'clock, *I have to get home.*

Nothing weird or perverted, as far as she knew—and the way the teachers and the other volunteers at the Senior Center gossiped, Wilma knew pretty much everything that went on in Boone's Gap. No ugly secrets or bloodstained bed-linen hidden in closets. Just fear. Fear so great that it excused them, in their own eyes, from participation in the pain of real life.

Then Bob had driven down to Beckly late one night to pick up some medicine for Arleta and had come around a curve into the path of a semi heading for State Highway 64.

Call Arleta, she thought. *And call Fred.* And though she didn't exactly phrase it thus to herself, it went through her mind, watching the graying, chubby woman minister to the corpselike man on the bed, that if Arleta were Fred's sole source of information about Bob's condition, he might not be getting the whole story. Not that Arleta would deliberately lie to the son who had deserted her twenty years ago, who had visited so seldom since. But seeing her, in her pink-and-green warmups—she had at least two dozen sets of variously colored sweat garments, which had, Wilma mused, pretty much replaced housecoats in American culture—chatting about the latest doings of the vengeful Veronica and the manipulative Christine and all the other characters of the mythical town of Springdale, it struck Wilma how terribly alone Arleta seemed.

Only her and her son. He trapped in a coma since May, she trapped by her love for him. And her fears.

Isolated, just the two of them, in that big bright machinery-cluttered room.

NEW YORK—8:14 A.M. EDT

It was early morning, and already they were out. Ruining everything.

Sam Lungo sat on his front-porch glider, in the shade of his scraggily elm, watching the world go by, or, at least, *his* part of it, the rectangle bordered on the west by Amsterdam, the east by Columbus, the familiar country beyond whose borders he did not venture. And why go anywhere? It was all the same, every place. He knew, he saw. Sally Jesse, Jerry, Ricki, the endless parade of vulgar people in black-and-white splendor on the old Dumont his mother had kept all those years, and which he had maintained since. Illuminated through the oil bubble in front of the screen, their grotesque faces distorted and true. Monsters, they were all monsters.

It was no different for the denizens of the block. He knew all of them, their comings and goings, their trashy little lives, their ugly, secret selves. And he knew their names, not just what they called themselves, but their *real* names, discovered by close appraisal over patient time. Mr. Blotches, the Varicose Lady, Yellow Teeth, Loose Ways . . .

They never came through his gate, into his front yard, onto his porch. His rambling Victorian Easter egg of a house was an anomaly on this block of brownstones, a gaudy interloper, like some odd trinket dropped by a careless god from the heavens. The adults never came, anyway. Their brats stole onto his property in the dead of night, threw rotten fruit and worse at his windows, scrawled their initials on his door.

Looking out at the front yard, Sam sighed, feeling the familiar churning in his stomach. Try as he might to keep it pruned, manicured, subdued, the devil grass would keep encroaching, the weeds and thistles smothering the careful order he fought to maintain. The gate and fence were showing signs of ruination, too, growing ever more splintered and worn.

He felt, as he had so often since Mother had gone, a sense of cataclysm coming on, rushing toward him, chaotic and malevolent. There was nothing he could do to stop it. Except watch, take note, remember. Mother had said there would be an accounting. If so, she hadn't lived to see it. And in the forty-nine years he'd been on this earth, Sam had grown ever more hopeless that justice would come.

"You there! You stop that!" Sam always tried for an authoritative tone, but more often than not it came out higher and more nasal than he intended. The Slave to the Mottled

Terrier was out again, tethered to that nasty little wretch that sniffed at his rhododendron and squatted where it was least wanted.

The Slave acted like he didn't hear. But he heard, all right. "You are breaking the law!" Sam shrilled. "I've seen you before!"

Reluctantly, the Slave tugged the protesting dog away. Glaring, Sam pulled the notepad from his shirt pocket, jotted in his cramped chicken scratches the specifics of event and time and day. It was all there, the microscopic history of this place, all the petty crimes they would want forgotten. But that would not happen.

He was the witness.

❦

It was one of those glorious summer mornings, in which the splash of sunlight against the buildings and the lulling breezes made New York seem both exquisite and livable. But to Cal Griffin, it spoke only irony. His mind was a battlefield, and he felt the previous night's dream like a black truth within—the choking stench of burning and blood, the screams that tore at him, his stillness, his failure of nerve.

Spurred by these, Cal had embraced an action he knew to be undeniably, shamefully right and set Schenk free.

But his masters would not concur.

As Cal emerged with Tina from their fourth-floor walkup along Eighty-first toward St. Augustine Middle School, the street was alive with joggers, folks walking their dogs, kids heading for school. An image intruded on him, of a chill evening not long ago. Mr. Stern had lingered beyond his usual departure time and gestured Cal into his cavernous, intimidating office. Stern was in a strangely reflective mood and drew Cal into conversation. They spoke of the prairies, so familiar to Cal and alien to Stern, of Tina and of death. Eager to impress, Cal had ventured onto the subject of tactics, of will and action, had become talkative, even expansive. Stern's eyes grew hooded. Then, frostily distant, he pointedly severed their brief intimacy, saying that frequently the most powerful action was inaction, that silence could be a blade.

Recklessly, Cal had jettisoned both. Stern would learn of it, of course, and the consequences would be grave. He'd never be able to match this salary, and word would spread like a black stain. *Five years ago, I wouldn't have cared.* But now, he was afraid.

He glanced at his sister, pacing beside him in her school grays, book bag with its toe-shoe insignia slung over her shoulder. What could he possibly do, say, to maintain the sanctuary he had so carefully constructed for her? Tina had been only four when her world had been blasted away, and he had stepped in to be her anchor, her rock. Now he felt perilously seamed and cracked. And most alarming, a voice inside seemed to be calling him to release, to shatter, to see what emerged.

His eyes lingered on Tina as she glided weightless beside him, her face a mask of indifference, counsel only to herself. With a shock of recognition, Cal realized that—outside her protective world of dance—she had duplicated his own stony mien, the impassive barrier he used to shield himself from the sea of humanity.

"You there! Yes, you!" The voice cut across Cal's thoughts like a scythe—a man's voice, but querulously high.

Sam Lungo, their neighbor, sat on his porch like some Buddha gone to seed, glaring at them, domed head glinting in the sun. Tina groaned. It was a familiar sight, and normally they would have continued on, Lungo's abuse splintering against their backs. But surprisingly, Cal stopped and turned. Tina paused, uneasy.

"You *wadded* that." Lungo brandished his gangrenous walking stick in the direction of a spot on the sidewalk just beyond his yard. "The other day. You wadded that up and just—just *excreted* it."

Cal gazed near his feet and spied the crumpled Snickers wrapper. He hadn't tossed it, of course. Nevertheless, he scooped up the offending paper and started off again.

"No." Lungo surged up to them with his odd, hunched crow's stride. "No. You *apologize*."

Tina murmured incredulously. But Cal peered back at the little man, walled against the world, insulated from empathy, and saw himself.

"I'm sorry," Cal said, for Sam, for the futility of years.

But Lungo, unused to pity, took it for mockery. He flushed, and his mouth twisted to a vinegary scowl. "Get out of here," he hissed. "Go on!"

Cal turned and walked stiffly away, as if bearing a wound. Tina dogged after him and, when she was able to catch his eye, gifted him with a smile.

Lungo saw none of this, busied instead transforming them into one more outrage in his pad, as he whispered his venomous, as-yet-unanswered prayers.

WEST VIRGINIA—8:35 A.M. EDT

"Fred, what's going on?" Bob reached out, grasped his brother . . . not exactly by the hands, because in addition to being entangled in the equipment that kept him alive, Bob—the physical part of Bob—was closed down. Not dead, but on hiatus, like an engine barely ticking over. His mind and thoughts and soul, the Bob that Fred had protected all through their insular childhood—the vague, helpless, gentle little photographer, the voracious reader of everything from Aeschylus to Wolverine who could barely speak to anyone he hadn't known all his life—these were trapped in that body, entangled in it the way the body was entangled in its machinery.

The way Fred was entangled by distance, by obligation to be elsewhere. By the walls around the Source in its gloomy complex of bunkers and Quonset huts and the mazes of barbed wire. By his colleagues' endless squabbling.

"I'll take care of you," he said. "I'll take care of you."

Illusion? The self-delusion of an exhausted man, dozing

at his desk and wishing with everything in him that he was home where it was safe? That he was with the only person in his life he'd ever truly loved? The fantasy that Bob was able to talk to him again, rely on him again for help and support as he'd done all his life?

The comfort of forgiveness for leaving Bob alone?

Would this room be so clear to him if he hadn't known the house from birth? He could get up—he knew he could—and walk out into the downstairs hall, with its gloom and its smell of mildewed carpets, turn right to the living room with its curtained shadows or left down the hall to the kitchen, sunlight, clutter, burnt toast and Mom's TV perched on the untidy counter and the view across the weedy yard to Wilma Hanson's blackberry bushes.

Like the old commercial: *Is it real or is it Memorex*? Was all this—including Bob's hand, warm and trusting in his—something he was creating for himself, no more real than a computer game or a stage set?

For he could clearly see his office around him. Feel the pressure of his buttocks on the gray-and-black desk chair. Glimpse the orange and green glint of computer lights and surge suppressors, the steady blink-blink-blink of the red lights on his phone, and hear the low subliminal humming of the Resonator locked behind the maze of walls.

No, he was there. And he was here.

And that was what the Source was about, too.

Healing Bob. Maybe in time healing Mom, leading her gently back to the real world that she'd always feared. He'd deserted Bob, deserted Mom. He was a better driver, better at coping with the world in general. He, not Bob, should have been in the car that night. But now everything was possible. Everything was going to be possible.

"Fred, I'm scared. All this stuff—Mom didn't even hear me when I talked to her. I feel so cold. What happened to me?"

"You're going to be all right."

"She didn't even see you. She looked right at you sitting there and she didn't see you."

"That's because . . ." How to explain it? He could feel the Source right now, the curious, elusive energy that seemed to permeate the air. He was breathing it into his lungs. No, that wasn't right. Maybe just absorbing it into his flesh. Drinking it like sunlight. And that vibration was what let him be here, holding Bob's hand.

And what let Bob be aware of him.

"That's because Mom's tired," he finished. "Don't you worry. I won't let anything happen to you, and I won't go away."

SIX

Cal Griffin was drowning.

The multitudes surged about him, overwhelming, pressing in, jostling him as he struggled along Fifth, a phantom mirrored in the dispassionate glass of Saks and Versace and Dior. The unseen, massed humanity of his dream was garishly replicated in the morning sun. Snatches of Italian, French, Japanese and every mutant strain of English whipped by amid an endlessness of Carnegie Tech T-shirts and Bernini, body piercings and haute couture. The delicate, luxuriant weather had proved fleeting; the humidity was coming on now, air thick as tar, pregnant with the promise of storm. Cal felt sapped, every breath a labor.

He remembered a time when, newly arrived from Hurley, he had acknowledged all who met his gaze with a smile and nod of greeting. Recently and so long ago. When, how, had it faded to anonymity and silence?

Now, today, he searched the faces hungrily for connection as they blurred past. But their eyes evaded, and in their kaleidoscopic jumble of dress and manner, their forced hilarity and dynamism, he read artifice and fear.

He thought again of the dream, the screaming ones in the

blackness. If light were suddenly to flash bright across that scorched plain, what might those faces reveal?

When Cal had delivered his sister to the nuns at St. Augustine, set incongruously in the Village, the ancient walls seemed to whisper "citadel . . . sanctuary." A grim contrast to the dark tower of Stern, Ledding and Bowen to which he now strode.

The machine will stop; it will come to a grinding, shrieking halt. And then what? The dream mocked him. The unspoken certainty of the ones in the dark that he *could* aid them if only he would, the unassailable power in the sword and himself. It was absurdity. He had no power, only expenses, debts, obligations and a queasy moral sense that had suddenly kicked in to yank the rug from under his feet. As heat shimmered off the concrete, Cal's head swam. He was seized by a sensation of inexorable velocity, of something uncontrollable racing toward him.

The Stark Building, that Déco-Nouveau-Gothic monstrosity of steel ornament and worked stone that looked blue or black or green depending on the light, loomed ahead at Fifty-sixth like an executioner.

Cal regarded it uncertainly and slowed, shrank from the coming moment. He scanned the masklike faces for a spark of recognition, found none. Then turning, he saw, beyond the clamor and haste, a still, lean figure that met his gaze and knew him.

"Calvin, my friend!" The shout was exuberant. "No rest for the wicked, eh?"

Late or not, Cal headed for him, a candle in the storm. "Doc" Lysenko grinned from behind his gleaming aluminum cart as he slathered mustard on a bun.

"What have you got for a condemned man?" Cal fished out limp singles as he neared, not caring about the food—the churning in his stomach negated any hunger he might have felt—but eager for the word of cheer, the balm to his spirit.

Doc nodded at the steaming array of franks turning on the grill. "Here? Atherosclerosis." His vocabulary, as always, was good but the accent—Odessa by way of Kiev and

Afghanistan—thick. As ever, he moved with precision and ease, the smooth, unthinking routine of assembling the dogs, handing them off, making change for customers who often didn't say a word, miss a step, even look at him.

The herd bulled past, the swarm blind to the mysteries around them, the wonders. To step out of its rush, to be still a moment, to *see* . . .

"Being a physician isn't helping you as an entrepreneur," Cal ventured.

"In Leningrad—sorry, St. Petersburg—I'm physician. Here, my degree's toilet paper."

Cal scrutinized him as for the first time, the second-hand jeans and condiment-spattered apron, the Yankees cap turned backward. What chance, what calamity had washed Doc here? The question, when asked, would invariably be dismissed with a laugh and an evasion. But no camouflage could belie the refined complexity of that face, the probing glance like a scalpel. His cheeks were pale and smooth, his eyes so weary and lined, a face at war with itself. And those astonishing hands with their long, delicate fingers. Surgeon's hands, slopping mustard and kraut.

Cal felt a swell of kinship. Aliens, the two of them, in lives too small, on the run. But from what? To what?

He became aware that Doc was staring at him, his head cocked questioningly. "Condemned for what crime?"

It took Cal a moment to comprehend, but before he could answer, a blare of horns shrilled over the buzz of the crowd.

Cal looked up to see the mass of pedestrians sweeping through the crosswalk, narrowly avoiding the onrush of traffic, a screaming chaos of taxi, truck and bus—and one individual mid-street, trailing the others, strolling unaware.

Cal dove through the obstacle course of bodies, grabbed the tall, rangy figure and quick-stepped him onto the opposite curb. A semi dopplered behind them, wind wake tousling Cal's hair.

Cal stood trembling, sucking in air. Unable to speak, he gestured wildly behind them at the diesels and SUVs and taxis hurtling past. The other glanced about, seeming to see the street for the first time. Only then did Cal recognize him. A street character. "Goldie," the shopkeepers called him, no name beyond that. They'd spoken, the man refusing Cal's proffered coins, explaining in a patient, patronizing tone that he was a scavenger, not a beggar.

"I'm glad you're here." Goldie pulled the straw cowboy hat with the five aces in the brim low over lamplight-auburn eyes, high Cherokee cheekbones, as cool as if he stood in a park. "We need to talk."

Cal's gaze darted to the Stark Building, its revolving door a summons. "Listen," he said, not unkindly, "there's somewhere I need to be." He nodded toward the thirty-fifth floor.

Goldie craned his neck, then gestured offhandedly toward a steam grate. "Personally, I prefer the subterranean."

A subway roared by below, shoving air before it like the howl of a beast. Cal felt a tremor of unease. He'd heard of the Mole People, the pale outcasts who inhabited the less-traveled corridors of subway and sewer, the dark city under the bedlam of the city he knew.

Cal offered, "Maybe later."

"Later will not do." Goldie stepped in abruptly, political buttons, free promo pins and other pop-culture accretions clattering on his padded electric blue vest. "Be gone to ground then, man, we all will. Been reading the paper lately? Fire, flood, earthquake. Scary times."

"Yeah, pretty scary," Cal agreed, trying to ease past. Goldie cut him off, sliding sideways, staring down at him with jangly intensity.

"I will show wonders in heaven and signs in the earth," Goldie's voice exploded into a shout as he switched from Cal to the studiously not-looking pedestrians rushing past. "Blood, fire, vapors of smoke! Your old men will see visions!" It was Revelation, of course. What other book did lunatics read?

Cal seized the moment to duck under Goldie's out-stretched arm toward his office. But steely fingers clamped on his coat sleeve and yanked him back, nearly off his feet. Goldie shoved his face ominously close. The smell of him was musty and thick, his gaze lucid and dazzling. In a whisper like a talon strike, he warned, *"Your young men will dream dreams. . . ."*

Cal felt unaccountably stripped of all defenses, seen. It wasn't just the words or the look, but something deep and enigmatic behind them.

"I'm telling you this 'cause you talk to me, don't just look through." Goldie brought his lips to Cal's ear. "No such thing as coincidences. It's omens, Cal. Something's coming." His eyes suddenly went flat and distant, as if his mind had disengaged from the street and was plugged into some other landscape, some other time. "Metal wings will fail, leather ones prevail."

Bad poetry now, Cal thought, uncomprehending. *Where did that come from?*

Goldie's eyes returned to him now, back in the moment. He released Cal and stepped aside. "You keep your head low."

Cal nodded mutely, turned to the doors. Just before he entered, he glanced back. Goldie was still there, watching him.

"I'll see you later," Cal murmured.

"If there is a later," Goldie replied, still and gray for all his outrageous color. Cal faltered, missing the revolving door, and had to wait for it to come around again.

Herman Goldman watched the young man vanish into the building, lost among all the identically suited men. He doubted he'd been believed, certainly not fully, not enough. It didn't surprise him, but how could he not have tried? He wiped a bit of powdered sugar from his stubbly chin. Time to find another Gillette in the endless cornucopia of trash receptacles.

How much they discarded, he thought. How little they *saw*. The street was emptying as the Others fed themselves into the towers like so many termites. He hardly ever thought of when he'd been one of them. He hadn't known himself then, hadn't known the many worlds that made up the one world. But which was better, he wondered, knowing or not knowing? Blindness could be a blessing, sight a terrible burden.

His legs suddenly felt watery. He reached for a nearby wall. Heat radiated off the pavement, and the din of the city hammered at him. *What a world, what a world. Who would've thought a good little girl like you could destroy my beautiful wickedness?* No, that wasn't right, get a grip. He envisioned the sturdy brown tomes of the *Britannica* from his childhood, opened Volume One and began reading. *This letter has stood at the head of the alphabet during the whole of the period through which it can be traced historically.* It was all there, all still in his mind. Mother and father might shriek their invective at each other, a bruising clash of legalese and psychobabble, an endless verbal car wreck, but he was safe in his fortress, perched on the closed lid of the toilet under the sixty watt, big book on his lap, transported. Order from chaos. It had saved him, made him a survivor. Words had power.

Time to get home, to hunker down and wait. There was still time, at least a little. He turned into a narrow alley that shielded him a bit from the noise. His nostrils flared at the hot garbage smell emanating from the dumpsters. Funny how, even now, he had such an acute sense of smell, how easily his nose was offended. Shambling along, feet cushioned in his over-large New Balances by wadded newspapers, he mentally ran over the possible routes home, discarding Rockefeller Center for Grand Central. This time of day there'd be less scrutiny, easier to slip into the darkness. Just be careful not to touch the third rail.

He heard a rustling behind him, an odd, whispery sound, and turned, intrigued. Wadded candy wrappers, stained sheets of the *Post* and bits of excelsior that had tumbled out of the dumpster were starting to swirl about in a mini-tornado, gathering speed. *But where was the wind?* They seemed to be moving of their own volition. With shocking abruptness the force grew, edging the dumpsters back and forth on their wheels, their heavy metal lids rising and then banging down, again and again. His skin pricked, and he noticed a smell of ozone in the air. *Not yet; please, not yet.* Although he had been expecting it, he found that he was terrified. Above him, he heard a crackling, snapping noise— *and it ain't Rice Krispies*—and looked up to see blue electrical discharges whipping about in the sky. Dark clouds roiled, casting a yellow-gray pall. He felt incredibly small and, worst of all, *observed*.

The blue lightning was increasing in ferocity, slashing in all directions, with a sound like ice sheets splintering. And behind it, another, greater sound, a low *roar* that vibrated through him and grew in power, rumbling the ground. He wanted to run, to hide. A desire that seemed to come not *from* him but to *drive* him overwhelmed him. A compulsion to emerge from the shelter of the alley, to *see*.

The pavement beneath his feet was heaving now, buckling, as if some massive serpent below were struggling to burst forth. He fought his way to the alley mouth, peered out.

The sky was alive with blue lightning. It spat its hatred down at the city, frenzied wild fingers reaching out to every spire. The roar was deafening now, a spike through his head. He clapped his hands to his ears, but it did nothing. The roar changed pitch, rose higher, became a scream.

The buildings, the buildings were melting. Like ice cream cones on a hot day, dripping down, the entire city was liquefying. Proud towers turned to slag as the lightning danced its mad dance and the clouds enfolded it like a shroud.

Goldie's mouth was open, and he was screaming, too, though he could not hear it against the shriek of the city. He folded in on himself, arms covering his eyes, rocking, all armor torn away. In what he knew were his last moments, he surrendered to it, realizing that no matter how much he prepared, how much he might *know*, in the end it would do with him whatever it wished.

He opened, and the world fell away.

There was a jolt, and he heard that he was the only one screaming. He clamped his mouth shut and cautiously opened his eyes.

The buildings stood upright; the men and women went about their business; the cars surged and huffed, going nowhere.

"Your old men will see visions . . . ," Goldie murmured, shakily finding his feet again. He wasn't that old, not really. But Jehovah, Moloch and Jupiter—not to mention Jerry Garcia, his personal god—he *felt* old.

The lobby was hell. Or, more accurately, purgatory.

As Cal entered, he found himself jammed up against a throng of dark-suited men dragging on cigarettes, women hopping from foot to foot, exchanging Nikes and Reeboks for heels—all crowded riotiously together, buzzing discontent and impatience.

He quickly saw the reason: a bank of elevators lay inoperative, a workman bent over the maw of one with a lamp, the top of the cab visible at floor level. A litter of tools lay near an open red toolbox, along with big metal hooks and blocks of wood.

Cal scanned the opposite row of elevators. They were working, but the lights above revealed them on distant floors—twenty-seven, thirty-two, thirty-five—tauntingly static, as though nailed there.

"What's up with this?" "This fucking city . . ." "C'mon, c'mon, c'mon . . ." The angry, brittle voices swirled about Cal. But one voice held sway.

If there is a later . . .

It was the kind of apocalyptic ranting you heard on New York streets every day, but the words dogged him, lodged in him with rough conviction.

And resonating within him, too, in a voice his and not his, a response.

There would be a later, cast in darkness and blood and screams. And a sword. And he would rise to it.

Or not rise . . .

Cal thought of Stern, thirty-five floors above, all fang and claw, waiting, and a sudden thrum of passion flared in him, a determination to stand in opposition.

Dangerous, dangerous, dangerous . . .

"Hey, asshole, how 'bout you play with that later and let the rest of us do some *real* work?"

The words seized Cal's attention. He saw that a lean executive was standing over the workman, red-faced, fists balled in challenge. The suit was Cal's age, had the same hair, the same clothes, might well have been Cal.

The day before.

For a moment, the crouched figure didn't move, and Cal wondered if the man had heard. Then he set down the work lamp and turned. With surprise, Cal saw that it was a woman with shaggy, short-cropped hair and a grease stain on one cheek. Even through the scuffed brown trousers and baggy denim shirt, Cal could discern a slender form with broad, muscular shoulders. Her face was all strong lines and clear, disdainful eyes. The patch on the front of her shirt read "Colleen."

"Hey, cut the lady some slack." Cal was surprised that it was his voice. Without intending, he had spoken.

The young woman turned on him. "Listen, hotshot, I need a personal savior, I'll ask for one, okay?"

Derisive laughter bubbled from the crowd. Cal flushed hot embarrassment. An elevator opposite *dinged,* and its doors slid open. Cal was carried along with the press of bodies into the car, the mass that needed to be somewhere, whether they wanted or not. He saw the young woman over their heads for just a second, turning back to her labors. Then the doors slid shut, and she was gone.

IN THE AIR

Nobody asked her questions at the car rental return.

Nobody asked her questions at check-in.

Nobody asked her questions at security.

(*Am I really going to get away with this?*)

It was part of Jerri Bilmer's job to look unconcerned, to blend in with other caffeine-deprived morning travelers jostling along the concourse. To stand in line in the Kigali airport or at a bus stop in Baghdad without even a quickening of breath while RPF or Republican Guard came around checking papers and ransacking luggage at random. To appear, not innocent—they always go for those who look innocent—but simply as part of the background. To appear like nothing, no one, with microdots or little rolls of fiche burning holes in her purse strap or shoes.

Thinking about something else helped.

But this wasn't like Kigali or Baghdad or Port Sudan. For the first time since she was a recruit, Bilmer felt a skittery sense of being out of control, of waiting for something to happen and not knowing what the hell it would be.

Bilmer floated restlessly, uneasily in the vicinity of the gate without sitting down, listening for boarding, watching the standbys. Pretending to look at magazines, books, candies, souvenir-covered wagons and shot glasses inscribed with the Royals' logo. Straining all her senses, without the slightest idea what she was looking for.

She didn't wear the sunglasses that so many of her colleagues favored—*I mean, how obvious can you be?*—so it was more difficult to scan the concourse around her, but she saw no threat.

Or at least, saw nobody who looked like Russian mafia or Serbian nationals.

But what would this threat look like?

Stay cool. Stay cool and you can get away with anything.

Jetway.

Boarding pass.

Seat 12-A.

If the plane should lose cabin pressure during flight, these oxygen masks will drop down. . . .

One of the most useful talents in an agent, some friend in the department had told her once, is the ability not to sweat. Taking her seat, she mentally tagged the possibles, the ones to watch out for: the guy in the green T-shirt with the computer, maybe. Not your typical businessman. Or maybe one of the businessmen with laptops? Clones of one another, easy disguise. The old dude with the cane, maybe. Had she seen that woman with the backpack before?

Follow the rules and be ready, she thought. *Be ready for anything*.

Takeoff. Square brown fields with the green circles of center-fed automatic watering equipment. Gray-white roads and cars like hurrying bugs. Coffee service.

At least lifting off from Basra or Beirut you could exhale and lean back and think, *safe*. (Well, if you weren't flying Aeroflot anyway.) Could these people get her at Dulles? On the taxi into D.C.? McKay said he'd send someone to pick her up if she wanted, and she'd told him what she'd wear, but she had no intention of doing so. Not after what she'd seen at the Source.

She angled her foot so her toe was always in contact with her purse under the seat ahead of her and tried to look interested in the copy of *People* she'd bought, while the men in suits read their reports or worked on their laptop computers and the guy in the green T-shirt got out his Powerbook and started to play hearts.

For all his reputation as an idealist, Stuart McKay was a President who worked well with Congress, who knew the shortcuts and could get things done in a hurry. Bilmer had heard him described as a mixer, a pourer of oil on troubled waters, or, if you listened to his enemies, a compromiser. *And he'll need it*, thought Bilmer. *He'll need to pull all the strings, to call in all the favors, he can, if he's going to cut off Sanrio's power before . . .*

Before what?

It scared her, that she didn't quite know. Nor had she any clear idea of what McKay might be able to do against the little group of physicists in their South Dakota fastness. Call them back to Washington on a pretext and arrest them at the airport? Cut off the electricity to the installation in the Black Hills? Nuke the place before they got their field, or whatever they called it, into place?

She settled back in her seat and turned pages, pretending to read.

The old dude with the cane fell asleep, or pretended to. The broad with the backpack read a book. *What else was in the backpack?* The Mississippi River below, then the Ohio, then the Appalachians. Stroller Mom in the seat behind Bilmer read *The Velveteen Rabbit* to one child—*the more you love and are loved, the more real you become*—while another squalled endlessly, peevishly. A man two rows in front of Bilmer kept up a loud-voiced catalogue of the Hollywood celebrities with whom he'd worked, to the intermittent gasped punctuation of a sweet female voice.

Nothing.

"Ladies and gentlemen," said the captain's voice from the cockpit, "we're starting our descent into Dulles International Airport. The time in Washington is approximately 9:17, eastern daylight time. Your flight crew will be coming by to collect cups and napkins. Please bring your seats and your tray tables back to full upright and locked position."

The plane tilted, banked. Below, the green-dotted sprawl of streets, brick houses, parks, baseball diamonds. The glitter of water of the Chesapeake country. To the west the low green ripple of the Alleghenies, and beyond them . . .

"Hey," said Bilmer's seat mate, sitting up and looking past her at the windows. "What's that light in the sky?"

SEVEN

"He's breathing fire," Janice Fishman warned from her desk as Cal Griffin pushed through the double doors into the lobby of Stern, Ledding and Bowen.

The secretaries and mailroom boys and paralegals were chattering on their headsets, scribbling notes, rushing about under herniating weights of paper. Cal dodged them, slid up to the closed conference room doors, gleaming like twin coffin lids. Through the glass on either side he could see the meeting well under way; Ed Ledding and Peter Chomsky and Anita La Bonte were there, as well as the other associates—with one notable exception—silent as stone heads around the big table. The familiar black-suited figure strode up and down like the predator he was, holding forth, his words cloaked to silence by the glass, his back momentarily to Cal.

Cal's fingertips brushed the heavy wooden doors and paused. He wanted to be calm, but his heart was jackhammering; his brow and upper lip glistened with sweat. Curiously, a phrase drifted into his mind, one that at first he couldn't place. Then the memory came of their mother reading by Tina's bedside; he heard it, muffled and musical, through the walls of their wind-whipped home.

Whether I shall turn out to be the hero of my own life, or whether that station will be held by anybody else . . .

Cal steadied himself, eased the doors open and stepped through.

"—cells working in harmony, you get a hummingbird, an orchid, a humpback whale." Stern was speaking quietly, as he always did when most dangerous. "In mutiny and rebellion, all you get is cancer."

The others had spied Cal and tensed. Sensing this, Stern turned to face him. "Ah, Mr. Griffin. Word of your morning's handiwork hath preceded you. Should we give you a ticker-tape parade? Perhaps a party with clowns?"

Indignation flared in Cal; he opened his mouth to speak. But Stern raised a preemptive finger. "No. Not a word." He closed, glowering with eyes impenetrable as mirrored shades. "This is not Woodstock. I am not Mother Teresa. So the only relevant issue is—"

His words cut off as the tremor hit the room, like the flat of an immense hand smacking the building. The walls shook violently; the floor lurched. Cal staggered, barely managed to keep standing as he clutched the table and felt something pass through him like a great wind. Stern grasped the wall for support. Bunky Hegland and Seth Harris tumbled out of their chairs, amid a babble of shrieks and gasps. The overhead fixtures swayed, and the lights went out, plunging the room into darkness.

Cal shouted, "The table! Get under the table!" En masse, they dove beneath the thick slab—all save Stern, who stood frozen by the wall. Out of the corner of his eye, Cal thought he saw a blue light surge about Stern, an eruption that flared and was gone. But he couldn't swear to it; his eyes were still phosphor-flashing from the sudden shift of light to dark.

The tremor continued, rose in rhythmic, undulating vibrations, the walls swaying and groaning, the floor bucking. Distantly, Cal heard glass breaking, the thud and clatter of objects, impacts dull and splintering. Huddled under the table, he felt the warmth of bodies mashed against him, the rise and fall of rapid, shallow breath. There were no screams now, only grunts with each concussion, wordless murmurs of incomprehension, the need for it to stop.

Cal found that he had his arms draped over two others, he couldn't tell whom, instinctively sheltering them. The intimacy of the dark, the clamor, the proximity of bodies all held an echo, a resonance of his dream.

But it was real. As the blood pulsed in his ears, his bones and flesh and teeth shuddering, all he could think of was his sister.

The shaking began to subside, the cacophony of distant sounds racheted down. The voices about Cal whirled up in sharp whispers, collided, broke upon each other. "Earthquake, my god—" "In Manhattan?" "Explosive device—" "Big gas main over in, my cousin—" "Vertical fault lines, right under—"

The creaking of the overhead fixtures slowed, the glass tubes cooling, extinguished. Cal crawled out from under the table, motioning the others. "Come on."

They followed, as he shoved open the big doors and rushed out into the bullpen. It was brighter here, daylight filtering from the open doorways of Ledding's and Bowen's suites. Paralegals and secretaries were helping each other up, dim shambling forms in the gloom. Somewhere a man or woman—impossible to tell—was sobbing quietly.

Cal grabbed up a desk phone, held the receiver to his ear—dead.

"Who's got a cell phone?" he shouted.

"Here!" Janice Fishman handed off her Nokia, and Cal punched in the number of St. Augustine, hit send. Nothing.

"Where the hell are the emergency lights?" That was Paul Cajero, panic fracturing his voice.

Cal cast about the room, made out the misty shapes of Bob Williams Jr. and Chris Black holding cell phones to their ears, shaking them ineffectually. By now, Anita La Bonte had fished a portable radio from her desk, and Paul Leonard had retrieved a flashlight from the utility cabinet. Inexplicably, they weren't working either.

Cal felt a vise tighten around his heart. He had to get onto the street, see how widespread this was, get to a working phone, *if there was one,* make sure Tina . . .

A soft moan issued from the conference room. Cal turned to it. Through the open doors, he saw the figure within, slumped against a wall, alone.

Cal entered and drew near. In the murky light from the doorway, he could see Stern sitting motionless on the floor, face averted. Stern grew aware of him, angled his head slightly, eyes nearly closed.

"Do you need a hand up?" Cal asked. The sight of Stern so still, emptied of his hectic, decisive energy, shook him.

"No," Stern said languidly, indifferent. Shock? Cal couldn't see any obvious injuries, but that meant nothing. Stern grimaced, shielded his eyes from the dim light.

"Hey, everybody! Look!" Barbara Claman's Marlboro rasp sang out from the common room. Stern turned his head away dismissively. Cal withdrew.

He found the rest of the staff massed with Barbara by the window in Russ Bowen's suite, peering down, strangely subdued. He squeezed through them, squinted at the daylight.

On the street far below, and on all the streets as far as the eye could see, the cars, trucks, cabs and buses were still. Tiny figures emerged from pygmy vehicles, lifted hoods, stood stunned and disbelieving. "They're not working either," Janice muttered incredulously, needlessly. Her voice held awe, and fear.

Cal let out a long breath. His eyes lifted to the heavens—and he froze. "Oh, my God," he whispered.

The others turned to him, saw the dawning horror on his face.

The objects looked almost like toys, so many miles distant, and they were lovely, really, glinting in the sun, all twisting and angling downward.

"The planes," Cal said. "They're falling out of the sky."

WEST VIRGINIA—9:17 A.M. EDT

Fred felt it grab him at the same instant every machine in Bob's room went dark.

There wasn't even the steady flamenco of alarms that you saw in TV movies when the hero's wife or mother or best friend went into seizure in the emergency room. Just no lights, no readouts. Even the backup batteries had gone dark. And Bob's mind, screaming, screaming for help . . .

Bob, I've got you! Fred caught him, seized him, reached out into the dark into which he was falling and held on, even as he felt the horrible cold dragging at him. . . .

They were children again; Bob had fallen into Cherry Creek during the floods of '63, racing current ripping him away. Fred had managed to grab him, hook his own arm around the remains of the old dock, while the cold water hammered him and icy numbness bored deeper and deeper into his flesh.

I won't let you go! I won't let you go!

And the child-Bob pressed into his chest, clutched at his arm with nerveless fingers. He couldn't breathe or think. He only knew that he couldn't let go.

Roaring in his ears, in his mind. Weightless swinging over a void, and that terrible, ghastly dragging at him, drawing him back to the Source. Voices screaming, thunder in his brain: Sanrio, Wu, Pollard. *Come back here! Come back! We need you . . . !*

Bob screaming his name.

He'd deserted Bob once before. He would not do it again.

Fred reached out, gathered everything the Source surrounded him with, all that power, all that light, and poured it into Bob's still heart and still lungs and dying bloodstream and brain. *I won't let you go*!

And in his ears and heart and brain and soul, the world screamed.

❧

Roof fall, thought Hank in a second of blind, hideous panic. *Floor heave. Explosion.* His hands fumbled automatically at the Self-Contained Self-Rescuer—the respirator—hanging at his belt.

"Fuck a duck!" howled Sonny Grimes from the darkness behind him, and for some reason the man's yowl of protest steadied Hank, centered him. As soon as he yanked the SCSR's strap tight, he hit the levers of the shearer, though the thing had ground to an instant, shuddering halt already.

Hollow in the respirator's filters, Gordy Flue's voice said, "C'mon, Sonny, where you gonna get a duck down here?"

And Ryan, "What happened to the headlamps?"

Silence. A million tons of mountain and darkness deep as the end of the world.

Hands shaking, Hank fumbled the flashlight from his pocket. He heard something clatter, small and metallic on the floor, and Gordy cursed. He guessed the others were doing the same.

He switched over the toggle, and he might as well have flipped a tiddly-wink for all the light it summoned. "Son-of-a-bitch batteries," said Roop McDonough as Hank shook his own flashlight, took the fresh batteries from his pocket, tried again.

Zip.

Hank felt himself trembling, sweat on his face and bile in his mouth. The smell of coal dust was thick in his nostrils, his lungs. Every man at the face knew that a flame here could be the last light any of them would ever see. *Aftershocks,* he thought. Wasn't that what happened in California and Japan? The earth calmed down and then went on shaking, on and off, for days?

Ryan Hanson spoke again. "How come all the helmet lights went out?"

"Everybody okay?" Hank called into the blackness, and Al's voice and Tim's echoed in response. Hank hit the toggle on his radio and got nothing—no surprise there. By the stillness of the air he knew the vent fans had quit working, too. "Anybody hurt?"

"Yeah, I slipped in it when I pissed my pants." Gordy again, and the unwilling laugh it got was like the breaking of an iron band around Hank's throat.

"What happened to the batteries?" asked Bartolo. His voice was moving. He was feeling his way along the wall, Hank guessed, toward the tunnel that led back to the main.

"Coulda been some kind of electronic pulse," said Ryan. His voice struggled to retain its calm before his seniors. "Like they say a nuclear attack would cause."

"Nuclear attack?" Panic edged Roop's words. "You think . . . ?"

"Fuck, who'd drop a bomb on West Virginia?" cut in Grimes, exasperation further chipping at the terror, breaking it up like a boulder into manageable chunks.

"Could be something like the same thing, I meant," Ryan amended hastily. "You know, that would put out electronic equipment."

"A mile down?"

"A battery and a bulb ain't exactly what you call 'electronic equipment,' butthead."

"Hey!" Hank pocketed his useless light. "Doesn't matter what put them out. They're out. We'll find out what happened when things get working again. Everybody get to a wall and work your way around to the entrance of the main. Let's get back to the elevator and maybe find some lights that work."

Nobody said what everybody was thinking: What if there was a roof fall in the main?

If there was, they'd find out soon enough.

Stumbling and slipping on the rolling masses of shale and coal, Hank worked his way back along the face, the curved gouges in the rock sharp and rough under his fingers. In the darkness the men kept up a banter, cursing or making jokes to cover their fear ("Hey, let's play Marco Polo!" "Fuck you, Gordy") and Hank marveled again at their capacity to deal with terror, emergency, God knew what.

We're not dead. We can deal with the next ten minutes.

"Got here," called out Tim, presumably from the entrance.

Very suddenly, Hank's hand encountered damp, slightly greasy cloth and the warmth of a shoulder. "That you, Tim?" He could have hugged the man.

"Ryan?"

"This's me."

"Gordy?"

"What, my good looks don't glow in the dark?"

"Smells like shit, it's gotta be Gordy."

"Sonny?"

"Who the fuck else would it be down here?"

Al, Roop—voices out of the darkness, hands touching hands. *So far*, thought Hank, *so good. Don't think about what it means.*

The men linked hands and felt their way along the wall. Whenever they encountered a box containing another SCSR, they took it, slinging it onto their belts. In addition to the danger from methane, without the fans working, the air would go bad quickly and there was no telling how long they'd have to wait for rescue when they reached the elevators.

If they reached the elevators. Thank God, thought Hank, Applby had gone over to long-wall mining in the new section. He couldn't imagine trying to grope their way to the downcast if they'd still been doing room and pillar, with the mazes of crosscuts and subsidiary mains. At least there wasn't anyplace to go but straight back. And another little prayer of thanks that a respirator worked by compressed air and wasn't susceptible to whatever had knocked out all the batteries. His greatest dread, as he led the way along, was that every second his fingers would encounter an unscheduled wall of loose rock that would tell them they were well and truly screwed.

As they walked, Ryan was still trying to figure out what had happened to the batteries. Others proffered suggestions of who to blame: management fuckup, Arab terrorists, Chinese bombs. Grimes rode the boy unmercifully, jeering at his speculations but offering nothing of his own except obscenities. Hank wanted to punch him but kept silent. Any speech was better than none, against this terrible blind silence and the racing puzzlement that filled his heart.

A faint scuffling of bodies, of voices in the dark ahead. Hank called out, "Yo!" and Andy Hillocher's voice replied.

"Hank? You guys got a radio?"

"Deader'n a road-kill skunk."

There was appropriate commentary on both sides.

"Roof's holding stable, anyway."

"Well, be sure to write that down for the geology boys," retorted another sarcastic voice—Dixon's, Hank guessed from the slight intonation of black speech. "They'll be glad to hear it."

"*I'm* glad to hear it," snapped Hank. "Who all's here?"

After an endless crawl through darkness, Hank's groping hand felt the corner of the wall and, cautiously removing his respirator, he smelled water and wet rock. A little farther on, his hand encountered the edge of the unmoving conveyor belt that led the way toward the downcast. "Hang on a minute," he said. "Everybody shut up for a second."

When the voices ceased, the silence flowed back. Terrible silence, horrifying in its completeness, broken only by the slow, infinitesimal drip of water leaking from the pipes and, at long intervals, a far-off tapping and creaking.

"That's the mine breathin' in her sleep," his dad had said. And his grandfather had made spooky eyes at him and whispered, "It's the tommy-knockers. They digs in the mines, too."

One of the company boys in engineering had once explained to Hank what those noises really were in terms of ground water and weight distribution over the rock. But when he heard them, he always thought of his granddad, sitting in the warm corner between the big old iron kitchen stove and the cellar door, cradling a shot glass in his hands.

"What you think you're gonna hear down here, asshole?" demanded Sonny Grimes.

"Maybe Superman and Batman talkin' about how they're gonna find us," retorted Hank. There was something in the air—the coal dust, maybe—that made him itch all over, and his head ached something fierce. He was in no mood for Sonny.

A little farther on they found the tram, dead on its tracks and empty. They encountered the men who'd been in it at the downcast, after Hank laboriously worked the manual openers on the three sets of airflow-control doors that guarded the elevator. "That better be somebody we know," Gene Llewellyn's voice called out from behind the third set of doors, and of course Gordy couldn't resist and let out a horrible growl that fooled nobody.

"Get your hand off my ass, Gordy," retorted Lou Hanson, and there was general laughter.

"They know we're down here," Brackett said comfortingly, as everybody shifted to make room, and they counted off names, made sure it was the whole shift. "Even if the emergency generator up top got knocked out, they'll have another one in place inside a couple hours. This isn't like the old days."

No, thought Hank, scratching absent-mindedly at his shoulder. It isn't like the old days. *In the old days there's no way we'd have been trapped a mile under the ground.* The Green Mountain mine was a slope, not a shaft, and you could walk out, provided you weren't cut off or buried yourself.

In the old days, too, there were things that worked without batteries.

"What about it, Gene?" asked Andy Hillocher. By the sound of it he'd removed his respirator, to save on air, something he was pretty safe doing here by the shaft. Hank had already taken his off, because the straps itched like fury. "You're the company egghead. How come all the headlamps went out?"

"Beats the crap out of me." Llewellyn tried to sound jaunty but didn't quite succeed.

"There any record of gas in this part of the mine?" asked Hank.

Llewellyn's voice replied from the darkness. "If there's been a floor heave, there could be gas anywhere; you know that."

"Okay," said Hank. "But even with a couple of respirators apiece, things are gonna get pretty stuffy pretty quick. I think somebody needs to take a look around outside. I mean a *look*."

There was silence. They knew he was right. But they all had the miner's inborn horror of fire below the ground.

"After you close that third door behind you," Gene said at last, "you count to three hundred before you light that match. There shouldn't be dust this close to the downcast, and if there's gas, you're not going to make it that long and nobody has anything to worry about. Anybody in here got a problem with that?"

"I got a problem," groused Sonny. "Why the hell don't we just wait till the company gets its butt in gear and comes down after us?"

"Because they might not, asshole," Hillocher retorted. "And if the ceiling's getting ready to cave in or there's water pouring down the walls or something, I'd kind of like to know about it while there's still time to shift our sorry asses someplace else, okay?"

There was a little more argument, but at length Hillocher handed his lighter and a twist of paper—it felt like a page from a magazine—to Hank. Hank cranked open the doors, cranked them shut and cranked open the next pair, and the next.

"Fuckin' asshole's gonna blow us all up," Grimes muttered.

"So sue him."

The doors shut off their voices.

Beyond the third set there was the dim smell of coal and rock dust, of wet rock and oil from trams and machines.

And silence.

Hank listened again to that silence and let it fill him.

On the other side of the downcast, he knew, would be the

mains leading into the older sections of the mine, the worked-out room-and-pillar areas where black crosscuts intersected the rubble of roof falls and controlled collapses that had occurred as the men had retreated after taking every fragment of the supporting coal. But no sound, save for the drip of water, the creak of the tommy-knockers.

Behind him, muffled by three sets of doors, he heard Brackett ask, "Some other kind of gas, maybe? Does anybody smell anything?"

"You mean other than the shit in Hanson's pants?"

"Oh, fuck off, why don't you, Sonny?"

"Does anybody else have a headache?"

"I'm gettin' a headache listening to Hanson's crap about Arab fuckin' terrorists and nuclear warfare."

Hank had a headache. Not the same as he'd had from his brushes with firedamp in the mines, but a strange sense of tightening, a weird ache in his neck and back and in some deep center of his brain. Looking back toward the doors—toward his friends—he felt a curious unwillingness to return to them, a sense that he'd be more comfortable here in the dark, with the tommy-knockers. Hank lit the spill of paper, but he had to force himself to do it. The light showed him the tunnels, the silent machinery, the pipes slowly dripping water. Everything as normal.

Quickly he blew out the flame. The light of it, he found, hurt his eyes. He wondered if that meant anything.

Shaking his head a little, he made himself go back.

EIGHT

WEST VIRGINIA

"Arleta? Are you there?" Wilma sprang up the front steps of the big white house, tried the knob with fingers barked and bloody from having been thrown off her feet by the earthquake. Behind her, old Mr. Swann from the trailer court and young Shannon Grant—to whom she'd been talking when the quake hit—waited anxiously, ready to give whatever help might be needed. Only a few years ago Shannon had been one of Wilma's students, and Wilma fully expected to one day see Shannon's daughter Tessa, currently two years old and perched on her mother's hip, in her classes as well.

The knob wouldn't turn. Oddly, it didn't rattle, as it would have if the door were locked. It felt frozen, jammed hard. Wilma pushed inward. Nothing. "Arleta?"

"We're all right here, Wilma." Arleta's voice, behind the shut door.

Wilma tried to look through the window, but the curtain was drawn. "Arleta?"

"We're all fine."

She must be terrified, thought Wilma. Like the cats, skittering spookily around the shadows, fearful of everything, and why not? The house wasn't supposed to move. "Can you open the door? Are you hurt? Is Bob okay?" There were, of course, backup batteries on Bob's machines, but every battery in Wilma's house seemed to have been affected, and in Shannon's, too.

"We're all fine, really." If it hadn't been for the unmistakably human timber of the voice Wilma would have sworn it was a recording. *Poor Arleta!*

"What about Bob's machines?" she persisted. "How long do the backup batteries keep running? Do we need to get an emergency team here or something?"

Still that stilted, wooden tone, still that sense of . . . what? Something odd, Wilma didn't know quite what. As if it wasn't really Arleta. "Bob's machines will run for forty-eight hours without any problems. Don't worry. We're fine."

As Ryan would say, thought Wilma, *my ass.*

"I have to go now. Bob's calling for me."

"What? Arleta?" Wilma gripped the doorknob again, shook it. *Bob? Bob's in a coma.* "Arleta, let me just . . ."

Behind her, Mr. Swann gasped, put a hand to his chest and leaned suddenly against the railing. Shannon caught his elbow as he staggered. "It's nothing, I just felt sorta bad." The neighbors were all coming out into the street now, the Stickneys and June Culver and old Mrs. Weise. She saw Jim Stickney walk over and get into his Jeep Wrangler, then get out again a few moments later.

Shock because of the quake, thought Wilma. Californians got used to them, she'd heard—didn't even bother to get out of bed, most of them. But the Appalachians weren't supposed to shake.

She got Mr. Swann into her living room and sat him down on the couch. Shannon and Rae Ann Stickney and Gerda Weise followed them through the door uninvited, making soft-voiced inquiries: Was everything all right and did much get broken and were the batteries out in your radio too? Their faces showed something Wilma hadn't seen there a few moments ago: bafflement. The expressions of people faced with something they've never encountered, something far wider than an earthquake.

"It's not just batteries." Shannon was still holding Tessa's hand. "That old hand-crank generator of Jim's won't go, either. We were going to drive over to the pithead and see if everything's all right there, and. . . ."

Wilma realized how deep the silence was. The refrigerator was still. The battery-operated clock wasn't ticking. Nor were there the sounds she had been half-listening for in the distance, the wail of emergency sirens.

Nothing. Stillness.

She began to understand that what had happened was very different from what she had thought.

NEW YORK

The sky was clear now, save for a few twisting vapor trails, already dissipating, melting into the clouds.

Cal had not seen any of the planes hit ground; the buildings had blocked his view. But they *had* crashed; how could they not have? Most on the periphery of the city, away from its heart, so perhaps . . . He caught himself trying to force the disaster into the smallest possible proportions.

As for the buildings, none had collapsed as far as Cal could see, though many were fractured and a few tilted at treacherous angles.

It's omens, Cal, Goldie had said. *Something's coming.*

Cal shuddered, and the desperate urgency to be on the move, to reach his sister, drowned all else.

The legal staff, drawn together in the dim light of the common room, had learned soon enough that, of all their technological marvels, only lighters still worked. Most of them had children, parents, spouses and others of variable significance. Despite their misgivings at leaving the relative safety of the building (now that it had stopped shaking), they, like Cal, were eager to brave the stairwells and be gone.

Only one question delayed them.

"What about Mr. Stern?"

He remained secluded in the conference room. Since Cal's exchange with him, none had ventured to disturb him. Yet to leave without informing him, gaining his sovereign consent . . .

They milled uncertainly in the gloom, Janice Fishman and Paul Cajero and Tom Sammon and the others. The lowly ones who made the office go, the exalted few who jockeyed for position and coveted partnerships. Darkness veiled their expressions, but Cal could read their fear.

"I'll do it," he said.

As he cracked open the conference room doors, Cal could see in the weak light from the outer office that Stern had not moved. He sat slumped against the wall, eyes half-closed, a black stillness.

Cal entered, hunkered down. "Mr. Stern?"

Not looking at him, Stern said, "Hm?"

"How are you doing?"

"Got a bitch of a sinus headache. Tell Naomi to get me some Sudafed." He scratched one arm languorously but relentlessly through the black fabric of his coat sleeve. Somehow, more than the planes careening out of the sky, the buildings drunkenly askew, this strange diffidence spoke most powerfully to Cal of calamity. Earlier, he had thought himself a rock perilously seamed and cracked, but it was Stern, not he, who had shattered.

"Looks like power's out all over the city," said Cal. *No need to elaborate on the cars and planes, keep it simple.* "Everyone wants to head out, find out what's happened."

"Not five yet," Stern mumbled absently, still not looking at him.

No, it's not five yet.

Cal visualized the vaulting, unreinforced brick walls of St. Augustine, tried not to picture his sister crushed beneath them. . . . .

I'm not Mother Teresa. This is not Woodstock. But it was sure a hell of a lot like Mount St. Helens and Hurricane Andrew and Armageddon all rolled into one, *so why aren't you getting it?*

Cal forced down his anger. Stern was clearly, however elusively, injured. The crackling blue lightning Cal had glimpsed about Stern as he himself had dived beneath the table could readily have been some electrical discharge spat from the wall sockets as the juice cut out.

"Come on now," Cal said firmly, grasping Stern's arm, hauling him up.

With a mad shout, Stern tore his arm free, so violently that Cal staggered, was nearly flung off his feet. Stern plopped down sullenly, staring at nothing.

"Your skin itch?" he asked idly.

Cal backed slowly to the doors. "No," he said quietly. "Does yours?"

Still looking away, Stern muttered, "No."

Cal's back brushed the doors, and he stopped. He might get Paul Cajero and Ed Ledding and Chris Black in here to help deal with Stern, try to wrestle him down the stairs. But Stern would fight them every step of the way, he felt certain of it, and precious time would be lost.

"Look," Cal sighed. "I'll get someone to send back help for you, okay? I've got to go now."

Stern didn't turn, but something at last seemed to register. "Leave, and you're terminated."

Cal gave a mirthless laugh—the dreaded words at last.

The coffin-lid doors murmured softly against the carpet as they closed behind him.

Stern was glad Griffin was gone. His chatter had been irritating, almost as maddening as that damn itching. But it felt muted now, hushed in the darkness and the quiet. Calm descended over him as he floated on a gentle sea, its waters embracing him. All he wanted was to remain awhile, to let the feeling wash over him.

But then a dim memory came to him. The Bernero-Vivante deposition was later today. What time was it getting to be? Dreamily, he lifted the Piaget on his wrist to eye level, glanced at its face. In the gloom, he caught a reflection of his eyes in the glass.

I should be frightened by this, he thought. But he wasn't, merely intrigued, and far removed. He continued to stare at his own eyes looking back at him, their irises no longer the familiar black. Vaguely, it occurred to him that his choice of clothing no longer matched the color of his eyes.

For that, he would need yellow.

"Easy there. Nobody's got to hurry now." Cal's voice betrayed none of the sick urgency he felt. Cautiously, they descended the stairwell, Anita La Bonte and Barbara Claman and about ten of the others holding their lighters aloft, offering a timorous, close illumination. The fire doors at each floor blocked any light; other than the scant blue flames all was blackness. It lent their party a hushed intimacy. As they had ventured down, their group of thirty-odd had been joined by others with the same imperative, had swelled to more than seventy. On floors above and below them, they could hear similar parties, moving with the same blind tentativeness. Their feet shuffled on the steps, a dull thudding like an army of golems on the march. When they spoke, even in whispers, their voices echoed back, a loud, jarring assault. So they were quiet, by and large, their reeling thoughts held checked within.

Tina will stay at St. Augustine; she will wait for me. An image loomed before Cal of his sister fleeing into the streets for home, being swept up and lost in the mass of ten million souls vomiting from their buildings, flooding the thoroughfares and washing her hopelessly away.

No. She'll know to wait. She's level-headed, smart. He summoned the memory, three years back, of when, newly arrived from Hurley, Tina had tripped and burned herself on the radiator. She had cried out just once, then been quiet through the mad rush to the emergency room, the long, chaotic night. Silent and watchful and calm, far calmer than Cal had been.

But that had been an event prosaic and knowable, if unpleasant. This was something new.

And yet . . .

The nightmare clamor in the dark, the feel of the sword hilt, so right, the invitation to know himself at last.

Your young men will dream dreams. It's omens, Cal. Something's coming. . . .

Cal's Midwestern common sense rebelled. Disasters always pricked some feeling of déjà vu. But that didn't make those real premonitions, any more than some fake psychic on TV telling the viewers to—

Mike Covey suddenly cried out, missing a step. Anita La Bonte grabbed him.

Covey, who had taken credit for the brief that had been shipped in the night pouch to the Rome office, the brief Anita had sweated blood on till three A.M. four nights running all so he, and not Anita, might be the golden one to make the jump from fifth-year associate to contract partner.

Forgotten now, or at least put aside.

And not just the two of them. Tom Sammon's simmering resentment at Gilley Gray's "jokes," Janice Fishman's certainty that charm alone advanced Maria Bryant, all the petty slights and wounds, the long-held grudges melted in the white heat of catastrophe, fear . . .

Not the cold dread they lived with every working day, that kept them strangers, the persistent hum they finally stopped hearing, though it permeated everything in their lives.

Even hell, Cal realized, might have small patches of heaven.

The door to the hall flew open as they hit the sixteenth-floor landing, a mass of bodies blindly surging in. Blundering, cries, shoving in the darkness. Paul Cajero's arm was bumped, and his lighter clattered away, going out.

"Watch it, there's people here!" Cal cried out.

Everyone within the stairwell stopped where they were, while those still in the hall jostled and shoved. A discord of words, grunts, the tang of fear—the second group parted and their leader stepped up, carrying a lit candle, appraising Cal coolly.

"Who made you safari guide?" she asked. Even in the dimness, Cal recognized the denim shirt, the toolbelt slung low on her hip like some *Home Improvement* fast gun.

"Guess the same guy who made you one," Cal said. The corner of Colleen's mouth twitched in the hint of a smile, and Cal could see she had a dimple in one cheek.

She raised a heavy crossbar. "Been liberating folks stuck in the shafts," she explained. "You in the hall, hang back till we're clear." Both groups shifted around, adjusting themselves. Her eyes swung back to Cal. "So . . . ," she said, and it was both question and challenge.

"How about, I take point," Cal offered.

"—and I ride drag and pick up the strays." She nodded. "Yeah, okay."

His eyes followed her as she edged back into the throng, becoming indistinct, a silhouette. Paul Cajero was still scrabbling for his lighter. Cal spied its dark shape, scooped it up and flicked it to life. Paul murmured thanks, his face ruddy in the dancing light as they descended, their shadows in pursuit.

What struck Cal first as he emerged onto the street was the absence.

No diesel fumes, no din of engines or construction equipment. And no sirens, not even in the distance.

The silent, inert vehicles stretched along Fifth to infinity, their owners spewed onto asphalt and pavement, sweat smell discernible in the air amid the dust of fallen debris. The neon hubbub that normally blazed on storefronts—HOT GIRLS! GET YOUR BAGELS! PHONES FOR LESS!—lay dark.

Torn and tumbled men and women hunkered on curbs, pressing kerchiefs and wadded shirts to a host of injuries.

Above the buildings, Cal could discern pillars of rising smoke drifting across the sky. *The planes.* Despite the asphalt's baking heat, he shivered.

He was already on the move as he plotted a route to Tina. The major streets were choked, a strangling knot of humanity. For a moment, he considered the subways. Power would likely be out there, too. And in the blackness, shadowy forms waiting, eyes watching.

I prefer the subterranean, that homeless man, Goldie, had said.

Cal jettisoned the notion, quickly formed a grid in his mind of back streets and serviceways that led more or less directly to St. Augustine. He was heading purposefully toward a nearby alley when a voice called out behind him, throaty and loud.

"Hey, hold up there!" Cal turned to see the lean, muscular figure making a dash for him from the revolving door. Eighty flights on that concrete StairMaster hadn't taken a bite out of *her* vitality, apparently.

Colleen Brooks caught up with him, breath hardly labored. "Listen, what I said earlier—"

"It's okay," he said, still moving.

"I was outta line." She fell into step, shrugging, abashed. "Trouble with my love life."

Cal slowed, disarmed by her directness.

"What can I say? He puts up with me." Her eyes swept over the street scene with cool curiosity, then returned to Cal. "So, you got plans for the Apocalypse?"

"My sister. I take care of her." They had reached the alley mouth. He needed to get going but found himself surprisingly reluctant to end the conversation.

"She far?"

"St. Augustine. On MacDougal."

"Get some water before you go, 'cause that'll be a freakin' long walk."

Cal knew this and had planned to, but he nodded his thanks. He turned to go, then the doubt came to him that perhaps this fierce, competent girl might be hanging with him to avoid facing something fearful ahead of her. "You need . . . help of some kind?"

Colleen gave a wide smile, the first he had seen, and it so changed her, lightened her, that Cal had a glimpse of what she might have been had her path been less corrosive, less needful of guard. She shook her head. "Not from around here, are you?"

"No," Cal said and smiled, too. Colleen nodded knowingly. They began to drift apart, Colleen moving off in the other direction. "You keep your head low," she said.

Cal stopped, startled.

Keep your head low. Amid his wild prophecies and seeming knowledge of Cal's dream, just before zero hour, Goldie had said exactly those words.

And *metal wings will fail, leather ones prevail. . . .*

The planes had fallen out of the sky, but what the hell did "leather ones" refer to?

Coincidence, it was all coincidence. And yet, for a fleeting instant, Cal had an image of the three of them somehow tethered, their destinies twined.

"Yeah," Cal murmured to Colleen as she headed off. "Yeah, you, too." Then the alley enfolded him, and he was running.

NINE

WASHINGTON D.C.

The Joint Chiefs of Staff—or those of them as happened to be in Washington in late summer—arrived at 11:45, according to the eighteenth- and nineteenth-century clocks that continued to tick smugly in the Green Room and the Blue Room and the Red Room after everyone's quartz-movement Rolexes froze up. Larry Shango, who'd grown up with a Basin Street boy's mistrust of the uptown whites who spent more on a pair of shoes than his daddy could make in a week at the restaurant, had to smile.

An inner smile, since it was really none of his business to have an opinion about anything.

By 11:45 there was little else to smile at.

His eyes had been on McKay when the building started shaking—when the Japanese delegates, with the promptitude of long practice, had gone under the furniture or into the doorways and the aides and the folks from the Department of Commerce had tumbled like pins in a bowling alley. He'd seen the look on McKay's face. Later on, as the FBI and Secret Service cordons snapped into place around the White House and the National Guard started to arrive, sweating from the double-time march through the car-clogged streets, he'd kept nearly as close an eye on the President as on the men and women around him.

And by 11:45 he was pretty sure he was right.

McKay wasn't surprised.

He was, however, scared damn near shitless. And it was a couple of hours before anyone else got that scared.

"Reports are still coming in via semaphore and other nonelectric sources, but these conditions seem to prevail up and down the East Coast and as far west as Denver." General Christiansen set his papers on the table and glanced around at the other advisers, civilian and military, with pale, small watchful eyes. He had a hunter's tan and the air of a man who'd make you remake your bunk three times just to let you know he could. "No word yet from the West, but according to our sources, portions of Mexico and Canada seem similarly affected. We have no launch capability, no defensive capability at all."

"But what *is* it?" asked Dr. Perry, the stout, normally jovial physicist who headed up McKay's recently revived Science Advisory Board. His voice cut across the gasp and stammer of panic that Christiansen's announcement had triggered. "The things I've been hearing are absurd. There's no way—"

"Once you've eliminated the impossible," Christiansen cut in, "then whatever's left is probable . . . only maybe we'd better not eliminate the impossible just yet." A riff on Conan Doyle and not bad for a crisis, Shango thought. He hadn't known Christiansen had it in him. He noted, however, that while the general's mouth formed the ghost of a smile, his eyes stayed cold.

"All right, gentlemen," McKay jumped in. "Here's what we have to ascertain, right now or sooner—"

A babble of conflicting opinions, defensive statements erupted, which McKay's voice rose over, forcing silence. "Is this a natural disaster or man-made? If man-made, is it deliberate attack or accident? From within the U.S. or elsewhere? Is it worldwide, with the same effects? And are those effects strengthening or easing?" He addressed Christiansen.

"Ed, with the reports you're getting in, try to nail down specific times the alteration occurred in the various locales; maybe it'll help us track its locus, which direction it spread and how fast."

Christiansen nodded, whispered something to an aide, who jotted a note. McKay opened his mouth to add something, then thought better of it, Shango saw.

And just what aren't you saying? Shango wondered, dogged by the certainty of the words under the words, the poker hand held but not yet played. His eyes moved from face to face as they responded with the familiar round of finger pointing, before McKay again corralled them back to order.

It was Shango's job not to have an opinion, but a childhood of watching his mother and her church-lady pals in the tenants association and various neighborhood committees had left him with an insatiable curiosity about unspoken truths, hidden alliances—about who they'd run to and whisper once the meeting let out. His mind touched this and from long practice dodged away again, concentrating on the task at hand.

Watching the men in the room. Never mind that these were the highest brass in the DoD, watch 'em anyway. Watch the windows, the backs of the National guardsmen visible through them. Something massive had happened, and there was no guarantee what was next, and this man, this paunchy balding white guy with the pleasant Oklahoma drawl, was his responsibility.

He knows something.

Shango perceived that McKay was searching the faces of the men and women who flowed in succession into the Oval Office—group after group—for some sign as to who else knew.

The lights weren't on by noon. The White House command post sent over every available agent as soon as they showed up—most had started walking toward Foggy Bottom the minute the ground quit shaking—and there were anti-sniper posts in every building that overlooked the White

House, but it still put Shango's teeth on edge when McKay insisted on opening the windows. The men loosened their ties and took off their jackets and the women looked like they wished they could shed their pantyhose. Having grown up in New Orleans without benefit of air-conditioning—or indoor plumbing, until he was five—Shango wasn't much bothered by the heat. But while mentally calculating sight-lines from the windows every time McKay moved and watching each flicker of motion outside, he was deeply conscious of time's passage. The emergency generators should have come on-line long before this. First in the White House, then in the government buildings all around it.

He didn't hear helicopters, sirens, nothing, though the humid air was laden with the far-off tang of smoke. Only the voices of the National Guardsmen and a growing clamor of distant voices in the Mall and in the streets.

Things were down too long. Way, way too long.

The gang from FEMA came and went, then came back with horrifying preliminary reports typed on old manual typewriters or printed by the clerk with the neatest handwriting. A squad of reporters, who asked every kind of damn-fool question and had the frightened look of people who didn't want to believe what they've been hearing. Lobbyists from two major oil companies and a multinational arms firm demanding explanations *right now*. The House Majority Leader and two or three senators who, Shango knew, were high up in the councils of McKay's party, responsible for his election—the men who truly set party policy, who pulled the strings. Anyone who could possibly work himself into the schedule did: Al Guthrie and Nina Diaz were worn to a frazzle, trying to triage priorities when everything was vital. McKay listened to them patiently: baffled, angry men, men deeply concerned with the long-term goals they'd worked all their lives to achieve. The heat became unbearable. Someone came in with jugs of water that tasted like metal and the unwelcome information that there wasn't a toilet in five miles that would flush.

And everything the President said, every plan and motion he requested, was aimed at stockpiling, digging in, guaranteeing stores and supplies. In the eighteen months McKay had been in the White House, Shango had observed that he wasn't a survivalist and wasn't inclined to panic.

Yet he had the air of a man who knew for certain that the lights weren't going to come back on.

NEW YORK

She had been there, on the broken curb in front of St. Augustine, solemn and watchful. As Cal had prayed.

Tina lifted her head at his approach, and he read in her eyes not relief but confirmation. She knew he would come. Wordlessly, she rose swanlike and fell into step with him for the long walk home.

From block to block, neighborhood to neighborhood, the city rearranged and reasserted itself. Those newly returned home assayed the damage, cleared out shattered crockery and picture frames, righted rockers and bureaus. TVs that had pitched off tables and stands or had remained stock still, undamaged, were unresponsive and mute. As was every automobile, refrigerator, light bulb, electrical device of any kind.

Against their silence, a deluge of voices roiled up and overflowed onto the streets, full of shaky speculation, edged with fear and bafflement, leavened by uneasy, occasionally boisterous humor.

As they reached Eighty-first and Amsterdam, Cal felt the tension in his shoulders ease, the tightness of breath release. It was a scene they had encountered on dozens of blocks, but the faces here were familiar, the buildings known.

At the crown of the street, Elaine Jamgotchian was sweeping litter and dead leaves out to the gutter, while Sylvia Feldman leaned on her walker in the shade of an anemic maple, complaining (as she had on so many thousand other days) that her useless son Larry hadn't yet shown up where could he be no doubt with that useless half-blind mulatto wife of his what did he see in her.

Cal smiled at the prosaic simplicity of it, and the toughness underlying it. He murmured greetings, received assurances they were all in one piece. Tina stood by, all huge eyes and attentive distance. Like heat-seeking grandmother missiles, the women turned their attention on her. Under prodding that brooked no evasion, she finally offered the intelligence that, while she herself was unmarked by the day's experience, Mallory Stein had suffered three broken ribs and several other students had gone MIA.

And you couldn't tell me this? Cal thought fretfully but said nothing.

He had gotten her home.

Mr. J., Elaine's husband, sidled up in the standard-issue workpants and pajama tops he'd worn ever since they'd downsized him from the dockyard. His deep-grooved face was brown and sweaty, which accentuated the white of his beard and thinning hair. "We're doing all right, God bless you," he told Cal in his soft Armenian accent. "It will all be fine soon as they get everything going again."

Soon as they get everything going.

Cal didn't say what nagging intuition, or dream logic, kept hammering at him. Instead, he glanced at his sister, saw her paleness in the lowering sun, felt weariness radiating off her. It surprised him to see her stripped of her usual vibrancy. Normally, the walk they had just endured wouldn't have taken a notch off her stamina. But then, it had been a day of surprises, and the emotional toll had undoubtedly worn on her.

Cal excused them, and together they headed toward the sturdy, weathered welcome of their fourth-floor walkup. An Amoco tanker truck lay diagonally across the street where it had quit, its cab door open, the driver apparently long gone. *Not like anyone's gonna steal it.* The two of them had to step up onto the opposite curb to ease around it.

"You there!" The voice sliced through the humid air.

Tina groaned. Cal turned to Sam Lungo as the smaller

man bulled up, still in his long-sleeved white shirt buttoned tight at the wrist. Cal saw that Lungo's woolen suit pants were dirt-stained at the knees, a fine patina of dust on his face and body. He seemed unaware of the dustpan he held, with its shards of what looked to Cal like something that once been a Hummel.

"I need you to get my bookcases back against the wall. I've asked everyone, and no one will help me. My house is a shambles."

And the rest of New York, incidentally. Cal thought fleetingly of Mr. Stern, that similar, unnerving tunnel vision.

Cal looked to his sister. Her eyes beseeched, beckoned toward home, and he felt his own exhaustion like a shroud.

"We've been walking for hours. Maybe later . . ." Cal nodded to Tina, and they turned to move off.

"Problem with you is you're selfish!"

Cal turned back.

"I'm giving you a chance to make amends!" Lungo's voice was that of a pleading, petulant child.

Cal struggled for calm. "Did it ever occur, did it ever *dawn* on you there might be *something* in this world—" Exasperation overcame him, and he fell to silence.

Lungo's gaze faltered, slid off Cal to sweep over the street. Piles of wreckage. Empty cars. Neighbors helping neighbors, some bloodied, some in shock.

"Is that yes . . . or no?"

Ingrates, petty little ingrates, so self-involved, so *important*.

It was every bit what he had expected, Sam thought, watching Griffin vanish into the brownstone with that pasty girl. Why, he looked like he'd just swallowed vinegar. And no word of parting, whatever had happened to manners? Holier Than Thou just yanked that Bound for Juvie sister of his and hustled off to his no-doubt crack-den hovel. It was pathetic, really, the sorts one was forced to live with, the insults one had to bear.

Sam waited a moment, with the strange hope—one he didn't even admit to himself, really—that the young man might come back, might help him, after all. But nothing happened, of course, nothing at all. Slowly, eyes still on the building, Sam withdrew pad and pen from his shirt pocket and began to write.

At last, they found their way to their apartment, by the light of a donated candle. Cal unlocked the deadbolt, swung the door wide.

Muted light filtered through the blinds. Several framed prints were askew, and three Perma-plaqued certificates had tumbled to the floor. All else seemed pretty much intact.

Cal looked at his sister. She sagged on the doorframe. The consummate performer, she had retained her composure until out of her audience's sight.

"Let's get you to bed."

"No," she said grumpily. "I'm okay." Then, cutting off his protest, offered a compromise. "Couch."

Cal ushered her into the room. They moved past the bulky old Grundig phonograph, an icon from their childhood still resting solidly atop the scarred oak end table by the sofa. He was relieved to see it unharmed. Mom had disdained television, refused to have one in the house, but had played endless LPs of Mozart, Beethoven, Tchaikovsky, the magic rhythms that had first set Tina to movement, making a world to shut out the cold.

But for now, like the lights, like every mechanism across the city, it was only an icon of the past.

Cal moved to open the blinds. From the couch, Tina cautioned, "I've got this monster headache."

He glanced back. In the dimness, he could see the clammy sheen on her forehead and cheeks, the pain crease between her brows. *And the air in here won't help any.* It was leaden and still. Keeping the blinds closed, Cal reached around and opened a window. "You eat lunch?" he asked.

Tina hesitated. "I lost it somewhere."

He headed for the kitchen. "I'll make you a sandwich."

She nodded absently, seized the remote. She aimed it at the TV, pressed useless buttons, then let her arm fall, a dead weight.

In the kitchen, light sifted through the gauzy curtains, making it easier to see. Cal turned the taps on the faucet, switched on the range. No water, no gas.

"This is so weird." Tina's pained voice was barely audible from the living room. "Everyone in the world with a direct line to everyone else . . . Now it's just the street where you live. We can't even see if Luz is okay or anything."

Cal nodded, said nothing. He opened the ancient, defrost-it-yourself fridge and saw that it had done a pretty good job of defrosting itself, water dripping from the freezer and in-undating most of the food. There was some veggie baloney, though, sealed up tight. He tore it open, sought out bread and lettuce.

Reaching for a dull bread knife from the drainer, he re-called the sword from his dream. *Whatever that was, you ain't it.* As he laid slices of rye on the breadboard, tore hunks of lettuce, the tumult of the unseen dream crowd again pressed into his consciousness. Certainly it had been a day of tumult. And earlier, leading all those people safely through the darkness, there was that strange sense of being exactly where he belonged, becoming *who* he—

"Cal?" Tina stood in the doorway behind him, a paler shadow in the gloom. "You think it's just here, or bigger?"

"I don't know." He smelled the mayo; it was still okay, so he started slathering it on the sandwiches.

"Think it'll last long?"

"I don't know, Tina." He managed a reassuring tone. "Let's hope not."

She nodded, hugging herself. He laid aside the knife and went to put an arm around those delicate shoulders. "It's okay to be scared. You'd have to be crazy not to be." Then he added, "And you'd need your bookcases put back against the wall."

She smiled. He gestured at the two identical sandwiches. "Any preference?"

Her smile faded. "Sorry. Guess I'm not hungry."

Cal almost said, *But you always are.* Instead, he offered, "Probably the heat."

"Yeah." As she averted her eyes from the kitchen window, Cal felt her shudder. "The heat . . ."

WEST VIRGINIA

It was Ryan Hanson who said it first. "What if they don't come?"

"What if you just shut the fuck up, asshole?"

"*You* shut the fuck up for a change." Ryan's voice was sharp in the darkness. "Look, I mean, let's face it. Somethin' weird's goin' on."

"No shit, Sherlock, when'd you get the first clue?"

"Sonny," Hank said wearily, "cool it, okay? I think you're thinking what I'm thinking, Ryan. Anybody else thinking that?"

There was silence, as if their thoughts were in danger of bringing their fears to pass.

Every one of them guessed that no ordinary power outage, no Arab terrorist or Chinese bomb, could account for the failure of the radio, the headlamps, the electric power of the tram. After three hours of waiting in darkness at the foot of the downcast, every one of them guessed, too, that whatever was wrong was wrong up top as well.

Most of the Cokes and coffee in their thermoses had been consumed. Gordy had gone out and unscrewed one of the water pipes in the tunnel, refilling as many thermoses and cans as he could. The men were saving their SCSRs, but Hank felt dizzy and sleepy and knew they'd have to start using them soon.

And then what?

"So what do you think?" asked Llewellyn the engineer.

Hank said quietly, "I think we maybe need to think about ways to get out of here."

"What're we gonna do, climb the fuckin' elevator shaft?" demanded Sonny. "Be like fuckin' Bruce Willis and go up hand over hand for a fuckin' mile?"

"You rather stay down here?" retorted Hillocher. In the past hour or two the camaraderie had worn thin as the darkness had seemed to thicken, weighing on every man. The close, stale air of the tiny vestibule stank now of sweaty coveralls and machine oil, of coal and the cigarette smoke that permeated the hair and clothes of half the men.

"Bite me, asshole."

"Hey!" Hank interposed, for the dozenth time. "Whoa! We're in enough trouble; let's not start taking pokes at each other."

"Well, this guy's an asshole."

"So don't talk to him."

"I don't even wanna breathe the same fuckin' air as him."

"So don't," snapped Hank, feeling as if a steel ball bearing were growing like a cancer somewhere in the middle of his brain. "Get the fuck back into the tunnel if you're so goddam picky about who you want to sit next to." Hank's bones ached as he crawled to the manual door crank again, and there was a quick burst of yellow light as Gordy, who had a lighter, rekindled the little torch so he could see.

Grimes, shrinking back from the flame, seemed even more repellent to Hank than ever.

"You stupid fucker, you want to blow us all up?"

"You can blow me . . ."

"*Shut up!*" roared Hank. He got the door open a crack, and Grimes was through it like a roach under a baseboard. "Anybody else want out?"

"Yeah," grumbled a man—Dayton—"I gotta breathe better air or I'm gonna die."

Three or four others joined them, crowding and pushing from the back of the group while others cursed or muttered. Hank doggedly cranked the vent door shut, then cranked open the next set, and so shut and open to the next, all the while wondering why the hell he got suckered into doing work like this for assholes. He'd been eating aspirin until he was nearly sick to his stomach, for all the good it did him, it was as if the part that hurt wasn't a part that any medication could touch.

He itched, too. The conversation in the tiny room had gotten on his nerves, and in his heart of hearts he was annoyed that Sonny and the others had had the idea of going outside before he did. Damned if he was going to sit out there in pitch darkness in that company.

He cranked the doors shut, but it was a long time before he opened the next set to rejoin Ryan and Llewellyn and the others in the vestibule before the elevator doors.

Until Ryan had spoken, Hank had been half-dreaming about Wilma. Dreaming about the sixties: the summer before she left for college, the summer when it had seemed, for a time, that they really would get married. The Summer of Love, people called it later. And he'd been so sure of her love. The last time he'd been really sure about anything. Maybe the last time he'd been dumb enough to think he knew what was going on in another person's head, just because he wanted so badly for her to be thinking the way he was thinking.

Dreaming about the tunnels. About being alone in the cool darkness with the tommy-knockers. When Hank dreamed about being in the mine—really dreamed—more often than not it was the old Green Mountain pit he dreamed about and going down the steep-slanting galleries with the skip cars heaving and rattling on their narrow-gauge track to the top.

Crouching in the darkness between one set of doors and the next, Hank realized that there was a part of him that didn't really want to leave the mines. That didn't want to go back and deal with whatever was happening above the ground.

Let's not go there, he told himself grimly. When Wilma had gone away to college—when he'd faced the fact that she'd been trying to tell him, most of that summer, that she didn't really want to settle into the life of a miner's wife—he'd gone through a bad time, a time when it had been hard to even get himself out of bed in the morning.

At intervals in the ensuing years he'd gone through similar times. Times when all the people in the town had seemed to him distant and trivial; when he drank a lot, watched a lot of TV. Only the concerns and conversations of those idiots in the 4077th or the *Hill Street* police station had proven equally unreal and unimportant, equally unable to pierce the darkness inside. The staff therapist, after Applby Mining had gotten a staff therapist, had pointed out to him that it was during such times that he signed on for a lot of overtime. But she'd connected this fact with a desire to lose himself in the only work he knew.

What he'd sought, he understood now, was being in the mine itself. Being in the darkness. Not having to deal with anything but the dark, and the rock, and the silence.

With a sensation like waking up, he realized he'd been dreaming again. He cranked the door open and wormed through to the warm room that smelled rankly of his friends and fellows.

"I think I can get us through the old part of the mine to where it connects up with the Green Mountain works," he said. "The air here's bad, and we've got, what, three or four SCSRs apiece? That's three or four hours, and I'm willing to bet there's not gonna be anybody coming down that shaft. Gene," he said to the engineer, "what's the gas situation in the old part of the mine? Do you know?"

"Pretty good, as far as I know, there's been no seepage reported," Llewellyn's voice came through the close darkness. "But we're talking about miles of tunnel down there."

"Then we take turns being canary," Hank said quietly. "We use the respirators as long as we can and work our way in the dark as long as we can. I'm pretty sure I know the way: there's only a couple of long mains, since they robbed out the last of the rooms and brought the ceilings down. If our canary passes out, we backpedal like hell. If he doesn't, we light up every now and then and see where we are."

Greg Grant said, "You're shittin' us. You know your way around in the dark like that?"

"Kid," Hank said softly, "I was *born* in the mine."

"Besides," said Ryan, "you want to end up like those cats you read about, where somebody dies and they starve to death in the apartment or wherever because nobody's remembered they're there?"

Of course Ryan would think about cats, Hank thought resentfully, his bitterness surprisingly strong, even after all these years. *Sneaky little vermin.* And with the bitterness, the old sense of angry bafflement, that Wilma would rather be a sour spinster living in a houseful of cats than have a real marriage and a real husband.

Who has days and weeks when he can't get out of bed, he thought. *And who doesn't want to put two words together to talk to anyone he hasn't known since he was a kid.*

Llewellyn asked wonderingly, "You think you can do it?"

Hank considered for a moment, tracing his memories of all those years underground. In spite of his feeling of fever, they were clearer in his mind than ever before. Each area opening into each older area. What mains had been collapsed, what mains only abandoned when the digging had moved on. Even the really nasty areas they'd worked back in the seventies, where there'd been three feet or less of seam, where they'd dug those god-awful tiny rooms and scraped coal bent nearly double—they were all as vivid to him as the rooms in his apartment, in the trailer he'd occupied before that, in his dad's cheap little company-built shack.

"Yeah," he said, amazed a little at himself. "Yeah, I think I can."

Hank had a drink of water, the thermoses were low again and would have to be refilled before they started their hike. Most of the men took a final pee into the elevator shaft ("Hey, you shoulda thought of that before you left the house!" joked Gordy), and Hank turned his attention to the tedium of cranking the manual controls on the doors once more. The air in the vestibule was sour and stale, and there seemed little point in conserving air that wasn't moving anyway, but the locks that prevented air loss were still in place: crank open, through, crank shut, crank open, through, crank shut. . . .

It had been at least an hour since he'd put Grimes and his like-minded pals out into the tunnel. They'd gripe, almost certainly, about the long trudge ahead of them, and Hank found himself looking forward to knocking Sonny's head against the nearest wall.

The third door opened, and Hank thought, *Just say anything, Sonny. Anything at all.*

But there was only silence as the doors opened. Hank stood, trembling, wondering if they were dead of methane gas and then wondering, as he lit the spill again, whether he'd go up in a bellowing blast of flame.

But there was no gas. And there were no bodies. In the light of the single flickering flare, the tunnel outside was empty. Sonny Grimes and his five companions were gone.

TEN

NEW YORK

Jesus, it's like a cave in here. As Colleen Brooks entered her apartment, what she half-laughingly thought of as her spider sense snapped onto full alert. When she'd left that morning, the drapes had been open. Now they were shut tight, the place dark as night. And what was that smell? Dank, musky, something she could almost but not quite place. "Hey," she called out, "any survivors?"

"Hi, babe." It took Colleen a moment to locate the sound, make out the shape on the lounger. Rory sat like a pile of stone.

"Why's it so dark in here?" She strode toward the drapes, grabbed the pull.

"Don't. My eyes are killing me."

Colleen's foot bumped something that rolled into the near wall, made a glassy *clink.* She felt around with her toe, nudged more of the same. Empties.

"Three in the afternoon. *Man!*" She glared at Rory, knowing full well he couldn't see her in this gloom.

He chose not to respond or was too fogged out to get it. "Pullin' a half-day?" he asked dully.

Shit, yes. Case you haven't noticed, the whole friggin'

city's closed. Don't get into it, girl. She sighed, unstrapping the heavy tool belt, feeling her way to the sofa to lay it down. "Yeah, but there's gonna be an elephant's dump to clean up when they get the power back on."

He said nothing to that, so maybe it had occurred on his radar screen that something was going on in the larger world. She added, mostly thinking aloud, "But it's the cars, too. Like a damn graveyard. You looked outside?"

"Huh?" he responded vaguely.

This was getting old even faster than she was. Stepping cautiously—she didn't need to tear her foot open on some damn Budweiser shard and add stitches to this royally cocked-up day—she headed for the bathroom. "I'm gonna take a shower."

"Good luck. Water's off."

Great. "And I don't suppose you thought to go out and buy some?" She caught the acid edge in her voice, just like her mother, and hated it.

"It's . . . bright out." He managed to sound surly and whiny at the same time.

"Bright." And now she heard her mother in her head: *You sure know how to pick 'em.* Yup, when the woman's right, she's right, even though she'd been dead from cancer, burned to ashes and dumped at sea, lo these eleven years.

So what now? Colleen plopped down on the sofa, felt the spring pressing her butt through the tear in the leather. She stared at the Rory shape on the lounger opposite, heard the slow rasp as he scratched his arm, over and over. Bitterness filled her. She hoped it was the beginning of some loathsome skin disease, that his worthless hide would bubble and peel away from him like steamed chicken.

Then she repented, thought again of the man he had been. Or was her memory, as it had so many times, playing her for a fool, imprinting an image of someone she had wanted, needed so hungrily that she had tried to assemble him from defective parts?

It had been a long day. And, Christ, it was shaping up to be a long night.

WEST VIRGINIA

They searched for Sonny and the others for nearly an hour.

Then they went on.

It was four in the afternoon by that time, and most of the respirators the men had taken from the walls at the time of the power-out were exhausted. While hunting for Sonny, they gathered every other SCSR they could find, but still they were short two or three apiece for a trek of what could easily extend on into the night, if they could find their goal at all. If it hadn't been for the batteries going out, for the utter, unexplained failure of every source of power, Hank suspected most of the men would have remained by the downcast rather than undertake the crazy quest through the blackness of the worked-out mains.

He certainly would have.

But he knew the way. It was long and complicated, yet it was clear in his mind, over the grinding of the headache, the feverish dry heat in his bones. Like the road from Boone's Gap down the mountains and on into Pittsburgh that he used to drive a couple times a month to visit his sister Thea and her kids. Turn here, turn there, this gas station, that burger joint on the right.

He knew it. He felt he had always known.

"Maybe they just got tired of waiting for us?" Ryan blew out the single flame as the men joined hands again, linking together in the dark. "I mean, Sonny'll walk away from some guy waiting on him at a Burger King if he thinks they're taking too long to serve him."

"Yeah, but where's he gonna go?" asked Brackett.

"And the others wouldn't have been dumb enough to go with him," Bartolo pointed out reasonably. "Could—you don't think something could have—have *happened* to them, do you?"

"*Happened*?" repeated Llewellyn. "What do you mean, *happened*?"

"I dunno. Just—well . . ."

"You mean," said the engineer, interpreting the note in his voice, "do you think *something* could have *got* them?"

"Well," said Bartolo, meaning, Yes, that's what he thought.

"You mean like those worm things in *Rodan*?" asked Gordy, as Hank followed the wall of the old main unerringly into the blackness. And with the blitheness of one who knows perfectly well there was nothing down in the mines except themselves, he related the plot of that cinematic epic for the benefit of everyone who hadn't seen giant rubber maggots devouring unconvincingly shrieking Toho Studio extras on the late night movie.

It was the headache, thought Hank, as he made his way on ahead. He didn't know why he thought this, but he knew it was true. All he wanted, now, was to walk away also, to disappear into the cool darkness. To be alone. He knew that was what they'd done.

That didn't give him a reason why they hadn't come back.

Feeling the wall, Hank took comfort in the rambling monotone. It was as good, he thought, as having someone counting—a way of gauging by sound whether the air was bad without reminding everyone that's what they were doing. Remembering the way the main ran on for hundreds of feet before the floor began to rise, before the first of the submains branched out into the worked-out areas where they'd collapsed the roofs back in '89.

Seeing it in his mind again, the way he'd walked a thousand times.

Remembering.

God knew whether the passageways would still be open. Roof falls had a way of spreading. But he knew in his bones they would die, waiting for rescue by the shaft.

"You okay, Hank?" Ryan asked him, the first time they

stopped and lit a quick flare to take their bearings. That was when they reached the first of the old caved-in submains. Hank blinked, flinching from the light, raising his hand against it.

"Put that out," he said. "I can remember how it goes better in the dark." Somehow the memories were clearer, and the light confused him, hurt him.

"Okay." And he heard in Ryan's voice a note that hadn't been there before.

Shock. Shock and fear.

"Hank . . ."

"I'm okay."

Long silence. Whatever the boy had seen by the brief quick blinding light, Hank knew he didn't look okay.

Hank added, "I'm just real tired."

"Sure," agreed Ryan.

What the fuck had he seen?

"Everybody still with us?"

"I think a giant maggot got Gordy."

"Good."

"Hey, I saw this movie once where there's these things in the sewers of New York City . . ."

They moved on.

Crosscuts. Old vent shafts. Submains and rooms whose entrances were now simply rubble walls. Hank remembered them with the odd ease of one recalling that a pool hall used to stand where a parking lot was; it was like walking to the old elementary school on Front Street, though he hadn't done that in over forty years. Clearer and clearer the memories came, the awareness of where walls lay in the dark, the sense of changing air, of shifting smells. Sometimes it seemed to him that he could see the walls, see the passageways they passed.

And looking back, he was both shocked and not shocked to see the men behind him. Dimly, and with a sense that was not exactly sight. Black with coal dust, running with sweat under their grimy hardhats, their useless headlamps, eyes moving, shifting blankly, hands linked in a chain. Ryan, Greg Grant, Roop, Lou. Llewellyn with a frown between his brows as if he were trying to work out in his head what was going on. Al Bartolo with tears running down his face, fighting not to sob with fright. Hillocher . . .

Dear God!

In the darkness Hank wasn't sure if he was seeing correctly—if this were a dream or a hallucination. But somehow he knew it wasn't.

And somehow he understood that, in a way, he was seeing what Ryan had seen in the brief flare of the light.

Dear God, did he look as bad as Hillocher?

He realized he himself was slumping that way, slouched forward in a way that should hurt his back but didn't. In fact it hurt him to stand up straight. Had his hair gone wispy, thinning away like that?

Did his eyes look like that?

And across the darkness, for a moment his eyes met those milk-white bulging eyes with mutual recognition, mutual sight.

He turned his head quickly. *No*, he thought. *No*.

Hallucination, fever, headache.

But he found his way unerringly in the dark.

There was a crosscut to the mains that had been made in the seventies, where the seam dipped sharply upward and narrowed to a few feet in height. It was over a thousand feet, and Hank crawled in the lead, groping in the darkness that was no longer quite so dark, and behind him the men crawled, each holding onto the ankle of the man in front. That was almost the worst, with the rock scraping their heads or their butts if they raised up even a little, and the smell of the coal dense and choking around them.

Voice echoing in the tiny tube, Gordy Flue started to sing.

You'd have thought it would be something like "Dark as a Dungeon" or "Sixteen Tons."

But Gordy Flue took up "Doo Wah Diddy," and everybody joined in.

After about three hundred years and a thousand miles and a zillion choruses of "Doo Wah Diddy" the shaft widened out again, and Ryan cautiously lit up his little torch and counted heads. Hillocher was gone.

"Fuck, he was right behind me!" cried Gordy in distress. He turned back to the gaping throat of the tunnel, wet ponytail hanging like a dead onion top on his shoulders. "I thought he was hangin' onto my pant leg!"

"Even if he let go," pointed out Lou, "he couldn't get lost. It ain't like there's a lot of places to go. Andy!" he yelled back down the shaft. "Andy, you okay?"

"He didn't look good," said Ryan. "He was bummin' aspirin all the way before we started crawlin'."

"I'll have a look for him," said Hank. "You wait here."

"I'll go," said Ryan. "You sit here and rest."

Hank moved instinctively back from the flame of the torch. He could see, in the mirror of the boy's eyes, what he must look like.

Ryan crawled all the way back down the shaft, over a thousand feet. The young man was so skinny that Hank, crouched at the top, could always see the glimmer of the light he held out ahead of him. Could see it growing brighter and brighter as he crawled back.

Hillocher wasn't in the shaft. Hank felt no surprise. "What happened to him?" Ryan kept asking, "What happened?" It was as if Hank knew something in his marrow that the others didn't know and couldn't know.

"Put that out," he said. And he led them on, into darkness.

II

BECOMING

ELEVEN

NEW YORK

As the sun set and the royal blue of evening muted into black, Cal finally opened the blinds. Now the two of them sat on the couch he had repositioned by the window, gazing out at the night.

No rock music blared, no salsa. None of Bill Lundy's show tunes filtered up from beneath, nor was there the echoing, omnipresent cackle of sitcoms. Below, not a soul was on the street, and cars stood where they had stopped, untended and still. Opposite and all around, voices wafted through open windows flickering with candlelight or glowing with the steadier flame of a Coleman lantern. Intimate, intent, companionable.

Beyond, the familiar outline of skyscrapers stood against the stars, flat as cut-out posterboard. There were few lights in their soaring heights, and small wonder. Here on Eightyfirst, the brownstones were all five stories or less. It would take a hardy soul to climb those darkened stairwells to the twentieth floor, or the fortieth.

"Maybe God just got bored, wanted a change," Tina mused, sipping lukewarm lemonade. Her fever seemed to have eased a bit, after her rest. She stretched a leg with easy, unconscious grace, working the ache out, her foot in a straight line with ankle, knee, thigh. "I mean, why should TVs work? Why should anything?"

She turned to Cal, curling the leg back under her. "Think you're out of a job?" Finally, *finally*, she lifted the sandwich beside her and took a bite.

Cal shrugged. "Mr. Stern was pretty shaken up. Maybe it'll slip his mind."

Leave, and you're terminated. Stern had been unequivocal, and the words had felt like a cleansing rain. But no need to get into that now.

"If you go to work tomorrow . . . Hey, what if there's no school tomorrow? What if there's no school *ever*?".

Cal smiled. "Don't count on it."

Tina pretended a pout, and then the dark thought came. "They wouldn't close the SAB? I mean, there'd be no reason to."

Cal felt the tightness in his stomach. If his premonitions were even half right, then when the School of the American Ballet might again hang out its shingle—

"Well, I dunno. But you'd have to take a day or two off anyway. You're a sick little cookie."

"No. I'm fine." She was adamant, almost angry. "I can't miss practice. I'd never catch up."

Concerned, Cal brushed her bangs aside to put a hand to her forehead. Her hair was sweat-soaked, her fever flaring with her upset.

She tried to wriggle free of his hand. "Leave off, Cal."

"Let's decide this dispassionately, okay?" He stood, took a few quick steps toward the bathroom. "How 'bout, if it's still working, we let Mr. Thermometer—"

The crash of glass outside stopped him. He turned to see Tina rise and step to the window. Cal covered the distance in a few strides, eased her out of the line of sight. "Stay back."

Shouts echoed from the street, the words indecipherable. Cal had to peer sharply down to locate the source in the sullen dark.

"Oh, man," he said, dismayed. Tina was edging laterally, trying to see, but he kept her back from the window.

"What is it? What?"

"Patel's." The market's windows were broken, the shattered glass glinting on the pavement. He could make them out now, eight or ten men and women, pulling at the bars on the windows and doors, struggling to pry them open. He thought of the snowstorm that had socked in the city last winter, this island where every saleable item had to be shipped in, how hoarding had flared like wildfire, the shelves stripped clean of milk and bread and Pampers.

And this was no snowstorm.

Past the market, dim shapes flitted along the darkness of Broadway, barely seen except where one or two bore makeshift torches.

Cal glanced over at Tina, her face pale and scared. "It's okay," he said. "They'll be gone soon."

A staccato sound echoed up that Cal didn't recognize at first. Then it clicked in: hooves, horse's hooves. A raspy voice boomed, "Back off, all of you!"

This time, Cal let Tina join him at the window. Even from a distance, Cal could see that the cop was a big man, a slab of meat made even more imposing by the added height of the horse. The looters stopped like figures in a strobe, watching him. He gave the reins a shake. The horse cantered forward, closing the distance as the cop drew out his nightstick.

Then as if a switch had been thrown, the looters surged up over the cop. Shouting and cursing, they grabbed at him, tore away his nightstick, snatched at the reins. Panicked, the horse reared with a scream, dumping the beefy man off. He hit the ground, with a thud that Cal felt in his bones.

Maddened, the horse was kicking, spinning. The looters ducked and collided to avoid it, gave it a wide berth as it reeled and then ran off into the night. The cop struggled to get to his feet, slipping on wet pavement. A sharp cry—Cal couldn't tell if it was the cop or one of the others—and they were on him again.

"Stay here." Cal was headed for the door.

"*No*, Cal, don't." Tina grabbed for his sleeve. "I mean it."

"It's okay. I'm just gonna . . ."

"Gonna *what*?"

She echoed his own thoughts; he didn't know, either. He rushed to the kitchen. In the darkness, he peered at the drainer, caught the dull glint of metal. Reaching out, his hand closed on the cool plastic handle.

Tina's eyes went wide as he emerged with the big Ginsu knife in his hand. A few quick strides and he was at the door, unlatching the chain, snicking back the deadbolt. "Lock it behind me."

He shot her a last, quick look. "I'd call 911 if I could," he said, an apology, and was out the door.

Cal took the three flights full out, two and three stairs at a time, grasping the wood banister as he swung around on the narrow descent, breathing hard.

His palm hit the door onto the street, sent it flying, and he leaped the final few steps onto the pavement. The hot smell of garbage, a chaos of voices, the sound of blows.

They were thirty, forty yards off on the corner, and at this distance, all he could make out was a dark mass of struggling bodies clumped together. For a mad moment, he had a sense that he was looking, not at a group of people, but an impossible, inhuman beast, flailing legs and arms, howling its rage through gashes of mouth.

Then the illusion was gone, and Cal could see the big cop on his feet, a wounded bull ringed by wild dogs. They were hanging on his arms, his neck, pulling at him, pummeling him as he wheeled about, trying to drag him down. Booty from Patel's littered the sidewalk around their feet: useless batteries, packages of cereal, burst cartons of milk. The cop was trying to drag his gun clear of the holster, but other hands interfered, grabbing and clutching.

He shoved them off, yanked the pistol clear in a wide arc.

But one of his attackers smashed a big hair spray can into the cop's face. He roared, and the gun went flying end over end toward Cal. The automatic bounced once, twice on the asphalt and lay still, twenty feet away.

Bellowing curses, the cop battered at his attackers, keeping them busy, their attention on him and not the weapon. Only one came after the gun, a rangy teen in black jeans and a Misfits T-shirt with a grinning death's head on it. He saw Cal's knife, skidded to a stop, still poised to leap.

Cal raised the knife. *Get back.* The youth feinted left, Cal swung the knife, and then the blade tilted at an odd angle, fell free of the handle and clattered to the pavement. *Shit.*

Misfits straightened. "You buy that from TV?"

Cal felt sick. "Yeah."

"They all crooks, man."

Incongruously, Cal noticed that Misfits' hair was patchy, with bald spots showing, cut to look like a radiation victim. *Why would anyone want that?*

They stood eyeing each other a moment and then, both with the same thought, dived for the gun. Stomachs and chests skidded along the rough asphalt. Cal landed closer, his outstretched hand inches from the blue-black metal, while Misfits' fingers clawed at an impossible ten-foot gap. *Not a chance!*

Cal reached as Misfits' black-makeup-rimmed eyes bloomed desperation, went glassy—*and the gun slid from beneath Cal's fingertips and jumped into Misfits' hand!*

Still on his belly, Cal looked at the gun in cold astonishment. Misfits, too, was peering at it amazed, an expression that melted quickly to pure, nasty joy.

Scrabbling to his feet, he locked his spooky raccoon gaze on Cal and ever so slowly pulled back the bolt.

I'm dead. Cal knew in the time it would take him to stand or roll out of the way, he would be shot.

There was a muffled *whack*. Misfits let out a cry, went down on one knee, revealing a figure behind him hefting a big wrench. Cal was astonished. It was the elevator me-chanic—what was her name? *Colleen*—from his office building. She raised the wrench for another blow.

"You fucking cunt!" Misfits swiveled to get a bead on her, but she brought the wrench down again, putting her weight into it, laying into his shoulder. He screamed and stumbled sideways, clutching the gun with both hands, stag-gering into a crazy, frantic run away from them. Cal could hear him spewing a litany of physical acts and body parts as his footfalls faded off down the street.

Colleen had already turned, plunging toward the fray with wrench swinging. Cal rolled to his feet and joined her, grappling, kneeing, twisting arms and wrists.

"Vamoose! Get outta here!" Colleen's voice was as cool and unyielding as marble. The looters fled, slipping on bro-ken booty, scrabbling up a few boxes and vanishing into the night.

Cal straightened, gasping with the adrenaline rush. "Did you see that? With the gun?"

"What?" Colleen, who wasn't even breathing hard, knelt by the cop. He sat wheezing on the curb, slumped like a sack of potatoes.

"You all in one piece there, friend, or are we gonna have to fetch the Superglue?"

"Nah, I'm on top of it." He coughed wetly, spat, struggled to rise, sat down again with a grunt.

"Take it slow," Cal advised. "No one's on the meter here." Still seeing the muzzle of the gun, he thought momentarily of Tina, looked up at his window. It was dark within, but even so he felt her eyes on him. He lifted his hand, tried to keep it from shaking. *We're okay.*

The cop felt along his bruised jaw, touched his bloody nose gingerly and winced. "Damn, they broke it."

A box of Kleenex lay where one of the looters had dropped it. Cal tore it open, handed the cop a wad of tissues. "Here."

"Thanks." The cop was breathing easier now, and, in the moonlight, Cal could see he was older than he had looked in the heat of battle, fifty at least, face all furrows and hard wear. "You two were a couple of knights in armor."

Cal shrugged it off. "I live right here."

"Me, I'm just down there." Colleen gestured toward the far end of the block. Then, noting Cal's surprise, asked, "*What*?"

"Nothing, it's just you live somewhere, you have no idea—"

"We don't exactly belong to the same clubs," she said coolly, and it brought back their meeting in the lobby, forever ago this morning.

The cop tried to stand again. Cal gripped him under one arm, Colleen the other, until he was sure of his footing. He waved them off, grateful. "You better get back indoors."

"You have any idea what's going on?" Cal asked.

A hard cast came over the cop's face. "No, but it's a holy mess. Some of my boys saddled up, headed over the Queensboro Bridge. It's the same there. Same as far as the eye can see. Could be the whole world, for all we know. It's down; everything's down."

Cal glanced at Colleen and was gratified to see she looked as chilled as he felt. "But, hey," she was saying, "the government's gotta be—"

"What government?" The cop stared into the night. "Without phones, computers, they can't even collect their damn graft." He glanced at them and stopped, rancor evaporating to—pity? He forced a mirthless smile. "Nah, discount that. I'm just having a bad night. I hear they're mobilizing the National Guard. It'll take time, but it'll be all right."

Cal nodded, unconvinced. The cop cast about, spied his fallen hat. He slapped it against his tree-trunk thigh, set it on his head. "Gotta go find my horse."

On the wind, Cal caught distant, unidentifiable sounds that might be screams, might be anything. He turned to the cop. "You wanna come upstairs?"

"I'd love to, but long as the city's paying my health plan. . . ." He'd found his nightstick, nestled against the curb.

He swung it around on its strap, *thwap*, into his palm. "You watch your backs, hear?"

"Back at you," Colleen said. The cop nodded, turned the corner onto Broadway and was gone, echoing steps soon lost on the wind.

Cal brushed himself off, caught Colleen looking at him, shaking her head. Her appraising eyes said, *Not bad, lawyer boy.* Or at least, he wanted to think they did.

"You want some lukewarm lemonade?" he asked.

WEST VIRGINIA

Up here, where no coal had been mined in twenty years, there was no dust. The SCSRs had run out long ago, so they would be out of luck if they ran into gas now, but according to Llewellyn there had been little in this area of the mine.

"Shut up a minute," Hank said softly, and the men shut up. Their respect for him, he noticed, had grown as they'd moved along; as he'd gotten them through the tangle of caved-in tunnels and worked-out rooms and submains that went nowhere—if not easily, at least steadily, more and more confident in the dark. In the silence that followed Hank could hear a dim swift shuffling and could smell something elusive, half-familiar.

"What is it?" Ryan edged up closer behind Hank.

His voice sounded higher above him than it should. Hank tried to straighten a little out of his comfortable slouch and found that he couldn't. Only this morning he'd been able to look at Wilma's nephew almost eye to eye.

"D'you hear it?"

Ryan shook his head. Hank could see him do it, though no flare was lit.

"Tell the guys to keep it down, okay?" whispered Hank. "And maybe we might want to have a light now a little more often."

"Is that safe?" Llewellyn asked.

"Maybe safer than not," returned Hank, though he could

not have said what it was that he feared. "Everybody keep a hand on each other. If nobody keels over, we know it's pretty safe for a quick look."

"I like your definition of 'pretty safe,' Culver."

"You got a better one?"

A pinlight of yellow. Hank could see—squinting and backing off from the glare himself—that nobody liked it much, though it was a comfort in the dark.

Ryan swallowed hard. "You mean all that crap Gordy was talking about . . ." He let the words trail off and averted his eyes. He bit his lower lip, a childhood filled with every monster movie from *The Thing* to *Alien* playing fast across his face. "Jesus."

"Look," Hank said quietly, trying to keep as far from the light as he could. "You know and I know there's nothing down here but us. My daddy and my granddaddy and your grand-daddy too and goddam near everybody else's—they worked here all their lives and all they ever saw was each other. But a couple of things happened today that nobody or their grand-daddies ever ran across in their lives. And lately I've heard things, sounds that shouldn't be here. And I think maybe it'd be a good idea if everybody could see what's around them."

Ryan nodded, scared but accepting. *Accepting what?* thought Hank. Accepting the fact that Hank had been mov-ing through the old mains with perfect ease, able to identify scratches and minor malformations of track and rock and abandoned bits of machinery in the dark?

Accepting the fact that Hank could hear things the others couldn't?

Although God knew, as the flame was blown out again, the men were noisy enough, chattering loudly about baseball and TV and the movies, trying to cover their fear. Trying to pretend that each and every one of them wasn't thinking: *If all this is going on down here, what the fuck are we going to find when we get to the top*?

That had been in Hank's mind as well. Maybe that was the source of this feeling inside him, this dread of leaving the dark of underground. This feeling that this was where he wanted to be, where he wanted to stay.

To hell with the world of traffic noise and stink and management directives and health care plans. To hell with glaring sunlight and cold. To hell with people who asked questions that were none of their business. To hell with Wilma and her kitty cats.

Darkness. Peace.

Provided, he thought wryly, *I could find something to eat down here*.

He was just glancing back to tell Ryan they might want to light up again for another quick look when a black, deformed Something flung itself out of the crossing tunnel and smashed at the boy's head with a club.

Ryan must have heard or sensed something, for he was dodging, flinching, even as the cluster of dark slumped forms bore him down. Hank heard the hard whack of the club on the boy's shoulder and heard Ryan yell and knew the blow hadn't brained him, as had been intended. Ryan yelled again, a scream of pain, as the things seized him. In the darkness Hank could see them, five or six crouching troll-like things, huge eyes catching the far-off reflection of the torchlight.

Hank was running, bounding down the tunnel, as the things dragged Ryan into the crosscut from which they'd come—a vent shaft back into what was left of an old room-and-pillar main. The others behind Llewellyn clung and blundered together in shock in the darkness, groping and scrambling for lighters and paper.

Hank was quicker. He slipped through the crosscut bore, seeing the things ahead of him clearly, easily, in the pitchy black of underground. Ryan was struggling, flailing with his right arm, his left clearly useless. Broken collarbone. Hank grabbed a handful of mud-colored clothing, elbowed the flat, gray face that came around to gnash undershot teeth at him; kicked hard at a bent and crouching groin. The narrowness of the seam gave him some advantage, since all six of them couldn't come at him at once. They had weapons, wrenches and hammers from toolkits; edged metal tore his arm.

Kicking, snarling, he managed to shove down one of the attackers and get to Ryan, dragged him away, thrust him in the direction of the torchlight that appeared in the end of the seam. "Go!"

Stumbling, Ryan fled in the direction of the sudden tiny flare of new-made light.

Hank kicked, cursing, at the things that clutched at him and felt another slash on his arm, and the hot wetness of blood. Bartolo's voice yelled, "Hank!" behind him and the light came closer.

The attacking things squinted against the flame, snarling, rage and hunger warring with pain and fear. They fled stumbling, loping, swallowed into the blackness of the shaft.

"Hank, you okay?"

"Gimme a minute!" yelled Hank leaning against the wall, trembling so hard he thought he'd fall. "I'm okay! Just gimme a minute!"

The light stopped, though its ruddy glare continued to flicker over the coal wall. Hank kept his back to it. The cold of the rock under his shoulder steadied him. His blood felt hot, running out over his arm and soaking into his shirt and coverall. His headache had returned, and with it wave after wave of dizziness that he knew had nothing to do with the wound, nothing to do with his earlier fever and aches.

Or nothing obvious, anyway.

"What the fuck were they?" he heard Gordy demand, and Ryan gasping over and over again, "I don't know. I don't know."

"Jesus," said somebody, and somebody else, "Oh, man. What the hell'd they want?"

"What you think they wanted, meathead?" demanded Roop McDonough's voice. "They're these things wanderin' around down here a mile below the surface, way too far from the nearest take-out, what the hell you think they wanted?

Took one look at us and thought, *Hey, it's Pizza Man! He delivers!*"

"Fuck," said somebody.

Hank thought, *Fuck.*

They were right. They hadn't even seen what he'd seen, and—hungry, angry, strange animal instincts whispering in his own bones—they were right.

What the hell had happened? The words came back to him, echoing in circles, riding over the chopped meaningless yammering of the men.

What had happened to him?

And what had happened to Sonny Grimes, whose mutated features he had recognized on the slumped, huge-eyed troll he had just fought?

NEW YORK

He couldn't stop his hands shaking. But then, he had always been prone to physical manifestations of anxiety.

Dr. Louis Chernsky stood by his desk, drapes open, picture window revealing the blackness that had settled on the city like a shroud. An aromatherapy candle sat atop his desk, flickering pitifully, exhaling a pine scent that utterly failed to soothe him.

He shook out two more Xanax, filled a paper cup from the cooler and gulped them down. He nearly choked as a chuckle sounded from the shadows near the door. A denser silhouette stood framed against the dimness spilling from the hall.

"Still here. I always figured you had no life of your own." The voice was thick and husky, halfway between three packs and throat cancer. Chernsky shouldn't have been able to recognize it, but the scorn was familiar.

"Mr. Stern."

Stern walked slowly into the room, seeming to draw the waiting room's shadows with him. There was an odd stiffness to his movements, as though his bones had broken and been reset strangely. "I need a session, Louis. I seem to be going through some changes."

The candlelight touched him, and Chernsky gasped. Stern's appearance was shocking. It wasn't just that his black suit, ever so immaculate, was scuffed and torn, sleeves mere tatters. He seemed *larger* somehow, more muscular. And his face, lined and pitted now like distressed leather. The wavering candlelight cast hard shadows on distorted bones: the eye sockets more sunken than before, the nose and brow and cheekbones more pronounced.

Chernsky had a sudden vision of the gargoyle he had seen by moonlight atop Notre Dame years ago. *If it could move and walk* . . . Chernsky had to stifle a giggle, felt hysteria rising. Stern tilted his head quizzically, and his eyes—in the yellow light, it was hard to tell—*but were they yellow?*

"You, uh, should see a physician," Chernsky said.

"This time of night? Emergency room would be hell." Stern belched, a sound far louder and deeper than it should have been, it came up from the depths of him and assaulted the room. "Pardon me. I have got the *worst* heartburn."

"What do you want?" Chernsky became aware he was wheezing thinly. He longed for the inhaler in his desk but didn't dare to look away from his terrible visitor.

"Answers would be nice." His lips edged into a smile, but his eyes stayed cold.

"I—don't have any." Chernsky tried to swallow, found he couldn't. Stern was right up to him now.

He ran a pointed nail delicately across Chernsky's cheek, not hurting him. "No, that's right, you're *process* oriented. Has to come from within, new experiences to discover."

With a cry, Chernsky tried to bolt from the room. Almost at the door, Stern rose up behind him, yanked him back by the collar of his coat. Chernsky screamed, feeling himself pulled off his feet by a strength far beyond anything he would have thought possible.

In the part of him that was the detached observer, he watched as he flailed and shrieked, the thing that had been his patient shaking him as a dog worried a doll. Then, flying through the air toward the big glass pane, he thought of Susan, of the Winnebago, of Zion and Yellowstone and the decals that went on the back bumper. There was a shattering that filled the world and a coldness of air like a blow and a falling that was all waiting.

Stern stood back from the jagged, glinting hole, counting the seconds. He didn't need to see it; it was sweeter this way. One Mississippi, two Mississippi, three . . . From twelve stories below came a sound like a bag of glass breaking. He sidled to the broken pane and looked down, saw the sprawled figure in the splash of moonlight, even more silent than it had been during their sessions.

"We have to stop now," Stern said. "I gotta tell ya, it felt different . . . but good."

TWELVE

Rioting started in Petworth as soon as the sun went down. Maybe someone had gotten scared, thought Shango; thought to do a little hoarding when it became clear no lights were on and no cops near. Grocery shelves might be empty tomorrow, and no money to pay prices suddenly escalated to profit from the panic.

Maybe the Army, guessing what McKay may have guessed, had tried to lock the stuff down. Childhood in the projects had taught Shango everything he needed to know about the fear that stalked Washington's squalid ring of slums and the violence that lay just below that fear.

From the window of the duty room of headquarters, across the street from the White House, Shango could see the glow of fire in the sky, hear the steady beat of boots as National guardsmen double-timed it down the streets. More National Guard showed up at about the same time to harden the cordon around the White House itself, and through the trees Shango and the other agents could see the ruddy light of torches illuminating the grounds.

"Fuckin' mess," said Gabriel Cox, the shift supervisor

who'd been on duty since eight that morning, when the chief didn't show.

Shango had to admit that was a pretty succinct summation of the situation.

Emergency shelters had been set up in the lobbies and hallways, the conference rooms of every office building along the Mall and in the classrooms and lecture halls of George Washington University for commuters stranded downtown. Some hardy souls had set out on foot around noon on the long trek to Georgetown, Manassas, Arlington, Woodbridge, but the majority of clerks and bureaucrats had stayed put, confident that transportation would be restored. From what he'd heard from the other agents since coming off duty at four, Shango gathered that frustrated and furious crowds had intermittently gathered around the offices of Eastern Bell, shouting for service to resume.

They'd remained there until it dawned on them slowly that not being able to phone their families was, in fact, the least of their worries.

Shango himself felt little actual concern for his own family. Home, to him, was a peeling blue double shotgun on Ascension Street near the Mississippi where his sister lived, his Georgetown apartment was just a place to shower and sleep. He knew perfectly well that seven or eight of his mother's church-lady buddies would look in on her and that in case of a real emergency his sisters and brother would take care of her. They'd band together like they always had and get each other through.

He smiled a little in the dim glow of the candles that had been set around the duty room in the elaborate candelabra sent across to them by Jan McKay: centerpieces from any number of White House dinners. The golden light reminded him of nights in his childhood, when there'd been a little hiccup between NOPSI's electricity cut-off date and Dad's paycheck, or when Georges or Betsy or Andrew had roared through town and water had stood in the street up to the porch. Dad would bed everyone down in the living room on blankets and tell stories in front of a dead TV, taking all the voices and the special effects himself, a thousand times better than anything on *Star Trek* or *MASH*.

Funny, he thought, what the glow of a candle could do.

"So what do you think?" Cox looked up as Witjas, one of the younger men, came in with the hand-printed list of agents: who had checked in, who lived where, who might be expected to show up tomorrow.

"I think anybody who hasn't shown up by this time isn't gonna." The young man tossed the papers on the gray metal table. "I was just out. Looks like more fires in Anacostia."

"Oh, great," muttered Cox, trying to sound pissed instead of scared. "What the hell is it about your people, Larry? Things fuck up, and they start wreckin' their own neighborhoods." He turned back to Witjas without waiting for a reply—which was fortunate, since Shango made it a point never to reply to Cox's attitude on blacks. "How many have we got?"

The half dozen agents in the duty room put out their cigarettes and put down their half-eaten sandwiches and gathered around, divvying up shifts for the night: so many for the embassies, so many to work the White House perimeter, so many for inside. Many of those, like Witjas, who'd walked in from Falls Church and Bethesda had brought sleeping bags and changes of clothing under the assumption that they'd be staying for as long as they had to. When things hadn't straightened out by about noon, Cox had passed out pens and paper and told them to start writing reports about everything they'd observed on their way in, and these had been forwarded to the emergency command post in the State Department building.

"You mind going back till midnight?" asked Cox, glancing up at Shango. "I'd feel safer if there was a fourth guy over there, and we're gonna be spread thin."

"Fine with me," said Shango. "Beats listenin' to Witjas snore in the conference room." *And you talk in here.*

Witjas gave him the finger as he left the duty room and descended the stairs.

No lights showed from the windows of the West Wing, but when Shango reached there—it must have been ten by then, though his watch had stopped at 9:17 that morning, like everyone else's—he found the corridors and conference room still glowing with candlelight, stuffy after a day of no air-conditioning and the nightlong burning of dozens of small flames. When Shango came in, Agent Breckenridge was just showing Nina Diaz and Ron Guthrie out of McKay's office—McKay's press secretary and the White House chief of staff, part of the inner circle of advisers and friends. McKay had walked to the office door with them and looked like ten miles of bad road: shirt soaked with sweat, jacket and tie long gone, lines that most men didn't develop until their sixties printed deep on his face. Past his shoulder Shango could see into the candlelit Oval Office, where chairs had been pulled up close to the desk and every surface was littered with papers and reports. Shango wondered whether any word had yet come in from the agents who were guarding McKay's son up in Maine.

There were still a dozen people sitting in the hall waiting to be seen, a couple of the big-name lobbyists from the oil companies and arms manufacturers, but mostly military: grim-looking young corporals with folders on their knees. Messengers.

Not, by the look of them, bearers of any kind of good tidings.

McKay turned his head and met Shango's eye. And smiled—relieved?

"Mr. Shango," he said. He was always scrupulous about knowing the names of the men on the White House detail, and about calling people Mr., an odd little formality left over, Shango assumed, from his army days. The next instant a frown creased McKay's forehead, "But you're supposed to be off shift."

"Mr. Cox thought an extra man here might be helpful."

And he saw understanding change the President's blue eyes.

"As it happens," said McKay, "I was thinking of sending a message asking you to come back for a few minutes. Steve," he turned to where Steve Czernas, his deputy chief of staff, sat in the chair closest to the office door. "Mr. Breckenridge, if you'll excuse us, please."

Breckenridge—one of the older men on White House detail, thin and tough and very silent—glanced at Shango and stepped out into the corridor to let Shango and Czernas pass him and go on into the office. McKay shut the door.

"Mr. Shango," he said, "I understand you scored at the top of your class in the training center."

"Not in all areas, sir," said Shango, hands folded before him. He was a little rumpled and tired, but with his tie tied and jacket on he still looked more businesslike than the Commander in Chief. "But I was in the top five percent, yes, sir."

McKay smiled. "What you scored tops in was survival and escape and evasion."

"I grew up black in the Deep South, sir."

McKay grinned.

"I'm going to ask Mr. Richter—or Mr. Cox, if Mr. Richter hasn't come in yet—if he would second you to special duty. Would you be willing to undertake that?"

"Of course, sir." Shango felt a slight prickling of his scalp and thought, *Here it is. What he's known all along today that no one else has known.*

He glanced at Czernas. Like Shango, he was still neat, Yale tie knotted, navy blazer unrumpled, chin smooth as Pamela Anderson's tit, and yet, beneath his almost dandyish sleekness, he had the elastic, broad-shouldered fitness of a young man who works out diligently. He'd often been on those long road rides, zooming out ahead while McKay stayed obediently back with the Secret Service boys.

"This isn't anything I'd ask of anyone if it weren't an emergency," McKay went on, and for an instant Shango could see him, thirty years younger, huddled in cammies by firelight in some Southeast Asian base camp, sizing up who to send out on patrol. "Jerri Bilmer was supposed to come into Dulles this morning, with some papers and possibly film, that could hold the key to what happened today."

Bilmer. Shango remembered the way McKay had kept his cell phone beside him that morning, the way he'd sat tense on the exercycle seat, conscious of it, listening for it. Recalled, too, McKay talking to Bilmer at that garden party last month, just before Bilmer went on vacation.

"When was her flight due in?" asked Czernas, and McKay's face seemed to settle a little in the wavering candlelight.

"9:20," he said.

The glance that went around was almost audible. *Oh, fuck.*

"She's wearing black leggings, black sneakers and a red sequinned sweatshirt. She'll have a black purse with her and some kind of travel bag." McKay took a deep breath. "Find her. Get her here. If you can't find her alive . . ." And there was a hesitation, an understanding among them of what they might have to do if her plane hadn't touched down by 9:17. "Bring her purse and her luggage. This is vital. This is . . . this is to *vital* what the Nagasaki blast was to a damp sparkler. Understand?"

Shango thought, *Oh, shit.* His uncle had been one of the cops to clean up the wreckage after a Delta flight had come down on a New Orleans housing project in the seventies.

"About a month ago," the President went on, "I heard a rumor that what I'd been told was a minor project of energy research called Source was receiving clandestine sums from both the Department of Defense and the CIA—"

Czernas opened his mouth, glanced sidelong at Shango, then back to McKay, with *Aren't there too many people in this room*? written all over his handsome young face. McKay's eyes met his, long and steadily, then he continued deliberately, "far more than any minor research installation should have been getting. I couldn't get a straight story out of either DoD or CIA, and in fact I got substantially different stories from each person I talked to. I still don't know if they thought what they told me was the truth. The reports I've received over the past eighteen months—and the reports Source has been turning in since the Reagan administration—were all carefully tailored to make the project look like something other than it was."

Czernas looked over at Shango again, tightened his lips, and then asked, "And what was it, sir?" Shango said nothing and didn't react. He understood already why McKay was telling them both this.

"That was what Ms. Bilmer was trying to find out. We agreed that whatever day she came in, from whatever direction, she'd be on the 9:20 Houston flight, United Airlines 1046. She planned to change planes a couple of times, in case anyone was a little curious about which direction she came from. I don't know her starting point, other than that it was somewhere in the West."

"It shouldn't take more than a few hours to get to Dulles by bicycle," said Czernas after a moment. "I biked here this morning. My backpack should hold enough water for the trip."

"I'll lend you my backpack," said McKay to Shango. "You can carry water."

"Excuse me, sir," Shango said quietly. "I'm not sure taking bikes is wise, at this point. There's rioting down in Anacostia and in other places as well. There's still no transportation as far as I've heard. Bikes may make us a target."

"Can we really afford the time it'll take to walk?" replied Czernas. "Would the risk be that much greater, to justify the delay? We'll both be armed."

McKay hesitated. "Speed is of the essence," he said at last. "And even more than speed—getting back here with those papers. With that information. That's why I'm sending both of you. I *must* get whatever it is she has. And I must get it soon."

"Yes, sir," said Shango. Already the buildings had the faint smell of sewage, of plumbing that wouldn't work, of water that wouldn't come through pipes. First it'll be water, thought Shango, and then it'll be food, if something isn't done. He knew the Army and the National Guard were already stockpiling supplies. That would cause further trouble.

"I've written you an authorization, as Commander-in-Chief."

"That won't cut any ice with Jerri Bilmer," said the aide. "I mean, she'll know us by sight, but she wouldn't trust Jesus Christ if he showed her the holes in his hands. If some of the other services are involved in the cover-up, she may recognize us and vanish in the crowd. Is there anything we can give her, to let her know she can go with us?"

Shango thought Czernas was referring to another document, but after a moment's thought, McKay reached into the open collar of his sweat-stained shirt and drew out a little ball-link chain that still bore a slip of punch-printed tin.

Shango had one like it, in a footlocker at his sister's place. The sign of someone he used to be.

McKay coiled it down into Czernas' hand.

"Mr. Shango," he said, turning to the agent, "Czernas is in charge of this mission, but you're both responsible for its accomplishment. If one or the other of you should not be able to complete this task, I charge the other one to complete it. My authorization will let you take whatever you need, do whatever you must." And Shango saw in his eyes exactly his own thoughts about what had happened to every plane in the sky that morning. "But find her and the information. Bring them back."

"We'll get them," said Czernas. Then he grinned his boyish grin and added, "Heck, by tomorrow they might have got the cars running again, and this whole thing'll be a snap."

"They won't," said McKay, and there was in his voice a

note of sureness and sorrow that turned Shango's heart icy with dread. "They won't."

NEW YORK

One hundred three point two. *Shit.*

Cal shook down the thermometer, gazed at his sister. Her hair was plastered to her brow in thin strands, clung to the side of her face. She turned her head on the pillow with a bleary, fevered intensity. By the bedroom's candlelight, she looked like some refugee child, fragile and very pale.

"How's the head?" he asked.

"Light," Tina whispered dreamily. "Like if I let go, I'd just float up and up."

When he and Colleen had entered the apartment, they had found Tina leaning against the window frame, staring out at the night as though the fight was still raging. He'd called her name several times before snaring her attention, and then she'd turned to them with an eerie slowness, seeming to summon herself back from a long distance.

He had touched her face, felt an alarming heat. Then he'd gathered her in his arms, as he had so many times when she was little, and carried her to her room. In the gloom, his foot had found a heavy volume—the Nijinsky diary, fallen from the nightstand in the tremor. He had nudged it aside and set Tina softly on the bed, a feather.

Colleen hadn't said, "Maybe I should go." She'd just gone to the kitchen, soaked a dish towel in water from an Evian bottle and brought it to him, along with the aspirin. Then she had withdrawn to the living room, silent, waiting.

Cal shook the thermometer again, guided it toward Tina's mouth. She groaned a protest. "Just one more time," he said, "just to—"

He stopped, startled, as he spied her hand resting atop the covers. In the moonlight it appeared bloodless, translucent, faint tracings of veins beneath the skin.

Tina followed his gaze. "Looks like I'm turning into one of those fish you can see through," she murmured, but he could hear the fear beneath.

Tightness gripped his chest, and he had the wild thought that vampires had gotten to her, drained her. He pushed it away, held the thermometer before her mouth. "Just to be sure."

She nodded this time and took it.

"Any better?" asked Colleen, when Cal emerged from his sister's bedroom. He raised his eyes, and his face in the candlelight seemed older than it was downtown this morning, when he was just another fresh-faced life-support system for an Armani. Not that his suit was an Armani, she thought, looking around at the threadbare apartment, the shelves of law books, the fencing trophies treasured on a shelf. CALVIN GRIFFIN, they said. CLASS OF 1992. HURLEY HIGH SCHOOL.

Where the fuck was Hurley?

"Worse," he said, and his eyes looked old and weary.

She remembered the tone in his voice when he'd said, *My sister*, on the street that morning. *I take care of her.*

Yet he'd stopped to ask if she, Colleen, needed help. If she was okay.

She could see the tremor of his hand as he set the thermometer down on the edge of the pass-through into the kitchen. She wanted to put an arm around his shoulders and tell him, *She'll be all right*, but that might be bullshit. For all she knew, the poor kid might have the plague.

And hanging around here wasn't exactly the greatest health move for *her*, either. She held no special immunity from whatever the hell *it* was.

But surprisingly, this didn't worry her. She felt calm here, comforted even, although she couldn't have said why.

Cal Griffin stood still, looking bleakly at her—no, beyond her, to nothing at all. She said, "Try the phone."

"It's dead." So was his voice, his eyes.

"Try it."

He opened his mouth to snap but saw her point—things could come back on at any time—and picked up the receiver. Even as she watched him try not to smash it against the wall—of course it was dead as stone—Colleen realized she'd been prepared to go over and pick up the phone herself, assuming he'd simply say, Oh, fuck off, it's dead, why bother. Like Rory did. She'd almost forgotten that there *were* people willing to listen to her. Willing to change their minds or their attitudes.

I've been around Rory too long.

She looked at the framed photos on the wall: a slim, solemn, fair-haired boy with worried eyes, an ethereal slip of a dark-haired girl, on a shabby front porch with a tired-looking woman. That was the only photo that contained Mom. The rest were just Sister and Young Mr. Suit: college graduation, him getting another fencing trophy, Sis in ballet tights, a series of recitals, a brittle clipping from some local paper, with her looking so innocent and fragile it made your throat hurt—all the prettiness Colleen had envied as a girl, without the spite that the pretty girls so often showed.

And another, just the two of them, hand in hand.

"I have to get her to a hospital," said Cal. "She's burning up."

Colleen glanced back at him. Voices carried up to the fourth-floor window. Looters had returned to Patel's, picking over the goods scattered on the sidewalk and on the street.

"Roosevelt's the closest." Not knowing how to speak of comfort, Colleen took refuge in the practical, which was always the best course anyway, she thought. "Fifty-ninth and Tenth. You got something to carry her in?"

She saw the young man flip through half a dozen possibilities in a second, picking them up and discarding them like her dad checking out bolts of different sizes, looking for one that fit.

"There's grocery carts at Patel's," he said.

Colleen nodded. Close, and the looters wouldn't be fighting over them—not yet, anyway.

Cal drew a deep breath, made a smile and held out his hand to her. "Thank you," he said. "Thank you more than I can say." And there was that brisk lawyer tone in his voice that added, *We're done here.*

I won't ask you for anything else.

"I'll get the cart," said Colleen, ignoring him. "Can you get her down the stairs?"

Cal closed his eyes briefly. Colleen could see the relief on his face, that he wouldn't have to do this alone. He said, "Thank you," again, the voice of a friend.

WEST VIRGINIA

"There is nothing unsafe about those tunnels!" Norman Mullein pitched his voice to carry over the voices of the men and women crowding the wet gravel yard between the office and the pithead. "There hasn't been a flood, there wasn't a cave-in. . . ."

"How would you know?" yelled Anne Flue, in tones at least an octave lower than the mine supervisor's.

"And destroying the elevators in attempting to clear the downcasts would only halt production and put everybody out of work for weeks."

"Like them dying down there wouldn't put 'em out of work for longer?"

Wilma stood back from the crowd, arms folded, watching the faces of her friends and neighbors and feeling oddly detached. The sky still held its light-drenched blue brilliance, but, with the setting of the sun behind the green spine of Pigeon Ridge the valley that held Boone's Gap was beginning to fill with shadow, and twilight was, she found, having a curious effect on her.

With the coming of dusk the world seemed to take on different colors. The company compound, with its clutter of green-painted buildings, its tall angular pithead, its cyclone fences strung as though to keep the crowding woods at bay, looked strange to her now. Over the scents of coal and mud and machine-oil other scents tickled and whispered and murmured in her brain. Scents of the woods. Scents of the night.

". . . wait another few hours and everything will be all right. We're overdue to hear from the power company. . . ."

"Overdue?" hooted Ulee Grant. "My nephew just got back from biking down to Beckley, and he tells me everything's out there as well. And he says you can see smoke in the sky, off from Charlestown and way off in the north towards Wheeling, and you know what else? He says the whole day, he didn't see one airplane, one helicopter; he didn't see one working car on the road."

"To hell with this!" Hazel Noyes, Wilma's next-younger sister, planted a booted foot on the edge of the porch and hoisted herself up to stand at the same level as Mullein. "So we can't get the elevators out of the shaft? I guess that means we've got to go in some other way."

"Now, wait a minute!" protested the supervisor, looking as if he might shove her off the porch in sheer irritation.

"Everybody, get food, get water, get blankets, and get all the candles and lamps you can," Hazel went on. "Meet me over at the old Green Mountain pithead."

"That's company property!"

Hazel raised her eyebrows and mimed a moment of stunned surprise. "Gosh, and here I thought all these years you'd turned it into a state park when you were done with it!" Hazel had had her nose broken by Applby's goons on a picket line when she was fifteen: Norman Mullein did not impress her. She turned back to her friends. "It's a slant mine, not a shaft. Candy, can you meet us there with maps?"

"Those maps are company property!" protested Mullein. "Miss Leary, I forbid you. . . ."

"Oh, button it," snapped Candace, springing up the

steps and pushing past him. "I quit, okay?" She went into the office.

"Get water," Hazel was repeating. "Get lamps . . . Blankets . . ."

Wilma slipped away into the shadows, dusk swallowing her up as the crowd scattered.

Dusk did strange things to her thoughts. She was conscious of movement everywhere, of wildness in her heart and in her veins. As she passed the cars and pickups, stopped wherever they'd been at 9:15 this morning, she felt an odd indifference, as though such things meant nothing to her anymore. It was the time of night when she'd ordinarily have started thinking about getting a flashlight, but she knew there weren't any and it didn't bother her. She had no trouble making out shapes—in some ways they were clearer.

In all the shabby little houses along Front Street, people were lighting candles, waiting for moms and dads, husbands and wives, to get back from the pithead with news. Half of those houses had only had electricity for fifteen or twenty years anyway, and many of them still had wood stoves: the company had built those houses back in the forties, then sold them in the seventies to the miners who'd rented them for decades.

She turned the corner, climbed the long hill of Applby Street.

And slowed her steps at the sight of the big white house on the corner amid the honeysuckle.

Or at the non-sight of it. For a moment it seemed to her that all that was there was a kind of shadowy vacancy. Then she saw it again, but she saw, too, Boone's Gap's single patrolman, Glen Abate, making his methodical way down the street. Checking on houses, knocking on doors.

He walked past the Wishart house as if he didn't see it. Didn't remember it was there.

Didn't remember that there were people in it who hadn't been accounted for, that a man he'd gone to school with lay in a coma in the downstairs bedroom, dependent on machines that *had* to have failed when everything else did.

And for some reason, Wilma wasn't surprised.

She climbed her own front steps, the cats curling and rubbing against her ankles as she came into the porch; walked down the hall to the kitchen and opened cans. Somebody—probably Eleanor of Aquitaine, who was a savage little huntress—had brought a dead mole in as a present, and for some reason the smell of the blood touched a chord in Wilma, not of disgust but of intent and savage eagerness.

I'm not feeling like myself, she thought.

But that was a lie.

She felt more like herself than she'd felt since childhood. She felt light and springy, dazzlingly aware of small noises that she could identify with a weird clarity as tree mice, lizards, cicadas. And with each identification, she felt a strange delight and a dizzying impulse to go and catch them in her hands.

Perhaps what had happened wasn't entirely bad, if it freed the spirit like this?

Across the yard, the white house appeared and disappeared in the dusk.

Wilma sat on the back porch steps for a time and watched it. She could hear the birds whistling and calling their territories in every bush and tree of the vast thick-growing yards, and knew they were absent from the Wishart yard. The fireflies, which prickled the cobalt velvet of the summer dusk more thickly than they had in years, came nowhere near that house.

There was light—or something that wasn't quite light—in the window of Bob's ground-floor bedroom.

We're all right here, Arleta Wishart had called through the door in a voice unlike her own. *We're all fine.*

And, *Bob's calling me.*

Bob, locked for weeks in the silence of his coma?

He has to be dead, she thought. She knew that no battery in the town was working.

So why that prickling down her spine, that animal sense of wrongness when she looked toward the house that Glen Abate apparently didn't see?

Wilma got to her feet, picked her way through the deep grass toward the house.

The light in the window wasn't fire. Nothing of the golden warmth of kerosene or beeswax or any flame. It was violet, cold and pulsing rather than flickering, and as she stepped forward into the rank beds of honeysuckle she felt a pressure, a tightness in her chest, as if the air around the house were suddenly hostile and alive.

Anger. Anger and terror.

Go away! Go away! Go away!

She called out cautiously, "Bob?" Edged another step closer, her tall body crouching, limbs drawing together in a sort of lithe feral readiness, to spring or to flee. The air clawed and crinkled on her skin, and she prickled, nostrils twitching. Before her the honeysuckle stirred in the darkness, and from the leaves, from the thin glabrous flowers and the tough vines, came a kind of hissing, as if the plants themselves stirred and lashed against the ground.

She saw it move, ripple and rise, and she thought, *Stranglers.* The very scent of the flowers changed to a warning stink, the pungence of blood and death.

Slowly she withdrew. On the lawn behind her, Sebastian, Imp and Eleanor crouched in a line like three sphinxes, tails twitching slightly, huge eyes seeming to glow in the dark. Crazy with the craziness of cats in the night. Aware, as she was aware, of the lizards in the ferns, of the birds in the trees.

The honeysuckle stirred again, and Sebastian opened his red mouth and hissed.

Careful, soft-footed, alive to every whisper in the dark, Wilma circled the house to the path by the back door. Something in the house was aware of her. Something in the house followed her around the walls with its consciousness. Something in the house crouched down into itself, gathering darkness.

Arleta was in there, thought Wilma. Arleta and Bob—and Arleta was still alive even if Bob wasn't. She had a momentary vision of them, the pale chubby, helpless little woman in her pink sweats, her soft fair-haired son helpless in the bed.

Her friends, whom she could not desert.

She edged down the path, tense and ready to flee.

Under her feet the concrete shifted suddenly, the ground jerking, breaking. The two slabs of broken path yawned open, and she sprang back as they snapped shut like jaws biting at her ankle; the path jerked again, like a snake's back rippling. Wilma leaped back, not even fully aware that she shouldn't have been able to clear eight feet from a standing start. Her feet hit the ground, and she darted forward again in a long-legged springy run.

She grabbed the back door handle, moving fast, dragging on it with all her strength. Though the door had never had a lock on it, not even a hook, it refused to budge. Some terrible strength pulled against her own, though she could look through the screen and see nothing in the dark dusty clutter of old couches and boxes of romances heaped there. Behind her she heard a rustle, a whooshing green-plant heaviness of moving air, and reaching up she slashed and clawed at the screen where it was loose on its crazy old nails, bringing it down in a great tearing curl.

With weightless strength she swung up, through and into the porch, hearing in her mind the screaming desperate voice, *GET OUT! GET OUT! GO AWAY!* The darkness seemed to slam around her, a crushing fist, smothering. Dust and panic and something else, something terrible. Wilma dodged an instant before a cardboard box slammed heavily against the wall by her shoulder, the violence of the blow splitting the ancient glue. Paperbacks snowed to the plank floor, then rose up again like mad birds, flying at her face, shoving, suffocating. Wilma backed, dodged, nimble and very fast, instinct beyond words telling her to keep moving and changing direction, but whatever was in the porch with her was strong and fast as well.

Fear pounded on her, fear like a whirlwind—her own fear and a fear that seemed to come with that terrified scream. She grabbed the doorknob that would let her into the kitchen, and it was scalding hot under her hand. She jerked back, and one of the old couches swung at her legs like a battering ram. She sprang on top of it, up and over, ran as it tipped, plunged out through the window screen again. Fell, rolled, was on her feet and fleeing.

It was only when she sat once more on her own porch steps, panting and shivering and staring through the darkness at the white house that she could still see perfectly well—see with the preternatural clearness with which she still saw every leaf of the honeysuckle, every blade of the grass, through the night's gathering gloom—that she thought, *How the hell did I survive that*?

Softly, silently, the cats padded up to her through the gloom. Clinton levitated in a weightless spring to her shoulder; Mortimer butted the side of her knee gently with his flat furry skull; Isabella coaxingly dropped a mostly dead bug on her foot and touched her with a gentle paw. Wilma scratched scruffs, stroked backs, rubbed chins, drawing from them the comfort of company, the uncomplicated love that never disappointed her, never made demands that she wasn't prepared to fulfill.

It seemed to her years since the morning whistle had sounded in the mine, since she'd taken her shower and opened cans. She guessed now what the others didn't, that the lights might not be coming back on.

Good thing I have a manual can opener.

Except, of course, she thought, *when we run out of cans.*

She looked across at the darkness of the Wishart house, at the eerie purplish phosphorescence flickering in its window, and whatever was there looked back at her.

Voices in the street. Shannon Grant and Marcia

duPone—friends and neighbors, reminding her that whatever else had changed, there were things that hadn't.

Wilma closed the back door and returned to the dark of her house, to gather up water, food, blankets for those who would need them. And she felt whatever was in the Wishart house aware of her as she stepped out the front door to join her friends.

THIRTEEN

NEW YORK

Big Eddie was cooking, and that was that.

Didn't make no never mind if it was World War III or the biggest fuckup Municipal or the Man Upstairs had ever pulled. Nothing he could do about it. He'd just left that fucking Metro bus of his on Forty-second and Sixth where it had up and died, come home and hauled the barbecue right out onto the street. Now he stood like some black Moses in a chef's hat and apron, keeping the coals red hot and dishing out the good stuff.

He'd started the ball rolling by grilling whatever was thawing in his own freezer. Pretty soon folks from next door and down the block and around the corner were popping up with armfuls of burgers and dogs and chicken from their own kitchens. Better to cook it up than let it just rot. And some cats had gotten out their conga drums and saxophones and acoustic guitars, and it was sounding fine. Folks were scared shitless, hell yes, but it was also a damn good party. And not just the folks from the neighborhood: anyone could play; this was New York City. Big Eddie saw Asian dudes in pinstripe suits, a couple of them Orthodox guys, some Italian chicks still clutching their shopping bags from Bloomie's and

Bergdorf's. All mixing with the local talent, the brothers and sisters, Puerto Ricans and Vietnamese and just plain white guys. Everybody keeping it cool, right here, right now.

"That smells damn good." The voice behind him was a gutter rasp that made Wolfman Jack sound like a soprano. Big Eddie turned to see a long, lean figure hugging the shadows between two buildings.

"Tastes better than it smells," Big Eddie said. "So whyn't you just come on up and get yourself some?"

Unsteadily, the figure emerged from the shadows into the mellow light cast by the paper lanterns donated by the corner sushi bar. Eddie could see the guy was even taller than he, better than six and a half feet, a white guy with a dark complexion and really bad skin, wild black hair, and Raybans hiding his eyes. His black suit—looked like it had been expensive once—was torn to shit.

"Man, what happened to you?"

"Dunno," Stern said vaguely. "I'm all turned round."

Even through the smoke curling up redolent of meat and juices, Big Eddie's nostrils caught the tang of the dude's odor, some funky dinosaur smell or weird shit.

"Well, lemme get you set up here." Big Eddie heaped chicken wings and a burger, some potatoes and corn on a paper plate, held it out to him. The dude's hands had been jammed in his pockets, but now he had to pull one out to reach for the plate. Light fell across it, caught the glint of a white-gold wristwatch. Eddie saw long, rough-ridged nails and a hand all blotchy and bubbly, like it was erupting from within.

Big Eddie yanked back his hand, dropping the plate. "Geez, man, you're sick! What the hell you got?"

"I don't know," Stern said with absent neutrality. Man, the dude was trippin'.

"Well, keep your distance. You go over there, I'll slide something to you."

Stern tilted his head, regarding Big Eddie, and an insolence bloomed on his face that made him at once seem more together and formidable. "I don't take orders."

"You wanna eat, you better start." Big Eddie kept his eyes on the other man, not backing down, as he assembled another plate.

"Friend," Stern said, and there was no friendship in it, "you can kiss your tip good-bye." With a sweep of one big arm, he sent the barbecue tumbling, meat and spuds and cobs all flying, red-hot coals spilling out. Big Eddie yelped and fell back, swatting the burning stuff away.

"Motherfucker!" Now others were coming on the run, yelling at the crazy sick asshole. "What the fuck is your problem?" More and more of them, surging together, tattoos and silk ties and brow studs and Versace, moving fast. "Mess him up, mess that fucker up!" Stern lurched away, broke into a run, sunglasses flying off his face.

And they were after him.

Sam Lungo heard the mob coming from behind his lace curtains and heavy oak door, screaming their trash talk, their obscenities.

It had been a frightful evening, jumping at every creak of the old house, every distant crash and yell. The anguish and fury of the night had shrieked outside like a storm, shuddering windows and doors. Huddled in the dark, he had witnessed Patel's being smashed and torn apart, seen the wild ones descend on that mounted policeman in all their hunger and fear.

He had felt the briefest stirrings of sympathy, a fretful impulse toward action, but then Patel's had always gouged, their prices twenty, thirty cents higher than any supermarket. And as for that policeman, well, the police never did a thing when you called them, never did their job.

Then Cal Griffin and that dykey girl from down the street had appeared, driven the mob off. Sam had watched, silent and still, as they had helped the bulky old cop to his feet, murmuring like his own caring children, obviously solicitous, though Sam couldn't hear the words.

Sam's heart had pounded so fiercely then that he feared it

would burst his chest, be launched through the glass to land wetly at their feet, longing, longing. . . .

To have someone care about him, to have a protector, to be seen and heard and known, not an outsider or pariah, excluded from all confidences and joys.

The shouts and footfalls were louder now. Sam pressed his nose to the glass, squinting at the darkness. They were still around the corner but coming closer, and fast. The first one appeared, a huge, bony man in a tattered suit, gasping, stumbling, clearly frightened. Why, he was being *chased*.

The first of his pursuers emerged behind him, rounding the corner, a big fat man with a baseball bat. The one in the suit turned on him just as Fat Boy swung the bat at his head. Incredibly, Torn Suit caught the bat in his hands, snapped it in two—*crack*—and cast the pieces aside.

Now it was Fat Boy's turn to be scared. He backed as Torn Suit advanced on him. Torn Suit grabbed him by the front of his T-shirt, then threw him. Fat Boy flew a good twenty feet, bounced off a wall and sprawled in the gutter.

The other voices were loud now; any moment they'd be here. Torn Suit spun about, looking for escape, a way out.

Sam threw open his door. "This way! Quick!" Torn Suit didn't hesitate. Several bounding steps took him across the street and into Sam's house. Sam quickly shut the door, careful not to slam it. He motioned the other deeper into the room, away from the windows, then hunkered by the glass, careful not to be seen from outside.

The pack of wild ones was on the block now, a smorgasbord of surly, flushed faces. They crushed flowerbeds, knocked aside trash cans. Slowing only a bit, a few helped Fat Boy (who wasn't dead, surprisingly) to his feet, evaporated down the street.

Sam waited a moment to make sure they were gone, then turned to his visitor. Torn Suit was little more than a silhouette in the black room, massive and still, his head tilted to one side as though evaluating him.

Sam had kept the room dark so as not to draw attention.

Now he lit one of Mother's oil lamps; thank heavens she'd saved them.

But then she had saved everything.

The wick caught, and yellow light flared up, casting its glow over his guest. Sam let out a sound that was a little like a laugh and a lot like getting punched in the stomach.

Torn Suit was magnificently ugly, beautiful really, face all crags and angles and rough, leathery patches. No, not leather . . . he recalled the cast he'd once seen of a tyrannosaur's skin, with its ordered rows of ridges and bumps, so powerful and impervious. And the eyes that peered down at him, they gleamed like the twenty-dollar gold pieces Mother had shown him when he was little, the ones he'd never been able to find after she died.

"My," Sam said softly, "what *are* you?"

Numbly, Torn Suit searched in a breast pocket, handed him a card. *Ely Stern*, it said, *Lawyer*.

"Oh," Sam muttered. "Of course."

Stern regarded Sam with a bemused expression. "Why'd you help me?" His voice sounded like a tuba lined with sandpaper; it raised the hairs on Sam's neck.

Slowly, Sam approached, stretched out tentative fingertips to touch Stern's sleeve, feel the hard muscle beneath.

"I need someone strong," he said.

Sam had been a boy when Mother had bought the intricately carved Art Nouveau bookcase. It had taken three big men, sweating like pigs, to wrestle it into the house and against the wall.

But Stern lifted it off the floor where it had fallen and replaced it as easily as if it were cardboard.

"Holy cow," Sam giggled.

"I play racquetball Tuesdays and Thursdays," Stern murmured. He still seemed about one sandwich short of a picnic, but he was coming around. His pyrite gaze washed over the velvet and scrollwork furniture, the heavy wood bureaus and the dolls. Mostly the dolls. Sam had put them all back in place, as Mother would have insisted. Miraculously, not one had broken. They lined the tops of chaise longues and etageres, massed every surface in their pinafores and sausage curls, bisque cheeks and glass eyes, the Gaultiers and Brus and Jumeaus.

"What's with the dolls?" Stern asked.

Sam grimaced as if ashes were on his tongue. "My mother. My late mother. She left me all this."

Stern's eyes glinted off the silent audience staring out like children's corpses, like contemptuously amused ghosts. "She must have been bent."

Sam barked a laugh; and in the heavy, airless room it reverberated off the walls and furniture. "Don't get me started."

Stern grinned at him, a horrible, exhilarating grin wider than any human mouth should have been, teeth curved and razored like a shark's.

"You got anything around here to eat?" he said.

"Jeez, what I'd give for some WD-40," Colleen said, and Cal had to agree. The front wheel on the shopping cart was wailing like the unquiet dead.

They had turned onto Tenth now, only five more blocks to Roosevelt Emergency. He had expected the wide avenue to be packed, but they'd seen few people, mostly wary souls who walked fast and gave them a wide berth, plus a scattering of grim men guarding shops and restaurants with handguns and rifles.

The front wheels of the cart hit a hole, and Tina gave a small moan.

"It's okay, baby," Cal said, not slowing. He reached down and stroked her shoulder. She seemed barely aware of him. In the moonlight, her face had a blue sheen. She was breathing in ragged gasps, struggling for each breath. Cal gripped the bar of the cart tighter and increased his speed as much as he could. The pavement in the street would have been smoother but there wasn't room to get the cart between the stilled cars.

Colleen kept pace alongside, her long, easy strides matching his, the big wrench held loosely, an extension of her arm. He saw she was watching him. "What?"

"Nothing," she said. "You're just not what I'm used to." And what might that be? *Trouble with my love life*, she had said outside the Stark building, and she'd been in no hurry to get home since she'd descended on that punk with her handy cudgel.

"So what's with you and elevators?" he asked, trying to make it sound light, to speak of anything other than the breathless dread he felt, to cover the heartrending rasps from the huddled figure in the cart, mindful of the street, the air, the night.

"Dad was a grease monkey in the military; guess it got into my blood." She scanned the shadows ahead. "Heart got him when I was fifteen. Ma and I didn't exactly see eye to eye, so I packed up my tools soon as I could, hopped a bus east."

"And never looked back," Cal added. He was working hard to avoid the ruts in the pavement, but the front wheels twisted with almost willful contrariness. He kept up the pace, urgent, headlong, his legs aching from the forced quick-march. He found he was holding the metal bar with a white-knuckle tension that sent pain shooting up both forearms. He loosened his grip, just a little, and the discomfort eased.

"Well, you study history," Colleen's voice mingled with the night breeze, "you might just have to learn something from it." Her face clouded. Then she said, "So what's your story? Where're your folks?"

For a moment, Cal considered evading, painting some *Brady Bunch* scenario to be spared the recital of the gory details. Then he nodded toward Tina. "Dad ran off when she was born. And when she was four, Mom . . . got killed."

He braced for the pitying gasp, the familiar questions. But all she said was, "How old were you?"

"Eighteen. But I wasn't gonna let anybody split us up. I got myself declared her guardian, had everyone swear I was responsible."

Colleen's eyes slid over again to appraise him. "They were right."

No, they weren't. I became a fucking lawyer and left her till all hours with nannies and au pairs and all sorts of faux parents who weren't—

Colleen shot up a warning hand. He stopped short, brought the cart to silence. She was peering into the darkness ahead, listening keenly. Now Cal heard it, too, a shuffling of many feet, a scurrying. And something more, murmuring voices that sounded predatory, expectant.

Cal pressed down on the bar, lifting the squeaking front wheel off the asphalt, keeping it mute. He crab-walked the cart behind an overflowing dumpster, out of sight. Mercifully, Tina was quiet, eyes shut. He and Colleen crouched down.

Small, huddled figures appeared in the intersection, moving quickly along Sixty-second, speaking in soft, eager tones, whispering and chuckling like naughty children.

Children? Their silhouetted heads seemed abnormally large, their arms too long. Their clothes flapped loosely, bunched and oversize, and they moved with a strange, lithe step. Cal caught the glint of what looked like a rifle barrel, held straight up, in their midst. Then they were gone.

Cautiously, Colleen emerged, stepped to the cross street to make sure. A moment later she waved Cal forward. He eased the cart out, drew up by her. Her eyes mirrored his own thoughts, betraying incredulity and—something he hadn't seen before in her—fear.

Cal tried to reassure himself they were just people, fleetingly glimpsed, misperceived. But something deep in his gut belied that. His sense of events stirring, of the world altering, grew stronger, more insistent. This darkness, this silence, wasn't just some outage, some one-shot event, to be righted tomorrow.

This *was* tomorrow.

Colleen was still peering down Sixty-second, wary and uncertain. "Come on," Cal said. With an effort she tore her attention away, and they continued down Tenth.

Cal tried to lose himself in forward motion, enveloped in the terrible rhythm of his sister's tortured breath. But the image of those huddled dark shapes, moving so swiftly, so purposefully, would not be banished. In his mind, it became all of a piece somehow: the malformed, twisted ones speeding on their errand; the dream of darkness, of blood and the sword, the multitudes crying for him to *act*; the homeless madman warning of the catastrophe to come, which *did* come; Stern, muted and deflated, crumpled on his office floor, so like Tina in that fevered flatness, now that he thought of it.

And that punk in the T-shirt, reaching for the gun.

Unreality seized him. It was as if the dream had not ended, merely transformed, and he was snared in it, changing.

Tina moaned again, snapping him back to the moment. He murmured reassurance, then glanced at Colleen, prowling silent alongside, certain again in action.

"Colleen," Cal began, still on the move.

"Yeah?"

"When you hit that guy holding the gun on me . . . did you see anything?"

"Red."

"No, I mean," he searched for words. "I thought I saw . . . something."

"Like what?"

"Like—" he hesitated and noticed that Colleen had stopped in her tracks, was staring ahead in astonishment.

He followed her gaze and saw them, in the hundreds, men and women all jostling, pressing forward, struggling to get into the great, dark building as desperately outnumbered fig-

ures in lab coats, scrubs and a scattering of security uniforms strove to keep them back.

They had reached the hospital.

A steak a day, cooked rare, Mother had demanded for both
of them. Blood to feed the blood.

But what do you do when the electricity cuts out and six
months' worth of prime cut is turning to a soggy mess in the
freezer? You let it go, that's what you do, and you attend to
your guest. *My guest.* When had he ever used that phrase,
when had he had call to? Never.

Sam bustled back into the dining room, hefting the platter with its great hunk of meat. Stern sat at the table, immense and dark and incongruous before the lace tablecloth,
the linen napkins, the silver.

"Got a whole freezer of these," Sam said. "Just be ruined
if the power doesn't come back on." He set the heavy plate
on the table. "I'm not sure how we can cook—"

Savagely, Stern snatched the meat and downed it in a single, vast inhalation. Sam yelped in surprise, took a step
back, almost falling.

Stern's eyes fixed on him, and, for a terrible moment,
Sam felt like a rabbit caught in the searchlight glare of a
wolf. Seeing it, Stern chuckled, and his eyes lost some of
their edge. He held the platter out with one sharp-nailed
hand. His dagger teeth caught the lamplight as he intoned,
dragon's voice attempting a childish falsetto, "Please, sir . . .
may I have some more?"

Blood was in the air, and things worse than blood. The
hospital was suffocating, bedlam in the crowded, narrow
corridors lit by candles and whatever else the hospital staff
had scrounged up. Cal even spied a menorah casting its
glimmering light on the triage teams bent over forms on
gurneys.

Cal had cautioned Colleen to stay outside with Tina while he ventured into the labyrinthine building in search of aid. But gaining the ear of a doctor or nurse was impossible; each rushing medic was besieged by supplicants, deafened by pleas. Initially, they had tried to quarantine those who seemed infected by this strange new disease or diseases. But the masses had soon overwhelmed them, and all systems had broken down, replaced by a frantic improvisation.

The wounded and ailing sat or stood wherever they could, some rocking, some moaning, others silent and numb. One boy of ten or so lay cradled in his mother's arms, his hair half-fallen out, eyes huge and vacant as he chanted television listings in an endless drone. From the woman Cal learned that there were many cases of odd fevers, inexplicable pains, alarming growths beneath the skin, as well as those directly injured by fire and quake. And not anyone here to tend them or explain.

Cal thought of Tina, out in the cart, fever consuming her like kindling. Panic swirled about him, and he felt his own panic rising to meet it. *She's slipping away from me, she's slipping away, and there's nothing I can do.*

No. I won't accept that. He fought his immobility, bulled through the crowds, collared a blank-eyed, wispy internist named Marquette, forced his attention. Keeping a grip on the man's arm, Cal barked out Tina's symptoms, demanded advice, treatment.

But Marquette began gabbling about what happened when the quake had hit, the emergency generators and backup batteries failing. Operating rooms had turned into hell-black chambers of horrors, with not even the light from flatline monitors to show the gaping cavities of the suddenly stilled bodies on the tables. Every operating room had been in use, with teams frantically, hopelessly trying to keep hearts and lungs going.

Not to mention the nightmares in the ICU and the incubator room off Maternity. . . .

Screams had echoed down the corridors long before the newly maimed and diseased had descended on them.

"You want advice?" Marquette finished shrilly. "*Take her home.*" He tore free of Cal's grasp and plunged into the mob, was swallowed up.

Cal stood silent, alone amid the mayhem and noise, the families crouched with their wasted, broken ones. His eyes stung, and he found he had to will every breath. He summoned calm, focused on a single thought.

I've got to get her a doctor.

Somewhere in this fucking city, there had to be *someone*.

But every doctor would be under siege, unreachable. It would be exactly the same as here.

Unless somehow he were unknown. Unless—

Unless his degree wasn't worth toilet paper.

Doc. Who had fled Russia, abandoned his practice. Who joked about atherosclerosis and heart attacks as he dished out franks and praline-covered coconut. *I don't even know where he lives.*

But I know where he works.

If he's there. At this hour . . .

On the first night after the end of the world? He just might be.

Cal found Colleen near the alley that led to the delivery entrance, away from the crowd. Beside her, Tina was a tight-curled knot in the cart, blanket thrown off, eyes half open. She made no response as Cal approached.

"It's hopeless in there," he said and looked down at his sister. "Tina?"

Colleen touched his arm. "She can't hear you. Fever's got her."

Cal ran his fingers through Tina's matted hair, along the blazing smooth brow. "There's someone I know, a little. He used to be a doctor. I think maybe he'll help, if he can, if I can find him."

He cast a desperate glance at Tina, remembering the endless trudge from Eighty-first. It took so long to get her anywhere, and she was burning, fading away even as he watched.

"I'll stay with her," Colleen said. He hesitated. "It's okay. We'll be safe. We'll wait over there." She gestured across the street.

"Over there" was a concrete playground. Cal spied flares and torches, hustling dark forms, some in uniforms, erecting tents and uncrating supplies.

"National Guard," said Colleen. "Started setting up while you were inside. It's for folks whose buildings got wrecked or who can't hack the climb, whatever."

She closed the gap between them. "We'll be here when you get back. Get a move on." He nodded and turned away, caught his stride, leaving them behind. The night air filled his lungs.

It felt good to run.

Toward the end, Stern had gotten a little daintier. He was no longer swallowing the bones.

They lay heaped on the platter before him, between the German porcelain candelabra. He held the last, teeth scraping the final bit of meat from it. Then he tossed it on the pile and belched. "There goes my cholesterol."

Across from him, Sam perched on his chair's edge, fascinated. The freezer was empty now, but what did that matter? "You remind me of Hoss on Bonanza. He liked to eat. And no one messed with him."

Stern nodded solemnly, regarded his strange dark hands with their stiletto nails. "No one messes with the big guy . . ."

"That's right!" Sam bounced to his feet. "They respect power. They respect what can *hurt* them."

The oil lamp behind Stern had died, and Sam stepped into its pool of shadow. "I remember the blackout in '65," he said, voice high and fast. "This dark that just went on and on, and no one to tell you what was right or wrong except you. I remember thinking, What if this just goes on forever? But then the next day came, and it ended."

He strode to face Stern, peered at his craggy face. "But this is different, isn't it, Ely? I mean, there's you, for instance. Blackout wouldn't explain you."

Stern scowled, looked beyond Sam at the blackness, at nothing. "My therapist, those slugs on the street, they thought I was sick. I'm not sick." He stretched expansively, rippling muscle visible where coat seams had burst. "I'm becoming."

"Becoming what?" Sam asked, reverent, enchanted. Wanting, himself, to *become*. To become anything.

Stern rose like a tower. "I'll know when I get there."

Sam timidly reached up, nearly to the length of his arm, and daubed a linen napkin on Stern's mouth. "You got a little . . . blood on your lip." God, he was magnificent, and terrible.

"Thanks." Stern turned from him, striding out of the dining room toward the living room, the door. *He was leaving.*

"Wait! Wait!" Sam overtook him in the front room, blocked his way. "You go out there, it will be just the same, everywhere. They'll chase you, hunt you down. They never appreciate what's different, what's special. I *know*." The words cascaded out, pleading. "We can help each other. You can stay here. I can keep you safe, hidden, get you food."

Stern cocked his head, eyed him with a lawyer's caginess. "And what's your percentage?"

Sam's heart thrilled. As a child, he'd seen *The Thief of Baghdad* and for years after had fantasized about having its huge, forbidding genie at his command, to do his bidding. *What is thy wish, O my master?*

Sam plunged a hand into his pocket, withdrew the dog-eared notepad, one of so many, with their hundreds and thousands of notations, all the days and weeks and years of outrage and insult.

"There's some people I'd like you to meet . . . ," he said.

Cal found himself swimming against a tide of humanity, every cross street hopelessly clogged with folks making their way toward Central Park, drawn by the glare of the huge propane lamps of the National Guard encampment there.

Cal darted into an alleyway behind some restaurants. It reeked of rotted vegetables, spoiled meat, but mercifully there was no one in sight. He dodged spilled trash cans, leaped over rubbish, picking up speed.

"Yo, Ginsu!" The voice echoed off cold brick. "Where's your girlfriend?" The alley was pitch dark, but there was no mistaking the haircut in the reflected candleglow from a window above, the shirt with its grinning death's head.

Cal slowed as Misfits swaggered toward him. "Get a load of this," he said. He extended a hand.

The trash at Cal's feet quivered, whipped about as in a sharp wind, and Cal felt himself gripped hard, pulled by a powerful suction. He struggled, but there was no fighting it. It swept him up, hurled him toward the open hand, which caught him by the throat, squeezed tight.

Misfits bared ragged, nicotine-stained teeth in a delighted grin. "Magnet Man, just like with the gun. Didn't know I could do it till tonight. Been wastin' my time in vocational school." He winced. "Man, my ribs hurt."

He raised the police automatic, held it an inch from Cal's face. "Am I glad to see you," he said.

FOURTEEN

"Wait!" Cal shot out a desperate hand. Misfits fired. But there was no bang. Instead, the gun gave off a weak spark, like a lighter not quite catching.

While Misfits was still doing a double-take, Cal reacted, stomped the younger man's instep. The youth doubled over. Cal twisted in his grip and elbowed him in the mouth.

His advantage was momentary. Misfits lunged back at him with a kick that knocked Cal sprawling and drove the breath from him. Conditioned by years of TV and movie fights, though, the young man couldn't give up the idea of a gun. Instead of advancing, Misfits fired again.

And again, the fizzy little flash, the ping of a bullet falling out of the muzzle.

Cal rolled to his feet and fled, stumbling on his first stride but then leveling into speed he hadn't thought himself capable of. Misfits fired after him: *pht-clink, pht-clink, pht-clink.* Feeble flashes in the dark.

Leaning against an alley wall later, belly hurting more than he'd thought possible from the youth's kick, Cal thought about the encounter.

Magnet Man, didn't know I could do it . . .

Had he really seen what he'd seen?

Defective gun? But he'd seen the spark. And it hadn't jammed, he'd heard the bullets fall.

One defective bullet, maybe, but all of them?

The gun moving along the pavement . . .

Being dragged into the young man's grip . . .

Planes falling out of the sky.

He took a deep breath, straightened up. His palms were bleeding from hitting the pavement, and his elbow was bruised from Misfits' teeth.

The image of Tina came flooding back to him, and the horror and chaos of Roosevelt. Cal hurried up the alley, jogging at first until the pain in his belly eased, then running full out again, like a man pursued by the darkness he'd all his life tried to outrun.

WEST VIRGINIA

They still don't know, thought Wilma, her long stride keeping easy pace with Shannon Grant's hurrying feet, with the small scuttling Marcia duPone. *They still don't understand*.

She didn't understand either, not exactly. She would have been hard put even to explain the suspicions and speculations that circled through her mind. But she knew to her marrow that what had happened wasn't a power outage.

Something had changed. Whatever had driven her out of Arleta's house—and it was a consciousness, a blinded screaming hammering rage-filled Something—wasn't part of a world where power outages or earthquakes or cave-ins, or even nuclear war for that matter, were what you had to worry about.

She carried a two-and-a-half-gallon bottle of Allegheny Spring Water and a canvas bag filled with candles, lamp oil and three disassembled colored-glass oil lamps. Anyone who lived for any length of time within driving distance of a dozen Appalachian craft fairs picked up colored-glass oil lamps: impractical for the most part, but an inevitable gift at Christmastime. Shannon had two in her satchel, plus another, burning, in her hand. Marcia brought only one, having decided that food was more important.

"It's only been since nine this morning," pointed out Shannon, eyeing the old woman's collapsible shopping cart of canned tuna and bags of day-old bread.

"I grew up in the Depression, honey," announced Marcia, in case Shannon had somehow neglected to assimilate a statement she'd heard four times a day since birth. "And I know there's nothing worse than being hungry. If I feel that way, and my Gus feels that way, and God knows my Tommy feels that way, you know half those men down there feel that way."

Shut up, thought Wilma, not in impatience, but because her new awareness brought her sounds from the darkness around them. Her mind snapped away from uneasy concern about Arleta and Bob as she thought she saw something run, dodging nimbly between the stranded cars, across the bottom of Applby Lane in front of them. There was a ruffle and scurry in Gerda Weise's lantana bushes to their left, and a smell.

Coal and ground water. Tobacco and grime.

Alien flesh.

"Mother used to take all of us down to the bakery, where they'd give us day-old bread for a nickle, and we'd all bring our pillow cases. . . ."

It was impossible to hear, but Wilma thought they were being paralleled on the other side of the street as well. Her night-sighted eyes could see nothing, but sounds came to her from the other side of the dark houses, the crunch and skitter of stooped bodies slipping through backyards, the creak as something heavy went over Carl Souza's fence. The muffled grunt-grunt-grunt of snuffling breath.

"Marcia," she said softly, touching her friend's sloped shoulder, "could you be quiet a minute? I think I hear something following us."

Marcia stopped in her tracks. "What? Following us?

What the hell would be following us? For God's sake, everybody in this town is in the same boat."

"What is it?" asked Shannon, stopping and holding up her lamp.

"Middle of the street," said Wilma, hearing it coming, fast, through the dark screen of the Souzas' overgrown yard. Her two companions looked around blankly while she saw—and clearly they did not—the clotted mass of hedge and laurel jerk and twitch, heard the slash-slash-slash of running feet and smelled trampled herbage and wet-coal stink, sweat stink, alien stink racing toward them through the undergrowth. "Middle of the street!" she yelled again, grabbing each of the other women by the arm and thrusting them toward open ground.

"Wilma, what the . . . ?" Marcia planted her feet, then let out a shriek as the slumped grubby thing burst out of the dark of the hedges and grabbed for her throat.

If Wilma hadn't already been shoving her, the older woman would have been killed, for the thing's hands, clutching at her shoulder as Wilma yanked her clear, were hugely strong. As it was, Marcia screamed again in shock and terror and pain, and something else raced out of the shadows between the Ure and Dixon houses across the street, grunting as it reached for them with apelike arms. Wilma saw round, huge blinking white eyes reflecting the flare of Shannon's lamp and went for them instinctively, her hands bent to claw.

Fast, fast, scratching at the face of the thing that was tearing at Marcia and her parcels, grabbing with her hands and raising a foot to dig at the belly. And when the thing reeled back and fled, she turned, pounced, clawed at the second attacker. The next second it too was running, for Shannon had sprung forward, swinging the lamp. The glass chimney came loose and fell with a ringing smash of glass, and for an instant the flame, streaming long and yellow like a ribbon, showed all the women what only Wilma had seen in the darkness: feral faces, hairless heads, bulging white eyes filled with sullen hunger and rage.

Then they were gone. Wilma stood up, panting, blood under her nails and a weird singing exultation in her heart, as if she'd tasted forbidden fruit and found the taste divine.

"Oh, my God," Shannon was gasping, her short dark curls tangled in her eyes, "oh my God, what are they? Did you see them? Did you see their faces?"

Marcia, sobbing in a welter of dropped bread rolls and tuna cans and torn bags, was beyond speech.

"Tessa!" Shannon cried. "I have to get back to my mother's; I left Tessa there with her cousins."

"Tell them to light lamps there," Wilma said quietly. "It ran from the fire. But get Beth Swann and Clare Greene and everybody else who isn't at the mine already, get them together in one house, with all the light you can manage."

"But what are they?" demanded the young woman, hesitating, torn between her husband's danger and her child's. "Where did they come from?"

"I don't know what they are," Wilma said, thinking of the strangeness of the night air and of the terrible thing that had attacked her on the porch of Arleta's house. "But by the smell of them, they came out of the mine."

Shannon and Marcia left the rolls and tuna on the sidewalk where they had fallen and headed back to the neat little Front Street house where Shannon's mother, Ardiss Hillocher, lived. Striding along Front Street toward the grimy collection of brown-brick buildings and abandoned filling stations that comprised old downtown, Wilma looked back to see the two women hastening up Appalachia Road to the trailer court, the gold spot of Shannon's lamp outlining them in light.

Before the women had gone a dozen yards, Wilma saw dark bent shapes creep from the Souza yard and start picking up the bread and the cans. She halted, standing alone on the sidewalk. She felt curiously little fear; she could smell and hear clearly and knew there wasn't any danger near her.

She heard them grunt to one another, gutteral noises almost like words. Then a scrunching, ripping crinkle of metal and the smell of tuna (*divine greasy wonderment exploding in her hindbrain*!). She'd seen the cans and knew they weren't the little single-serving tear-opens but the big six- and nine-ounce size that required a can opener.

She walked on. She heard, smelled, sensed others of the creatures moving through the night, heard their grunts and recognized the characteristic musky scent of their bodies and the fact that some of them smelled of coal and others didn't. They smelled of engine oil, of dust, of industrial soaps. Of beer and cigarettes.

Enough people were walking along Front Street through old downtown that the creatures didn't attack there, though Wilma was aware of them scuffling through the grimy alleys, the empty lots beyond the range of the torches. She felt, as always, a stab of profound sadness as she passed the store where she'd bought her school clothes, its window painted dark green and transformed into one of the town's sleazier bars; as she saw the drugstore across the street where she'd lovingly combed through the rack of paperback books every Saturday, closed down since the end of the coal boom in the seventies. The restaurant where she and Hank used to go for ice cream after school on Fridays was boarded up; the record shop, where she and Hazel had picked through stock for such rarities as Glenn Yarborough and Rod McKuen albums, had "Antiques" painted on the window but actually only sold junk.

So much gone, she thought. So many places and people, vanished in that sparkling stream of time.

And Arleta? she thought. What had happened to her friend, what had happened to poor Bob, when electricity had failed, when Power had seized the white house among the honeysuckles?

There were about three hundred and fifty people gathered in front of the sagging cyclone fence that ringed the old offices, the rusted ruin of tippling shed and machine housings. The buildings were rankly overgrown, there'd been talk for years of rehabbing them for a "regional crafts market and antique mall," but nobody'd come up with the funds to do so. The bobbing sea of candle and lamp flames passed across brick and concrete defaced by the scribbles of years of kids. The searchers, who'd straggled a little as they'd come out of the sorry squalor of old downtown, now bunched tighter at the sight of those plywood-covered windows, those chain-locked doors. Even after all those years the place stank of coal, the black dust dyeing the earth underfoot. Wilma well remembered the filthiness of everything west of Front Street in her childhood, before the union and the federal government had forced Applby to institute dust control.

She remembered, too, her mother telling her not to go near the miners' children because they were "dirty." Remembered Sue Hillocher telling her in a whisper, "My daddy's got black lung, and they say he's gonna die."

And he did die, the following year.

Norm Mullein was still with them, presumably to protect the weather-worn sawbucks and rusted machinery from further vandalism.

Candace Leary was there too, bless her efficient soul, and she and Hazel were already hand-copying portions of Candace's big map by torchlight.

"How we gonna go down there if we ain't got flashlights?" asked Katy Grimes. "You can't take no open fire into the mine."

"Same way the old-time miners did," said Hazel. "One person out front with a canary in a cage, to check for gas. There shouldn't be dust up at this end; it hasn't been worked since '77."

"But how'll we find our way through to where they are?" asked someone else. "Wasn't it all caved in?"

"Most of it was," volunteered old Mr. Swann, who should have been home in bed, thought Wilma, recalling his queer fit on Arleta's doorstep that morning. "But there's shafts and crosscuts left. I know, 'cause I helped retreat out of those sections. We can probably get through. Got to keep just one candle or so at a time, though, specially once we get down deep."

"Will they still be alive?"

"We're talking about . . ." Candy looked at her watch, then looked around her for help, since like nearly every other watch in the town it said 9:17 if it said anything at all. Every digital had simply gone blank.

"About twelve hours," said Theo Morrison, one of the two hikers who'd come into the town at around noon with word of fire toward Lynchburg. He snapped closed the silver pocket-watch he carried and put a worried arm around his wife.

"There's respirators down there on the walls," added Candace. "And we got more up here, lots more." She nodded toward the crates beside her.

"What do we do if we meet more of those grunty things?" asked Ed Brackett, whose face bore the bruises and cuts of a fight. "They all but killed my boy Steve."

The boy, one of Wilma's students, looked up at mention of his name, from where someone was bandaging a horrible gash on his arm.

"It may not be enough to keep guard on the town," added Carl Souza. He hefted his rifle. "We don't know how many of 'em there are, or where they are, except they can see in the dark and they're strong as the devil. What if there's an army of 'em?"

There was a fast, scared ripple of talk then, people trading experiences, showing wounds. They jumped out of the dark at me. . . . They was hiding in the Sawyers' yard. . . . They took and tore my shotgun clean in half before I could get off a shot at 'em. . . . The terror in the air was volatile, like gasoline or alcohol, only needing a spark.

She was not the only one, Wilma realized, who was beginning to understand that this was not simply a matter of a power failure, of waiting till the lights came back on.

Someone was talking about monsters, another of invasion, and how the Communist Bloc had only pretended to break up and collapse. Someone said demons and God. Wilma thought, *No. You're wrong.*

She didn't know what was right, but none of them had encountered the thing in the house on Applby Street.

There was still blood and skin under her fingernails, and it occurred to her that that was the first time since childhood scuffles in the schoolground that she'd physically fought another living being. She'd always been mild-natured and aloof, shrinking from contact. Even Hank's kisses—though she'd longed for the warmth of his closeness and the strength of his embrace—had been something she'd had to overcome her nature to achieve. And he'd felt it.

Hank. The thought of him filled her with a piercing regret.

And he was in the mine. With Ryan. With Lou. With men she'd taught when they were children, young men whose fathers she'd gone to school with, as she'd gone to school with Hank.

"Looky here!" yelled Katy Grimes. "Look! They come out already!"

And everyone ran to the rough blue-gray cliff of the old mine entrance to look.

Around World War II, Applby had put in a donkey engine to drag skips up the mine's steeply sloping tunnel, replacing the mules. At that time the tunnel floor had been paved for forty or fifty feet down, and what had been a huge cave cut into the mountain's flank had been finished with concrete, so that it resembled an enormous culvert, strung with electric lights. Time and weather and a million pairs of passing boots had had their way, however, and the pavement was invisible again under a layer of mud.

In the glare of the torchlight there was no mistaking the scuffle of fresh tracks, nor the print of men's workboots.

"Some of 'em come out," Katy repeated and brushed back her snaggly blond hair with the back of her arm. She was a hollow-eyed, too-thin girl who would have been stunningly pretty if she'd either washed or smiled; she'd never even made it as far as Wilma's classes. Her sister, Annie Flue, joined her, holding her torch aloft.

"So why didn't they come down to town?" she asked, puzzled. "Look at 'em, looks like they all sort of scatter every which way."

"They got to knowed there was men left back in the mine."

Torchlight gleamed on the puddles between the rusted rails as those who'd tried to follow the tracks regathered slowly around the tunnel entrance. Someone touched the cyclone gates that had guarded the tunnel, now thrown wide. The snapped chain lay in the mud.

"What you make of this?" asked Ulee Grant, kneeling to shine his light more clearly on the mud.

The prints of workboots, going back in.

And a mangled empty tuna can.

Voices sank to a whisper, baffled, then to silence.

"I guess we'll find that out," said Hazel, "when we find 'em."

Candy started passing out maps and balls of string.

"It's a real labyrinth," Hank had told Wilma when he'd first gone to work there in '67. "They been digging under that mountain since just after the Civil War, and there's miles of played-out galleries and rooms where the face collapsed back before anybody was born. They took up the tracks in most of 'em, but all they've done since is just put a couple of sawbucks in front of 'em, to keep us from taking the wrong way down. It dips real steep just about where Pidgeon Ridge goes up, and there's whole sections that mostly caved in. God knows what's in there now."

God knows, thought Wilma, looking down at the tracks, then into the darkness.

"You won't have to worry about anything till you get down to the last section, where it dips down here." Candace Leary pointed to her map. Farther back from the pithead, the little gangs sorted themselves out, making sure each group included someone with string, someone with candles, someone carrying a canary or finch or budgie. Someone with water, with SCSRs. Someone with a gun.

"This is where they tried to put a vent shaft through to the new diggings. The fan engines got took out after the cave-in, so you don't have to worry about the electricity going on all of a sudden and the fans starting up. After that you'll have to spread out and search. If somebody did try getting through that way, they'll have got lost in the dark."

"What if those grunter things are down there?" Carl Souza shifted his rifle in his hands. "We can't shoot 'em in the tunnels. The ricochets'll kill somebody."

"And what if they cut the string that leads us back to the vent?" That was Lynn Fellbarger, who ran the antiques store. "What if there's another earthquake and a cave-in?"

"Then stay on top of the ground," retorted Hazel, picking up a lamp. "This isn't a Disneyworld ride."

Movement in the tunnel—far, far away in the dark. Wilma stepped into the wet concrete circle of its maw, gazing, listening.

Voices.

Al Bartolo's. Gordy Flue's.

"They're there," she said. She turned. The opening behind her was a circle of golden light. "They're there, I can hear them!" she called out, and the lights streamed in, glistening on the wet of the walls. "Al!" She raised her voice in a yell. The echoes of it bounded away into the blackness, piercing decades of silence there. "Gordy!"

"GORDY!" bellowed Annie Flue, who had a voice like the chimes of Big Ben. "GORDY!"

And blessed, blessed in the distance where the echoes died away, "Son of a bitch, you see it? Lights!"

"They're there," she said again. She was nearly lifted from her feet, carried along as if on a tide, men and women crowding around her, shoving to get to the men. The echoes of their voices drowned any further sounds from the tunnel, but she knew the men could see the lights, would come to them.

And they did. Pressed against the wall, Wilma sensed more than actually saw the first contact with the missing men, when the surging mass of bodies in the tunnel going down stopped, shoved and milled a little, holding up candles and lights to keep them from being overset. Struggling, hugging, touching: she saw Della desperately hugging Ryan, hugging Lou. "My God, my God." Annie and Gordy, Shannon and Greg, Gina Bartolo sobbing in Al's arms.

More mobbing, pushing, surging back toward the entrance with Candy yelling, "Let us through! We got 'em; now back out and let us through, for Chrissake!" and someone else from the back of the crowd saying, "We couldn't have done it without Hank! Hank, fuck, he can see in the dark! You know he can fuckin' see in the dark? Hank—Hank, come on."

And Hank's voice, "No, no, let me be."

"Whoa—whoa, hang onto him!"

"What's the matter?"

"Couple of the guys went like this, turned back into the tunnels. . . ."

And someone else, "What the fuck happened? What the fuck's going on? Looks like a fuckin' Greek wedding with all these candles."

Even before they reached the end of the tunnel, the wave of joy, of rescue and recovery, had turned to an undertow of fear.

"Whaddaya mean, the cars ain't runnin'?"

"Batteries are all dead down under the ground too."

"These things attacked us in the dark."

"Smoke? Smoke in the sky? How do you know it's not bombs? Lynchburg—there's an airport in Lynchburg; first thing they're gonna bomb is airports."

Wilma smelled it, the rank smell of terror and rage, above the coal and the mud and the sweat. For hours these people had clung to the goal of rescuing the men from the mine; getting back their husbands, their fathers, their sons. Their hearts had told them—though their minds would certainly have conceded differently if consulted—that everything would be all right if only they could do that.

Now, suddenly, everything was not all right again.

Not all the men were there. Garbled stories were traded, of horrible things that attacked out of the darkness. "Where's Andy?" Leah Hillocher kept asking, baffled. "Where's Andy?" Something was wrong, terribly and terrifyingly wrong, and they were trapped and lost as ever in a world of darkness and fear.

The noise in the tunnel mounted as voices shouted theories at each other. The men and women who spilled out into the muddy and cut-up ground in front of the tunnel surged back and forth, puzzled and angry, already gathering into cliques even before the last of the men whose rescue had united them emerged into the candlelight.

And as they emerged, silence fell.

When the lights struck Hank Culver, slumped and bent and hairless, with his huge bulging milk-white eyes and snaggle-sharp teeth, cringing from the light in the grip of Roop McDonough and Jeff Swann, realization struck the mob like an indrawn breath. Wilma could almost hear the flicker of each individual candle, the crying of a cricket on the hill above the tunnel mouth.

"My God, what happened to him?"

Hank's widowed sister-in-law screamed.

Someone said, "Fuck, he's one of them!"

Carl Souza brought up his rifle, and Wilma sprang at him, though nearly twenty feet separated them: sprang and reached him before the barrel was leveled, and with a quick swat of her hand knocked the gun aside, wrenched it from his grip. Someone else brought up a gun, and she reached him, too, spring-spring-snatch, shocking him by her speed.

Then she was standing at Hank's side. "One of *them*?" she said, furious disbelief in her voice. "One of *who*? One of the things he just saved them from in the mine?"

"What if it's a disease?" Norm Mullein had backed as far away as he could without getting outside the torchlight. "I mean, *look* at him! What if it's contagious?"

"Them things . . . ," stammered Carl Souza. "Them things that come out of the mine. Them grunty things. . . ."

And Hank cringing, turning his face from the terrible revelation of the light.

"Well, God for*bid*," Wilma said in an awful voice, "that anybody should risk themselves by touching their husbands or brothers or sons when they might have a disease. Isn't *that* the most terrible thing in the world." She flung the second rifle—Kyle Dixon's—into the mud.

She turned to Hank. "Are you all right? Do you feel all right?"

He nodded, not speaking, shielding his white unblinking eyes from the sea of candlelight, made as if to retreat into the mine again, but stopped, and behind her in the shaft Wilma heard the rustle of bodies, smelled the acrid pungence of the others, changed and mutated and savage. Waiting for him. Hungry, and robbed of their prey.

He turned back and looked at the people who were no longer his own. And they looked back, aghast and frightened beyond anything they'd ever known. Norm Mullein put his hands over his mouth and began to laugh, a cracked, shrill, awful sound, tears running down his face.

Wilma took Hank's arm and walked forward toward the gates of the pithead, toward the dark town beyond. The candles parted. She and Hank walked through an aisle of silent people, friends and neighbors; through them, and into the night.

FIFTEEN

NEW YORK

The trash cans along Fifth were all burning, not for warmth but for light. Cal was thankful; it was easier to spot the line of weary, rumpled people that stretched from Fifty-seventh down past Fifty-fifth and terminated at the familiar cart. Wrapped in a localized fog of steam, it looked dreamy, unreal. The cotton candy and chocolate bars and salted pretzels were all gone, but the propane tank was still firing, and the rich smell of cooking juices wafted out.

"Here we are, *matuskha*. Sorry, we're out of mustard." Doc handed a frank to a birdlike old woman, who nodded thanks and withdrew. He must have been feeding people for hours; where had he gotten the supplies?

"Making a killing, Doc," Cal said, stepping up to him.

The Russian's eyes brightened at the sight of him. "They're killing me," he grinned ruefully, continuing to assemble and dispense hot dogs as he spoke. "It's free, everything free. To each their need. That was written above the blackboard in every classroom in my school. Sounds good, neh?"

Cal's face darkened. "To their need . . ." *Tina*.

Doc's quick-moving hands slowed, paused. "What, my friend? What is it?"

Cal told him, at least the relevant part. The older man hesitated only the slightest bit, then selected someone standing nearby, a carrot-topped teen with an earnest, open face. Quickly, he showed the boy how to keep the tank going, cook the meat, dole it out. He turned back to Cal.

"Show her to me." By his tone Doc might have been at a clinic somewhere with a hundred thousand dollars worth of hospital backing him up: confident and gentle. *All will be well.* The two of them hurried from the cart, past the burning cylinders of trash, their smoke spiraling into the empty black sky.

The faded, cracked tile before the entrance read N.B.C. "National Biscuit Company," Doc explained, his voice so casual he might have been giving them a tour. "Or so they tell me."

Cal knew it was an old doctor's trick to keep him and Colleen calm, and he appreciated the effort. Since they had reached the Guard encampment, Cal had let Doc take the lead, had been relieved, in fact, not to have to make decisions for a time. Tina, wandering in her fever dreams, had been only dimly aware of Doc's probing. "Best you come with me," he'd said afterward. "Now, at once." Neither Cal nor Colleen had asked questions. They had merely trusted.

This deserted block of square brick buildings would normally have been choked with trucks and workmen at this time, with dawn drawing near. Doc led them around the side of the building to a padlocked metal door, withdrew a key from about his neck. Colleen held aloft the Coleman lantern she had scored ("Don't ask").

"In here." Doc swung the door wide. Cal lifted Tina from the shopping cart and carried her in. Doc followed, Colleen bringing up the rear, throwing a last, keen glance at the walkway behind them.

Tina lolled in Cal's arms, a bundle of sticks, and he felt hollow, lifeless. Images collided in on him: Tina beaming in a pirouette, vibrant in a grand jete, rushing to pointe class early to steal a glance at the New York City Ballet rehearsing, brimming with life and surety and purpose.

She was his world, his whole world.

The windowless cubicle had been a storeroom once. Now it housed a mattress, a microwave, a radio. "You *live* here?" Colleen asked incredulously.

"As little as possible." Doc slid the bolt. "Put her there, please," he instructed Cal, nodding toward the bed.

Cal placed Tina gently on the mattress. She mumbled a soft protest, then was still. Doc produced a medical bag from under the microwave, bent over her. Colleen stood behind with the lantern.

"Is she allergic to any medication?" Doc asked Cal, not taking his eyes off the girl, examining her with gentle, deft hands.

"Not that I know of."

Doc nodded. He withdrew a syringe from his bag, filled it from a small bottle and administered an injection.

"Penicillin. Don't tell anyone I have it." He handed Colleen the used syringe. "Rinse the needle in alcohol. We may need it again." She hesitated, revulsion plain on her face. "There's some in the bathroom," he prompted firmly, brooking no argument. She withdrew, taking the lantern with her, casting them into shadow.

"In Ukraine," Doc told Cal, "we don't count on supplies." At the bathroom doorway Colleen set the lantern down, so as not to leave them entirely in the dark, then went into the other room. Doc closed his bag, gazed into the face of the unconscious child.

"Do you know what it is?" asked Cal.

"It's like a lot of things. But there are some symptoms I don't know. The skin. Translucent . . . strange." He drew Cal from the bed, lifted a beaker off the floor. Brown liquid sloshed in it. "You want some Chock Full o'Nuts?"

Cal shook his head, which made it throb. Now that he was letting down, all the bruised and abused parts of him were screaming their outrage.

"Come, Calvin," Doc coaxed. "In former Soviet, when there is only waiting, men drink. I never acquired taste for vodka, so . . ." Cal shrugged, relenting. "Good." Doc lit a can of Sterno, set the beaker on a rack atop it.

He looked back toward the bed. "At the cart, I heard people talking. There seem to be lots like this."

The horrific corridors at Roosevelt reared up, all the listless, frail ones and the others with their strange agitation and gray skin. "Radiation, you think?"

Doc looked thoughtful. "Not like any I've seen."

Cal's eyes met his. There was something unsettling about the weighted manner in which the man had said the words.

"I was in Kiev," said Doc, after so long a silence Cal thought he wasn't going to continue, "when Chernobyl came. They summoned me to treat the"—he struggled for the word—"bystanders."

Doc turned away, stared into the darkness. His voice was a whisper, barren. "They died by thousands, melting like ice in fire. We placed them in soldered zinc coffins, buried them in concrete." His eyes returned to Tina. "You know, I thought, No more doctoring. *Good.* No more playing Santa Claus with my big empty bag."

"I'm sorry." *Sorry.* The word sounded to Cal like he was offering a Band-Aid to a gut-shot man.

Doc brushed away the apology. "How could you know? Real doctors don't bury themselves with their patients."

Cal reached out, grasped the Russian's shoulder. Doc flinched—*when was the last time anyone touched him?*—then relaxed, his melancholy gray eyes full of gratitude.

They stood a moment in the silence, then a soft sound of sliding metal drew Cal's attention. He turned just in time to see the front door ease shut.

Cal caught up with Colleen as she reached the street. "Late for a train?" he asked gently.

Colleen looked away. She had left the lantern behind, but the sky was growing lighter, and he could see the tentativeness in her eyes, the remnants of old wounds.

"I've always known when to exit stage left," she said. "You got yourself pretty well set. Russkie there seems a good guy. Me, I'd just be in the way."

He stepped closer, caught the strawberry shampoo scent lingering in her hair, the tang of sweat and grease. Through the long night he knew he'd have fallen to despair if she hadn't kept him going, pushed him to action. *In the way?* Jesus Christ. Struggling to say what he really meant, all he could come up with was, "I think you'd get an argument there."

He gazed at her clear, watchful eyes, set in that strong face with its high cheekbones and broad forehead, and was aware of the lean, efficient body under her T-shirt and overalls, the tool belt low on her hips. Standing near her, emotion flared in him, powerful and primal, so sudden it surprised him.

She sensed it; he saw the slight shift in her stance, heard the quickening of breath. This was a turning point, he thought, a moment where what he said would either send her away or draw her near, and he very much wanted her near. They had spoken little since he arrived with Doc, and that had all been to the task at hand. He had said nothing of his run-in with Misfits or of the gun, of his dawning suspicion as to what was happening.

And as he reflected on it, he knew that all he had to bind her to him was the truth.

"There's some things I need to tell you," he began.

"Yes?" She tilted her head, and there was challenge in it, and shyness.

He opened his mouth to speak, but there was a clattering from another block that sounded like a tin can, bouncing off a car door. He tensed and saw his own wariness mirrored in her eyes.

"We're exposed here," he said and drew her into shadows.

WEST VIRGINIA

"I don't understand what happened." Hank sank onto the bed Wilma had prepared for him in her downstairs guest room. It was the first time, she realized, that he'd been in any room of the house but the kitchen and, occasionally, the living room. Since her return from college she'd kept him at a distance, sensing his resentment, not able to explain her longings and her fears.

Neither had attempted to kindle a light, though Wilma had candles. "What happened to me, what happened to Sonny, and Andy, and the other guys that left . . . what happened to you."

He touched her hand. The cats, who had padded soundlessly into the front room when Wilma had come through the door, lay across the foot of the bed and over the threshold, blinking their golden eyes. They'd always been fond of Hank, who had in times past muttered ill of them as their numbers multiplied and he himself had played less and less a part in Wilma's life.

Now he stroked Imp's head and chuckled a little as he said, "I never seen anybody move so fast in my life."

"I was scared for you," said Wilma. "And Carl Souza never had a lick of sense with that gun of his."

"No," said Hank. "That wasn't just . . . 'scared.' What happened? To you, I mean?" He regarded her with round opal eyes. "Are you okay?"

Wilma nodded. "I think so," she said, interested that Hank alone could see the change in her. Perhaps it was because Hank had changed so terribly himself. "I'm not . . . I don't hurt anywhere. And I don't know what happened. Something." She ran her hand along Dinah's back as the elderly calico climbed into her lap.

"You always were different," Hank said softly. "I mean, it never showed. I'm glad it's had a chance to finally come out, whatever it is."

Around them, the town was falling silent at last, exhausted men and women returning to their homes, locking the doors, blowing out candles and lamps. Now and then Wilma would hear disjointed exclamations as people came home to find that the grunters had raided their kitchens, their back-porch freezers and cupboards—exclamations of anger and alarm, for who knew when trucks would be coming into the grocery stores again? But mostly there was silence, in which the singing of the crickets was undisturbed by even the whisper of cars on the road or the far-off roar of airplanes in the sky.

"Thank you." Hank touched her hand again and took his as quickly away. "I roughed up Sonny and Andy and the others in the mine pretty bad. They may get over it, and they may not, but right now I think that's not a good place for me to be."

"Do you want to go back?" she asked.

He stared into the darkness, stroking the cat, his face in repose once again, curiously still Hank's face. "I don't know," he said at last. "In a lot of ways . . . it's quiet. There's too much noise up here. Too many people. I always was a hermit, you know." And she laughed, because that was one of the things he'd grown angry at her about: she had too many friends, too much family. Too many things that took her from him. She was always out, always doing. "Too much going on. Under the ground it's . . . it's simple. But just because I don't like everybody don't mean I want to spend the rest of my life with Sonny Grimes. There's people up here I love."

"I know," said Wilma.

Their eyes met.

"What does it mean?"

She shook her head. "I don't know what any of it means," she said. "But whatever happens . . ."

Her hand closed around his, and for a moment they sat in the darkness, looking at one another with changed and seeing eyes. She saw Hank's nostrils flare and knew that he, like she, sniffed the coming of dawn.

The first new day, she thought, of the rest of . . . what?

"Whatever happens," she finished, "things are not going to be the same."

SIXTEEN

NEW YORK

Patrick Francis listened to the night.

It was silent outside now, which was a relief, considering the crescendo of shattering and screams earlier. He hadn't even ventured to look through the window, just hunkered in the darkness, cradling Oreo as the little black-and-white terrier trembled and whined, stroking him and assuring him that it would all be okay.

Not that Patrick felt any such assurance himself.

He'd been up when the earthquake, or whatever it was, had struck, had been up all night, in fact, working on the De Vries documentary, running the tapes. This latest stuff was terrific. Patrick had begun the questions innocently enough, something on *Crime Boss*, then had led the elderly director into the more sensitive area of his marriage to Velinda Lane, the greatest of his leading ladies, and the most tragic. And incredibly, Anton had opened up, revealed details he'd never told *anyone* before.

It was all so incredibly rewarding, this journey he'd embarked on a year and a half ago, set in motion by a chance meeting at a dinner party. The one-eyed old man in his wheelchair had been so taciturn at first, so glitteringly acid.

But as they had come to know each other, as trust had been painstakingly built, Anton had opened to him like a puzzle box, revealing mystery upon mystery. The great noir director, unspooling his visions of a world in chaos, a universe of random, cruel coincidence. Chance meetings that led to anguish and death.

He wondered what Anton would have to say about today's events. Thank God he was at that festival honoring him in Lausanne. Patrick hoped and trusted that it was out of the danger zone, but, thanks to the phones being out, he had not been able to confirm it.

But Anton was a survivor, as the Nazis had discovered before he'd ventured to Hollywood and nine wives had learned since. He could hear that familiar, Hungarian-accented croak now, chiding him, "Worry about your own ass."

Okay, he'd do that and tell himself the current situation was just a speed bump on the road, nothing to get too bent out of shape about. Thankfully, he'd had the computer off when it had hit, lost none of his notes or transcripts.

Oreo was staring up at him now, an acute, querying look in his eye. It had been hours since they'd ventured outside, and the little dog was long past due. Patrick cocked an ear toward the door. All quiet on the western front.

Quickly, he leashed Oreo up, threw open the door and stepped out into the warm night air. Instantly, the terrier pulled to the nearest minute square of grass and let go. Blissful relief. Dogs were so simple, they brought things down to the basics—love and need, hunger and fear. Pure primal emotions, the same as in Anton's films. Black and white simplicity.

Oreo continued, intent, inquisitive, drawn by the panoply of scents. Patrick grew nervous as they drew near a familiar gingerbread grotesquerie, its windows black fathomless eyes. Sam Lungo was the last thing they needed tonight, erupting like some demented figure from a cuckoo clock, ranting and cursing.

Patrick drew Oreo to the far side of the street, breathed a sigh as they cleared the property. The little dog paused at a railing, seemingly magnetized, again lifted his leg.

He stopped abruptly. Hackles rising, he began barking wildly.

"Sign says curb your dog," a voice behind Patrick purred, husky as a semi engine. "But I guess it's too dark to read."

Startled, Patrick turned and found himself craning his neck up at a dark, angular face. He gasped and stepped back. At first, he thought it might be a mask; no face could truly *look* like that.

But as he peered closer—Oreo pulling madly on the leash, barking crazily—Patrick saw it was real, indisputably so, even in the moonlight.

And God, it looked *evil*. The bones of the man's face were spiking out from under the skin, and the skin itself erupted from eyes and nose and mouth in reptilian patterns like bizarre, relief-map tattoos. His shiny black hair flared in a wild spray off his head, scales interspersing it like the devil's own cornrow.

Patrick began edging back toward his apartment, dragging Oreo. The dog kept up an insistent growling, barking and baring of teeth at the other, who broke into an easy stride behind them.

"This your regular route?" he asked in an offhand tone.

"Yeah," Patrick fought to keep his voice even, not stopping. Oreo was ballistic, a wolverine. Primal emotions, pure simplicity.

"Good," the other said ominously. "I just wanted to be sure."

A world of chaos. A universe of random, cruel coincidence.

Patrick stopped and turned, facing the nightmare. "Listen," he said over the ear-ringing, staccato yelps. "I live right over there. I just want to go home."

"Who doesn't?" the other's voice was affable. He gestured toward the flat. "Be my guest."

Hauling Oreo, Patrick hurried toward the brownstone, his

eyes fixed on the other, who stood motionless. Finally, he reached the building, turned to the door.

There was a rush of sound behind him, Oreo screeched in frenzy and fear, and Patrick felt a wet agony in his back, a slashing that severed skin and meat. He heard the crack of bone and gave a truncated cry, fell crashing onto the pavement.

It's like a movie, he thought, and felt the absurdity of it, and the truth. Oreo's cries sounded distant now, muffled, as sensation faded, the last frame threaded through, the projector light damped. And then his mind and heart were stilled.

Stern rose from his work, exultant. To begin a thing and end it, to conceive and execute. It was delightfully straightforward, elegantly simple. And best of all, it was just the beginning.

The little dog was howling mournfully, backed against the doorframe. Stern stepped over the broken, wet form on the concrete and approached it. Its eyes grew huge, and it pressed itself back into the wood, dropped its voice to a whimper. Stern extended one long, clawed hand, dripping glistening red.

"Nice boy," he said and patted the dog's head.

Colleen Brooks gripped the rough iron railing on the fire-escape landing across from Doc's warehouse, glaring out at the night. Below, the shadowed street angled off toward the faint sheen of the Hudson, and everything was so still it was as if she were in a model of the city, not real at all.

"Why'd you tell me this? Why the hell are you telling me this?"

Cal Griffin stood behind her, saying nothing. But then he had said enough.

The Magnet Man. Bullets falling like little turds . . .

She wheeled suddenly, reaching toward his head. He caught her wrist, stopping her.

"I want to see how hard that guy hit you," she said.

He released her, scowling. "Not *that* hard."

"Yeah, well, maybe we oughtta have Doc Moscow be the judge. . . . Jeez, Cal, don't you know how this *sounds*?"

He nodded somberly, and somehow his very seriousness made her all the more angry.

"*Shit*." She turned from him again, considered the night. Dawn was coming on soon, the sky was inching lighter. She caught a silhouette of movement, discerned a hawk hanging in the air, its wings spread like great fingers. Did it see a changed world, or the same one, as far as its needs were concerned?

All that had happened today tumbled through Colleen's mind, the stalled elevators and blackened stairwells; the long trek past the miles of dead cars and trucks; hearing that cop's bellows in the night and wading swinging into that mob; that weird, dark clump of odd-shaped kids-who-might-not-have-been-kids moving fast down shrouded streets. . . .

And the pale, delicate girl, whom she hadn't really even met yet, on the mattress across the street, burning up with fever.

Colleen felt suddenly as she did in those dreams that assaulted her on so many nights, where she'd be working in a shaft atop a secured car and the joists abruptly gave way and she was falling, plunging into a bottomless shaft, back in that awful helpless child place where there was *nothing* she could do but hold on tight and fall endlessly into the blackness.

Was she angry because she didn't believe him, or because she did?

She knew the answer.

So what to do now? Sit in the dark with the windows drawn, like Rory, shutting out the world? The world was always right there with you; you couldn't outrun it, not really. By choosing or not choosing, you made your world, and your life. There was no standing still—or sitting still, for that matter, despite what Rory might say, there in his Barcalounger as the hours and days and years melted away.

And the image returned to her of the lobby this morning, before the storm came down, and the young man in the suit speaking up for her when no one would. And later, when he asked if she needed anything. And later still, when he asked without asking for *her* help.

Maybe she was falling; maybe they all were. But they could choose to fall together, perhaps somehow even stop the fall, or at least slow it.

"I DON'T NEED MORE CRAZINESS IN MY LIFE!!!" She shouted at the night, and it rang off the buildings.

But then, they hadn't asked her, had they?

She turned back to Cal and was gratified to see his mouth hanging open. "Okay, I believe it, every last fucking bit of it." She dragged her fingers through her short hair. "I mean, it's not as if a lawyer would *lie*. . . ."

He smiled then, and she liked what it did to his face.

The sound of a metal door creaking open echoed down the corridor of street, drew their attention. Doc stood in his doorway far below, bidding them return.

They descended the iron stairs, as the second day began.

Sam just didn't know what to do with himself.

Pacing in the airless, cluttered living room, so alive with shadows and ghosts, frozen in time, he awaited Ely's return.

A genie. His genie. To do whatever Sam commanded. And what had he wished for, so ardently desired, after the endless humiliations, the long, yearning years of frustration?

He had fantasized so many times in his loneliness, scrawled tiny, cramped miles of notes. All the shifting population of his life, the denizens of his street who swarmed like rats. How delicious, how dreamily satisfying to kill them all, one by one, ever so slowly, to maim and mangle them and, at last, at last, to make them pay. Judgment day.

But now here it was. And when he had shown Ely the infinity of notepads, indicated the offenses and slights, babbling his cherished daydreams, he found his exhilaration cooling to . . .

Fear.

This was no fantasy now; no, no, this was *real*. And to really do what he had longed for, why, why . . .

It would be monstrous.

He had tried to backpedal then. He just wanted Ely to scare them, really, to make them feel small and helpless and ridiculous, as they had made him feel so many, many times.

But Ely, towering over him like some gaunt god of scarecrows and desolation, had merely snatched the pad from him and chuckled. Then he had risen like an avenging angel and departed.

Sam contemplated running after him, overtaking him in the night-splashed street. But then the image of the one who had chased down Ely before, whom Ely had seized and sent hurtling to break against a wall, came to him with sickening vividness and shattered his resolve.

He fidgeted in his room in an agony of waiting, unable to be still, sweat gleaming on his brow and lip, saturating his armpits; his own smell disgusted him.

Then, after ten, fifteen minutes at most, he heard the frenzied barking, the awful shriek of what he knew must be a man, and other appalling sounds—like someone cracking wishbones, but much louder. Terrified, furious, he tried to block it out, tried to convince himself that whoever it was, they *deserved* it. But the conceit wouldn't hold. A dreadful nausea stole over him, and the room tilted, strobing pinpoints of light flashing before him in the darkness. He sat down on the velvet settee, breathing hard. Then he gained control of himself.

He might have gone to the window, gained final certainty, but there was no need. He knew.

Now a heavy trudging sounded, and Sam realized Ely was returning. Sam's heart raced, his breath came fast and shallow, and suddenly he remembered the *rest* of *Thief of Baghdad*: how the genie, once released, had proven malevolent, how it had been impossible to get him back into the bottle, how what he had wanted to do more than anything was to *kill*.

For the first time in forever, Sam desperately wanted Mother there, wished he could summon her hard, merciless spirit back from the grave, to stand between him and this malignant force he had so recklessly invited into his home.

Outside, the porch slats groaned as Stern stepped onto them. Sam was seized with a wild urge to rush to the door, throw the bolt, lock it tight. But that would only make Ely angry, and it wouldn't stop him.

The footfalls ceased. Silence, only the crickets in the night. Sam held his breath.

The doorbell rang.

Under it, another sound erupted in the room, and Sam was laughing, giggling hysterically.

Ely was one for details, oh, indeed he was, such a precise touch, so taunting, so scornful . . . and so clearly a summons.

The cruel meaning of it fell in on Sam like the roof collapsing, like the weight of rafters. Here was no liberator, no deliverance, merely another tormentor, the crowning one, without peer. Oh, it was funny, to die for . . .

Tears sprang to Sam's eyes, stinging, and he found his laughter turning to shrieks, which he stifled, panic blossoming like a wound in him. His feet leaden, he walked to the door, threw it open.

Stern stood on the threshold, his incredible bulk filling the doorway. He stepped through, ducking his head under the frame. Sam moved aside, making room, and then eased the door shut.

He saw that Ely was holding something out to him. A leash, a short leash.

"That pooch can run with the wolves now," Stern said.

Taking the leash, Sam found it sticky with congealing liquid. Then he spied Stern's carmine-soaked hands.

"I'll try not to touch anything," Stern mocked.

Crazily, needing to say *anything* to stop from screaming,

Sam found himself murmuring, "Bloodstains are a terror to get out."

"You should read Heloise," Stern replied and swept through the living room toward the bathroom.

Woodenly, imprisoned, Sam fetched a pitcher of water, found Stern before the mirror, stripped to the waist, appraising himself in the glow of the oil lamp. Sam could see that he hadn't been imagining things; Ely *was* even larger than he had been before running his dread errand, bonier and more muscular, his face continuing to extend, his skin to roughen. Skeletal projections erupted at surprising points all over his torso, and Sam noted odd protrusions beginning to press out below Ely's shoulder blades. *I'm becoming*, Stern had said. He most certainly was.

Sam raised the pitcher over the basin and heard his voice, leeched of emotion. "Hands. Ely, your hands."

"Hm? Oh." Stern extended his hands over the basin as Sam poured. Water flooded over them, dripped off the thick nails that, Sam saw, were growing more like talons, true claws. The blood washed away, swirled down the drain.

"Quite the night's work," Stern mused. "How I put myself out for you." There was merriment in his eye, ironic and mean. *This is your doing, Sam*, it said. *Not mine*. The genie doesn't get the blame.

Ely was lording it over him, in his own house, because he could, for no other reason than that. Power, it was all about power, who's top dog, who rules the roost. Just like everyone else, just like Mother when she had been here, and even after.

A raw heat of outrage ignited in Sam's chest, shot into his cheeks and eye sockets. For one mad moment, he almost took the pitcher and smashed it into Stern's grinning gargoyle skull. But the fear, the years of obsequiousness and invisibility, stayed his hand, and the moment passed. He bowed his head, shame and regret choking him.

"There now," Stern said, as the last of the defiled water fled down the drain. "All gone."

Numbly, Sam set the pitcher beside the basin, held out paper towels. Stern patted his hands dry.

Stern's eyes returned to the mirror. He ran a hand along his craggy, saurian chin. "Used to have the worst five o'clock shadow. Looks like I won't have to shave for a while."

Sam was only half-listening now, rooting about in the hall closet for the item Mother had put there so many years ago. *Why keep that?* he had complained to her. *Who will ever use it?* But she had saved it as she had saved everything, and, in this at least, she had been right.

"Here, Ely," Sam said in a hushed tone, returning to him. "It was my father's. He was six-five." He unfurled the heavy material in his delicate hands.

Stern felt the faded terry cloth between his fingers, drew it from Sam. The robe was as soft and shapeless as the man who had once inhabited it. Stern shrugged into it, glowered down at Sam. "What was your mother? A circus dwarf?"

Sam felt the blood in his cheeks, averted his eyes. "We all have our shortcomings."

Stern turned back to the mirror. "Gotta develop a thick skin," he said.

Mother had called it the guest room, though they'd never had any guests. Sam had always thought of it as the discard room. But now he had a guest, one that he could not discard.

Stern lay in the narrow oak bed, pulling the moth-eaten covers up, trying to get comfortable—impossibile given his size and shape. Sam hovered by the bedside oil lamp. "There anything else you need, Ely?"

Stern shook his head, then belched, a low rumble. He winced painfully.

"Still the heartburn?" Sam's tone was solicitous, if flat. He found his thinking was musty, as though wrapped in cotton wool like the keepsakes Mother had so carefully placed in boxes and stored away in the recesses of the attic. He felt curiously withdrawn, as if moving through a dream. *I'm trying to escape*, he thought, *I'm trying to escape in my mind.* And in some hopeless core of him, that seemed the only way.

"I don't get ulcers; I give them," Stern mumbled. His searchlight eyes were at half-mast, and, as he stretched, groaning, Sam could sense the bone-ache weariness of the—*man*? Well, no, that wasn't quite the word, not precisely, not anymore. Nor was *guest*, either, but that was how it was.

"You've had a busy night, Ely," Sam said, patting him on the shoulder and feeling that it was someone else saying and doing these things. He blew out the lamp, plunging the room into darkness, the drapes drawn tight against the coming dawn. "Tomorrow's another day." He withdrew, closing the door behind him.

Stern turned toward the wall, drew his legs up until he was curled in a ball. He was warm here, hidden. The pounding in his head had eased back some, and he felt the tempest of the day's events fading in his mind.

He woke; he didn't know how long later. Prickling danced over his skin, then erupted in a fierce blue energy. He didn't need to open his eyes, he could *see* it through his closed eyelids. It surged over him, pulsed through his veins, filled his mouth and lungs. He fought to scream but was paralyzed, immobile as it whipped about and within him. And in that instant, that ferocity of *being*, he realized that he had known this feeling before, earlier, in the office. *At the beginning.* And he knew too that it had not gone and returned but had merely resurfaced, was always now with him. He was becoming, and this vast, elemental current was the medium of that becoming. He relaxed then, and the energy drew back into him, continued its patient work. He exhaled a long, slow breath and opened himself, accepting. He slept.

WASHINGTON, D.C.

It had been a damn long night.

Crossing the dew-soaked lawns to the buildings of the Old Executive Office—where every available bicycle had been stored—Shango felt the same tension that he'd known as a child in hurricane weather. He remembered clearly how it had felt to cross between the run-down brick buildings of the Washington Street projects when the first jagged gusts of rain would come in, cold and strange feeling in the summer heat. Rain and then still. Rain and then still, but in the stillness you could feel the storm to come. Seeing through every window all the TVs tuned to the weather, those colored maps and the crawling ribbon of warning across the bottom of the screen that said, IT'S ON ITS WAY AND IT'S GONNA BE BAD.

Why did he feel, at the end of this night of riot and fire and fear, that he'd only felt the first cold splatter of preliminary rain?

"At least we don't have to worry about lugging guns," said Czernas, very trim and sleek in black biking shorts and a microfiber shirt. His smooth, sculpted shoulders shifted under the straps of his backpack. "Or about being shot at."

Word had come in fairly early in the night, about the guns. Shango had gone out behind the White House after he'd gone off-shift at midnight, and tested both of his personal handguns, the Browning and the P7, with the same results: *nada*. He remembered McKay's reaction, when a Guard captain had told him about this.

Again, nada. He hadn't been surprised.

"Might do for you to carry one all the same." Shango halted in the dark area between the torchlight along the White House walls and the lighted perimeter, and fished his P7 from the holster at the small of his back. "Things changed once. They might again."

Czernas obediently stashed the weapon in his backpack, where he couldn't get to it in under a minute, but Shango said nothing. He guessed the aide was in his mid-thirties, a couple of years older than himself, but he found himself unconsciously thinking of him as younger. This might have had something to do with the other man's boyish blondness, but Shango didn't think so.

He was a rookie. He might know politics, and he might know campaigning, and he might know who was important and how to get things done, but he wasn't hard. There was no core of iron inside.

"You have family here in town?" asked Czernas as they climbed the steps. "Someone to leave a message for?"

Shango shook his head. "You let President McKay check over any message you left, to make sure it doesn't say too much?"

The aide looked surprised, then flustered. "Oh," he said. "Oh, I guess—well, I left it with him."

And if he was smart, he burned it, thought Shango, recalling what the President had said about not knowing who was behind the Source funding. In the face of a fuckup this monstrous—if that was what it was—the scramble for deniability would be lethal and thorough.

As Czernas showed the guard McKay's authorization, Shango reflected that he was damn glad he'd kept his own life field-stripped. Even in ordinary circumstances he traveled with little more than he carried in his backpack this morning, and he lived the same way.

No photographs: not of parents, siblings or the house he grew up in. Now, *there's* a Kodak moment that you never see on commercials. An advantage, when you had a job to do.

Even at this hour of the morning people were coming and going in the long main corridor where they stored the bikes. There was a guard checking papers there, too, by the light of a half-dozen candles. National guardsmen were bringing in more—commandeered from God knew where—even as messengers were taking them out. Shango picked thin-tired racing models over the heavier off-road bikes, checked to make sure the tires had been puncture-proofed, and got spare tubes from

the guardsman in charge, while a makeshift moving crew—
National guardsmen, regular Army, and whoever else had been
rounded up from stranded office-staff along the Mall—moved
computers, phones, and chairs out of the offices around them
to make room for incoming supplies of water and food.

"I got us a survival-blanket apiece, and a first-aid kit."
Czernas came over, a bare-kneed superhero. "We may have
to go beyond the airport to find her. Anything else we'll
need?"

"Just water and food." Shango's pack was already
weighed down with those and he guessed his companion's
was, too. He kept his voice even but the sense of impending
chaos pressed more closely than ever.

IT'S ON ITS WAY AND IT'S GONNA BE BAD.

"What about weapons?"

Czernas had a big hunting-knife sheathed on the outside
of his pack—the National Guard was stockpiling the contents of every sporting-goods store they could reach. Bows
and arrows, fiberglass crossbows, knives, hatchets were all
being brought in, as well as horses from the wealthy countryside across the river: wagons, pleasure-buggies, harness,
fodder. Shango had a couple of knives in his pack already, as
well as one sheathed on the outside where he could get to it
fast, but he knew a desperate man can go on fighting for a
long time with a knife wound. And he'd never quite trusted
guns. *Only an idiot carries a gun,* he remembered his father
saying to one of his punkier uncles. *All a gun'll do is make
you think you can handle something you can't.* Uncle Mar-
quis had ended up shooting a cop in a panic and was probably still at Angola—Shango could guess what had happened
there, and in other prisons, when the lights went out.

But he smiled at the recollection of his father.

John Henry Shango. He'd boxed weekends around all the
small clubs in Orleans and Jefferson parishes and could double up a leather kicking-bag with one blow of his fist. When
he'd first heard his father sing "John Henry," Larry had seen
his father as that doomed, wonderful, steel-drivin' man.

So he said, "Wait here," and hunted around for the utility room, where the guardsmen had put all the tools they thought they were going to need: axes and bolt-cutters and lengths of cable and chain. There was a sledge there with an eight-pound head, with a long enough handle to give Shango reach on a man with only a knife in his hand, heavy enough that a small man or an unskilled one couldn't use it against him: it swung with his arm like a motherfucker.

He slipped it down through the hand-loop at the top of his backpack, so the head rested high between his shoulders.

He'd spent a day and a night watching people deal with the fact that everything had suddenly stopped working. Christiansen and the Army boys in a panic because no missiles would fire and maybe someone would be dropping them—which hadn't happened so far. People in the Mall, on the streets, screaming for Metro transport and telephones. The corporate suits frantic because suddenly there was no power to run anything and no way of getting what they had to sell to people who wanted to buy it. Every guardsman and soldier holding his useless rifle thinking, What do I do if someone comes at me?

This was one item, thought Shango, that wasn't going to quit working.

Czernas was waiting in the hall with the bikes.

"Ready to go," Shango said.

Outside, horses neighed in the hot night. The White House looked dark in its ring of torches. Shango couldn't see light in any of the windows, but he was willing to bet McKay wasn't sleeping.

For eighteen months he'd lived his life as an extension of the President's, keeping tabs on appointments, travel, people in his life; on likely threats or difficult situations. Sometimes he felt weirdly akin to those fixated "quarterlies" he and the other agents checked up on every few months, people who'd made threats against the President, some of whom could have told *him* where McKay was going to be and do. He remembered one woman in St. Elizabeth's, back before

Shango was on White House detail, rambling gently on about Hillary Clinton's wardrobe and how certain of her dresses matched Bill's ties.

As he and Czernas carried the bikes down the front steps, he felt a deep uneasiness. There were other agents on the job, good agents, he knew. Men he'd worked with for years and had trusted with his own life: Cox and Breckenridge and the others.

But he sensed he was leaving McKay in danger. More danger than even McKay realized.

He glanced sidelong at the young man gravely pulling on Pearl Izumi bike-gloves, adjusting straps on his airflow-grooved helmet. An idealist, as McKay was an idealist, but without McKay's experience. A pain in the ass and possibly a danger on the road. But he was the friend McKay trusted to find Bilmer, to get her or her information back safely.

And it was Shango's job to back him up. To make sure that the job got done, no matter what the cost.

He had been chosen because he was the best at what he did.

And because he was best, he felt disoriented to be riding away from the President into the darkness of pre-dawn and the smoke of burning that marked the rising of the new day.

SEVENTEEN

WEST VIRGINIA

Thunder and darkness. Lightning that hurt the eyes.

And even so, it was nothing to the darkness Fred saw, as through a window. Nothing to the light that seared forth out of that dark, like a searchlight, into his mind.

WISHART

The cold-water drag of the current redoubled, like the current of Cherry Creek, the wildness that would separate them. Desperate, desperate and scared, Fred clung tighter to his brother's arm, to the dock. The dock? But it was as if he saw them all standing on the dock, Sanrio and Wu and Pollack, only it wasn't three people or five people or ten people or all those people who'd been in the project when Hell had broken loose there in a roiling, glowing flood, streaming out of the Maze in a shattered firefall of exploding glass.

It was One.

WISHART

And the tolling of the voice was like the sounding of a huge bell. Only it was his own voice. His own face on the thing on the dock.

I can't leave Bob. He'll die.

But even as he said it, he drew the power from it, from

that One; the power to keep Bob alive. Every light on those useless machines was black and dead, hunks of expensive metal closing in the downstairs bedroom, looming around the bed; and every light, every flash of electrochemical brightness in Bob's imprisoning flesh was dark also. The only light was what Fred poured into it, out of his self, his strength and the borrowed brilliance of the One.

COME TO US

I can't leave Bob.

They didn't hear. They never did.

COME

Twisting, dragging, clutching . . . And he fought them. *I can't. He'll die. I can't.*

Hell. Agony. Tearing him apart. Drawing him down into something that was worse than dying, worse than living—the loss of self into that all-devouring malice and power. The loss of who he was. Eaten alive.

Then slowly the vision faded, and Fred was in the downstairs bedroom still, clinging to Bob, who sobbed like a child in his arms.

Don't leave me.

I won't.

Stillness, and the peace of momentarily being out of pain. But because he was part of the One, because his thoughts were entangled in the shining awfulness that was growing in South Dakota, Fred knew it wasn't over. It was gathering strength, calling to itself everything that would serve it, and he knew it too well to believe that it would give up on him. It had Sanrio's cold single-mindedness; it had Wu's dogged patience, which had taken her through fifteen years in a re-education camp; it had Pollack's skill in finding alternate solutions to problems.

It wanted to be whole. And to be whole, it would eat him. Make him be it, whether he wanted to or not.

I have to fight. I won't leave Bob; I won't become part of that thing, that One, that Source. . . .

In his heart he could almost hear Sanrio's voice—or

was it his own?—whisper, *But you are part of us, Fred. You ARE us.*

Bob would be taken away, never to be seen again. And *he* would be taken. The terror was suffocating.

I have to fight. Somewhere, somehow, I have to get the strength to fight.

NEW YORK

Tina dreamed, and the dream was a swarm.

She couldn't see them, but she could feel them, all blue— somehow she knew they were blue—scurrying like bugs' legs, tiny bugs all over her, and inside her too, frenetic, insistent. They whispered reassurance, a cicada hum, soothing words she could almost but not quite discern, lulling her, wafting.

Even so, she tried to fight, but she was so weary, so leaden. *Time to wake up,* she urged herself. *Time to wake up now.*

But she lacked the will, felt sapped by the cocooning presence. *Rest*, it sang to her, unspeaking, *rest and grow strong.*

As Cal and Colleen approached through the dawn shadows of the street, Doc stepped from the doorway and drew them aside. "How is she?" Cal asked.

"Sleeping. Her fever's down a bit. Not out of the woods yet, but . . ." He trailed off. Cal sensed his reticence to draw conclusions, to offer false hope. Still, it was hopeful. Doc stretched the stiffness out of his back and yawned hugely.

"You should get some rest," Cal offered. "We can spell you a bit."

"Thank you, Calvin, but not just yet." Cal could make out the stubble on Doc's chin, the dark patches under his eyes. Morning at last, and relief swelled in him. No telling what the day might bring, but it had been an interminable night.

"What the hell's that?" Colleen said.

Cal turned to her. She was staring up at the sky, toward the west, and he saw now that strange, dark clouds were roiling in from over the Hudson, blanketing the sky, moving with alarming speed. They weren't like any stormclouds he had ever seen. Blue lightning played over them, slashing, ferocious as crazy bullwhips. Then the discharges began to hammer down on the city.

"Inside! Get inside!" Doc thrust them toward the door. A yellow-gray pall swept over them; the clouds were directly overhead. Now they heard the thunder, a wind-whipped howl that battered their skin, shuddered the pavement under their feet. And piercing the roar that filled the world, another sound, high and terrible.

Tina was screaming.

The thunder smashed into Tina like a blow. She bolted up in bed, eyes snapping open. But what she saw was *not* the room about her, no, no, it was, *it was—*

Blurred streaks like blood smeared on a mirror. Men, women, booted, hooded, gloved in marshmallow white, running, shouting. Machines spinning, pinwheeling sparks, a thrumming rising to a whine and then a wail. *This is not right; this is not how it's supposed to be.* A rectangular door lined with lights. *A gateway.* And something emerging, slashing into existence, all colors and none, a whirlpool blaze of pure, savage power. The men and the women tumbling over each other, pitching headlong to get away, but the whirlpool surges up, seizes them and spins them back into itself. Faces shrieking as they melt together, a chaos of eyes and mouths, not dead but alive, not many but one, and screaming, *screaming.* And Tina was screaming, too, because this was not a dream, this was real, *oh, God, it was real—*

Hands gripped her, arms wrapped around her; someone was shaking her as she screamed and screamed.

Cal held Tina as the shrieks tore from her throat, her eyes shut tight.

"Sh, sh, it's okay," he soothed, but she didn't know him, couldn't stop. "You're safe. You're safe, kiddo. You're safe." Keeping his own panic in check, he felt when the grip of her terror broke, when she clutched him, shaking, her face buried in his chest. Finally she quieted, eased into sobs.

"I saw." She couldn't get the words out, gulping for breath. "Cal—Oh, God, Cal . . ." She turned her face up to him, and Cal's blood went to ice. For even in the weak light from the doorway and the guttering lamp, he could see that his sister's eyes, including the whites, were now a brilliant, incandescent blue, pupils mere vertical slits.

Uncomprehending, afraid, he held her as she gasped out, face damp with tears, "I saw . . . I *saw*."

Sam dreamed that the evening had been a dream. He awoke to a bellowing nightmare.

The roaring shook the rafters, and Sam came on the run, rubbing sleep from his eyes, disoriented and afraid. By the time he reached the guest room, all the ghastly, bloody events burst full upon his memory, the pitiless invader in his midst, the cold reality of it all.

Stern was sitting up in bed, blinking himself to wakefulness, breathing hard, covers thrown about. He'd even kicked out one of the oak bedposts, sheared it clean off.

Sam masked his horror, forced calm into his voice. "Goodness, Ely, what's all the ruckus?"

Stern turned his eyes like molten sunlight on Sam, and his expression was beatific. "I saw a vision," he said.

"In the west . . . it was in the west." Tina was all cried out now, finally drowsy.

"What, honey? What did you see?" He brought the blanket up under her chin. Her eyes were nearly closed, heavy with exhaustion, but Cal could still see their vivid aqua, like windows onto an ocean floor.

"I . . . we . . . I . . ." Her eyes dipped closed as she whispered, "Wish . . . Wish . . ."

"What is it, honey? What do you wish?" Cal's eyes burned, a cobweb ache in his chest.

"One to the south. Wish . . . Wishart . . ." And then she was asleep.

Cal stroked her hair, soft as down. It too had grown paler, blanched like her skin. He ran his fingers along her cheek, found the skin warm but not searing as before. He straightened, swiped his hand angrily across his eyes, wiping away tears.

"You don't have to tell me," Cal said to Doc. "There's no shot for that."

Colleen stepped to the open doorway. "Sky's clear. The storm's gone."

"If it was a storm," Cal said. "I don't know what anything is anymore."

"I'd say that's a good philosophy to live by at present," Doc said softly, watching Tina.

Cal drew closer to him. "What is this? What's happening to her? You saw her eyes."

"We're in unfamiliar terrain, Calvin. Who can say what the rules are?" He studied the sleeping girl, quizzical. "To the west and to the south . . ."

Asleep, Tina's face was serene, and in her marble whiteness Cal had the dreadful sense that he was looking at her corpse. *I can't save them. I can't save the people I love.* Mom had died; he had been helpless to avert that. Now Tina was being swept inexorably away.

Despair rose in him. But at the same time another sensation surged up, strangely familiar. *Fight*, it insisted, *fight even though you don't know what you're fighting.*

"Can she be moved?" he asked Doc. "Back home to Eighty-first, then out of town? Away from here?"

The Russian was quiet for a time, his eyes returning to Tina.

"Her fever's gone, but who knows if it will return? And what is happening to her is continuing to happen." He shrugged. "On the other hand, if power doesn't return—if the world doesn't return to the way it was—this city's a hungry beast, Calvin. A day, two days . . . it will begin to devour itself."

Cal nodded, his mind racing. Where would they go? Back to the prairies, the plains? Was this same nightmare happening there?

He didn't know. He was just going on a feeling.

But in the past twenty-four hours, it had served him to trust his feelings.

Colleen's eyes met his. *You really want to do this?*

He nodded. "Don't think I'm not open to suggestions."

She smiled. "I've got some stuff I think you can use."

Her flat was just down the street from his, the next block over. He'd passed it a thousand times, but he'd never known she was there.

Once Cal had gotten Tina safely settled in his apartment, Doc watching over her, he and Colleen had walked the few dozen yards to Colleen's place. Her brownstone was much like his own, a relic of the previous century: weathered brick and mortar, decades of paint layers, railings of curlicued black iron. Once through the heavy oak door with its leaded stained glass, Colleen led Cal up the narrow wood staircase past silent apartments to the fourth-floor landing. Musty sunshine filtered through a dingy skylight. The thick odor of cooking cabbage filled the stairwell, and Cal wondered how they were managing it.

At her door, Colleen slid her key into the lock, slipped back the bolt. She eased the door open and stepped through soundlessly, alert. Cal followed her in. The living room was airless, dark and still.

"Hello? Rory?" Colleen called out. There was no response. "Guess he's out." She tried to make it sound neutral, but Cal heard the relief in her voice.

She threw the drapes open, and light flooded in, twinkling dust in the air. Cal blinked against the sudden brightness, turned from the window and nearly jumped: rows of hunting knives in holders covered the walls, flanked by spears, fiberglass and wood bows, quivers of steel-tipped arrows. Colleen had vanished into the bedroom.

"Your guy's a real macho jerk, huh?" Cal called after her.

Colleen returned, carrying an empty cardboard box. "Most of those are mine," she said, nodding at the arsenal.

"Oh." And it made perfect sense, of course it did—and that there were no guns. Cal remembered the weekend warriors in Hurley, with their hats like Elmer Fudd, their assault rifles with the extra clips. But Colleen, with her sense of honor, would demand a more level playing field, pitting will and muscle, fang and claw, against that of her adversary.

And he felt sure that whatever she killed, she ate.

"It also happens to be the stuff I thought you could use." She shoved the carton against his chest. "You ask nice, maybe I'll show you a trick or two."

"You know, once upon a time, I was Midwest regional junior fencing champ, three years running."

"Someone throws Errol Flynn at you, you'll do great." She began removing gleaming blades from the wall, selecting a bow, piling them into the box. "We're not talking some effete rich boy's sport here, slick. Where you're going, you might not always be able to find dinner wrapped in paper and served in a sack. Might just have to run it down and wrestle it." She handed over quiver and arrows, replacement barbs, then moved to the far end of the room, started rummaging in drawers.

"Got a tent I can spare, and some thermals. That one's Rory's," she added, as Cal fished out an elaborate blade of the double-deluxe super-duper Special Forces variety, complete with brass knuckles on the hilt and hacksaw on the back. "He's a sucker for the really big ones. Goes through sporting goods stores like Sherman going through Georgia, but then they just collect dust."

Cal set the box on a weight bench. His eye fell on a photograph atop an end table. It showed Colleen in Gore-Tex and microfleece, victorious atop a snowy peak. "You climb, too."

"Hey, you ain't got money or looks, you gotta do something." She tossed a bundle of tent barely larger than a paving stone down by the box.

Cal thought to correct her on the looks part but, feeling sure it would be rebuffed, said nothing. A man was standing beside her in the photo, a lopsided grin on his face, his arm around her. Rory, in all probability. A little roughneck with a knife at his belt (on a climb?) and a tattoo on his ungloved hand.

"Matter of fact," she said, turning toward a big wardrobe, "if I can find that gear, that's something else you can probably—" A figure burst from the closet as she opened the door, blundered into her, clawing and shoving. "*Jesus. . . !*"

But the figure bulled past them, frantic, as Cal sprang to Colleen's side. It lunged to the front door on bare feet. As it struggled with the bolt Cal saw that it wasn't human, at least not entirely so. It was five feet or less, wearing a brown bomber jacket and "I ♥ NY" T-shirt and jeans too big and bunched up; its skin was light gray, almost blue, its bald head huge, with tufted, pointed ears. There was a broad muscularity to it, in spite of its twitchy fear.

Colleen was staring opened-mouthed. "Rory . . . ?"

Now Cal too saw that, incredibly, the creature before them *was* Rory, unmistakably the guy in the photograph, but shrunken and altered to this thing before them.

Rory froze in the open doorway. He stared at them through milky white, bulbous eyes with vertical slits for pupils. "I-I-I don't want to live here no more!" With that, he ran thudding down the steps.

Cal dashed after him, but the little brute was devilishly fast. By the time Cal hit the pavement, Colleen close behind him, Rory was halfway across the street. But he was slowing now, reeling, shielding his eyes with his hands. *He's blind,* Cal thought. *The daylight's blinding him.*

Rory tripped over a discarded bottle and fell flat. Screeching hideously, he flailed his arms, legs kicking futilely. His fingers brushed a manhole cover. Desperately, he clawed at the edge, pried up the disc and *lifted it with one hand*. He scrunched into the open hole and vanished, the cover dropping back with a thump.

Colleen was beside Cal now. "That was my old man. I mean, I mean, he was never any beauty prize but he didn't look like—like—"

"His eyes," Cal said, and the anguish in his voice stopped her. "They were like my sister's."

Afternoon·sun slanted through the gauzy curtains and lay across Stern's broad shoulders and massive head as he squatted in the living room, too big now for the sofa, a blanket wrapped around him. He held the china cup delicately in his taloned hands as Sam poured, then took a sip and sighed. "I'm not human till I've had my coffee."

Sam thought, *That's supposed to be amusing.* And he sensed Ely had always been powerful enough to have underlings assure him that he was.

Even squatting, Stern was now taller than Sam. Sam could see that Stern's face was becoming more of a muzzle, teeth longer and sharper, brow more severe. His skin was continuing to alter, thicker now, its ordered trenches and rises gleaming like brown-black carapace.

Sam replaced the kettle in the fireplace. While Stern had slumbered—twelve hours, dead to the world—Sam had searched feverishly for the notepad that Stern had confiscated, but he had not been able to find it anywhere in the house.

No one messes with the big guy, but the big guy messes with them.

Stern had relished the murder he had committed, that much was crystal clear. To be released from the bottle, to have no limits, no limits at all.

And it was just the beginning.

While Stern slept, Sam had gathered up all the other pads, armfuls of them, some of the browned pages older than many of his neighbors, and burnt them in the fireplace. He had crouched before the flames, heat singeing his eyes, as the paper blackened and curled and fell to ash. Watching silently as the journal of his life was consumed, Sam had felt his own life was burning, being devoured to nothing.

But it had to be done; Ely mustn't read any more of it.

All the uncounted, solitary days and nights Sam had read and reread every scribble, reliving the old trespasses, weighted down with the familiar sense of impotent rage.

Impotent. He'd had no idea. . . .

Glancing back, he saw Stern contemplating one of the dolls near him, a 1910 Jumeau, her hair an eruption of blond curls, her dress a fantasia of lace. Stern ran his rough hand along her pale, perfect cheek. "All innocence when they're young," he murmured.

"I have some muffins I could get us," Sam offered.

"Later," Stern said, not looking at him, and Sam realized that Ely was holding the fugitive notepad in his other hand, beginning to flip through it.

He must have had it with him, Sam thought, perhaps in the pockets of the old robe he had outgrown in the night, which lay burst and discarded like a ruptured cocoon on the bedroom floor. "I feel like stretching my legs," Stern yawned, "making a new friend or two."

Sam forced himself to look directly at Stern, said almost inaudibly, "I think you've made your point."

"Point?" Stern's molten eyes glided over to him. "There's no point here." He stretched, and the muscles in his back made a sound like creaking leather. "And anyway, last time I checked this was *your* writing, babe."

He's right, he's absolutely right, oh sweet God. . . . How many names were in that pad? Dozens, hundreds maybe. Sam felt light-headed, and in his imaginings the slick wetness that covered his body was not sweat but blood.

Stern was still watching him with keen interest. "You got anything else you'd care to say?" There was a deliberate menace in his tone that made Sam's guts twist.

"Me?" Sam ducked his head, looked away.

Stern chuckled, then dropped his gaze to the pad. He skimmed several pages, then stopped, incredulity dawning on his face. He looked up at Sam, and his lips curled in a smile of sheer, delicious joy.

"This one," Stern said, "will be a pleasure."

OUTSIDE D.C.

Shango and Czernas reached the first plane before they even left Arlington County, just a few miles beyond Scott Key bridge. It was a JAL nonstop to Tokyo, a jumbo jet whose pilot had tried to put it down on a high school football field, Washington Parkway being jammed with cars heading into the city. The fat silvery monster had, not surprisingly, rammed into the auditorium and plowed through into the rank of summer-empty classrooms beyond. Charred patches on walls and grass showed where fuel from the ruptured tanks had sprayed, but there was surprisingly little evidence of fire.

"He said she'd be on a United flight," said Shango, as Czernas skidded to a halt among the dead cars on the parkway and swung his bike up onto the median, to cross to the driveway into the school.

People were milling around the walls. Shango could hear moaning, the low steady clamor of those exhausted by pain that would not cease. *No meds,* he thought.

There was no sign of the National Guard or any kind of transport, though he could see bodies lined up under the shelter of the back of the bleachers. Movement there in the shadows, big birds—ravens or crows—and probably rats. At a guess they'd put the wounded in the gym.

The still hot air brought them the smell of smoke and shit.

A small white woman in green sweatpants and a white tank-top was striding toward them, waving her arms. "Let's go," said Shango, making a move to turn his bike, but Czernas didn't follow. The aide's face was twisted with shock and pity. Shango added, "There's nothing we can do here."

Still Czernas waited for the woman, who had broken into a run.

Having mentally reviewed McKay's other friends, Shango guessed why the President had picked Czernas for the job. Press Secretary Ron Guthrie had to top out at two-eighty, and Nina Diaz, though slim and fit, would have been viewed as booty by the roving gangs of looters Shango and Czernas had encountered in the pillaged streets on their way to the bridge. But Steve Czernas, with his youth and fitness, had the idealism that in McKay had been chipped and filed by Nam and politics and years of responsibility.

Maybe in his youth McKay would have turned aside from a mission to help people in need. Or would at least have waited to see what the woman had to say.

In war, reflected Shango, that kind of behavior would probably get you and your men very dead, very fast.

The woman in the green sweats stumbled up to them, panting. "Thank God," she gasped, and caught Czernas' arm, as if fearing he'd flee. "You've got to get help. Find the National Guard, wherever the hell they are. They sent out two guys—two guys!—last night and said they'd get water and food and some meds, and since then there's been nothing."

She didn't look bruised or smoke blackened, though her face was grimy with dust and sweat. Shango guessed she was from one of the houses in the upscale development down the road. She had the slim body and cut muscle of a woman who worked out hard and often, but her face was lined, her hair white: she was sixty-five at least. She took a breath, and when she spoke again, her voice was shaky but forcibly calm.

"We've got a hundred and thirty-five people in the gym,

trauma, shock—there's a girl there who broke nearly every bone in her body when the plane hit. My neighbors and I have been trying to help, but there's no water, no electricity. Does anybody know what's happening? What's being done?"

She looked from Shango's face to Czernas' and back again, and behind her thick bifocals Shango saw other things: desperation, terror, husband and children and grandchildren who hadn't been heard from since yesterday morning. Her world in pieces around her. Compassion stabbed him like an assassin through the heart, and like an assassin he thrust it aside, crushed it.

It was a luxury they couldn't afford.

Bilmer was somewhere out there, maybe lying injured in some makeshift dressing station somewhere, maybe trying to hike in from Dulles by herself.

"Please," the woman was saying to Czernas. "Whatever you're doing, please turn around and go back to town and find the National Guard or whoever's in charge and tell them—ask them—to at least get us some water, a doctor. Doctor Vanderheide's been on her feet for twenty-four hours, and she was hurt in the crash, too. . . ."

"We can't," said Shango, seeing the struggle on Czernas' face. Seeing that he could not say no.

The woman stared at him with eyes that blazed in sudden hate.

"If we run into the National Guard at Dulles, we'll tell them to get out here, but we can't turn back."

"What are you, deaf?" The woman's voice cracked with sudden passion, her hard-held calm dissolving. "Or stupid? You want to come down here for a second and see what a man looks like who's still alive after having his legs and pelvis mashed to jelly?" Her voice rose to almost a scream. "You want to tell a ten-year-old girl whose back was roasted that she's going to have to go on hurting for a while longer? You want to . . ." She gasped, clutching at self-control, fingers digging harder into Czernas' wrist as he tried to draw away. Tears were running down her face, tracking the grime.

"Please," she said. "Please."

There were tears also on Czernas' face, mingling with the sweat in the hot morning sun.

Quietly, Shango said again, "We can't." And to Czernas, who seemed incapable of movement or speech, "Let's go."

The woman released her grip, stood for a moment looking at them both, her eyes the eyes of a damned soul who has been told that there isn't any way out of Hell after all. Czernas unslung two of the water bottles he carried and pressed them into her hands. "I'm sorry," he said.

The woman turned without a word and walked back down the drive toward the gym, slim and small and fearfully alone in the glaring sun. Shango swung his bike around and walked it back across the parkway, the heat from the asphalt baking his legs. After a long moment, Czernas followed.

NEW YORK

A melodic tinkling roused Cal from a profound sleep. Within the cocoon blackness of his still-closed eyes, he tried to remember if it was Sunday, if Mom would be cooking her banana-nut pancakes.

Then recent memory sliced the image in two, and he jolted awake. He pressed himself up, safety and certainty vanishing. The sound was coming from Tina's room. He noted Colleen and Doc had turned toward the sound as well, Colleen's hands poised over her half-made bedroll, a disheveled Doc blinking himself toward consciousness.

Cal rose. The others followed.

Tina was sitting up in bed, the Buffy poster on the wall behind her like some protective saint. In her lap, she held the music box that had been her mother's, clinking out tinny strains of *Swan Lake*. Her back again arrow straight, the sheen of her fever gone, she continued to peer downward, appearing clear-headed but lost in thought.

Tina looked up, her eyes that startling, unearthly blue, her skin eggshell pale. A line of worry etched between her brows, she lifted the box toward Cal. "Remember how Mom used to keep her jewelry in this?"

Cal nodded. The depository for the few modest but much-prized pieces that Cal had never seen his mother actually wear, only display proudly to the daughter they would someday adorn.

Tina eyed Doc and Colleen timidly, not recognizing them. Cal said, "A couple of friends."

He stepped close, put a hand to her forehead. Mercifully cool. She turned her head aside, as if unwilling or ashamed to be touched or seen.

Cal glanced over at Colleen and Doc. They nodded and withdrew. He turned back to his sister, saw that she was again contemplating the jewelry box.

"I wonder how it felt."

Tina's voice was so low that at first Cal thought she was talking to herself. Her eyes, however, met his and, with a small gesture of her head, directed his attention to the volume by her bed.

It was Nijinsky's diary; on the cover, the dancer in makeup and costume for *Afternoon of a Faun*, suffused with passion. Half man, half something else.

"I mean," she continued, "to go not just a little crazy, like my variations teacher says we all are. But to lose yourself . . . "

Her otherworldly gaze slid to the vanity mirror. In a voice flattened and opaque, she said, "Would you cover that up for me, please?"

Cal took a sharp breath but said nothing. He lifted a blanket and draped it over the glass. She nodded and eased back.

Cal sat down beside her, not touching her. "It's not just you," he said. "It's everything. Whatever this is, lots of people have been affected. They'll have to find a cure."

At last, something connected, sparked life behind her eyes. "It won't be like what I read about smallpox or—polio and stuff? Where they can save your life but. . . ."

Her gaze returned to the music box. She whispered, "No one will want to look at me."

"You're lovely." And she was, in all her pale strangeness. But from her reaction, Cal could see his words had been dismissed. Worse, regarded as a lie.

Finally, Cal said, "Look. There's gonna be an awful lot of people working on figuring out what made this happen and making it un-happen. In the meantime, though, because . . . well, for a lot of reasons, I thought it'd be best if we left the city for a while."

Surprise flared, then resistance. "But what about my—!"

She stopped, but he knew the unsaid rest of it. What about my lessons, my variations and barre work? The endless, obsessive attention to every nuance of the dance that might, just *might* secure the future she had so avidly pursued, that he himself had sacrificed so much for. To abandon that, jettison it? To leave the focus of her life like trash by a roadside?

Then her eyes dropped, and her shoulders sagged, and Cal's heart felt a greater pain than he had known.

"Okay," she said, and he saw her resignation, her hopelessness that it would ever be the same again, ever be what it was.

"Tina . . ." Her focus remained on the blanket. "*Tina*."

Sharper than he'd intended. Still, it won her attention, cracked through her glass shell to bring him a look, a presence that, for him, made her *Tina*. An instant in which he saw the exuberant four-year-old making up steps to a Beethoven sonata, the ardent nine-year-old helping him prep for the bar while wincing through her stretches, her every gesture now bearing the grace of a carefully choreographed move. The tapestry of their life together glowing in the spotlight of his sister's unyielding passion.

"Listen." His voice had again gentled. "Even if things don't go back, even if they get worse—especially if they get worse—people are still gonna need more than food and shelter to get them through." Cal reached out, touched her silken hair. "There's such magic in you, in what you can do. You know that, don't you? I watch you move, just across a room, and I find myself thinking, miracles are possible."

I don't know how to do this, he thought. And suddenly her arms were around his neck, very tight, and she whispered, "I love you, Cal. I love you."

And in that moment at least, he knew that anything really *was* possible.

Doc and Colleen were waiting for him in the front room. "We'll be leaving first light tomorrow," Cal said.

Doc put a hand on Cal's arm. "Calvin, maybe the penicillin helped, maybe not; there's no way to know. But I'd rest a good deal more easy if I could send you off with some medicines."

"You know what the hospitals are like."

"There's a man who owes me a favor," Doc answered. "If he's out of prison—" Cal started to protest, but Doc cut him off, heading for the front door. "Don't worry, I'll be quick."

Colleen fell in alongside him. "*We'll* be quick." Now Doc was the one protesting. Colleen lifted her sweater to reveal twelve inches of Green River toothpick sheathed at her belt.

Doc raised his hands in surrender. "I never argue with a woman who has a machete."

As she followed Doc through the doorway, Colleen paused, shot Cal a look. "Thanks for the adventure."

He returned the look, with gratitude. But in the turmoil of his mind, all he saw were eyes entirely blue.

He had stood in the shadows of Patel's looted market for some time now, gazing through the broken glass at the brownstone across the street, watching the woman, the dark man and the other as they appeared from time to time at a fourth-floor window. Now two of them emerged from the building into the hot slant of evening sun, headed off down the street, unaware.

That left just the one, alone in the apartment, as he had wanted it. Not that he couldn't have taken all three quite easily; the sweet hum in his arms and legs and chest told him that. No, it was just that he wanted to give this one his full attention, and all the time in the world.

Slowly, making sure no one saw him, Stern crossed the street and headed toward the apartment.

EIGHTEEN

NEW YORK

Cal's eyes felt like they'd been scooped out and boiled, his muscles complained like rusty hinges, but he was determined to get everything ready before it grew dark.

The pedicab stood in the living room, beside the recliner—the one Mr. Schenk had sat in a millennium ago yesterday morning. Cal had known of the stashed cycle three doors down, one of David Abramson's failed summer jobs, and had traded the NYU student his law books, stereo and coffee table for the bike, some food and water, and containers to hold them. Bedrolls and provisions were stacked neatly around it. It would be a bitch to wrestle the thing down the stairs in tomorrow's pre-dawn darkness, but only an idiot left things outdoors unwatched.

When he straightened up from stowing the knives and arrows, he saw Tina watching from the archway into the hall, leaning against the frame for support. She held out her music box, tilting it questioningly toward him.

"Sure," Cal said lightly, taking it. He pressed it between the folds of one of the bedrolls, made sure it was secure. The basic frame of the pedicab was a mountain bike with a wide range of gears: it would stand up to hard traveling, but every ounce of weight would tell.

"Funny how little you really need, when you think about it," Tina said. "It's like we've been carrying all this stuff on our backs; now it's just shedding away." She stepped a little shakily to the sofa and sank down with a ragged exhalation.

She's not well, not at all. He had been so relieved when her fever had broken, when she had come back to him, but the illness was still in her, still working, he could sense that. He sensed, too, her fear, her horror at what was happening to her. He wondered if she had, after all, seen the bands of slouched pale-eyed creatures that he'd glimpsed near the hospital.

"You're not gonna leave me, are you, Cal?"

"What? *No.* What makes you think that?"

"When I was little," she began quietly, "and they told me something had happened to Mama, I tried to imagine the worst thing that could happen, and the worst I could imagine was she had a broken arm." The light from the blinds cast shadow striping across her face, rendering her expression unreadable. "But she was dead."

Cal nodded, remembering the day, the helplessness he had felt. Tina reached out and grasped his sleeve, peered up at him with her cobalt gaze. "Sometimes things happen, and it doesn't make any difference if you're good or not."

Cal peered into her strange, troubled eyes. "I'm not gonna leave you."

A tapping sounded at the front door, and they both froze. Cal had given Doc his duplicate key, and neither he nor Colleen would have bothered to knock. Wordlessly, Cal motioned Tina toward her room. She rose and quickly moved to her door, slid out of sight behind it.

The tapping continued, insistent, as if sharp nails were drumming on the door. Cautious, Cal unzipped one of the packs, withdrew the buck knife Colleen had given him. He unsheathed it, crossed the room in a few soundless steps.

He was almost to the door when there was a harsh thud and the door exploded inward, fragments flying like shrapnel. With a cry, he stumbled back, shielding his face, wood shards bouncing off him. Dimly, he could perceive *something* squeezing through the ragged hole in the door, dark as some vast insect.

Cal gasped. The intruder was a monstrosity, reptilian and manlike at the same time, standing on two legs that bent in more places than a man's. It towered over him, head nearly grazing the high ceiling as it leaned forward, stalking toward him, elephantine footfalls shuddering the floor.

It paused and tilted its head, its yellow eyes considering him. Then the creature's long, projecting face split in a ghastly grin that revealed twin rows of steak-knife teeth.

"This is not Woodstock," the monster said. "I am not Mother Teresa."

Cal gaped, recalling the words, hearing in the thunder of that dragon voice a tone familiar from days and months and years endured. Now he could see, unmistakably, in the rough saurian planes of that face, the remnant—no—the *essence* of the man. "Mr. Stern . . ."

Stern nodded, pleased. *He wants me to know it's him*, Cal thought. *Whatever he's going to do, he wants it personal.*

Stern took another lumbering, gliding step toward him, relishing it. "I told you if you left, you'd be terminated." He belched, and, incredibly, a tendril of gray vapor curled out the side of his mouth. "Mind if I smoke?"

A nearby gasp drew both their attention. Cal saw that Tina was standing in the doorway of her room, jewel-blue eyes riveted on Stern, vertical-slit pupils staring.

Stern regarded her with his own changed eyes, identical pupils. "Lord of exiles and miracles," he whispered, voice trembling. "I thought I was the only butterfly in this brave new world."

He took a step toward her, one razored hand extended. She shrank back. "Don't be scared, honeylamb. You're looking at your future."

Cal flung himself between them, thrust Tina behind him. "Stay away from her!"

Stern paused, firelight eyes raking Cal. "I will, if you introduce us."

"She's my sister."

Stern weighed it, then flashed an obscene Cheshire grin. "Well, Mr. Griffin, may I have permission to take out your sister?"

Stern lunged with crocodile speed.

"Run, Tina!" Cal shouted, shoving her away. She darted into her room, slammed the door. Cal wheeled on Stern, the long knife blade gleaming.

Stern batted Cal aside like wadded paper. Scrambling to his feet, Cal saw Stern rip the door apart with two quick slashes of his monstrous hands, tear through the bookcase Tina had overturned within as a barricade.

Cal sprang after Stern into the bedroom, leapt on him from behind, bringing the knife down hard. He felt the blade jar aside on bone and gristle, saw Tina shrink back in terror, trying to wedge herself in the corner. Stern roared, more in outrage than pain, threw Cal off and spun on him, claws sweeping across Cal's abdomen in a wide arc. Cal sprang back and felt his shirt rip, the dagger points lightly scoring the skin of his stomach, just enough to draw blood.

Stern closed on him, and he stumbled back, knife leveled, desperately searching for some soft place under leather hide and bony plate.

A boxy object flew through the air, struck Stern on the back before crashing to the floor. Stern yelled, spun to face Tina. *The night stand. She threw the night stand.* But now she had nothing close to hand as Stern rushed at her. She fell back between the bed and wall, cowering. He bent over her, reaching out nightmarishly long arms.

Cal dove forward, but Stern twisted, gripped him and sent him flying across the room. Cal's head hit the wall with a terrible, resounding crash.

Tina screamed as he hit the floor, splayed limply.

Oddly, his mind felt clear, but he couldn't see the room anymore, only a flat grayness. He struggled to rise, to move his arms and legs, but it was as if the strings to them were all severed.

He heard the crack of the big window shattering, then a strange sound as of a great bedsheet unfurling, followed by a rhythmic whooshing of air that filled the world, then diminished, punctuated by the fading keen of Tina's screams.

In the last moment of awareness before the gray darkened and was all, Cal recognized that sound.

It was the sound of wings.

OUTSIDE D.C.

"You could have said you were sorry," said Czernas, after about two and a half miles.

Riding ahead, Shango was watching the cars on his left like a hawk, watching the trees that fringed the parkway, planning what he'd do if someone lunged at them from either direction. The bikes were thin-tired touring models, not mountain or hybrid. If they were forced off the pavement, they couldn't maintain escape speed.

Shango said nothing. *I'm sorry. I'm sorry you're dying, Mister. I'm sorry you're screaming in pain, sweetheart.*

I'm sorry you're never going to see your husband or children or grandkids again.

Something grated within him at those facile, worthless apologies.

I'm sorry I lent a friend the fifty bucks you were planning on buying the kids' shoes with, honey. They'll be okay for another two weeks.

As a child he'd learned to hate the words.

Sweat ran down his face. Far to their left, thin smoke rising above the trees showed the location of another downed plane. Shango wondered if he could determine whether it was a United flight by simply standing on top of an SUV and studying it through binoculars, and if his companion would feel obliged to ride over to the wreck to say *I'm sorry* to them, too.

Czernas persisted angrily, "We may not be able to do anything, but we don't have to treat people like they don't exist."

"She exists, all right." Shango braked beside a big silver-gray Washington Flyer in the number one lane. "She exists enough to have taken a liter of my water, which is what I'm going to have to give you to split the difference of what you'll be short." He slipped his hammer from the straps of the backpack, walked warily among the cars, as careful as if he were in one of the old New Orleans cemeteries, where the tombs cut your field of vision to about two feet. The rear wall of the cemetery backed onto the projects: the Park Service found dead tourists there all the time. The only difference was that the tombs weren't made of metal and didn't throw waves of heat.

"Well, you can keep your fuckin' water!" Czernas yelled from the shoulder.

Shango paused beside the searing, silvery wall of the Flyer's side. "I can't even do that," he said patiently. "Because if you collapse from dehydration, we stop, and since we can't stop, I have to split my water with you."

"I'll manage."

The fuck you will, thought Shango, but he let the quarrel drop. Yet it disturbed him, because he knew Czernas was right, or at least right in any context but this one. When you're pinned down by enemy fire, you don't sit there putting Band-aids on the bullet holes, you take out the goddam machine-gun nest and *then* care for the survivors.

The hot steel of the bus seared his bare knees and elbows where they brushed it. Even standing up on top, he couldn't see past the trees in the direction of the rising smoke.

Fuck. Another side trip, and it was nearly noon. If Bilmer started walking to Washington—given that her plane had landed at least three minutes early—she wouldn't follow the main road. They'd never find her.

He could see two more smoke columns, too, which might or might not also be planes.

Probably were. The countryside around Dulles would be littered with them. He put from his mind what that meant, in terms of death and lives shattered, of men and women like those the woman in green was trying to care for, with her two pitiful little liters of water, of people sitting in dark houses somewhere wondering if their mothers' or husbands' or grandkids' plane had touched down before the lights went out.

"You think he can do it?" Czernas asked, when Shango returned to the shoulder and mounted his bike again. "Turn this around?"

"Do you?" Shango took a drink, held out one of his bottles to Czernas, who shook his head. Shango unceremoniously draped the strap around the aide's neck. Czernas made a move to pull away, and their eyes met. Then the young man's lips tightened, and he looked aside and adjusted the strap to sit better on his shoulder, and swung onto his bike.

"I don't know," he said after a time. "Even if whatever Bilmer found is complete . . . The sooner we get it to him, the better. The quicker he can act. He has enemies, even in his own party; he always has."

For some reason Shango heard Cox's voice in his mind again, *Things fuck up, and they start wreckin' their own neighborhoods.*

But he couldn't even begin to explain to Czernas why he laughed.

NEW YORK

He hadn't ever liked her, Sam reflected. But then, he hadn't actually known her.

And now, surprisingly, she was his second guest.

The little neighbor girl, the dancer, sat mute in the corner, scanning the room with queer blue eyes. She was pallid as uncooked dough and sickly blue veins spiderwebbed out over her skin. He might have feared catching some awful illness from her, if he hadn't seen Ely first. She was "becoming" . . . something. If she didn't fade away to nothing first, crumble to white ash like his precious notepads, now cold dust in the fireplace.

Stern crouched on his haunches watching Tina, who stared back at him silently, doll-like amid the curled and coifed bisque figures.

"What's wrong with this picture?" he murmured contentedly. "Nothing at all."

It was only because Sam was watching her closely, looking for it, that he saw the lightning flash of fear across her face before she submerged it, masked it with indifference. *She's trying to be brave.*

Sam clucked his tongue. "We don't need her." And he didn't know, really, if he was saying this in an attempt to protect her or because he resented her presence; in some perverse way, he felt possessive of Ely's attention. The taunts, the malice, the contempt—at least they made him *visible*.

"Speak for yourself," Stern said acidly, and Sam felt the sharp prick of his scorn. Stern drew closer to his unwilling guest. "I thought I was a solo dance. Turns out I'm a *pas de deux.*"

Tina raised her head defiantly. "I'm not like you. I *won't* be like you."

"Look in a mirror, child. Oh, I admit, you don't have all the luxury extras yet, but give it time." Stern eyed himself in the aged wall mirror, its silvering half fallen away. "Symmetry, matched and balanced, the two of us . . . How little faith I showed, to think all this would unfold and I'd be left alone."

"You weren't alone, Ely," Sam demurred.

Stern's eyes slid over to him, narrowed to slits. "Sorry, you're not my type." He cast a critical gaze about the room. "And, frankly, I'm used to better."

"You have to change with the times." Sam heard the edge

of anger in his voice. He had barely slept since Ely had arrived, and he was finding it increasingly hard to hide his feelings.

"That's just what I've been thinking." Stern rose and strode to the window, swept aside a curtain. Twilight was falling—"magic hour," Sam had heard it called—and its melancholy light washed over Stern's face, emphasizing its monumental, grotesque beauty.

"Know why most people hire a lawyer? They don't want justice. They want *more*." His saurian head swiveled to regard Sam, and his twisted smile revealed ivory scalpel teeth. "I ran a business. I can run a mob."

Sam felt his stomach clench, a wave of nausea surge into his throat and mouth. "But if they *see* you . . ."

"Ever catch *Cyrano de Bergerac?* After she fell in love with his ideas, she didn't care what his nose looked like." Stern let the curtain drop, his eyes burning into Sam. "He just needed a front man."

Sam remembered the grade school play Mother had made him appear in, as J. Pierpont Morgan, of all things. He had opened his mouth to utter the first line and had vomited in front of them all.

And now, to venture out onto those riot-torn, killing streets—*a front man*—so naked, so vulnerable . . .

He said, pleading, "Ely, we're safe here."

"Mr. Mole wants to stay in his mole hole." Stern's lips curled contemptuously. "Well, I need room to spread my wings."

Astonished, Sam heard himself say, "No."

"*No?*" Stern's response was immediate and terrible, his anger igniting like a firestorm. Before Sam could shriek or move at all, Stern was upon him, grasping either side of his head in immense, taloned hands.

For an instant, Sam knew what it must have been like to be that man with the dog or the little girl's big brother in their last moments. Out of the corner of his eye, he could see Griffin's sister watching them, horrified and still.

Sam whimpered and prayed it would be quick.

But the pressure on his head did not increase. There was no cracking of bone, no finality. Instead, Stern peered into his eyes, and the gleaming yellow gaze flared brighter, blazed into a white-hot nuclear glare that flooded into him, hushed all the babble in his mind with a vast, powerful will. Sam felt himself fall away, all objection shattered to a mute, distant compliance.

"Say after me," Stern intoned. "It's a new world. . . ."

WEST VIRGINIA

Half sunk in sleep, Hank listened to Wilma moving around in the house.

The strange darkness of the morning was long gone. He'd been awake when it clouded over the new day. His headache had returned, fit to split his skull, a hammering sense of something, some Voice, shouting at him. Or a dream of someone shouting at him, terrifying, overwhelming, while he cowered before it, naked in this new strange body.

But that dream had fleeted away as quickly as it had come, taking its very memory with it. Later Wilma had come in and told him that lightning had struck again and again around the Wishart house, leaving great patches of burned honeysuckle and charred earth.

Now he heard her go out onto the porch and knew she was sitting on the steps, surrounded by her cats, watching and listening to the strange heat of the afternoon.

Drifting toward sleep, he heard with his new and preter-natural sharpness the footfalls of neighbors passing along Applby Street. No one paused near the white house on the corner, almost as if something prevented them from seeing the place. Considering some of the things Wilma had told him, he didn't even feel surprised.

Things are not going to be the same, she'd said.

Through the dense weave of the bedroom curtains he could

still see a pin-mesh of sun. Even that hurt his eyes. He raised his hands and looked at them. Huge hands, deformed bones growing still larger. The ache in the long bones of his arms informed him that his body still had a few more changes to make.

And Wilma, he thought, with a glimmer of delighted pride. Wilma lithe and strange and fast, Wilma with eyes that, like his, saw in the dark, quick and agile as one of her own cats.

Snotty as a cat, too, he thought, and grinned affectionately to himself. Why the hell hadn't he ever seen that, in all these years? And yet with a cat's strange all-accepting softness, unsurprised and undemanding.

Things are not going to be the same.

What was he now? A creature of darkness, like Sonny and Hillocher? But inside he hadn't changed—had he? The thought that maybe he had, or would later, was a frightening one. Would he turn on his friends and neighbors? Become what Sonny had become?

And what was Wilma now? What were we ever?

But he knew the answer to that. In a way, the sharpening of the differences between them made the differences matter less. She was his friend. She had always been his friend. And she had always been herself.

The thought brought him a measure of peace.

But you have no place in this world, whispered a voice in his mind.

It was a cold voice, and the thing it did to Hank's heart was a twisting pinch of bitter cold.

You're different from them. Alien. You've always been different and you're more so now. They will kill you for being different. Wilma won't protect you.

But she did. Hank argued with the Voice, for it seemed to be a thing coming from outside of him; like the voice that spoke in his head sometimes when he dreamed about the Devil of his Southern Baptist upbringing. *She kicked Souza's butt and got me here.*

To be her pet, sneered the Voice. He tried to look where it was coming from—he knew he'd drifted off to sleep and was dreaming—but he couldn't see it, exactly. His dreams were dreams of darkness, and in the darkness shone a bluish light; the light was a shield, hiding something darker still. *To be her pet like one of her fucking cats, so she could run your life the way she runs theirs.*

Come off it, thought Hank. *Nobody runs a cat's life and nobody runs mine.*

But the doubt was cold in his heart.

You'll have to kill her, the Voice said reasonably. *And the others.*

What others? He wanted to simply shut his mind off from the Voice but couldn't. Wanted to wake up and go outside and talk to Wilma, but the Voice held him in sleep. *I don't want to kill nobody.*

But you'll have to, said the Voice. *Or they'll kill you. Haven't you realized that yet?*

And he saw again the crowd by the gates of the mine, the torches burning in the darkness, the men with their guns and their clubs. Saw their faces and knew them: Carl Souza, Leo Swann, Ed Brackett, Jim Stickley. His cousins Sid and Ernie, and Aunt Claire, faces twisted with revulsion at the sight of him. In his dream they all stooped and picked up stones (*That area in front of the shaft was paved, there's no stones there!*). He saw the stones fly toward him, felt them thudding into his flesh. In the dream the men around the tunnel opened fire, bullets whining and pinging against the concrete, tearing like hot bees into his flesh.

No! he thought. *It didn't happen that way!*

You'll have to kill them, said the Voice, and it was hard to see why he shouldn't.

Who? he asked.

And he thought the Voice smiled.

We'll tell you, it said. *We'll tell you when the time comes.*

"She doesn't seem to have any fever." Shannon Grant's voice trembled as she touched her daughter's hand. "When she—when she started to get like this, I asked her what was wrong, and she said, 'It's all going away. He wants it. It's all going away.' " She swallowed hard, looked pleadingly up into Wilma's face.

Wilma passed her hand in front of Tessa's eyes. They neither blinked nor moved, only stared out ahead of her, not blank, precisely, but rapt, gazing into distance. "Tessa?" she said, and the child made no response. " 'He wants it.' " She turned back to Shannon. "Nothing about who *he* is? Or what he wants?"

The young mother shook her head, hastily slapped tears from her own cheeks. "Dr. Blair says he doesn't know what's wrong with her," she said, naming the only physician in Boone's Gap. "He says he can't find anything physical." Her voice cracked, and she looked quickly away.

"But wait," said Hazel, in grim imitation of a TV huckster, "there's more." She stood in the doorway of Tessa's tiny bedroom, arms folded, watching her sister and her friend with weariness in her eyes. "Terri Brackett says her son Billy's the same way. Just staring, no fever, doesn't move. She says his hands are freezing, and she doesn't like the way he's breathing. And Fawn Leary."

"All this stuff going on," whispered Shannon despairingly. "The guys in the mines, and Hank and . . ." She looked at Wilma again, as if she would have said something else, maybe something about why she'd thought getting Wilma to look at Tessa would be helpful, but didn't.

And Wilma understood.

She passed her hand over Tessa's dark curls, felt her face and her hands—both noticeably cold—and tilted her head a little, letting her own mind go a bit slack, relaxing into what she was more and more coming to realize was the cat part of her, or the part that was connected to her cats.

Tessa looked *wrong*. Faded. Pale. There was a smell to her, more dead than alive, a scent that prickled Wilma's nape with fear. If she'd been a cat, she would have taken her at once to hide in some dark place. But even then, she knew that hiding would do no good.

She brought her mind back, looked up at Shannon. "We just don't know enough about what's going on," she said. "Maybe it's time to walk down the mountain, see if someone in Charleston or Lynchburg knows what's going on."

"That's just it!" Shannon's voice shook, and for the first time Wilma noticed the bruises on the young woman's face, the tear in her plaid shirt and the scratches on her arms. "I tried this afternoon! I can't leave town!"

NINETEEN

NEW YORK

At first, consciousness did not return to Cal so much as pay a call nearby.

From the blackness, he heard others calling his name, a man and a woman. Then hands were touching him. But he felt unconnected to it, as though events were playing out in a distant room, some muffled TV show that had nothing to do with him, was none of his concern.

"Is he dead?" That was Colleen, voice tense.

"No," Doc answered. "Hold this." Silence, accompanied by further probing. "Superficial cuts to the abdomen . . . and a nasty bump to the head."

"Can we lift him onto the bed?"

"I'd feel more comfortable on advice of an X-ray, but—"

"Yeah. Right."

Cal felt his body lifted, deposited onto the soft mattress. Curious, this feeling of observing himself outside himself, this vague indifference.

"You're not squeamish, are you?" Doc said admiringly.

"No," she answered, the sound drifting away as silence reared up and emptied him.

❧

Later, a good deal later, a damp washcloth passed over his eyes and Cal decided to try opening them. Slowly, tentatively, he lifted the lids. Instantly, light tore at him and, with it, searing pain.

Jesus, his head felt like—

Like someone had fucking thrown him into a wall. And with that, he remembered, every last terrible bit of it. *Tina!*

He sat up quickly in bed, and, Christ, was that a mistake. The room wheeled crazily about, and Cal had to work very hard to keep whatever was still in his stomach more or less where it belonged.

Then strong, gentle hands were on him, easing him back onto downy pillows.

"Easy there, ace."

Cal squinted against the brutal light. A misty figure stood over him, a familiar lean efficiency.

"Welcome back," Colleen said.

Cal licked dry lips, tried for a response, but his parched throat managed only an incomprehensible croak. She brought a glass to his lips. He gratefully managed several swallows of water.

Probing beyond the curtain of pain, Cal could feel a bandage wrapped tightly around his middle, under it raw slashes of torn flesh like parallel lines of fire. Stretching slightly, he could also discern the protesting cries of ribs that he hoped were only bruised and not broken.

Doc joined Colleen by the bedside, glowering down at Cal with an affectionate, scolding air. "If it's of interest, you've got a concussion accompanied by a smorgasbord of assorted lacerations and other nastiness." As he spoke, he lifted the lantern in the dim room, scrutinized the pupils of Cal's eyes, made him track the flame. "We repeat this every two hours, to be sure."

Cal could see now that he was in his own room. He tried again to speak, succeeded in a breathy whisper. "Tina . . ."

Colleen and Doc glanced at each other, expressions darkening. "She's . . . gone," Colleen said.

Cal groaned and closed his eyes. Doc touched his shoulder. "Calvin, who did this to you?"

Cal forced his eyes open. "My boss."

"Geez, who do you work for?" asked Colleen.

"His eyes were like hers," Cal continued. "Only he was this big lizard thing." He could see the surprise in their faces but also that they believed him. Good. He didn't feel up to lengthy explanations. He thought of Tina, alone with Stern, and a wave of bleakness washed over him. "Why would he take her? He could have killed us both. He must've thought he *did* kill me. What would he want with her?"

"One crisis at a time." Doc gave a small, sad smile. "Do you know where he'd be?"

Cal looked out the window, began to shake his head but stopped himself as the pain flared. "I never heard where he lived. They could be anywhere. . . ." He slammed the flat of his hand against the near wall. "I need a damn psychic!"

And it was as if the thought emerged not from himself but was presented to him as a gift. In his mind's eye, he was back on Fifty-sixth and Fifth, in front of the Stark Building, with the gaudy, absurd figure standing before him, full of jangly conviction.

Goldie.

"It's omens, Cal," he had said. "Something's coming. You keep your head low."

In the immediate aftermath of the Change, it had seemed incredibly prescient. But looking back on it now, it could easily have been mere coincidence, the ranting of any street-corner crazy any day of the week.

If not for the *other* thing he had said, the phrase that had made no sense at the time. *"Metal wings will fail, leather ones prevail."*

The planes had fallen out of the sky. And in the moment before Cal had lost consciousness following Stern's attack, the sound that only now came clear, like a vast leathery bed-sheet unfurling.

Wings. Stern had wings.

Desperate, Cal ransacked his memory for the vital clue Goldie had left him, the offhand words. Then he had it: Goldie gesturing at the grate as the subway trains rumbled below. *I prefer the subterranean.*

Cal flung off the blankets, flailed to rise.

"Calvin, be careful."

"You're in no shape to do anything," Colleen said.

"You're right," Cal agreed. "Now will you fucking *help* me?"

In the end, the heat of his certainty melted them. He felt their hands under his arms, steadying him. Somehow, miraculously, his feet found the floor.

The room was whipping about but he could force it down, tame it. There. It was better now.

He took a deep breath, forced the pain in his head *back*. There was no time for it.

Darkness beckoned.

"Stay here," Cal insisted. "He's kinda paranoid."

He knelt by the grate with Colleen and Doc. Although it was only late afternoon, Fifth was barely populated, the stores closed up tight. The smell was worse, far worse, than it had been yesterday. A few timid passersby glanced their way curiously, then hurried on at Colleen's challenging glare. The crossbow and quiver of arrows hung easily across her back. Cal noted she was taking the weapon everywhere now, its polished steel and wood a fierce kind of beauty. It suited her.

And she was far from the only armed person he saw.

Colleen's crowbar eased under the grate, and now the three of them put their shoulders to it, forcing the barred covering up and off the square hole in the sidewalk. They dropped the grate clattering onto the pavement, then stood

over the waiting maw. A black murmur like distant ocean reverberated out of it, accompanied by a stale stink.

"This doesn't impress me as the greatest idea," said
Colleen.

"Yeah . . . sure wish I had a better one." There was no
way to track his quarry with any certainty. But whenever Cal
had seen Goldie, it had been around these few blocks; they
seemed to be his stamping grounds. Just maybe, when he'd
gone below each night, he hadn't gone far.

It was a place to start.

He peered down into the darkness, tightened the straps
of his backpack. "Wait forty-five minutes."

"Then?" Doc questioned.

"Then . . ." Cal realized he didn't have a then. Saying no
more, he slid into the opening.

It's like climbing into a grave. Cal pushed the thought away.
He focused on the task at hand, gripping the metal rungs set
in the concrete wall of the shaft, lowering himself—how
far? He couldn't see clearly below, couldn't gauge the depth.
As far as it took. That was all the answer he had, for any of
this.

The metal and concrete and air about him were sharp
with chill, but he felt flushed nonetheless, the wound on his
scalp screeching, his head an overinflated balloon. Everything had a muzzy edge of unreality to it. Glancing up, he
saw the world above was now no more than a distant square
of blue surrounded by blackness. Rung by rung, arms straining, he moved stiffly, as though needing lubrication. *Oil can,*
he thought sardonically. *Oil can what?*

He felt a subtle shift in the flow of air around him and
abruptly his feet found support. He released the last rung
and stood, gaining his balance. His eyes had adjusted to the
gloom, and the light from above cast a pallid radiance.

He was in a subway tunnel, was standing, in fact, on the
track itself, which snaked away into the darkness. Another

time, this would have been cause for alarm, but there was no roar of an approaching train, nothing save a hushed ocean-like murmur that was a sound and not a sound. His finger-tips brushed the wall and found no vibration in the stone, no rumble of distant engine and cars. A dead place . . . at least as far as the machines were concerned.

As all the world seemed to be dead.

He leaned against the wall and considered his options. How many hundreds, thousands of miles of tunnel serpen-tined under the streets? *I'm looking for a crazy man*, Cal thought. *Does that make me crazy?*

Cal shrugged out of his backpack and unzipped it. His probing hand found the cool glass and metal of the Coleman lantern. He withdrew it, closed up the pack and replaced it, then dug in his jeans pocket for the lighter.

Suddenly, his ears pricked at a strange flitting sound, here and there about him, like an immense, unseen hummingbird. He spun, trying to detect the source.

And then he spied it, in an arched recess against the tun-nel wall, twenty feet off. There, seeming to hover in the blackness, was the glowing face of a pale boy, eyes liquid blue, regarding him with wary surprise.

Cal saw him just for a twinkling, then the boy darted back into the darkness, face wild with fear.

"Wait!" Cal ran a few strides after him, lantern banging in his hand. The sound of his voice rebounded off the walls, frighteningly loud, his footfalls staccato accompaniment. But there was no sound of the boy running at all, just that odd thrumming tone, higher now, climbing in pitch, then cutting out to silence.

Cal reached the archway, saw that it was an opening be-tween inbound and outbound tunnels. He dropped onto the other side, eyes straining the darkness, alert for any sound. But there was nothing.

The boy, or whatever it had been, was gone.

Cal lit the lantern, watched its light spread slowly along the trackbed. Ahead of him, vast and still, lay a subway train, like a row of steel coffins. He moved cautiously along it, raising the lantern high to illumine the interior of the cars, the untenanted seats and straps, the ads for skin treatments and personal injury lawyers. "You may have been the victim of an injustice," one proclaimed. "Have you suffered a recent calamity?"

In the darkness, a pebble thwanged off a metal rail, sending up an echoing reverberation. Cal snapped to wariness. The boy? No. Something else. Listening intently, not breathing, he could make out a soft padding of many feet. Voices too, whispery, guttural. He had a sudden flash of the clump of shadowy figures he'd seen the other night on the street, moving in that queer, flowing rhythm. They had sounded like that. It had made his skin crawl; he'd felt an immediate, unaccountable revulsion.

The sound of their steps was growing louder, coming his way. And with their approach, their voices grew into a din of expectation, excitement . . . *hunger*.

Cal felt a stab of terror. *They know I'm here.*

He took to his heels, knowing he should extinguish the lantern but unable to bear being alone in the dark with these pursuers.

His flight spurred them, and they broke into a clamorous run behind him, shouting with frenzy and delight. Cal rounded a bend, could hear them closing. His free hand shot to the buck knife in its sheath. He pulled it free in a wild arc, heart hammering, the blood loud in his ears.

And then his foot caught on something, a wire strung taut. Abruptly, he was flying, tumbling headlong. He landed hard, breath knocked out of him, lantern and knife skittering away. He floundered wildly, fighting to rise, and something heavy fell on him from above. *A net; it was a weighted net.* Snared, he cried out in fear and rage, tore at the ropes. It held fast.

His pursuers slowed, watching. The lantern lay on its side some yards off, miraculously unbroken, illuminating a grotesque tableau.

They were perhaps fifteen in number, grunting among themselves, chuckling malignly as they drew near. There was something loathsome and furtive in the way they moved. In their too-big clothing, they looked like some demented, stunted street gang, pale as grubs, eyes milky white with slitted pupils.

Cal's eyes darted to his knife, impossibly out of reach. A bare hairy foot came down on the handle. Cal lifted his gaze to the figure, took in the baggy jeans, scuffed bomber jacket, ragged "I ♥ NY" T-shirt. With a thrill of surprise, Cal realized he knew this one.

It was Rory.

"I seen you." Rory's lips curled nastily, revealing stained icepick teeth. "You were with my chick."

Rory scooped up the knife. As he advanced on Cal, the others followed, pressing close. Cal struggled futilely against the net. They reached toward him with hideous malformed fingers, as Rory swung the knife high and back. . . .

Suddenly, from the far end of the tunnel came a flashing of lights and booming sounds, like myriad skyrockets going off. The creatures gaped, shielding their eyes. Astonished, Cal craned his neck to see through the netting.

A figure was approaching, fireballs of light shooting out of his hands and bouncing off the walls.

"BEGONE!" The voice was huge and commanding, God on the mountaintop—and a vengeful God, to boot. Terrified, blinded, the little brutes skittered down the tunnel into the darkness, their screams floating in the air and then evaporating.

The fireballs ceased. The figure reached Cal, bent down to him.

"Well. Hello, Cal."

It was Goldie.

He looked the same as ever, with his cascade of hair, electric clothing, cacophony of buttons pinned to his padded vest. Through his amazement, one of them caught Cal's eye: REALITY'S A BITCH.

"How—" Cal was gasping, breathless. "How did you—?"

Goldie wiggled his fingers. "That? Little something I just picked up. Doesn't do jack, but it scares the hell out of them."

Cal tried to speak, but he was overwhelmed.

"I can see you're a little freaked. Lemme help you." Rory had dropped Cal's knife in his flight, and now Goldie grabbed it up, started to cut away the net.

Cal felt sheepish, ashamed. "I walked right into their trap."

"Hm?" The net fell away, and Goldie helped Cal to his feet. "Oh no, this is mine." He grinned and handed him back his knife. "I'm very particular who comes to my place."

Sergeant Rodriguez hated this part.

He and the rest of his boys stood flanking the back of the wagon, the crowd around it like hungry locusts. His squad had been doling out the emergency rations for the better part of two hours here at Columbus Circle, handing out cans of evaporated milk, Spam and jerky and instant pudding, whatever the hell the government had gotten a lock on.

But now they were getting lean, and it was time to haul ass, move on. This whole thing had been one sorry drag, ever since he'd been called up on active. He'd been minding his own, doing the insurance salesman thing, saving for that SUV for Maria and the kids. Man just couldn't get a break, that was the gospel truth. And now that order had just come down about not using your weapon under any circumstance, what kind of fucked-up shit was that?

At his nod, Private Halloran closed up the back of the wagon. Corporal Fontana grasped the reins of the two big Clydesdales they'd commandeered from a circus in Jersey.

Seeing they were about to pull a Houdini, the crowd surged forward. Rodriguez, Halloran and Villanova closed ranks, blocking them from the wagon, rifles held loosely but brooking no nonsense.

Rodriguez raised his arms. "That's it, folks."

"What're you talking about?" That came from some red-faced Irish guy. "You still got boxes!"

"Yeah, for other destinations."

"Lies!" Irish pointed toward the two privates. "I heard 'em say we're the last on your slate." He turned to the crowd. "They're black-marketing it!"

Rodriguez shot Halloran and Villanova a look that scraped paint. Then he glared back at the crowd. "Back off! Now! Understand?"

"We understand you've got our food!" Irish loved the sound of his own voice. Jesus, he'd like to clip that asshole, just to make a point.

The crowd pushed forward dangerously as the soldiers held position, twitchy, rifles aimed. Then a voice shouted over the tumult. "Forget it! You're nothing to them!"

Startled, the crowd turned to the man behind them. Rodriguez stretched to see over their heads. A little bald guy stood twenty, thirty feet back from the crowd. Even from this distance, Rodriguez could see he was different from the others. He stood stock still, cool as gun metal.

"They'd kill you for a dime," the little guy said.

The crowd was focused on the little guy now, and Rodriguez saw his opportunity. He motioned to Halloran and Villanova. The three jumped into the wagon. Fontana gave the reins a shake, and the Clydesdales broke into a heavy stride, the wagon rattling down the street. Several people, empty-handed, chased after them a few steps, then gave it up.

The others closed in on the little man.

"So what are we supposed to do?" a dark woman in a sari demanded of him. "Starve?"

"No," he replied calmly, "you *learn*." He beamed reassuringly at them. Had they been especially discerning, which they were not, they might have noticed that his eyes were unreadable, opaque as stones.

"Stop whining for handouts," he continued, "waiting for

the ATMs to open. What are your bellies telling you? Things aren't getting better, they're getting worse! And they're gonna get worse yet. . . .

"Gather 'round, folks." Sam Lungo gave them a knowing smile. "We've got things to talk about."

You'll have to kill them, you know.

Fuckin' right I will. In his dream Sonny Grimes sat in the Copper Kettle Café and everybody was eating but him.

He didn't see the person at the table with him. Every time he looked across the table, someone was there, all right, but he couldn't get a clear look at them. Sometimes it just looked like a spot of darkness, like the pupil of an eye with no eye there, not even an iris. Just a dark that went straight back into his brain.

A dark that drank everything into it.

Sometimes there was nothing at all.

Just that voice.

Looking sulkily around at the other people in the restaurant, Sonny recognized nearly everyone he knew, everyone he couldn't stand, from his mother—young, as she'd been when his dad was alive, and knocking back Johnny Walkers with that creep who'd been her boss when he was a kid, the one who'd send him out of the house when he came over in the afternoon—to Hank Culver, the No-Smoking Nazi. As if it was any of his or anybody else's goddam business whether he smoked or where he smoked.

And all of them were eating except him.

Waitresses undulated between the tables, saucy little high school girls or chicks out of *Penthouse* and *Hustler*, with tight little asses and perky tits and big bedroom smiles: *Can I get you something else? A little more coffee? Would you care for a blow job with that?* He kept trying to catch their attention—they hadn't even given him a glass of water, for Chrissakes!—but they looked through him as if he weren't there.

Bitches, all of them. Assholes.

Over at the next table he saw that slob Arleta Wishart and her two geek sons, chowing down on a banquet that would have embarrassed that old Henry VIII guy who threw chicken bones on the floor in the movies. Roast chickens and bowls of chili and steaks so big they hung over the edge of the plate . . .

In his sleep Sonny Grimes twitched, his nose wrinkling in the darkness, for he'd gone to sleep hungry.

Pigs, whispered the voice to him out of the darkness. *Yes, pigs.*

A pretty waitress came by and smiled at him. KITTEN said the nametag on her size-D boob. He wanted to ask her what the other one's name was. "Can I get you something?" she asked, widening sympathetic blue eyes.

"Miss," whined Fred Wishart from the next table. "Miss, get over here right now and get me some more coffee!" He was waving a twenty-dollar bill. There was still coffee in his cup.

Kitten glanced back and forth between Sonny and the bill.

"Get over here now," yelled Arleta, "or we'll call the manager and have you fired!"

The pink lip tucked painfully between little white teeth, "I'm sorry," whispered Kitten. "It's my job, you see, and I have my mother and grandma to support."

She left him, stomach rumbling, alone at his dark little table, and Fred and Bob Wishart elbowed one another in the ribs and pointed to him, doubled over with laughter as they gave poor Kitten all kinds of orders to take this back and take that back, and get them this and that. . . .

You'll have to kill them, said the Voice softly in Sonny's heart, and Sonny thought, *Yeah.*

That'll suit me just fine.

TWENTY

As Shango and Czernas drew closer to Dulles Airport, the wrecks became more frequent, splattering the green countryside. Sweating, exhausted, Shango had a vision of the United States spread westward like some mammoth counterpane, strewn with burned wreckage, with scarred earth and ruined buildings, with smoking fields of metal and seats and burst luggage and charred rubber and soggy, crusted, fly-swarming fragments of people's parents, spouses, children, friends. He dreaded Dulles as a child dreads the coming of nightmare when the first premonitory stirrings of fright invade a dream. *This is going to be bad.*

He was right beyond his grimmest imaginings.

On the some ten thousand acres of Dulles Airport's runways, half a dozen pilots, those whose planes had already extended their landing gear, had managed to bring their planes in at a glide. Others, when their consoles went dark and their engines stopped, tried anyway, without the hydraulics or electrical signals to lower the gear, without instruments. One of these, an American Airlines DC10, had come down on top of an El-Al flight that was trying the same thing and the two planes had rolled, skidded, slid onto the next runway and into a third plane, a Lufthansa. Again—curiously—there was very little evidence of fire, only patches of blackened grass.

The moaning reached them first, like the outcry of hopeless ghosts, and as they came nearer, the growing stink of human waste, like a warning of still more terrible things to come.

The National Guard was there, trying to care for some of the injured and to keep a kind of order. But when, after nearly an hour of searching through the jostling crowds, through the reek of blood and piss, through the endless echoing wails of the injured, of men yelling in frustration and women holding children who wept or rocked and stared and scratched themselves in strange fevers, Shango and Czernas at last found the major in charge, it was clear that tallying the missing, rather than the wounded, dead and dying, was low on his list.

"Are you crazy?" he said, focusing bloodshot eyes on the two men. Soot blackened his face and his clothing; he was shaking with fatigue. "We haven't even gotten all the survivors out of the wrecks! Twenty-four hours we've been working and there are still people trapped out there, and you're asking me . . . Okay, put 'em in the shuttle garages." He turned to a worn and filthy captain, grim-faced and sickened. "See what else you can find for blankets and bandages. Start asking people for clothes from their luggage, anything. . . . Any word on the water yet?" This to another man, a civilian, dirty and beaten as all the rest.

The man shook his head; the major turned back to Czernas. "I'm afraid I'm going to have to commandeer those bicycles," he said. "We haven't had word from headquarters since midnight and. . . ."

Silently, Czernas produced again the authorization McKay had written for them.

The major said, "God damn motherfuckers. How the fuck many of you spooks are coming in? We've already had the CIA and the FBI—What?" A heavy-set woman, in what was left of an Anne Klein suit and a pair of Nikes, had come up behind him with another request. "Well, what the fuck are they? *Who* are they? Gremlins hiding in the goddam baggage tunnels?"

He turned back to Czernas. "I gotta go have a look at this," he said. "I put a guy on getting together a list of planes that aren't accounted for . . . Melker. Corporal Melker." His brow squeezed as if only with the greatest effort could he recall the name. "Stuff was in the computer. Christ knows where the fuck he— What do you mean, hold back a reserve?" He swung around on a green-uniformed major of the regular Army. "What the fuck reserve are you talking about?"

"I have orders that water and food are to be rationed."

"Well, I have fucking orders that water and food are to be given out to people who're fuckin' dying . . . !"

Shango turned promptly away, and Czernas followed. Four feet from the crowd around the major, a big Lebanese businessman grabbed the handlebars of Shango's bike, tried to thrust a handful of money at him; Shango shoved him and, when he wouldn't let go, caught and back-twisted the businessman's little finger. The man screamed and staggered into the crowd. "Let's get up to the tower," he said. "See what we can see from there."

Squads of exhausted National guardsmen and civilian volunteers were carrying survivors in on stretchers. Soldiers shoved a baggage cart half-full of half-empty water bottles, and were stopped by another officer with conflicting orders or maybe just his own opinion about what was best to be done. Someone had designated one of the shuttle garages as a privy—huge hand-lettered signs pointed toward it and requested that it be used—but it was clear from the smell, as Shango and Czernas crossed from the terminal to the tower, that these were not being heeded. Small groups of men clustered around the officers and soldiers, men in white shirts and dress pants, shouting in frustration at the conflicting orders, the miscarried information—the fear.

Fear was in the air. Shango felt himself bristle and

prickle, like a cat at twilight, sensing the rising rage as he sensed it sometimes in the bad neighborhoods of hopeless poverty around D.C.: danger. Rage that's ready to strike out.

He'd been away from the White House, from the President, from his job for twelve hours now, with God only knew how much longer to go. God only knew what was going on in D.C. The same kind of rage, he thought. The same frustration edging toward flashpoint with every miscarriage of supplies, every fuckup.

McKay was sitting in the middle of it. Waiting for the piece of information that might save them all, if he could get it in time.

The door at the bottom of the control tower stood open and unguarded. Shango slid his hammer from its place in the backpack straps and carried it ready in one hand, hiked his bike onto his shoulder with the other hand, led the way up the darkness of the concrete stair. Czernas followed, bike on shoulder—good high-quality racing models, neither vehicle weighed above twenty pounds. Late-afternoon light filled the huge square room at the top from four walls of windows, and beyond those the runways spread like a defiled map.

Shango counted, even as he set his bike down, clamping his mind shut against the horror and the implications of the count. Thirty wrecks scattered across the two-mile runways of Dulles.

Eight were United flights.

More dotted the green countryside beyond, as far as the eye could see.

"There a guy named Melker here?" he asked the lookout reservist, a tough-looking little grasshopper of a woman scanning in all directions with binoculars. She shook her head.

"You guys got any kind of map going?"

The other occupant of the tower, a white male civilian with his left shoulder strapped tight and a bandage on his head, beckoned with his pencil and said, "Help yourself."

It was an inch-to-the-mile scale map of Arlington, Fairfax, Loudon and Prince William counties, and someone had meticulously calculated and plotted the probable locations of all wrecks visible from the tower. Shango could have embraced the gentleman with the broken shoulder, Secret Service or no Secret Service, and never mind what people would say if they saw him kiss a white guy. The wrecks that had been gotten to on the runways already had been circled, but no notation had been made about what flights they'd been or if there were survivors.

"Please don't tell me you're from the Bureau of Statistics," said the lookout corporal, peering at Shango over the tops of her glasses, when he asked.

There was plenty of extra paper and pencils, to copy the map. Someone in the tower, thank God, had had the wits to install an old-fashioned manual pencil sharpener at his or her desk. Shango and Czernas started at opposite ends, marking every detail, not knowing what would be important to know later: Shango noted how neat Czernas' copying was, as if he'd had drafting classes sometime in the past. The growing slant of the afternoon sun turned the young man's drooping forelock to gold, glittered on the stubble of his cheeks.

Now and then Shango would get up, prowl to the windows, stand for a moment beside the silent reservist, edgy with the sense of growing danger. He noticed that not a wreck had exploded, and though many had caught fire and burned on the ground once the tanks ruptured, not one was burning now. Nor was there evidence of widespread fires, only sullen patches of ash. Was this something McKay would need to know, or had he heard already? *Gremlins in the baggage system*, the major had said. Toward the end of last night, rumors had filtered to the command post in the Treasury building about scrunched little mutants in the Metro, in basements, looting in the alleys in the rioters' wake. Shango could imagine what the military boys were making of that.

Down on a runway, a gang of men—a couple of women, too—accosted a group of reservists pulling a cart of what might have been food: a dumb show of shoving, anger, cross-purposes and frustration. Up in the tower, only the soft scratching of Czernas' pencil and that of the guy with the sling as he collated flight information and passenger lists.

The light was failing. Shango knew they'd have to spend the night at Dulles, guarding the bikes, guarding their water. Thank God he'd brought candles. He reviewed the buildings, what he could see from the vantage point of the tower, trying to find a place that wasn't crawling with humanity but wasn't so isolated they'd be trapped in a corner by scared or angry men, or by gremlins, whatever the hell the gremlins really were. Footfalls blundered in the dark stairway, and Shango had his hammer in his hand before a weary-looking guardsman appeared in the doorway:

"Verne? Palmerson? Major Walker's putting together a squad to get those last four planes before it gets dark. You, Blondie, Hammerhead, you better come too. He needs every warm body."

Czernas looked up, doubtful and torn, and Shango went to the door without a word and held out McKay's pass. The guardsman gave it one cold glance and said, "Well, excu-u-use me," saluted elaborately, and went downstairs with Verne and Palmerson, leaving Czernas and Shango alone. A few minutes later Shango saw a small squad, including the lookout corporal and the guy with the strapped-up shoulder, leave the base of the tower, heading out toward the farthest smoking wreck.

Still no sign of approaching vehicles. That meant no water, no food, no relief for the burned and broken and pain-racked. Far out on one runway someone had set up a depot of something—Shango couldn't tell if it was food or water or weapons or what—surrounded by men; there seemed to be an argument going on in front of it.

Night was coming on.

He and Czernas copied until it was almost too dark to see, Shango listening more and more intently to the silent stair-well as the minutes passed. Once he thought he heard noises and walked to the top of the stairs to see. But there was only dark and silence and the stench of piss from the dead rest-room on the landing below.

Quietly, he said, "We better get going."

A big section of Loudon County remained yet to be copied, but Czernas packed up his pencil and sheets without a word. Shango got a candle from his backpack and handed it to Czernas, wishing there were some way he could carry one too, in addition to the bike and the hammer. One light wouldn't be a hell of a lot, in that stairwell.

Gremlins in the baggage tunnels . . .

The flame danced and jigged with the updraft of the stair-well. Door at the bottom left open, thought Shango, strain-ing his eyes to look past the darkness, to look past the next turn in the pitch-black stair. Straining his ears as well, though all he could hear was the click and clatter of the wheels, as they slowly spun with the movement of being carried; the creak of backpack straps and the scrape of the coarse nylon on the walls. Czernas' breathing . . .

Czernas yelled, and as he and the bike crashed down into Shango's back, Shango thought, *They were behind us. Rest-room* . . . Weight smashed him, rolled him agonizingly down the stairs, metal, flesh, concrete jabbing and punching him. The light went out. Hands clutched, gouged in the dark. Someone kicked him, stepped on him. He heard Czernas yell his name and tried to lunge back up the stairs to help him, but the bike caught on something or someone and he was falling again, a man's weight falling on top of him.

"Shango!" Czernas yelled again and then cried out, a mortal cry, and there was a stink of blood.

He came to hearing men outside the stairwell door: "The fuck you're gonna get that bike!" "You said we'd flip for 'em!" "Yeah, well, you guys flip for the other one. . . ."

A moment later, dim and confused with echoes in the darkness, another cry.

Something hot lay against Shango's leg, limp and wet. He groped along the floor: it was Czernas, he identified the light nylon shirt. There was a lot of blood, but he could tell it wasn't pumping out anymore. He felt for his face, to see if there was breathing, and encountered the gashed throat.

All they wanted was the damn bikes, he thought, sitting in the silent dark. *You should have played possum. Why did you call out my name?*

Were you trying to get to me? To make sure I was alive? Was that why they killed you?

His backpack was still buckled to his body, though the water bottles and the outside knife were gone. His whole body throbbed and he guessed the only reason he wasn't throwing up was there was nothing to throw. He sat in the dark beside the body for a long time, listening to the far-off groaning of the injured in the main terminal.

IT'S ON ITS WAY AND IT'S GOING TO BE BAD. As if a door had opened before him into one of the lower rooms in Hell, he glimpsed how bad it was actually going to get.

Was that what McKay had seen yesterday at 9:17, when the earth had shaken and the blue lightning had crawled along the walls, and the lights went out?

If Bilmer was in the terminal still, alive or dead, he'd have to find her. To hunt patiently through the dying and the dead, to keep clear of the quarrels and fights over food, over water, over fear as the confusion and conflicting orders grew worse.

And if she wasn't there, he'd have to go look for her. Look for United Flight 1046, somewhere out in the green countryside that lay beyond the airport. Because McKay had asked him to.

Because if he had to leave McKay in danger, he had to bring back something to show for his desertion.

There was no point in staying longer at Czernas' side. His body would be picked up by a clean-up squad or rot where it lay; that was another one of many things that was no longer Shango's job. He rolled Czernas over, unbuckled his backpack and added it to his own, went carefully over the dark landing to make sure he wasn't leaving a water bottle that the thieves had missed.

Then he drew a deep breath, picked up his hammer and went down the dark stairs to the dark night outside.

He didn't look back.

WEST VIRGINIA

The mist started at about Blackbird Street, a hundred feet or so beyond the trailer court, where land had been cleared in the eighties for a housing development that never came through. It grew thicker among the trees beyond. It was a curious mist, white and thin, but it made little swirls along the ground and Wilma felt the skin on her neck prickle again at the sight of it—the smell of it. She slowed her steps on the cracked and disused sidewalk of Second Street and gestured Shannon, Ryan and Hazel to stay back.

Shannon said, "Be careful! The things I saw—the things that chased me . . ."

"Do you want my spear?" asked Ryan. He'd brought the makeshift weapon with him when he'd come to tell his aunt about what was happening to his eight-year-old brother, Louie.

Wilma only shook her head. "I'm not sure a spear will do any good." They'd already learned, to the chagrin of about eighty percent of the town's masculine population, that the guns weren't working. She moved forward cautiously, the white vapors swirling around her knees. The mist seemed to flatten the shapes of the pavement, the vacant lots, the trees behind them, into a pale matte one-dimensionality that was unsettlingly reminiscent of the expression in Tessa's eyes.

Dampness and cold. It was close to twilight, and maybe time was different; who could say? It was harder and harder to see the trees on either side of the road, but this was not because of mist. Rather, visibility itself seemed to be breaking up. The smell was stronger, cold, like the air after lightning, and there was a sound. Someone crying, she thought, crying at the end of an endless tunnel.

Wilma stepped back with an exclamation as a black flying cloud swirled out of the mist—crickets, cicadas, june bugs, driven as if in a wind. The insects enveloped her, crawling and clinging. Wilma beat at them with her hands, twisted, flailed, clawed the horrid things from her hair, but at the same time felt in each struggling little bug a helpless desperation.

She ran free of the whirling cloud, panting. The crying in the trees was louder. Women running, she thought. She had an impression of long black hair, deerskin skirts, wrapped babies clutched to naked dusky breasts, wailing in pain and terror. Through flesh gone transparent she saw their bones outlined in fire, and then they were gone.

A howling like wolves, like the winds of winter—like ghosts lost along the corridor from one world to the next. The mists around her grew dark with a darkness her night-sighted eyes could not penetrate, and the clammy air grew colder. Walking forward, Wilma saw a bicycle lying beside the road, a young man's body tangled in its frame. Stepping close, she recognized Bruce Swann, whom she'd taught English only a few years ago. Trying to leave town? Trying to come back along the Charleston road?

She shivered, alone in the mist and the darkening silence.

A blue flickering in the darkness, a sudden roar. *Hornets*, she thought, terrified. Swarms of them—she saw the flash of phosphorus reflecting off their wings as they swirled toward her. She ran, desperately keeping to the road. The insects veered and swerved in a pursuing cloud, trying to run her off the pavement, she realized. Trying to make her enter the crowding shadows among the trees. Fingerlets of blue flame licked up through the asphalt, singeing her hiking boots as she fled. More lines of blue flame crept down the trunks of the trees, crawled toward her, and she ran harder, breath coming in sobbing gasps.

A hornet caught in her long gray hair, stung the side of her scalp, the pain a red-hot needle. Under her feet she thought the pavement was moving, rippling, shifting and cracking, but she didn't dare look down. Ahead of her the road had changed, and she couldn't tell where she was: it looked like the squalid unpaved roads that led up to the hollows, like something out of the last century, muddy and narrow. Yet she felt pavement still under her feet. Another sting on her wrist, and she ran still harder knowing a swarm could easily sting her to death. The insects' maddened roar filled her ears, and above it, behind it, she sensed still greater desperation.

Something was in the woods, she thought. Something terrified, frantic, insane. Something that wanted her to leave the pavement and run into its darkness, down its throat.

Lights burned gold before her. The flame behind her roared up, and the hornets howled against it like black hail. Shapes waved and closed in through mist and darkness. Then the vapors thinned, and the shapes became definitely human, holding out their hands to stop, seize, calling her name.

"Wilma!" yelled a male voice, raised a weapon—a spear. "Wilma!"

She stumbled, panting, and looked around in the charcoal mists of evening. She could hear the hornets buzzing sullenly somewhere in the darkness behind her; her head and her wrist throbbed from the two stings. Her hair had come out of its habitual pins and hung down in a scraggly colorless mane over her shoulders, and she trembled where she stood, almost sick with shock.

"Are you okay?" asked Hazel.

She was back at the corner of Blackbird Street.

She had not turned around. She knew that. Had only run forward, continuing in the direction she'd been going . . .

And had emerged from the mist at her starting point, where Shannon and Hazel and Ryan awaited her.

She turned, looking back into the fog that was now dyed with darkness. A voice cried something—words in a language she did not understand—and far away, it seemed to her that blue flames crawled along the ground and then sank out of sight.

She supposed that there were worse things than coming back out exactly where she'd gone in.

She straightened up, still clinging to Hazel's shoulder for support. "Well, whatever it is," she said, "it doesn't want us to leave."

TWENTY-ONE

NEW YORK

With an urgency born of despair, Cal tried to tell Goldie of Tina, as soon as they had gotten clear of the snare and the pandemonium of the retreating nightcrawlers had faded to nothing.

But Goldie, implacable, waved him to silence and beckoned him deeper into the darkness.

Making sure no one was following, Goldie led Cal down echoing corridors, past tracks splitting off into lightless infinity, ancillary current rooms, blast-relief shafts. They eased between the rusted, stilled blades of huge fans, stepped lightly over corroded duct work, moved through silent power substations where ceramic transformers twelve feet high loomed lifeless as stone gods. Rats swarmed everywhere, and the darkness stank of raw sewage and the unburied dead.

At last, a narrow service stair opened onto cavernous space. Neither Cal's Coleman lamp nor the dim gray reflections of far-off daylight from some unseen grating could pierce its immensity, but the hush of the place spoke to its size. In the nearer reaches of wall, the lantern picked out surprising details: cracked, exquisite remnants of Florentine tile, twisting Nouveau railings, brass cuspidors. High overhead, a monumental chandelier of delicate crystal and gilt glinted in the lamplight. Elegant, top-hatted men, women in fine silks and embroidery had lingered here, certain in themselves and their time. Then the station, magnificent as a treasure room, had fallen to ruin, abandoned, forgotten.

Goldie turned to Cal, smiling. "Home," he said.

He threw what looked like part of a chopped-up dining table onto a smoldering campfire, and it flared again, its flickering warmth going a long way toward dispelling the chill that had crept into Cal's bones. Skewered meat cooked on a spit over the flames, skin crackling, the aroma of succulent juices thick in the air.

Now at last, Cal was allowed to speak. The words poured out as from a burst pipe, emotion choking his voice.

Goldie settled in an oak rocker by the fire, began meditatively strumming a guitar. "Bummer about your sister, man . . ."

"Can you help me?" Cal entreated.

Goldie's eyes grew bright. "Can I help you? Get a load of this." He stood quickly, guitar gripped by the neck, scooped up Cal's lantern with his free hand—and threw it on the fire.

"No!" Cal leapt for the lantern, but it was too late. The glass shattered, there was a *whoomph* of ignition. Cal felt the heat flash on his face, his eyes dazzled. Then, incredibly, the flame passed over him, dissipating, spreading like a ripple on a lake, and was gone.

The campfire guttered, nearly going out. Cal sat back on the ground, stunned. Wordlessly, he touched his brow and cheeks, felt nothing more than a tenderness like a mild sunburn.

"Where—" He swallowed, mouth dry. "Where'd it go?"

Goldie removed the spit from the fire, started eating off the skewer. "Good question. Somewhere else. When anything reaches a certain temperature, it just *vanishes*.

Like something's drawing it off . . . to power other things."

"What things?"

Goldie shrugged, held out the skewer with its blackened meat. "Hungry? You should try this. Not bad."

Cal hesitated. Around them hung a ring of smoke where the flame had spread, now misting away to nothing. "What is it?"

"Track rabbit," Goldie said through a mouthful.

"Track rabbit?"

"Rat."

Cal grimaced. Goldie laughed and settled back in the rocker. "Old-style thinking, my man. Thems on bottom gonna be on top now." He tossed another chunk of wood on the fire, throwing up a shower of sparks that danced in his melancholy eyes. "No more Invisible Man."

"Goldie," Cal began and suddenly felt absurd. "The other day, you said you could foresee things. Can you—can you see my sister?"

Goldie's eyes glided over to him. "Cal, I can see everything." He glanced about, as if to be sure of their privacy, then leaned forward in a conspiratorial whisper. "It was like this a long time ago. All the myths are true. Everything is true." He paused, then added, "Ask me how I know."

"How do you know?" Cal found that he too was whispering.

Goldie peered into Cal's face gravely, scant feet apart. Then the corners of his mouth lifted in a grin. A chuckle bubbled out. It grew. In the hushed blackness, a roiling, uncontrollable laughter spewed forth, raucous and loud. Goldie spasmed, held his stomach, bent double with hilarity.

Cal stared at him, unnerved.

Finally, when he could control himself enough to speak, Goldie gasped out, "I read between the lines, Cal, the stone lions. Up the steps into the vastness, where the books are. Signs everywhere but no one to see, no, it took a true omnivore, at liberty, so to speak, time to burn. The ancients got it, some of it, a bit at least. Eratosthenes and Iamblichus and Zhang Heng. Then the modern boys boogied in, R&B, R&D.... The Ordo Templi Orientis, Gurjieff, Von Liebenfels, Hoerbinger and Deibner of the Reich. A *grand jeté* over the Rhine to the Volga, and a Red *frisson* from Petukhov and Emelyanov. The Wall comes down and our own little burrowers join in, Kaiser Wilhelm to Popov to Arzamas to Sandia, spinning, spinning...."

His eyes were wild now, face glistening in the firelight. "Insanely simple, if you know where to look."

Cal's heart was a stone in him, face rigid. "I see," he said, measuring his words. He rose. "I'm sorry. I've got to go."

He was moving toward the entrance now, wondering how—*if*—he could find his way through the labyrinth without his lantern.

"Wait! Wait! No!" Goldie headed Cal off. "I'm going to help! That's what this miracle's all about!" His buttons clattered against each other as he waved his arms, nukes and whales and smiley faces.

Cal backed deeper into the room at Goldie's onslaught, bumped against something hard and uneven. He turned to it—and all thought of Goldie fell away.

Towering over him, unnoticed before in the gloom, rose an enormous pile of junk, thirty feet and more. Castoffs of every imaginable kind: baby buggies and stuffed blowfish, Lava lamps and hair dryers, tooled leather saddles, bus-station TVs in wire mesh, party hats, roulette wheels, even an iron lung. Scavenged from every part of the city for years, a dazzling magpie variety, a masterpiece of obsessive pack-rattery.

Cal ran his eyes along the hypnotic disorder of it, lifted his gaze to the ragged pinnacle. And now he could see, high above the pile in the distant cavern roof, a hole piercing to the surface. It was through this that the shaft of evening sunlight slanted in, dust motes dancing as it sliced golden onto the great heap of useless, coveted things, picking out one brilliant, incredible object.

It was a sword. Not ornate and loud, glittering its arrogance, but quietly assured in its darkened steel, the hand-worn leather of its hilt.

Cal knew it. It was the one in his dream.

A killing thing, he thought, designed to cut through flesh and muscle and bone. It filled him with dread. *If I take this, where will it lead me?*

Nowhere I won't need to go.

He clambered up the hill of marvels and refuse toward it, slipped back, found purchase and climbed. Eight-track players fell away under his hands, CRT monitors shifted and held. He pulled himself over jagged edges of plastic and metal and glass, got tangled in lengths of coaxial cable, tore himself free and kept climbing.

At last, it was within reach. He grasped the cool, welcoming hilt, felt it join to him, as much himself as his heart. He pulled, and the blade slipped smoothly from its prison of debris.

Cal slid back down, leapt the final ten feet or so and landed on solid ground, prize in hand. Goldie came up beside him, silent.

"Where did you find this?" Cal asked.

"Where do you find anything? Someone threw it out."

Cal made a few practice moves with it. It was deliciously, ominously heavy, and light.

"It likes you," Goldie said. "Consider it a gift."

Cal nodded thanks, self-conscious.

Goldie turned to the pile, rummaged about a moment, then pulled a second object free. He turned back to Cal, holding it in front of him, an offering.

It was the scabbard, secured to a belt with a strange worked buckle. Cal seized it, slid the blade effortlessly into it. He thought of Colleen with her crossbow, Goldie with his snare. *To each, by his nature.*

He held the belt out before him, hesitating at this last embrace, then thought of his sister. He secured it around his waist.

"Goldie," Cal's voice was contemplative. "Do you believe in dreams?"

"Very little else." He stepped close to Cal, his gaze calm now, voice sure. "I can help you. Trust me."

From behind his eyes, from the place where he lay curled and hidden, Sam Lungo watched himself and screamed.

Not that anyone could hear him.

Sunset was just settling over the street, washing everything in burnished tones of flame. The crowd had swelled, faces ardent and hungry, eyes gleaming. He held them in thrall, his voice liquid and easy, the words coming effortlessly.

Of course, it wasn't him, not really. It was Ely. Somehow, he had planted part of himself here inside, like a wasp laying its eggs in an insect host. Sam was merely a passenger, a dormant accomplice, like a paralytic after his neck had been broken or a torture victim clamped to a chair.

"What happened to values?" he heard himself call to the eager throng. "What happened to the Golden Rule? Ask the big shots—he who has the gold makes the rules!"

Shouts of agreement erupted from the crowd.

"They've been insulated by their life of privilege, their limos, their offshore tax shelters. But that's all over now."

Folks nodded, an ugly, avaricious look to most of them. In the back, a young man in dreadlocks shook his head. "This is sick, man."

Heads turned toward him, eyes spoke indignation and violence. The young man parted from the mass and was gone. The rest stayed rooted to the spot.

"Only one rule now, friends. Survival of the fittest. And the fittest aren't in Armani sweatsuits on the StairMaster. They're the ones who can smell which way the wind blows!"

Across the street, beyond the crowd, Sam spied a National guardsman listening uneasily, standing watch over a chained-up electronics store. *Ely is seeing this through my eyes*, Sam realized, and felt a distant echo of anticipation. Desperately, Sam tried to move some small part of his body by his own volition—blink his eyes, move a pinky—and could not. *Now I know why Pinocchio wanted to be human*, he thought wildly, and would have shrieked in hysterical, anguished laughter if he could have uttered a sound.

"It's a new day," Sam was saying. "No fast shuffle, no bait and switch. We take what's ours."

A guy in the crowd piped up, "What you talkin' about? Those soldiers got guns!"

"You're right." Sam leaned in, said slyly, "But we have an ace up our sleeve. Wanna know what?"

It was straight line and punchline. From the crowd burst a roar of affirmatives. Sam twisted around and pointed toward a shadowed space between the buildings. "Ely!"

Stern emerged from behind piled crates, stepped lightly onto the street beside Sam. As one, the crowd gasped and drew back. A few screamed.

He was an astonishment. The shredded flesh and pustules and oddly cracked bone had healed to a vibrant efficiency of muscle and claw, covered in tough, pebbled hide. In the darkling light, a muted iridescence gleamed rainbow off his scales of black and brown and ocean green. His folded wings swept high above his dragon's head like a cathedral arch.

Staring wildly at him, the crowd shouted, threatened to shear off, scatter, be lost. Sam extended his arms. "It's all right! It's all right! He's on our side!" Sam wondered how Ely could manage to work his own body and Sam's simultaneously. But then, in the time Sam had known him, Ely had proven himself a man—*thing*—of endless invention and resource.

The crowd quieted, but tentatively, unsure.

Stern's glance slid over them toward the horizon, a mirror of the dying sun. "A visual aid . . ." His voice was a rumble they could feel in their bones.

He swept forward. The crowd parted and followed in his wake, and Sam found himself being force-walked smartly to keep pace. Stern strode up to the guardsman. The man quailed but held his ground.

Stern cocked his head, allowed the hint of a smile. "I imagine you have a question."

Sam could see the guardsman was little more than a teenager, a boy playing soldier in an overlarge uniform. Pimples dotted his forehead, sweat sheened cheeks that had never known stubble. Sam felt a momentary flash of sympathy and sadness, knew there was no action he could take in his marionette state.

Stern held his gaze silent on the guardsman, awaiting a reply. The eyes of the multitude prompted. Finally, in a high quaver, the words came.

"What the hell *are* you?"

Stern's lips split into a broad smile, revealing those appalling, beautiful daggers. "Your death . . . if you don't shoot me."

Stern lunged. The young guardsman's assault rifle sparked. A fleeting but deadly silence—and the bullets fell, clunking like pebbles, rolling back against the guardsman's foot.

The boy soldier gawked. The only sound on the entire street was Stern's laughter, like the echoing footfalls of a giant. Then Stern grabbed the gun, snapped it in two, tossed the pieces contemptuously aside. The boy turned to run, but Stern reached out a taloned hand—almost casually, it seemed—and swept a terrible slanting cut that opened him wide. The boy screamed, and his legs gave under him. Stern caught him, sent him pinwheeling into a wall, where he sprawled, wet and broken and still.

A sound of revulsion rose from the crowd. But Sam suspected many were thrilled, too, guiltily pleased.

Stern turned to face them, and this time only a few

stepped back. "No man behind the curtain anymore. No army, no police." He straightened to his full height, spread his wings so they fanned out over them. In the streaks of the setting sun, they looked rimmed in fire.

"The only thing to fear . . . is us."

TWENTY-TWO

WEST VIRGINIA

Come to us, the voice—voices—whispered outside the windows in the darkness. *Come to us. You're one of us, and we need you, need you, need you if we're to be whole.*

If I/we are to survive.

Fred only clung tighter to Bob. He knew that part of him, the meat part, was still back in South Dakota, where he'd been when that swirling blue-white hideousness had burst the office door from its hinges, swallowed him up, flesh and bones and brain, as it had swallowed the others. He'd seen it happen, as if at the end of a long corridor, or through the wrong end of a telescope, while he'd clutched frantically at Bob.

And Bob had clutched at him.

And here he was, sitting on Bob's bed, holding his brother in his arms and feeling the cold unceasing pull that grew and grew and did not sleep or rest. The pull of Sanrio's will, and Wu's, and Pollard's, and that other Will that was greater than them all. It would pull him in, and he would cease to be himself, cease to be anything except a part of that Thing that was all of them now.

And he sent out his heart and his spirit, gathering, absorbing, drinking in strength and energy from the earth, from the air, from time. From the hearts of anyone his heart could touch, anyone who wasn't strong enough to defend against him, drinking it like coffee, to stay awake. To stay strong.

Just as the Source was doing.

He had to stay strong or Bob would die.

He had to stay strong or he'd be drawn back away and swallowed up.

He heard their mother's footsteps creak through the silence of the house. Followed her with his mind. Reached out to her—it was easy, for she was one of those his mind and spirit drank from, though there was very little warmth in her, very little light. He felt bad about it, bad about draining her, as he'd felt bad that first day when he'd made her go downstairs and tell people everything was all right and to go away. But he had to. He could see no choice.

If he let go, Bob would die. *He* would die. And *It* would be stronger by that much.

He followed her with a fragment of his consciousness, down the hallway—formed precise in his mind, with its new blue carpet and its green-and-white ivy wallpaper—watched as she went mechanically about her tasks. She made food for herself in the pale-blue kitchen, but she didn't eat it, left the sandwich forgotten on the counter beside three other sandwiches already curling and slimy in the summer heat. Filled another glass of water and left it to stand with the others beside the sink. He knew she couldn't go on like this but didn't know what to do. He couldn't release her. He needed every ounce of strength. The windows that looked out onto the side yard, and those opening into the junk-cluttered rear porch, were black with night now.

His mind drifted out over the town.

Drinking.

As with his mother, he was aware a little bit of those others whose energies he drank. Aware of what they saw through glazed, enraptured eyes.

He tried not to see, tried not to think. Guilt stabbed him, worse than the awful guilt of running away from his mother, from Boone's Gap, of leaving Bob there with that frightened, clinging woman who didn't want either of them to leave the house. He tried to tell himself that what he was taking would only be for a little while, and it wouldn't really hurt them. They were children, and children could take a lot.

He saw Dr. Blair taking Deana Bartolo's temperature, shaking his head while the girl's mother and older brothers looked on and whispered helplessly, their faces old and haggard in the gold flicker of candlelight.

He saw stumpy white-haired Marcia duPone trying to comfort Karen Souza, who could not stop weeping when she looked at her child.

He saw Shannon Grant—God, he remembered her when she was nine years old and mowing his mother's lawn!—in quiet-voiced conference with the Hanson girls, glancing every now and then at where Tessa sat like a silent doll. He was aware of the power glowing within Wilma Hanson and wanted desperately to touch it, to drink it, to help himself with it, but he could not pierce her toughness. He could only feed on the children, and on the whispering, ambient strength of air and earth and trees.

What is it? pleaded Bob softly. *I can feel it, I can feel it all around. What's happened?*

It's nothing, said Fred, and though he hadn't even a body anymore, he felt the familiar sickened clenching of his stomach. And then, *It's everything.*

His brother's grip closed tighter around him; he felt Bob tremble with the knowledge.

It's everywhere, Fred said, suddenly grateful to be able to speak of it, to share both the wonder of it and the horror. *I can draw it out of the earth, out of the coal; out of the blood that was spilled in olden times in the woods. Out of the trees themselves, and the animals—out of the shapes of the rocks and the stories the Indians made up about them.*

He thought, but he did not say aloud to Bob, *I can draw*

it out of the hearts of children, where it glows like little embers.

Maybe Bob knew that already. Or would come to know it and would hate him for it as he already hated himself.

I can draw it out of our mother's love and the fear that has dominated her life.

He heard the grunters, coming across the lawn.

GO AWAY! he screamed and tried to call the flames that sometimes burst from the ground when he called upon his powers.

They were coming, ravenous hunger in their white, glowing eyes. Their big knobbed hands gripped tools from the mines, from workshops all over town, from the trunks of looted cars. Their serrated mouths hung open, and they panted with hot little barks, like starving dogs. They'd dreamed about hunger, he thought. Dreamed about everything they'd always been denied.

GO AWAY!

On the porch his mother's romances stirred, fluttered their pages. The heavy couches shifted like restless beasts. Weary, aching, Fred felt the inexorable drag of the Source upon him grow stronger, but he knew what was happening and why. They were coming to kill Bob, coming to cut the cord that held him to this place so that he would have nothing to hold him to life. Nothing to be, or do, or want.

Only the Source.

MOTHER!!!

Arleta was in the kitchen when the grunters smashed the windows of the porch. She fell back against the wall, hands pressed over her eyes, as the house shook with the force of the blows against the door. Frantic, Fred caught up whatever could be used as a weapon and threw them at the attackers: the couches smashing through the windows like enraged bulls, the garden hoses wrapping around their legs and twisting, serpentlike, around their necks, squeezing tighter and tighter. The honeysuckle vines crawling and gripping, tripping and dragging down. Pouring, thrusting, flowing down nostrils and throats to suffocate, strangle, pinch off the circulation of the blood. The invaders writhed, screamed, tore at the tangling attackers while the broken glass of the windows rose in furious clouds, slashing and tearing, blood splattering on the grass.

Get out of here! Get out of here! Get out! screamed Fred, exploding phosphor and fire in the air all around the house, blinding the shrieking things held prisoner around the walls. *Don't ever come back!* Cans from the cupboard, broken jars from the porch, the toaster and the mixer and the waffle iron swept through the windows in a hammering whirlwind, cutting, gouging, tearing. And on the other side of town Tessa Grant screamed, clawed with blunt tiny fingernails at her own face and arms. Terrible and wonderful, Fred drank and tasted the deaths of the grunters around the walls, sucked the lives and the souls from their ruptured arteries, and the flame in him roared brighter.

GET OUT! GET OUT! GET OUT!

They fled, such as had survived, stumbling over the broken sidewalk that heaved and snapped at their legs, and he drummed them with fragments of the house, the furniture, the keepsakes he had known all his life, ripping at them as they fled.

"Get out! Get out!" Deana Bartolo moaned, twisting frantically in her brother Al's arms, and Al and his mother stared at one another in terror at the deep hoarse voice that came from the little girl's lips.

On her front porch in the darkness, Wilma Hanson watched the blue flickering skeletal things run down Applby Avenue, eyes glowing like demon lights. She thought they were the Indian women she'd seen in the woods, old memories of a massacre two centuries ago; the smell of their blood was very strong even from where she sat. The cats smelled it, too, bristling and crowding closer around her chair—and no wonder, she thought—but Carl Souza, hurrying along the sidewalk with a lantern and a makeshift pike, evidently didn't see them. He stopped in his tracks and set the lantern down, turning this way and that, looking for whatever it was he sensed or smelled or heard, but the things fleeted by him and he didn't turn his head.

The night was a humming whisper of needles, even after the three surviving grunters fled from the Wishart back porch, scuttered across the lawn and away into the dark.

The cats hissed softly, then turned and darted back into the shelter of the house.

Wilma stood, looked from the white ghostly bulk of the Wishart house to the dark doorway of her own, where the glowing eyes of her friends clustered like a carpet of fire-flies. "I'm afraid you all have a point," she said regretfully. "But Arleta is my friend, and I have to try."

She went down the steps and across the lawn toward the white house, cautious and listening to the night. There was neither sound nor smell of grunters, but something like greenish foxfire oozed up out of the ground and flowed ahead of her toward the Wishart house, a thin slip like a spectral earthworm; then another, and another. The night had teeth. She felt its breath on her halfway across her own lawn and stopped, knowing whatever was in the Wishart house would let her come no farther.

"Arleta!" she called out, to the gaping black rectangle of the broken porch door. She had little hope, after all this time, that Arleta and Bob still lived, but who knew? Who *could* know? "Arleta, are you in there? Are you all right?"

She smelled blood inside the house, and death, and a kind of slow steamy rot that probably came from the refrigerator. Her night-sighted eyes could just make out the shape of Arleta where she'd fallen, halfway through the door between the kitchen and the porch. There was a savage gouge on her tem-ple where something had struck her. The heavy breadbox, blood and hair gummed to its corner, lay smashed near the steps. It was clear even from that distance that Arleta was dead.

And Bob? she thought. Was his dead body in there some-where, still hooked to the machines on which he'd depended during the last few months of semi-life?

Wilma listened—for breathing, for movement, for the barest scratch or twitch of a moving limb, a groping hand. The porch door was a black mouth, the windows above it dead horrified eyes: the whole house was a frozen scream. She had a sense, for a moment, of something inside, crucified but still living, frantic and in pain.

And she felt it change, drawing strength from its own pain. Felt it remember just how strong it could make itself from the life that filled the world all around it.

But that strength changed what it was.

The darkness around her seemed to shift and settle into being something else. Then silence for a long time and the blue wicker of flame in the downstairs bedroom window.

In time, and listening now behind her with all her nerves, ready to bolt at the top of her speed, Wilma walked back to the house. "Hank," she called, as she mounted the porch steps, padded down the hallway in darkness. "I think you'd better get out here and have a look at this. Tell me what it looks like to you. Hank?"

She pushed open the door of his room.

He was gone.

NEW YORK

Moving with slow deliberation through Tina's room, Goldie ran his hands over her things, eyes locking on the myriad playbills of *The Firebird, Le Sacre du Printemps, Giselle* and the rest, the videos of Martha Graham in *Appalachian Spring* and Patricia McBride in *Sleeping Beauty,* the signed pointe shoes Tina had so joyously scored backstage from Wendy Whelan after *Swan Lake*, all the Danskin and Capezio leotards, the Grishko and Sansha slippers, the faux Degas bookends.

He lingered longest, it seemed to Cal, over the big vanity mirror, as he had over the one out in the living room, the glass into which Tina had poured herself, scrutinizing every

nuance of movement and position, every ecstatic and agonized pirouette, plié and grand jeté. That, and the Nijinsky
diary.

Cal found the greater Goldie's focus, the more he himself
fidgeted, wanted to scream. It had taken forever to extricate
Goldie from his undercity realm, and Goldie had insisted on
hauling along a huge duffel of odd items ("Never know what
might come in handy"), then had set about rigging certain "security devices" before entering the building. Cal had
protested—Stern had his sister; God only knew what he was
doing with her. But Goldie had gone off like a Roman candle,
had almost vanished into the open maw of a plundered restaurant's basement storeroom before Cal had overtaken him, ca-
joled him to return. All right, Cal had agreed fervently, Goldie
could set up any damn thing he desired, but please do it
quickly.

And, to be fair, he had.

Goldie reached the shattered window now, glided fingertips along the base. "Bad vibes. Your sister an Aquarius?"

"No."

Colleen, standing with Doc on the far side of the room,
rolled her eyes. Cal tensed even more. When he had
emerged with Goldie from the steam vent on Fifty-sixth into
the fading twilight, he'd been gone a full three hours—but
she and Doc had still been there, somehow sure he would return, as he too had felt certain they'd be waiting. Cal needed
their faith not to have been misplaced.

Goldie lifted his gaze from the jagged glass, peered con-
templatively out, the cool night breeze wafting his tangle of
hair. Then his eyes slid off, looking off at nothing, or perhaps something inward, distant and intense. It was identical,
Cal thought, to Goldie's expression long days ago, when he
had stood still and certain amid the morning chaos of Fifth
Avenue, before any of this waking nightmare had transpired,
when he had intoned, *"Metal wings will fail, leather ones
prevail."*

"That guy you're looking for." Goldie was speaking to

Cal now, without turning. "Big scaly dude, right? Eight, maybe nine feet tall, not counting the wings?"

Cal felt a flush of blood, urgency seized him. "Can you see him?"

"Uh-huh." Goldie's voice was maddeningly nonchalant. "You wanna see him, too?" He nodded toward the street below.

Cal, Colleen and Doc crowded around the window. The mob was still a few blocks off, hundreds of men and women, moving wild and slow. In the darkness, they seemed almost like a single, savage creature, but Cal knew this was a trick of the light.

Stern was another matter.

The beast stood at the heart of the crowd, towering over the rest, advancing in great, easy strides, a grotesque, ruined angel in the light of their torches. Cal felt a stab of chill certainty that Stern was their leader, had set the madness in motion.

Doc and Colleen stared, awestruck. As much as he had tried to describe Stern, Cal knew he had not come close.

"Sweet mother of God," Doc breathed.

"He's a mother, all right." Colleen's voice was flint.

Cal said nothing.

He simply turned, his eyes falling on the glinting, killing metal of the sword.

The noise swirled about him, and it was dreadful.

Sam's actions were his own once more, but it gave him little comfort. Instead, he felt adrift, abandoned to the chaos. In their frenzy, Stern's followers—they had thought themselves *his* followers so very recently, although Sam had not been allowed the luxury of that illusion—were spreading out like acid, wrecking everything they chose not to claim as their own.

They jostled him, shoved him nearly off his feet unnoticed as they bled past abandoned cars and the tanker that still lay slantwise across the road. They were dismantling his tiny world, and Ely had commanded it!

What would Mother have said, had she been there to witness this mayhem? That Sam had reaped the whirlwind, that he had invited it in. And she would be right, of course, as she had always been right, making him feel ashamed and small and wrong.

It was the old, familiar sensation, magnified a thousandfold, of cataclysm coming on, chaotic and malevolent, himself at ground zero, with nothing he could do to stop it. Mother had said there would be an accounting, had proclaimed it year after year. But she had never stated—hadn't needed to, he now realized—how, in that accounting, Sam himself would be judged.

At least, Ely had ordered *his* house spared. On a whim, it seemed, but Sam told himself he should feel grateful. Although who knew how long that whim might prevail.

A group seized on a lamp post, dragged it down with their brute weight, uprooting it. Sweating, grunting, they hefted it, rammed it against a heavily armored door, sent the barrier flying off its hinges. All the doors slammed in their faces all of their lives seemed to drive them, the unreasoning rejections and exclusions. Sam loathed them . . . and understood.

A roar went up as they poured into the fortress. Muffled screams sounded from within. From other dwellings, faces peered out from around curtains, silent and pale.

From the mouth of the block, Stern looked on in approval. Sam, wretched and heartsick, stepped gingerly over the glass and debris. He stumbled over a piece of rubble, and the sound drew Ely's attention. Stern's barracuda teeth glittered contemptuously; clearly, he had read Sam's mood. "Get used to it," he purred.

A tubby, olive-skinned man tore out of a building near them, a VCR in his arms. Stern swatted it away. "Leave it. It's useless!"

Ahead, the horde had flooded the street. Sam found his

view blocked by a wall of humanity. Suddenly, slicing through the clamor, a voice rang out, powerful and calm. "I used to work for a monster. . . . Now you're working for him!"

Surprisingly, the mob quieted, slowed its advance. Sam's gaze flashed to Stern. Outrage burned on that demonic face, but in the moment before Stern's fury seared it away, Sam spied what he prayed to see there: uncertainty.

Stern blasted through the mob. Sam slipped and wriggled after him, desperate to see what would happen.

Stepping free of the crowd, Sam could see Cal Griffin standing before Stern on the steps of his building, his hand resting on a sword at his hip. The pose should have been laughable, but it wasn't. Griffin seemed taller somehow, straighter.

Stern regarded Cal blandly, rocking on the balls of his feet. "Good golly, Miss Molly. I could've sworn I killed you."

"Where's my sister, you bastard?"

"Language, there are children present." Stern turned to his disciples. "Trash him."

Eyes blinked. A switch, rousing the mob from its torpor. With a cry, they surged forward, brandishing lengths of metal and wood, improvised weapons, comical and horrific. Sam scuttled for cover behind a trash can.

Cal dragged out the sword as Goldie joined him. "Now!" Cal cried.

Goldie made a broad gesture. "BEGONE!" Light dazzled from his hands. Stern's army fell back, many dropping into a crouch, shielding their eyes.

Then Goldie's display sputtered and went out. He turned to Cal, apologetic. "Gutter ball."

From behind a low wall, Doc shot up and hurled a Molotov cocktail at an open space in the mob. It exploded in flames, then dissipated like the fire in the tunnel. But it was enough to scatter them.

Screams echoed from across the street. Cal turned. A

waiflike redhead was being dragged from her apartment house by several burly men. They seemed to be gloating in their power, feeding on her fear.

Cal's hand tightened on the sword's hilt. So much had been taken from them, from them all, the innocents and the fragile. *I will not let this happen.*

And then he was moving, screaming a war cry, a bluff but knowing it wasn't a bluff if they refused to let her go.

He plunged into the group, flailing, all the techniques he'd learned momentarily blanked from his mind, his only ally a blind and absolute determination. The men fell back, one fleeing. But two kept their grip on the girl, and a third made a murderous swing with a length of pipe.

Cal ducked. The pipe sliced the air a quarter inch above his head. Cal shot up, blade held high, then smashed it down. It struck the pipe with which the man now shielded himself, threw off a hail of sparks and sent it flying. Cal was swinging wildly, using his weapon like a club, uncontrolled, unfocused, and then he realized—

I'm trying to kill these men. I'm afraid and out of control and only want them to die.

The realization pierced him like a bullet, both the viciousness of his thoughts and the white terror of impotence behind them.

Abruptly, his uplifted blade swung down into fencing position. And, with this quick movement, killing shifted from necessity into the option of last resort.

Cal lunged—a feint, designed to fall short—swordtip sailing toward one of the captors' breasts. The man flinched back, released his hold just as Cal parried the retrieved piece of pipe, slashed back down to graze the pipe wielder's arm and, without pause, arc back to the girl's second captor.

They loosed their prey, began backing away. The girl gasped, fled stumblingly into her building.

Cal turned again to the mob, and the next moment carved itself in nightmare. Confronting him was a vast sea of angry faces. Stern's dark army. They would do Stern's work, and leave Stern free to do as he pleased.

Cal's brief skirmish, terrible and terrifying, hadn't even marked the beginning.

Slowly, the mass began to close.

"Cal!" Doc sailed a trash can lid at him. He caught it one-handed, positioned it as a shield, stepped backward. Cal sensed the mob gaining courage with even this tiny retreat.

Something inside, deeper than thought, again cried out: *I will not let this happen.* He said, "The first one who moves . . . this goes right through."

He felt no longer himself but rather an electric wire of sheer will in this tiny, firestorm universe. Something in his eyes, his movement, telegraphed that single raw, unwavering message—NO—and he felt Stern's army begin to falter, lose their nerve. *It's not what I'm doing,* Cal thought. *It's what I'm being.*

With a mind-jarring shout, he leapt into their midst, managed to knock a few aside and plow through them to a wall, a guardian for his back.

His sword shot up before he was aware of having seen the two-by-four sweeping down. He blocked it, kept fighting, gradually inching back, losing ground. There were so many. Five driven off, ten more behind. Slowly, very slowly, he backed along the wall as the pack closed in.

"Let him be!"

The voice rumbled through the mob. Stern's army broke off. Turning, they drew apart like black clouds, leaving an open corridor between Cal and Stern.

"He's mine."

Stern flashed his murderous smile. Cal's gaze locked on Stern; he resumed edging backward along the face of the wall, nearer to his own building. Slowly, Stern closed in, taking his time.

"Goldie!"

Stern followed Cal's gaze, swiveled his head to regard the lanky figure. Goldie stood by the brownstone, clutching an electrical cord that ran up through an open window into the building. He gave it a sharp tug.

There was a sound of release overhead. A big, weighted net flew through the air, fired via some kind of improvised catapult from atop the building, sailed toward Stern.

Cal stood frozen. The whole street went still and watchful.

Stern canted his face upward. Taking a vast, deep breath, he hesitated, then exhaled a dazzling great gout of flame.

It blazed green like some hellish firework and twisted toward the sky, struck the webbing and seared it to nothing. The weights rained down about Stern, clattering harmlessly.

Goldie, still with the cord in his hands, said numbly, "I think we've got a problem."

This shouldn't be happening, Cal thought in the stunned silence. Not with what Goldie had shown him at the campfire, the explosion dissipating, the flame guttering out.

But then this was a new kind of fire, fed by where *that* fire had gone, and by the white-hot rage of this demon he had once served. A fire, like Stern himself, capable of anything.

Stern grinned at Cal. "Surprise." He reached out to him with razor claws.

Suddenly, an arrow flashed through the air. Stern gasped as it struck him in the arm.

Colleen stood beside the Volkswagen that had been shielding her, the crossbow in her hands, already reloading. She fired another shot.

This caught Stern in the shoulder, spun him. Cal seized the moment to dart past, get clear.

Stern wheeled on Colleen, glaring. "You *woman* . . ." He swept the arrows off his body, took a deep inhalation, the inferno rising in him.

Fluid crashed into him, drenching him. The scent of gasoline hung pungent in the night. Stern bellowed, twisted around to see Cal standing by the derelict tanker, still aiming its hose at him.

Cal's voice was low and deadly. "Try your fire trick now." He pulled a lighter from his pocket, flicked it. Stern cringed.

"Where's my sister?"

With a howl of rage, Stern grabbed a bus bench, ripped it free of the concrete and hurled it at Cal. Cal dove aside as it smashed to the pavement. Stern took off running back the way he came, scattering the crowd in his blind charge.

Cal was on his feet now, running, waving toward Colleen, Doc and Goldie. "Don't lose him!"

In the dim, creepy house, Tina stirred fitfully. There were sounds outside, but they seemed distant in the heat haze of her fever. She had been getting better, but somehow being near Stern had made the sickness flare with new ferocity. It churned in her like a living thing, worked its will. In her delirium, she saw blurry, indistinct figures, enticing her. Sometimes, she fancied they were Petrushka and Odette and the Firebird calling her to the dance, but then they would shift into other forms, some human, some not, and the place they beckoned from was a dark haven she had never known.

The front door burst open, rousing her. She opened her eyes to see Stern, gleaming with wetness that steamed off his hot skin. He tore down the gauzy curtains, wiped furiously at himself. "Damn, that stings!"

Footsteps sounded from outside. Through the open door, Tina saw Cal running toward the house, followed by the woman and man who had been in her room and also another man. She cried out to them, but Stern grabbed her up in his rough arms.

He brought his ghastly face down to her. "I'm sick of this dump. How about you?"

She fought to form words of protest but found she could only moan. Stern strode toward the window.

Sam banged the back door and burst into the room, wheezing hard. The import of the scene burned instantly into his mind. Ely was leaving, and he was taking the dancer girl with him—to whatever dark destiny he chose next.

Amazement washed over Sam, he couldn't believe it. The genie, the dread genie would be gone, and miraculously Sam would be spared, left alone. The dancer girl, it would be *her* turn to reap the whirlwind, wherever it chose to spin her, even tear her apart in its brute savagery.

But she hadn't invited it in. Sam had.

Ely was almost to the window, his broad wings stretching out. He would have to smash out the glass, perhaps even the frame, to fit through, but that would be nothing to him. No amount of destruction ever was. Sam hung back in the shadows, breathless and watching. The little girl hung limp in Stern's arms, and she looked so small, so fragile, not like a real person at all.

Her eyes opened, all depth-of-ocean blueness, and found Sam in the shadows. For just that moment, Sam felt swallowed in her gaze, recognized the desperation and despair there, the helplessness and humanity. Then her eyes slipped shut, and the connection was broken.

Hang back, the voice in Sam cautioned. *Do nothing, and they'll be gone.*

But his legs were already working, rapid, little steps that quickly overtook Stern. Sam stepped in his path, blocked his way.

"I can't let you, Ely," he said simply.

Stern advised, "Move aside, Mr. Mole."

Sam felt dizzy, sick with terror. His hand sought out an end table for support, and his fingers brushed the Loetz silver-overlay vase that had been Mother's favorite, a precious thing in a houseful of precious things that populated his life, that had never been his. Sam's glance held on Stern's face, so magnificent and appalling.

"I can't," Sam said.

The girl's eyes half-fluttered open, and Sam thought he

saw comprehension there, that she knew what was happening. Stern drew in a deep, warning breath.

Sam's fingers closed about the Loetz vase, and he brought it up in a swinging arc. The light in the dim room caught it, and it gleamed blue and black and green iridescence, like Ely himself.

Just before the flash, the sound like a furnace flaring to life, Sam saw the glass shatter against Stern's face, had time to think, *That will leave a mark.*

The dolls, in all their delicacy and indifference, watched Sam burn.

TWENTY-THREE

NEW YORK

Down the street. She had been there all this time, only three houses down, and he hadn't known, hadn't suspected.

From his living room window, Cal could still see the embers of what had been Sam Lungo's house, pulsing darkly in the night, wisps of smoke curling weakly, the stench of charred wood and flesh heavy in the air. In the firestorm that had enfolded it, the roof had crumpled, timbers falling in on themselves, throwing up a firefly swarm of sparks and ash. Mercifully, a breath of summer rain had come and quenched it, and the blaze hadn't spread.

The street outside was empty now, but it bore witness to the maelstrom that had passed through, windows broken, chunks of pavement gouged out, nameless fragments scattered wholesale as if some giant, willful child had played his roughhouse game, smashed his toys and moved on.

It was a new world indeed, one where men—or what had been men—could see in the dark, shoot light from their hands, fly. New gifts of power but, clearly, none of insight. Cal felt he'd been given no gifts at all, only a dream in which he'd seen the ridiculous sword that hung at his side, but what use had it been? He was a man, nothing more, and that had proved achingly inadequate.

Standing nearby, Doc caught Cal's expression. "If you'd like to crucify yourself, I could get some nails." But there was sympathy in his eyes, a forgiveness Cal could not grant himself.

" 'Scuse me." Goldie slid between the two of them, stepped lightly to the window. He cracked it open, lifted a potted plant from the sill and upended it without looking, dumping dirt and greenery onto the thankfully vacant street below.

The earthenware pot now empty, Goldie cradled it in one arm, gliding along the periphery of the room, his free hand outstretched, hovering above each object like a psychic metal detector.

"Déjà vu all over again," Colleen sighed, to no one in particular.

"Symbolism is very important when it comes to visions," Goldie said, not stopping, not looking at her. "You burn something as a token of what you want to see. In this case, we want to view something that, yesterday, sanity would have told us was . . . ah."

He snatched a copy of TV Guide off the television, said to Cal, "You won't be needing this." He dropped it in the pot. "And, um, if I could trouble you for a light. . . ."

Cal fished in his pocket, tossed Goldie the lighter. Goldie plopped cross-legged down in the middle of the room as the others looked on. He set the pot in his lap, then shot his cuffs. "Nothing up my sleeve."

He flicked the lighter. A thin blue flame shot up, which he angled to the edge of the TV Guide. The pages started to smolder, blacken, curl like moth wings aborning.

Goldie bent his head and began to mouth words under his breath quickly, blurred in a droning mantra. He repeated the incantation, gaining in speed and intensity. He rocked from the waist, davening like a Hassidic rabbi, eyes screwed shut, mouth working. Cal strained to make out the words, caught several syllables, a snatch of phrase. Something about not believing what you hear, only what you see. . . .

Goldie was intoning the lyrics to "I Heard It Through the Grapevine."

Colleen hissed, "This is such bullshi—"

"Shh," Cal cut her off. For the smoke rising from the burning digest was becoming something more, resolving into a vague, rectangular shape, a flickering cascade of light playing over it just like . . .

Snow, on a television screen.

The shape hovered above the pot, smoke framing it, the lilt of Goldie's words a soft, toneless music. In the darkened room, the light from it illumined their faces, stilled in wonder, even Colleen's.

The screen—for such it was—began to clarify into an evanescent image, shimmering as though seen through a rain-slicked window. Quickly, it gained substance, took on weight and solidity. The object was beautiful and ornate in its war of Nouveau and Déco. The gilded, dark gleaming stone stood cold against a malevolent night sky.

Of course it was where Stern would go. Cal felt the chill rise through his veins.

Goldie let out a soft groan. The image folded in on itself and winked out. The fire died, the magazine consumed.

Goldie opened his eyes. His face shone with sweat, and he was trembling. He looked up at Cal with regret. "Sorry, man, couldn't hold it."

"It's all right," Cal murmured.

The Stark Building—Stern's office, and his—stood waiting.

Cal and his cohorts advanced toward the building cautiously, alert for any assault, but it proved needless. The street was deserted, shut up tight, no light in any window. Fitful gusts spun bits of paper about their feet and ankles. A pale, uncaring moon lit their approach.

Drawing close, Cal peered at the brooding structure, towering over its neighbors, its stylized lightning bolts and stars of steel and gold whirling about doorframes and ledges. In his mind's eye, he had a vision of how this building, this street, would look in a hundred years, a thousand, vines choking its stones, birds shrieking from empty windows, as lost to memory as Angkor Wat or Machu Picchu had been.

This place had served its purpose, and now it was done, abandoned by those who had used it, left only to monsters.

The Stark Building's massive doors had been locked, but that proved no impediment. Colleen, as part of the maintenance crew, had a key.

The lobby, however, proved a surprise. When Cal had last seen it, it had been a vast, open space, airy and clean. Now it was a wreck, dust hanging thick, a charcoal stench in the air that caught at the back of his throat. Both the staircases and elevator shafts were trashed and scorched, ragged chunks of concrete piled high in them, tumbled like a storm of meteors, blocking all passage.

Stern wanted no visitors.

So now they stood outside again, staring at its black immensity, hard against the night sky.

"I don't suppose you have any spells to conjure up a helicopter," Doc said to Goldie.

Colleen set down her heavy shoulder bag and unzipped it. She withdrew coils of rope, nylon harnesses, bags of chalk dust, tapered aluminum wedges.

"I'll let you know what I find up top," she told Cal, securing her crossbow across her back. She took a step toward the sheer face, but he reached for her shoulder.

"Nobody goes unless I go," he said.

She scrutinized him with a baleful eye. "You ever climbed anything but a corporate ladder?"

Cal shook his head. Colleen pointed out that it was suicide for him to attempt a climb like this and, when Cal refused to be swayed, brought out every colorful epithet she could remember from a childhood of Air Force bases and low-rent dives.

Through it all, Cal was gently, maddeningly deaf to protest.

In the end, she handed him a harness.

Doc stepped up. "You know, I fancy a little exertion myself."

"Sorry, Ivan," Colleen replied, "just got the gear for Rory and me. Two's the limit."

"My first name is not Ivan," Doc noted.

"Someday, remind me to ask you what it is." She turned to Cal and smiled grimly. "Ready to climb, farmboy?"

"This city's finished."

From where he crouched high on the roof's edge, Stern could see pallid lights flickering here and there on the black, unknowable surface of the city, like maggots on a corpse. It was a dying thing, he had known that for years, had only forgotten it momentarily in the heady exhilaration of his new birth.

A gentle moan issued behind him, a sweet sound. He turned to see the girl stirring. She lay a few yards off, so delicate and untainted, nothing like the bitch predators that had circled him, smelling power and money.

A few long strides, and he was bending over her. She looked up at him with distant, appraising eyes. If she was afraid, she wasn't showing it. He liked that.

Her skin was pale as lace now, with only the finest mottling, a hint of robin's egg blue along her cheeks and brow, a porcelain tint that reminded him of a cup and saucer he had seen as a boy and coveted. Sweat fever damped her face, but it only highlighted her cheekbones and eyes.

"Excuse the rough handling. Feeling better?"

"Where . . . ?" She pressed herself partially up, drawing to the roof's edge to peer at a bottomless drop. Wind caught her fine, blanched hair, whipped it with insolent abandon.

"Where you can rest . . . and let it all go."

She cried out then as blue energy sparked out of her pores, splayed across her body in a mad dance. Her back arched at the white agony of it, and he felt a swell of sympathy, knowing firsthand her pain. With an angry snap as of an electric arc, it sucked back into her body and abated.

"What's happening to me?" Her words were gasping exhalations. "You *know*. . . ."

"Don't be afraid. It's just a transition."

"To what?"

"I don't really have to tell you that, do I?" The girl said nothing. Stern made his earth-rumble voice as soothing as he could. "Give in to it."

"That's what you want." Resistance flared in her eyes.

"That's what is."

His words struck home, he could see it. The fire in her eyes, like the color leeching out of her skin and hair, faded to nothing, replaced by an unreadable blankness that might have been despair. "To be . . . like you."

Like him, yes, the one he had been waiting for so very long, his own self mirrored back. But gentled, with none of the scalding rage that had ravaged every waking hour of his life. She would calm him, be a balm to his soul. And thinking this, it was as if a door in him were opening, and through it he could see the black emptiness that had been his life, the terrible loneliness he had ferociously denied. Emotion surged in him; he wanted desperately to slam that door.

He feared how much he needed her.

A shudder wracked her, and she fought hard to bite back a whimper. He drew up close, knifeblade hands hovering over her, a benediction.

"Soon you'll be past the pain . . . where no one can touch you."

Rory's leather climbing shoes with their sticky black rubber soles were a tight fit, but Cal managed to squeeze into them. Colleen eased into her harness, the black nylon looping around her waist and thighs, then she secured Cal's. She taped both their hands and chalked them.

As Doc and Goldie looked on, Cal craned his neck to stare at the mocking immensity of the building, water dribbling off the wild projections that made up its disturbing asymmetry.

Colleen studied him, her skillful hands loading the loops on her belt with slings, stoppers, the other vital paraphernalia. She thought of Cal back on his block, facing down that mob, driving them back with that absurd sword of his, so crazily determined that he had pulled off something that never in a million years should have worked.

Surveying this building, he had that same look.

She thought of her dad in his combat fatigues long ago, teaching her aikido and tae kwon do, telling her that practice and coordination and knowledge only got you so far. In the end, the one with the edge was the guy with the hunger, the one who needed something so badly that nothing, absolutely nothing, would make him stop.

Her dad, in his best moments, had been unstoppable. Rory had never been.

You that guy, Griffin? she wondered, and felt an old hope flare in her, which she labored to smother.

She turned to glare at the structure. Eighty-two stories straight up, with a cherry on top that breathed fire. She sighed. "Hell, if George Willig can do it . . ."

"George—?"

"Climbed the World Trade Center in the seventies. But then, he was fucking crazy."

Cal peered again at the summit, forever away. *Or maybe he just needed what was on top to go on living.*

"Show me what to do," Cal said.

Colleen went first, climbing quickly and elegantly, finding purchase for her hands and feet in tiny crevices, irregularities in the slippery, pitted stone surfaces. Cal stood on the ground, paying out the rope tied to her harness. This cord wasn't for climbing but rather for safety; every twenty feet or so, Colleen rammed spring-loaded devices—little aluminum plugs with plungers like hypodermics—into whatever crack or indentation would hold them, feeding her rope through metal cables in the cams, creating a network of braces to assure she would fall so far and no farther. A belaying device affixed to Cal's harness would provide the friction to slow the rope in case of a drop and allow the cams to do their work. As her belaying partner, Cal had the easy part of the job—keep a grip on the rope.

After a hundred feet or so, Colleen found an outcrop, a pigeon-fouled, scowling patriarch. She clambered atop it, anchoring herself with four or five cams at different angles. Then she fed her rope through a twin belaying device, and it was Cal's turn. He started up, tied to her rope, trying his best to replicate the hand and footholds he'd seen her use. The rain-slick surface was treacherous, and he slipped repeatedly, flailing wildly, somehow managing to find a hold and not fall.

It was a battle of inches. The sword banged against his thigh, throwing him off balance, and the banshee wind cascaded up from the corridor of buildings, snatching away his body heat. Before long, his fingers and biceps and throbbing head were shrieking protest.

"Let your legs do the work, not your arms!" Colleen shouted from above, voice nearly lost on the wind. "And try to rest your weight on your skeleton, not your muscles!"

Easy for her to say. But after a time he got the rhythm of the thing and it grew, if not easier, at least manageable. He surrendered his mind to the flow of muscle and bone, levered himself ever higher. He spied his hands, blisters coming on, bloody and raw as they slid up the rough, cold stone. He remembered how Tina's feet had been like that when she had first gone on pointe.

He reached the outcrop, pulled himself up trembling.

Colleen's eyes gleamed in the moonlight, appraising him. "How you doing?"

"I'm doing it."

"Are all your family this bonehead stubborn?" she called over the wail of the wind. Beneath her words he heard grudging admiration.

"My mother was . . . and my sister."

Colleen nodded.

They would rest here a moment, then continue. Another fifty feet and another and so on.

Stern could fly . . . but they could climb.

The waves were coming faster now and with greater insistence, labor pains of a thing giving birth to itself. The girl lay panting at the edge of the rooftop, her breaths shallow and rapid. Cool light oozed out of her mouth and ears, trickled from the corners of her closed eyes, dripped off her fingertips like blue quicksilver.

Stern had backed some yards off, wary of impeding its progress, and squatted, watching her.

"There's this philosopher, Hoffer," he mused, not knowing if she could hear him. "He said, 'What monstrosities would walk the streets were men's faces as unfinished as their minds.' Me, I thought, no—*beautiful*. Nothing more to hide . . ." He caught the smell of ions wafting off her, and something like burning flowers. "I always knew I was different."

She turned her head to him, opened her eyes against the pain, the liquid current washing over her.

"You knew, too, didn't you? Well, what if—" Under her gaze, he felt timid, fragile. "What if the lonely days for both of us were gone?"

At the fourteenth floor, Cal discovered the stairwell no longer blocked. He and Colleen took the rest of the journey upward inside the belly of the building, and so were able to recover strength. A service shaft on the top floor led to the roof. Crouching within the low structure, Cal insisted on taking point. So he was the first onto the roof, cracking open the shaft cover, hauling himself across the raised lip and stealthily dropping down.

He was surprised at the jumble that greeted him: a ramshackle penthouse of wood frame and glass that had seen better days; hulking, water-rotted packing crates; corroded fuel drums; big squares of tarpaper curling leprously across the deck.

His eyes scanned the dark contours, searching. A blue glimmering caught his eye. On the far side of the roof, maybe a hundred feet off, a pale nimbus, and in its midst the frail, prone form of his sister. Backlit by the gleam, turned from him, hunkered the brute shape of what could only be Stern.

Keeping low, Cal crept forward. He could sense Colleen close behind, unslinging her bow. Approaching, he discerned the croon of Stern's voice on the wind. "Away from this sinkhole, soaring like two damn prehistoric hawks . . . to the west."

Tina rose up on her elbows, the sickly blue radiance like mold glow on her. Her eyes were on Stern, she had not yet seen Cal. "There's a wave."

Stern straightened with excitement. "Yeah, yeah, that's right. You saw it, too."

"To the west and," Tina's voice came haltingly, Cal had to strain to hear it, "and the south, like an artery pulsing off it."

"We're tuned to the same station, sweetpea. The *whatever* that caused all this, it's calling us." Stern stood and stretched hugely, gazed out over the changed, dark city, the East River beyond. "Soon we're gonna own the world."

Another wave crashed upon Tina, and she crumpled with a strangled cry. The St. Elmo's fire flickered down to a mute guttering that licked at her skin. Her strange aqua eyes found Stern again, held on him as she whispered, "I don't want your world."

With a surprising burst of strength, she bolted upright, made a stumbling dash along the edge away from him, toward the open drop between buildings.

Stern gasped in alarm, shot an arm toward her, but she was beyond his reach.

Unmindful of himself, Cal shouted, "Tina, don't!"

Hearing him, she stopped, wheeled around, nearly pitching off the side. But she righted herself, just barely, and sank to one knee.

Stern too had swiveled to face Cal. "If you'd shown this much initiative on the job, I'd never have fired you." He took a single murderous stride toward Cal and drew in a deep, merciless breath.

The arrow caught Stern just above the collarbone, spun him so that the torrent of flame missed Cal by a good three feet. It raked across the tarpaper, igniting it.

Cal dove behind an exhaust outlet, saw that Colleen had managed to take cover behind a pile of crates. Stern rained a flamethrower stream of crackling green hellfire on her.

The crates burst alight in a glorious, mad consumation that no natural source could any longer have kindled, only Stern or some devil-kissed thing like him. Colleen scrabbled back quickly, gained shelter behind a concrete stanchion. Stern closed on her, the endless exhalation blasting the concrete white hot, fiery contrails ricocheting off it. Colleen struggled to reload her crossbow, lift it to aim, but the onslaught was too fierce; it drove her back against the roof's edge.

Stern swept aside the melted stanchion, exposing Colleen, leaving her defenseless. Cal took a running leap off the exhaust outlet and landed atop Stern's back. Stern screamed in fury. Twisting and bucking, he shot flame from his mouth like napalm, slashing across the roof. The penthouse caught like an oil-soaked rag, rusty drums detonated in volcanic plumes.

Then Stern's firestream cut off at last. Stern cursed and spun, trying to reach behind him, fling Cal off. But Cal dug his fingers into the armored ridges of Stern's shoulders, held on fiercely. The roof was an inferno now, sheets of angry flame dodging about them. Frantically, Cal sought out Colleen and Tina but couldn't see them as he careened atop Stern.

"Get off me!" Stern shouted as they lurched toward the edge. He leaned sideways like a swooning man and plunged over the side. Cal clutched Stern's neck, clinging to him. He heard a scream—Tina's—but it was swallowed in the wind that pummeled him. His stomach rose nauseatingly as the building fell away.

The black street rushed at them. Cal felt a ripple of powerful muscle beneath him, Stern's great wings unfurled with a snap like a bedsheet, and they were soaring, whirling and swooping, rocketing crazily above Fifth, the dark towers on either side grim cliff faces, dizzying blurs. Stern's wings pounded as Cal clasped the leathery furrows of skin, tightened his legs about Stern's massive waist. Harsh, staccato rasps were coming off Stern, beast sounds that might have been crazy, raging laughter.

Abruptly, Stern veered sideways, rammed into a building face, scraping along its edge. The impact flared pain flashbulb bright behind Cal's eyes, and he was flung loose, only saving himself by grasping a spur of bone projecting from Stern's spine. He clambered back, again locked his legs, hunkered down close.

Stern howled, threw himself from side to side against the buildings as they whipped by. The blood was loud in Cal's ears; he snatched breath as the wind tore past. And then Stern tilted up sharply, soared above the level of the buildings, wings hammering the air as he rose.

Stern slashed through the night sky, climbing fast, dozens, then hundreds of feet above the tallest spire. They were almost dead vertical. Cal grasped Stern as though trying to merge with him as the world fell away.

They pierced a cloud, and Cal felt the damp kiss of fog on his face. The steady rise and fall of Stern's respiration throbbed beneath him like a huge bellows, and he found himself matching his breathing to Stern's.

Almost lazily, Stern angled over, dipped below the cloud layer. He was gliding now, banking in a wide, descending spiral.

Then he folded his wings and dived.

The change was so abrupt, it caught Cal unawares. Blood rushed to his head, he fought to keep from blacking out. They were spinning, shrieking downward. Cal felt his body lighten, the pull of gravity ripped away under their savage velocity. In a rush, he saw clearly Stern's intention to hurtle toward the pavement, then pull up at the last minute, certain the momentum would wrench Cal free, smash him into the asphalt like an offending bug.

Stern was screaming now, a primal howl that matched the wind and challenged it. Cal found himself screaming, too, but he couldn't hear it over the din, only feel the raw outrage in his throat. Fighting down vertigo and panic, Cal made out a blazing rectangle rising swiftly to meet them, knew it for the roof of the Stark Building.

A sudden, desperate hope seized him. Stern was slowing his rate of spin now, gauging his target. Cal held his breath as the rooftop neared. He locked his legs about Stern more firmly, dared to loosen his arms. He sought out the scabbard at his hip, closed a hand about the wrapped leather binding of the hilt, eased out the sword as they thundered down.

The fiery summit was only yards away now, below and to the west of them. In an instant they would sweep past, and the moment would be lost.

Steeling himself, Cal gripped the sword in both hands, raised it high overhead and—with a cry that surged up from the core of him—rammed it between Stern's wings.

Stern screeched in anguish and surprise as the blade pierced through hide and meat, splintered bone. Blood geysered up, drenching Cal in a sickening hot stench. Stern's wings spasmed, flapping reflexively as he curled in on himself, tumbling.

It was the effect Cal had prayed for, as wind resistance slowed Stern's plunge, at least marginally. He tore the sword free, launched himself clear into space, toward the roof. Stern plummeted like a downed bomber, was lost in the blackness between buildings.

Cal smashed into the lip of the rooftop, went flailing across the surface, blasting through a curtain of green flame and halting thankfully on a bare strip of concrete. Shakily, he rose to his feet, slapping away burning ash, sheathed his blade. A blast furnace roar assaulted him, the heat was appalling.

"Cal!" He spun to see Colleen, smudged but unharmed, thirty feet off near a wall of flame. He ran to her, caught the desperation on her face. She nodded toward the barrier.

Through the flames Cal spied his sister standing on the precipice, the unbroken line of demonfire advancing, backing her inexorably toward the drop.

There was no way to reach her.

Colleen hocked a shaft into her crossbow. Her voice was grief, a whisper. "If you want, I could . . ."

"No!" Cal said. He cast about for some answer, some tool. But there was no water, nothing to quench or smother.

Through the leaping, killing flame, Cal locked eyes with his sister, saw terror there and a forgiveness that cut to his soul. She was moving her lips, speaking to him, but he couldn't hear her over the wail of combustion. Sparks of blue energy spat from her pores, flared swimming across her skin.

And then the fire surged up to her, and she reeled back from it, off the edge into space. Cal screamed. A blue flash like lightning erupted from her, and she was lost from sight. Flame shot off the roof in a long tendril toward where she had been, as though drawn by a vacuum, whipped about in midair, coalesced into a tornado of fire. It wheeled and swelled, drawing fuel from the rooftop, inhaling ravenously.

Like a molten sea emptying out, the fire gushed to the edge, cascaded into the whirlwind until the roof was free of flame, a wasteland of char and smoke. The funnel was spinning faster now, an impossible blur throwing off blazing fingers. It grew brighter and more frenetic, contracting upon itself, squeezing down to a pitiless core, dazzling white. Then it exploded.

The blast knocked Cal off his feet, blinded him. Dazed, the afterimage strobing in his eyes, he groped, found a handhold, the stone still hot, searing him. He dragged himself upright.

He could see a little now. Colleen stood with an odd light shimmering over her, childlike with awe. He followed her gaze past the lip of the building to the space beyond.

There Tina, or what had been Tina, hovered in a nimbus of light, an opalescent play of midnight blue, yellowjacket, carnelian weaving over its surface. Her face seemed broader yet more fine-boned than before, her skin blue-veined marble, lips thin and bloodless. Her ears elongated to fine points that thrust outward through hair that, albino silk, wafted about as if underwater. Her clothes too drifted weightless, the sphere of light about them seemingly a shield from the world's forces.

Cal thought of the boy he had glimpsed in the tunnels, who had fled at his sight.

Tina was regarding her hands abstractedly, the fingers El Greco long and nail-less, turning them this way and that. Then she glanced up, and her eyes met Cal's. They were all blue save the vertical pupil, with no whites showing, and blazed such a savage cobalt they seemed lit by an alien fire. Her mouth twisted in a bleak grimace, and he saw to his dismay that her teeth were triangular razors, like a shark's. *What are you?* he wondered. She seemed so inhuman.

But then she began to weep, and he knew he had not lost her, at least not fully. He stretched out his arms, coaxing her, and she came floating to him. His arms pierced the boundary of light and then his face, effervescence tingling on his skin. But Tina was solid, and his arms enfolded her as she cried.

Devil night. That's what old Granny Marxuach had called it, making him tremble and quake back when he was a little pissant on the *rancho*. All the demons and witches and hell shades take to the sky, so you better dig yourself under the covers and keep tight your soul.

But Papa Sky hadn't believed any of that crap for the better part of eighty years. Real life had been woolly enough.

His own brand of night had come on him back when he was straight and smooth-skinned and fine, his hair black and gleaming like oil. At first, it had been merely ripples in his vision like smears on glass, then a fog, and then darkness.

Still, it hadn't been all bad. He hadn't had to watch himself grow bent and lined and worn, a lank tree that had stood too many storms. And he had his axe, the 1922 Selmer alto sax that was part of his body, that he could make sing like Jesus himself humming. Blind as he was, he could still cut his own reeds, shaving down the Le Blanc bamboo with the straight razor he kept by his bed, in the one-room walkup he'd had since that glory night when he'd subbed for Johnny Hodges with Ellington at the Cotton Club.

How New York had changed since then. The elegance and grace and courtliness had sluiced away, leaving the young who had never known it desolate, abandoned, longing.

Of course, it had changed a good deal more in recent days, now wasn't *that* the truth. He could smell it in the wind, feel it on the air. And the stories he'd been hearing, like hophead D.T.s out of Bellevue. Some crazy badness was running the streets, no two ways about it.

But for some reason, no one messed with him. He'd gone about his business, gigging on street corners for quarters and dimes, that butterscotch sound booming up sweet and mournful along the concrete canyons. And the take had been *good*. The coins jingled warm in his pocket, a tambourine accompaniment to the tapping of his fiberglass cane as he made his way home along the uneven stones of the familiar alleyway. He'd sensed the desperation in the listening ones, their fear. They needed to be soothed, and maybe that was the answer: they hungered for just one thing that wasn't all screwed up, even if it came wafting off some old blind black Cubano.

And sometimes, when no one else was around, there'd be a soft shuffling of something in the corners, swaying to "Body and Soul," to "Stardust," saying nothing. He'd catch a musky stink at those times, and a shiver would run up his back. He'd be glad he couldn't see whatever it was that was hearing him.

Now it was late night, the summer heat leeched away and the cold seeping into him as he eased along the path like a shadow, his case clutched tight, the axe silent and drowsing.

Ahead of him, a low moan sounded, a timber that swelled and tremored through him. A hot liquid iron smell assailed him, like a whole lake of blood, like a slaughterhouse.

He was seized with a panicky, frantic urge to turn, bolt headlong away, never mind what he might plow into, what stick-thin chalky bones might snap.

But then the moan faded down, was broken by something like a sob of pure anguish. *This cat's in a world of pain.* Papa Sky's heart rose in him. *And he's alone, in the dark.*

Tentatively, he stepped forward. The tip of his cane found a shape along the ground, resilient and large. He could feel heat radiating off it, hear a raspy, resonant breathing.

Nervously, Papa Sky licked his lips, tongue running over the ridges of callus. "How we doin' there?" His throat was dry, the words shaky.

The breathing stopped, and there was a long, hanging silence. Finally, a voice croaked through the pain, "I've had . . . better days."

Papa Sky laughed, and there was tenderness in it. He bent down, put a gentling hand on the figure's back. Slick with blood, the leather felt hard as armor, bone projected at odd angles.

"Well, you just take it slow." Papa let out a breath that would have been exquisite through the axe. "We gonna see what we can do for you."

TWENTY-FOUR

NEW YORK

They got Tina to the apartment without incident. Fortunately, few were out on the lightless streets. She drifted between them as though air had become water, as though the gravity and atmosphere she inhabited were of an alien world.

Her tears subsided, Tina drew back from Cal, from, it seemed, his touch, and did not speak all the long way home. Stung, Cal ached to hold her but did not press the issue.

Once safely inside, Cal let Doc examine her. He changed his clothes, cleaned the congealed offense of Stern's blood off him as best he could, then joined Colleen and Goldie by the open window of the living room. Peering silently out at the night, they were drinking coffee made on the camp stove. Cal braced his shoulder against the side of the frame and let the cool air waft over him, grateful for the quiet. His mind felt washed out, his body leaden.

In the room behind, he became aware of a growing darkness. The shine about Tina that had cast the space in shifting pastels had softened. He glanced to where she sat curled on the sofa, or rather floated just above it, her face to the wall. Doc rose from her side and approached him. Even in the gloom, Cal could see his face was disturbingly pale, drawn. He motioned Cal off a bit from the others.

"Is she suffering?" Cal asked. "I mean, is she in pain?"

"No, I don't think so. Not physically." He looked to Tina, and Cal saw that Goldie had joined her, crouching by the sofa, his lips moving softly.

Doc turned back to Cal. "The plan you had before, it was a *good* plan. Smart people are leaving; they sense what's in the wind. High time for you to leave, too."

"And what about you?"

Doc looked toward Tina; pain flashed in his eyes. "Calvin, if my bag of tricks could help her—" He trailed off, shook his head. "Roosevelt General might have use of me. I don't think they'll be too picky about credentials."

Cal thought of the dreadful corridors crowded to bursting with the stunned, frantic ones. "You sure you want that?"

Doc nodded, then fell silent. Cal sensed a tension in him, as if he were deciding whether to speak further. Finally, he said, "There were those in Ukraine—Chernobyl—like a light had gone out in them. They could summon no hope, you understand? And they would want . . . an end."

"What are you trying to tell me?"

"Calvin, your sister, she asked if there was something in my bag that could—she wanted me to—"

The air in the room suddenly felt cold. Cal shivered. Doc's fingers brushed his arm. "I'm sorry, my friend, but I thought you should know."

❦

As he drew near the sofa, Cal saw that Tina had fallen asleep. The glow about her was gone and, cradled by gravity, she lay on the deep cushions, her hair like spun glass across the pillow.

Goldie squatted nearby, singing softly to her, a sweet, mournful hymn. "There is a balm in Gilead to make the wounded whole/ There is a balm in Gilead to heal the sin-sick soul. . . ."

Seeing Cal, Goldie cut his song off and rose.

"Thanks for finding her," Cal murmured.

"Hey, Mr. Keene, Finder of Lost . . ." Goldie's voice faltered; he grew serious. "Sorry, man."

Cal nodded. Goldie left them alone. Cal settled in the tatty burgundy recliner. Tina looked younger than her years and troubled even in repose, as ever. But she was terribly changed.

She wanted to die. Anguish flooded him. A vicious wind was battering her, trying to tumble her away, to sever them.

Whatever caused all this . . . it's calling us, Stern, that psychotic monstrosity, had said. Could it be true? If so, what in God's name did it want them for?

Cal felt a brightness on his face and jolted awake, realized he had dozed. Tina's eyes were on him, mosaic tiles, turquoise, unfathomable. Her aurora shimmered outward, and her hair drifted off the cushions as in a current.

"Tina."

She turned from him, toward the wall. An impotent rage rose in him at her despair. He fought it down, spoke softly. "I couldn't stop what happened to Ma, I couldn't keep us safe—but we're still here."

"Am I, Cal?" Her eyes found his, and her voice was a whisper. "Am I, really?"

"*Yes.*" He reached a hand to touch her, but she flinched, gaze averting, and he let it drop. Then, for a reason he could not have given name to, he added, "To the west and the south, there's a power."

Startled, she again faced him. "Yes." There was music in her voice, subtle tones accompanying. Her glance diffused inward, on memory. "In bed when I was little, I'd hear Mama's records through the wall. It was like the melodies were reaching inside, you know, like they were pulling me."

"And that's what this is like?"

She nodded. "Only . . . not beautiful. It's jangly. Scared and angry and sad. Sometimes . . . I dunno. Crazy. I hear it all the time, getting louder. Telling me there's something I have to do."

"What?"

She shrugged, not knowing. "But if I stopped fighting it, if I let go . . ." She looked at her bloodless hands, the nimbus casting shifting colors on her like stormclouds coming. "Near the end, when Nijinsky was in St. Moritz, he went for a walk in the snow at night. He heard a voice; he thought it was God. It told him to jump off a cliff into the darkness, that he wouldn't fall. . . ."

"Did he jump?" Cal asked.

Tina nodded. "A tree caught him; he hadn't even seen it. He climbed back up, went home. But it was the moment his whole life changed. He went from being what he had been to . . . what he became." Cal thought of the glorious, singular moment that had been Nijinsky at the height of his brilliance and prowess, and the forty years in the asylum that had followed. Tina's face twisted. "I don't want to go into that darkness, Cal. I'd rather—rather—"

"I know." He reached to stroke her starlight hair, and this time she allowed it. The pastel luminescence around her eddied about his fingers, sparkling off them. At the far side of the room, Goldie had settled near Doc and Colleen, strumming his guitar softly, the music drifting with no particular tune.

Within the corona of light, Tina's eyes had closed again, not sleeping but meditative. *She's hearing it even now,* Cal thought, this pitiless force with its grasp on her. *Perhaps on all of us.*

He wanted to run, take his sister and hide. Some dark hole, some mountain fastness. But *where?*

Where wouldn't it find them?

Then suddenly, her words registered. "Tina?"

Her eyes opened.

"It's getting louder . . . stronger?"

She nodded.

"When you say it's to the west and the south, is that one location, or two?"

She considered, cocking her head, seeming to listen to a sound he could not hear. "Two. The one in the south's weaker, kind of confused, like it's—" She intertwined her fingers, pulled at them as if battling.

"In turmoil?"

"Yes."

"Anything else? I mean, can you tell what it looks like, what it is?"

"I don't want to."

"I know, but *can* you?"

Again, that concentration. "No. Only—there's these words I keep hearing in my head. Wish . . . Heart."

"Sounds like part of a prayer. What do you think it means?"

"I dunno. Maybe . . . it's a place?"

"A town?"

She took in the thought, searching, but over what unsettled landscape Cal could not guess. At last, she whispered, "South."

"South," he repeated. "Tina, is this a place you can find?"

Her face flashed alarm.

"You feel it's growing stronger. Like something forming, but maybe not formed yet. Supposing—"

"*No.*" She shook her head vehemently. The aura about her flared up bright, and Cal felt an unseen force shove against his chest, press him and his chair several inches away.

Cal touched his breast. It didn't hurt but felt momentarily numb. He wondered how strong the power filtering through Tina might be, how controllable. Somehow, he managed to keep his voice calm.

"Tina, do you remember—maybe not, you were really small—when I came home from school and you were so upset because the Gage boys had set out those squirrel traps?"

She had withdrawn into herself again, behind the angry slashes of moving light. After an aching silence, she said, "I remember."

"We'd sneak out after midnight, you'd help me find them."

"And you'd break the lock from the inside, like they were super squirrels." Though she wasn't smiling, her face held an animation, a vibrancy, that summoned back a sweet ghost of what she had been.

He shook his head, the recollection was so vivid. "They were so damn *mad* and so damn sure it was a trick. Only—"

His eyes again met his sister's. And it was the two of them again, spliced in the tide of remembrance, before law school, before New York. Together, they said, "No more traps."

Cal smiled, the chilled hollow within him sparked warm. He didn't know if Tina had the strength to save herself, or the willingness to let him try. But he knew her heart, and what it encompassed.

"What I'm thinking about," he continued, hesitant, "is all the other ones. The ones who hear it calling, who *can't* resist." This time, she didn't look away. "What if—before it gets any stronger, while it's still in turmoil—we find it? What if—I don't know how yet—but what if, together, you and me, we could stop it? What if we could save them?"

She was gazing at him now, into him, weighing all the myriad hopes and dreads, the territories they had journeyed over and might yet encounter.

Doubt iced through Cal. Perhaps he'd just be hastening her death, or worse. But it was as if he were looking at an hourglass, the sand ever more swiftly running out. And he didn't know what else to do.

Tina's aura faded into its cooler colors. Concern etched her face. "It'll kill you, Cal."

He said nothing, let silence answer. Then he asked, "You think what Nijinsky heard was God?"

It wasn't what she expected. She contemplated it. "No."

"If somebody could've stopped that voice before he jumped off the cliff, what do you think would've happened?"

She stared at Cal through her shimmering haze, and he

felt, astonishing and harrowing, the current of her faith in him.

"He would have kept on dancing," she said.

Toward dawn, Tina fell into sleep at last. Cal withdrew from her side and sought out the others. He found them in his room. Doc lay across the bed, dreaming fitfully. Colleen sat curled in the big chair, napping, but with a wary tension that reminded him of a sleeping cat. Goldie sat cross-legged on the floor, still fingering his guitar. *When does he sleep?* Cal wondered, and the thought came back to him, illogically, *Never.*

Although Cal strove to keep his footfall soundless, the creak of the door roused Doc and Colleen. Blinking, they turned to him, inquisitive.

"We'll be leaving as soon as I can get everything together." His gaze swept over them. Strangers who had become so much more than friends. In words awkwardly, embarrassingly inadequate, he began, "There's no way I could ever hope to—"

"Listen," Colleen bounded from her chair, trying for an easy tone. "I been thinking of stretching my legs, so if you and Miss Emergency Flare could stand some companionship from the other side of the tracks—"

"No," Cal said, and it hit her like a blow, her surprise at his rejection cutting him to the heart. "It would be great, Colleen," he added quickly. "But there's been a change of plans."

Goldie lost just a beat but kept on playing, while Doc drew up beside them.

"At first, I thought we could run from this force that's gotten into Tina and Stern and who knows how many others, get somewhere it couldn't reach us, reach her. But Tina sensed—*saw*—it's far off, part of it to the west, part—the weaker part—to the south." Cal gazed through gauzy curtains onto the city. He thought of dying things, and the kind of life that fed on them. "If it can reach us here, I think it probably . . . I don't know where it's safe."

"And so what do you propose to do?" Doc asked quietly.

"She's still plugged into it. Like a receiver that's off the hook. If she can home in on it, we might be able to locate the part that's not strong yet."

"And then what?" Colleen's tone was glacial.

"Strike at the heart of it, if we can, and make it *stop*."

"This thing that can smash the world to pieces? That can shoot lightning from the sky? Boy, Griffin, it's not enough for you to launch yourself from the top of a skyscraper latched to some fire-breathing dinosaur—"

"That's why it has to be just the two of us."

Colleen's green eyes flashed protest. But before she could speak, Cal put his hands on her shoulders. "You've done enough."

All of Colleen's bravado deserted her then; she deflated. "Fine." She stormed out of the room.

"*Colleen . . .*"

Doc shook his head. "Calvin, my friend, I don't want to presume to tell you your business, but I'm going to tell you your business."

"Doc—"

"Kindly sit your behind in that chair and cease speaking." Doc cut off Cal's protest. "*Sit.*"

Sighing, Cal sat.

"You may have noticed that certain events have been transpiring around us, demanding we extend ourselves to new and surprising heights. I think we are in a process of transformation. Not physical, all of us, but . . . in other ways." Doc moved closer. "I know it feels terrible. Painful. Frightening. Some won't even survive, but that's how birth is."

"What are you getting at?"

"Calvin," Doc's tone now gently scolded. "Three days ago I was serving hot dogs on the street. I could smile, make jokes, but I was a dead man. Or at least, in deep coma. And Goldman here. A derelict soul, friendless, living—" He gestured the image away. Goldie continued strumming, seeming not to have heard. "And you. A timid rabbit in a business suit, denying who you are."

Doc's eyes shifted, followed Colleen's path of retreat. "As for her . . ." Cal caught something, or thought he did. A tenderness. "Well, you would know better than I. But my point is, we are all of us changing, perhaps rising to something we might only have dreamed of. A purpose. A *destiny*. Is any of this getting through to you?"

"I'm not going to lead you to your death."

"*Olukh*!" Doc erupted. "Didn't you just hear me ask you to lead me *away* from it?"

They glared at each other, the lilting tones of the guitar swirling between them.

"What about Roosevelt General?" Cal asked finally.

"A good doctor goes to the root of the malady." He shrugged. "Calvin, if I could have walked into that reactor, shut it down before its poison reached out to the men, their wives and children . . ." And here Doc thought of his own dear Yelena and Nurya, gone to aching memory. He did not tell Cal. Let the dead have their secrets.

"The pestilence spread because there was no containment vessel," Doc continued. "Here, perhaps, *we* can be that vessel."

He crouched before Cal, grasped his hands. "You are a leader, Calvin, that is your *self*. And if you deny it, you weaken any chance you might have for your survival or your sister's. It is arrogance and stupidity, two traits you have not evinced of late, so I would advise you not to start. If any of us care to follow you, *let us*."

Cal peered into the lined, compassionate face. "And what if I'm wrong?"

"Then you're wrong."

After a long moment, Cal nodded assent. Doc grinned. "*Speciba*," he said. "Thank you."

Cal rose. He felt like one big bruise. Only then did he notice the tune Goldie was softly playing, nodding to himself in the golden dawn light.

"Let's Face the Music and Dance."

Goldie lifted his eyes to Cal, and they were glistening.

He feared she might have left the apartment, but he found her in the kitchen.

"Christ, I hate instant coffee," Colleen murmured, tossing the flat, cold remnant of it down the drain.

Cal said, "I'm sorry."

She knew he wasn't talking about the coffee. They both looked down, avoiding each other's eyes. He moved closer. She took a step back.

"No water in the pipes, I'm startin' to reek like a pair of old socks."

"Try getting the smell of blood out of your hair . . ."

"Hey, the day's young."

Silence settled over them, oppressive. At last, Cal broke it. "Colleen, Doc and I had a conversation . . ."

She lifted her eyes, their brightness returning. "Yeah? Russkie set you straight?"

Cal nodded.

The tension in her shoulders relaxed. "So you're not gonna march into the mouth of hell."

"Well . . . yeah, I am. But Doc and Goldie are coming, too."

"Shit." She averted her face, and Cal had the impression that tears had sprung to her eyes. She swiped a wetness from her cheek and turned back. "You know, when the Wizard told them to get the Witch of the West's broomstick, it wasn't any fucking worthiness test—it was so they'd bite the big one and be fucking out of his hair."

"Look . . . I know it's crazy. It's . . . I just don't know what else to do."

"You'll die."

"Can't promise that for sure till I get there."

Colleen glowered.

Cal said, "Sorry I'm letting you down."

"You?" Surprise lowered her defenses. "You've been a brick."

"Sure you don't mean 'p' instead of 'b'?"

"Nah. I know the difference. You're talkin' to a connoisseur."

She gazed out the window then, the light full on her marble-fair skin, her eyes glinting jade. He watched her, saying nothing, wondering if she was reflecting on the long night and what remained for her in this broken city.

"Maybe hell's a real fun place," she said at last. "No way to know till we get there."

And though he felt weary and weighted and grim, Cal felt himself smiling as she looked back at him.

WEST VIRGINIA

A man named Jerome Bixby wrote a story called, "It's a *Good* Life," in which the inhabitants of a town were trapped in the tiny, completely arbitrary confines of their village by a child born all-powerful, unhuman and mad.

Wilma had always hated that story; hated the nightmare of helplessness it implied, the subjection to unknowable power and rules.

She thought of it many times, in the days and weeks that followed the grunter attack on the Wishart house.

Seven or eight people tried to leave Boone's Gap in the twenty-four hours that followed Wilma's attempt. Two made it back to town, scraped and scared and hornet-stung and exhausted, with tales of things heard and seen in the mist that started just beyond the confines of the town. Al Bartolo, who was gone three days, reported finding the bodies—or what he thought were the bodies—of Phil and Nancy duPone, who'd disappeared into the mist shortly before Al's attempt. He wouldn't say what had killed them, but he said over and over again that they were definitely dead.

No one and nothing came into the town. No news, no hikers, no supplies. On the third day Gordy Flue dug a garden in the ground that had been cleared for the housing development, planting beans, potatoes, peas: anything that would grow into late fall. Within days a dozen, then a hundred, followed suit. Hazel got the town council to push through emergency measures pooling and rationing foodstuffs and regulating water. Lookouts were posted daily with binoculars, scanning the blue summer sky above the white wall of the mists.

By Dr. Blair's count, thirty-five children were taken with the same malady that gripped Tessa Grant, that terrible symptomless silence. The night Deanna Bartolo slid into a fathomless coma despite all her mother's attempts to keep her from the void, Chrissie Flue cried out, in her sleep, screaming, "Don't! Don't!" before lapsing into absorbed contemplation of nothingness from which she could not be roused.

That night, Wilma walked the streets of the town in the darkness, until dawn stained the sky. Watching, listening, searching, though for what she did not know.

Shannon had brought her the news about Chrissie. Shannon, haggard, gray-faced with exhaustion, almost as gaunt as her daughter, who like every other one of the affected children had whimpered and struggled at the same time Chrissie was deadened. *It's spreading*, thought Wilma, after the young woman left her again, sitting on her porch in the darkness. *And it's getting worse.*

She put on her jeans and sweatshirt and set out on a patrol that had become almost routine to her, checking what she mentally termed the Hotspots of Boone's Gap. She met no one. Everyone locked their doors and shuttered their windows with the setting of the sun. This was partly for fear of the grunters, though at her suggestion, the town council laid out rations for them near the mineshaft and for the most part this had ended their raids on individual houses.

On her nightly prowls Wilma always had the hope—or the fear—that she'd see Hank, but so far she had not. Worry for him, and the aching sense of what could have been, settled in the back of her mind like a constant, like the arthritis in her wrists that had somehow vanished that first night of the Change.

But other things, too, now walked the nights.

Where Shenandoah Drive crossed Main Street, even the unimaginative saw blue lights flicker and bob. Some, like Ryan, said they saw what seemed to be human figures, or skeletons, dancing or writhing, and heard their cries. Only Wilma, evidently, could see the Indian women and their dead children clearly, could smell their blood thick in the night air. But she always wondered about the dead grunter Gordy Flue found there one morning on his way to weed his crops, the one they had all recognized, despite how dreadfully he had changed, as Joe Rance, who'd worked at the garage on Front Street and had disappeared that first day.

And on the unkempt streets leading to the old Green Mountain shaft Wilma saw nightly the ghostly shapes of the rioters of '37, heard the shouting of long-dead policemen, the crack of rifles and the slap of mahogany on flesh. Sometimes she had to take cover from the swirling cyclones of maddened hornets that whirled through the darkness, but not tonight. Sometimes there were other things, dark small things like clots of hair and bone and mist, impossible to see clearly. Sometimes only green crawling streams of energy that flowed up from under the soil, or out of the dark maw of the mine.

Tonight as she watched the trickling streaks of light from an alley behind a gutted store building, she felt the tension in the air explode and saw strange ghostly fire erupt in one of the abandoned cars that still littered the streets. Sparks ignited a blowing newspaper, carried the blaze into an empty saloon. Wilma turned and ran, pounded on the door of the city watch headquarters in the old high school. The fires spread, but never grew: instead they burned with the queer slow smoldering that everyone had become aware of in these changed terrible days. While the Fire Patrol was putting them out, others burst spontaneously into being nearby.

And beyond the fires, energy flowed and swirled.

She could see it, almost. Smell it, ozone sharp in her nostrils. Hear the crackle of it in the dark air, shouts and wailing and gunshots that blended into a deep soft rumble, like a monster breath. She didn't need to follow it. She knew where it went.

Only near dawn did she circle back, after visiting every one of those places in the town—and there were nearly a dozen of them—where she sensed energy of some kind was being drawn out of the ground, out of the mine, out of the past. Silently flitting from shadow to shadow, night-sighted eyes probing the darkness, she returned home, to catnap and rest for a day, to lie in the sun and wash, which she did with dampened facecloths six or seven times a day, not because she needed to but because it made her feel better. And in the darkness, as she turned the corner of Applby Avenue, she paused as she always did, shivering though the night was warm.

Shivering at the sight of the white house. At the smell of it. At what she knew from her dreams was inside.

Whatever it was, it was drawing energy, drinking it from every corner of the town. Drinking it desperately, frantically, racked and crucified and twisting in terror and in pain. Grunters had made another attempt to break into the house, and one of them could still be seen—Eddie Dayton, it had once been— dead just outside the porch, strangled with the garden hose. The smell was appalling even at night.

Did the grunters know something about it she didn't? Was that why they tried to kill it, making attempts that they had to know would only lead to their deaths? She wished she could find Hank and ask him. Wished, more than anything, that she knew where he'd gone, and if he was all right.

Whatever it was, she thought, it was definitely generating a chaos of old pain, old horrors renewed.

And unless it was stopped, Wilma knew in her bones, it would destroy the town and everyone in it.

NEW YORK

Cal draped a canopy over the passenger section of the pedicab so that, once inside, Tina could not be seen. The rough
blanket was thick and dark, and what little of her illumination leaked out along the edges appeared no more than the
glow of an oil lamp. Disappearing into its folds as it sat in
the living room, Tina seemed thankful to be out of sight,
shielded by this fragile barrier.

They would keep her hidden as much as possible. There
was no telling how many might be like her. Cal had seen at
least one other "flare"—Colleen's joking reference was
sticking, he reflected—in the tunnels under Fifth. But as
they traveled on their odyssey south, they would draw un-
wanted attention as it was; any stranger would, in this perilous world. The more they could avoid attention, the better.

In the gray chill of morning Cal, Doc and Colleen wrestled
the pedicab down four flights of steps, and everyone in the
building helped them carry duffels and backpacks and water
bottles down. They strapped the provisions onto the rusty old
bikes Goldie brought from his underground treasure trove—
or trash heap, depending on one's perspective. Colleen had
ridden shotgun to fetch them. On their return, neither had spoken of what they'd encountered on their mission. But Cal had
noted Colleen's relief at being aboveground, and the dark
stain on her shoulder of blood that was not hers.

Goldie was unusually quiet this morning, limiting himself to terse replies when pressed. Cal observed, too, that he
had jettisoned his familiar multilayered electric wardrobe in
favor of somber browns and blacks. Protective coloration?
Cal wondered. Or was Goldie afraid to be striking out into
the unknown, too?

The unknown, indeed. For while Goldie and Colleen had
been off on their errand, Cal and Doc had pored over every
map in the place, had borrowed dog-eared Auto Club guides
from Eleanor Sparks and the Jamgotchians, and had found
no town of Wish Heart or any like name to the south. Or the

east, west or north, for that matter. Whatever siren call might lie southward, be it in Mississippi, Orlando or Tierra del Fuego, they would be seeking it in the dark.

All they could plan with any certainty, for now, was their route out of the city.

"I can get you through the old test bore of the Brooklyn subway line, no problem," Goldie murmured, the morning heat starting to come on as they muscled the last of their supplies downstairs. "I know the guys who live there; they'll let us through."

Cal thought about the smears of blood he'd seen on the subway platforms, the snuffling of the crouched figures in the dark and the predictable unpredictability of Goldie's bag of tricks. "Uh, I think Tina would probably be better off aboveground."

"If we take the Queensboro bridge, we can work our way down through Brooklyn and across the Narrows on the Verranzano," said Colleen, adjusting her crossbow over her back. "We can be in Staten Island tonight. Cross to Jersey tomorrow. And then . . ."

Then what? Hope that Tina's line to Nijinsky's Voice of God or whatever it was didn't disconnect until they had time and fortune to find it.

Into the mouth of hell . . .

They told Mrs. Sparks and Sylvia Feldman and the other neighbors who crowded around them on the street that Tina—unseen, enfolded within the protective canopy—was resting now, had been utterly exhausted by the previous days' events. The tenants nodded solicitously, pressed sandwiches on Cal to give his sister when she awoke, brooked no objection as they bestowed extra cans of tuna, bottles of Gatorade.

Colleen stood watching this, part of her scoffing at their generosity. They'd regret it soon enough, when their shelves were bare and their bellies rumbling.

Yet surprisingly, she found herself heartened, as well. It was foolish of them, perhaps suicidal. But what she was doing was suicidal, too. And for what?

For him.

When her dad was a non-com at Offutt Air Force Base, she had come running in tears at some casual cruelty of her mother's. Holding her, rocking her, he had tried to explain that Jean lived in a world of coldness, that they two lived in a warmer clime. Colleen hadn't comprehended it then, nor even years later.

But now, looking at Griffin and the well-wishers who surrounded him, pointedly not speaking of their fear and uncertainty, offering what little they could, she had a glimmer of understanding.

There would be terrors ahead, Colleen was sure of it, homicidal, raging nightmares to make Stern look like a cartoon in the Sunday funnies. The world had turned into a grim, hard place, and it was still turning. That was real; that was *so*.

But how many of her neighbors would have turned out to bid her farewell? How many even knew she existed?

We make our world, she thought, *at least some of it*.

Maybe in days gone by Griffin had bartered his soul in increments to Stern. But through all of it, she felt certain, he had been a decent, caring man, and people had responded, been warmed by it.

Colleen anticipated a hard road ahead, full of nothing but impediments and adversaries and, almost certainly, a very messy death.

But, thanks to Griffin, there might be allies ahead, too, even new friends.

As she had become.

A world of surprises, and not all of them bad.

Bullshit, she thought, pushing it away. But the feeling stayed with her a good long time.

They set off, west across Manhattan, for the Queensboro Bridge. As they were leaving Eighty-first Street, passing the fallen, charred timbers of what had been Sam Lungo's house, Cal—pedaling hard against the weight of his sister and their baggage—heard a murmured litany from the canopy behind him. Reaching back, he parted the fabric and saw his sister within the halo of her phosphorescence. "For Mr. Lungo," she said. But whether she was entreating mercy for him of their mother's God, or of the thing that called to her, he did not ask.

Tina had told Cal of Lungo's last moments, of his valiant, futile act. *We're changing, all of us*, Doc had said, and it was true. A week ago, Cal wouldn't have dreamed Lungo capable of such a thing.

You won't be the last of us to die, Cal thought and, though his own faith had been shaken and splintered long ago, he sent a silent prayer alongside his sister's.

They made their way across midtown in the hard, merciless light, the concrete-amplified heat. The air, rank with sewage, thrummed with flies. The people they encountered moved quickly past, many openly carrying weapons or objects that could serve as weapons.

It took them two hours to get across the Queensboro Bridge. The metal span wasn't choked with people, not yet; that would come in the days and weeks to follow, if what Cal dreaded came to pass. Only three days in, most had not seized the initiative. But without water, without lights, with its food supplies hemorrhaging down the hungry throats of six million people each day, New York would soon be little more than just predator and prey. As it was already starting to be.

Dying things, and those that fed off them.

Already, the refugees heading outward numbered in the hundreds, perhaps thousands. Many no doubt lived elsewhere, had gotten stranded in the city and had finally jettisoned waiting for the fix that would reanimate the cab, the plane, the train. Scared people, angry people, desperate people, pushing shopping carts full of bottled water or liquor, confused people with satchels and suitcases and shoulderbags. A heavy-muscled fat woman with a mouth like a trap herded eight small children, each loaded with luggage, like little pack beasts on a rope. Three college kids pushed a dumpster full of bags of flour, books, blankets. An elderly man walked a bicycle so loaded down with bulging plastic bags that he could barely be seen. And everywhere, nuclear families and extended families and the haphazard, improvised surrogate families that outcasts from all corners had created in New York. White, brown, black, yellow people and every permutation between, helping one another, shoring each other up, trying just to get to the end of the bridge.

Then what? Did they know, any more than Cal himself?

As they came off the long exit ramps and pushed out of the crowd into the streets of Queens, Cal drew to a halt and glanced back. Manhattan gleamed in the sunlight, the Empire State and the Chrysler Building so regal and fine at this distance.

He remembered the day he and Tina had arrived here from Hurley, with such hopes, such dreams. The golden city.

"A zloty for your thoughts." Doc rolled up alongside. "I'd say a ruble, but everyone knows they're worthless."

"I guess," Cal struggled to find words. "It's hard to let go."

"Of the past."

"More . . . the things you hoped for." He thought of Tina's promise of greatness, the fire of her certainty in it. Perhaps all gone now, melted like snow.

Colleen was looking back now, too, and the image of Rory came to her. She felt a stab of regret, an unreasoning guilt at having failed and abandoned him, and wondered what subterranean passage he might be gliding through. *Hell of a way to end a relationship . . .*

Goldie, still oddly muted, peered back at the city.

"Anything you'd like to add?" Cal asked.

Goldie addressed the island, its silent spires. "We'll write when we get work."

Cal thought of Stern, of those he had led and destroyed.

Of Rory and his monstrous brethren in the tunnels. Of the lost and broken ones in the hospital corridors and on the streets. Of the rivers of blood that had burst upon them all and whose currents were now carrying them to who knew what dark source.

The Change that had smashed everything, that was devouring them all. A force of nature or something conscious and malevolent? *Scared and angry*, Tina had said. *Sad and crazy.*

That made it conscious, then.

"Whatever caused this," Cal murmured, "it's one sadistic bastard."

And we're gonna kill you, if we can.

They crossed the Verrazano Bridge the next day, with the smoke of a thousand individual fires curtaining the sky to the north.

III

CALL AND
RESPONSE

TWENTY-FIVE

"This way, I think," said Tina, when they crossed the third bridge, the one that took them off Staten Island and into New Jersey, and she pointed southwest, through a tangle of smoldering buildings, looted stores, gutted cars and smoke.

Cal cringed inwardly, and Colleen said, "Oh, great. We get to ride a nice straight line through Philly, Baltimore and D.C."

"Wouldn't surprise me to hear it's in D.C.," remarked Goldie, peering into a shaving mirror he'd mounted on his bike's handlebars and mopping hydrogen peroxide on a cut above his eyebrow. A pack of young men had rushed them as they were coming off Goethals Bridge, trying to take their bikes, the food, the weapons. It had been no more than a skirmish, but it was an indication, Cal thought, of what might lie ahead.

They avoided the cities. When they could, they avoided the smaller towns as well. Cal took to studying the map more closely and kept to the countryside.

Now and then they'd see bicycle messengers or fleet-footed rollerbladers streaking along the silent highways, heading for New York or the next town up the road that had a militia company, slaloming among the motionless cars. Once, they found the body of one such messenger, broken and bloodied and discarded, his wheels flown. Cal had cautioned Tina to stay in the folds of her canopy, but she had insisted on viewing the dead man and had remained silent, brooding, long afterwards.

"Whoa, whoa, whoa, hold up." Goldie shouted and was off his bike and sprinting for the weedy field before any of them could stop him.

Cal brought the pedicab to a halt alongside Goldie's fallen Red Ryder. Colleen and Doc coasted up behind him, puzzled and concerned. The balmy afternoon was melting into twilight, the hint of coming autumn borne on the calls of birds, the shiver of leaves, the breath of the wind.

They were just south of Elizabeth, riding down Highway 19, and hadn't been within hailing distance of a soul for two days. The very quiet, the lack of incident, made them all jumpy.

And now Goldie was wading among exhaust-grimed obelisks, the veined-marble cherubim, the bronze plaques spiderwebbed with patina as with some skin disease. He glided, a shade, between the shadows of mausoleums, stepped daintily amid snaggle-toothed headstones.

Then he stooped and began digging in the dirt like a dog. Cal walked over to him, spoke softly. Goldie murmured a word of reply without glancing up.

"This is very not cool," Colleen said, watching from the roadside with Doc. She cast wary glances at the row of silent houses beyond a grassy rise on the opposite side of the highway, the periphery of a small town. Her shoulder muscles were tensed coils. "Field glasses," she said, and Doc handed her the binoculars. She scanned the windows of the silent, squat structures as Cal came up. "People at the windows, watching us."

"They can watch all they like," Cal said, "as long as they don't do anything."

"With the elimination of television," added Doc, "their options for diversion are somewhat limited."

"Yeah, well, let's hope they don't like their entertainment interactive." She wheeled on Cal. "So what's the story here? We adding grave robbing to our list of accomplishments?"

Cal contemplated Goldie, still rooting in the earth, a considerable pile of dirt forming behind him. "I don't think so."

"You don't *think* so? What did he say?"

"He said, 'Render unto Caesar.' "

"Oh great, perfect. Well, here's what *I* say: we tackle him, hogtie him and haul *his* ass and *ours* out of here while we've still got something to haul. Or better yet, we leave him here."

"No."

"No?"

Cal looked at her evenly, shook his head.

Colleen opened her mouth to snap something—or maybe to bite him, Cal thought, seeing the sudden fury in her eyes. Then she abruptly turned and stomped off, away from them and from Goldie too, past the chiseled markers and pillared tombs.

Cal started after her, but a gentle hand touched his arm, and there was a voice like music.

Colleen drew up by a sweet gum tree and glowered at the sun-burnished, twilit clouds. Nearby, a Carrara marble angel stood atop an ornate Nouveau pedestal, its arms beseeching the heavens, wings spread wide. A plaque read, "Never to Forget Our Great War Dead," followed by a list of names— boys from the town over the hill, no doubt—all nineteen, twenty, twenty-one.

Tina flowed toward her, effortless as mercury, the blades of grass quivering as if electrified where she passed.

"You shouldn't be where you can be seen," Colleen murmured.

"I can't hide all my life." The luminous clouds refracted through the lens of her aura, sparked brilliance.

"You got me there, kid."

Tina looked away, and Colleen followed her gaze. Goldie was still engrossed in his digging.

"You really hate him," Tina said.

Colleen was startled by her bluntness, felt a stab of guilt. "Nah, it's not that, it's—he's slowing us down."

"Maybe where we're going . . . it's good not to hurry."

Colleen rubbed a weary hand over her eyes. "Look, I feel sorry for him, I do. It's not his fault. But he's not in control. He could draw attention, maybe get us—" She stopped as she spied the blossoming look of pain and shame on Tina's face.

He's not the only one to draw attention. Colleen cursed herself; her mouth should have been chained up years ago. But then Tina particularly, with that astonishing grace, made her feel like an awkward, insensitive brute. And yet she had to admit to feeling a growing kinship with the girl, seeing in her tentativeness, her shyness, a reflection of her own concealed inner landscape.

Tina was looking off toward a bank of clouds. Colleen reached a tentative hand to touch her, then withdrew it.

"You know who Martha Graham is?" Tina asked, still studying the clouds.

"Unless she invented the cracker, no."

"She said, 'Dancing is a call. . . . Free choice doesn't enter into it.'" She brought her ice-fire gaze to Colleen, gave a melancholy smile. "Do you think we have a choice in life or are we just fooling ourselves?"

"I think . . . we can't choose what happens to us. But we can choose how we act." Colleen's eyes returned to Goldie. He stood now, brushing the dirt from his clothes. He held a wrapped parcel under one arm.

"Maybe some people can't." Tina gazed beyond Goldie to where an evening mist was rising, and her voice was a whisper. "No matter how hard they try."

Colleen and Tina found Cal, Doc and Goldie gingerly unwrapping the oilskin-bound package Goldie had dug up. Inside were more layers of paper and fabric in various stages of decomposition. Then finally, the object itself, dried-out wood and rusty metal.

It was a musket, *Springfield 1857* just discernible on the pitted metal screwed to the wormy stock.

"*This* is what you needed to dig up? It wouldn't even work if guns *did* work." Colleen snapped. "How 'bout you tell me why, Gunga Din? And don't give me that 'Caesar' crap."

Goldie straightened, hefting the weapon in his long-fingered hands with their thick nails like gray stones. "I have absolutely no idea."

They swung west to avoid Philadelphia, traveling through the green sweet farming country that was being stripped of its horses and cows. Skirting Bala Cynwyd and Merton Station and Havertown, they would draw near travelers, scuffed and weather-worn, groups of two or three or four, mindful to keep their hands open and in sight, their weapons stowed—and Tina carefully hidden.

Sometimes Doc would dress wounds, administer simple remedies he had picked up from medicine chests of abandoned homes, first-aid kits from automobiles and RVs. Goldie might sing or dance to lull the children, do simple tricks of pretend magic—or real magic feigned as pretend—while Colleen hung back, keen-eyed, and Cal questioned the adults.

None of them had heard anything of a power to the west or the south. No, Wish Heart meant nothing to them, nor any combination of words sounding like that. Yes, they had disturbing dreams, naturally, but nothing like the revelations that had been visited upon Tina and Stern.

Curiously, as Cal and his companions journeyed on, they encountered none of the altered ones, by day or night, although some of the men and women they interrogated admitted to having heard of such creatures, and a few had even seen them, fleetingly.

Everyone they spoke to confirmed that the Change had

come over the land at the same time, and that it stretched as far as anyone had seen, or that anyone they had talked with had seen. As to what it might be, or what had caused it, most had a theory, running a tabloid gamut from alien invasion or government conspiracy to warfare between the gods. Some were stated boldly, others offered with grave doubts—but none with the least hint of proof.

"It is like a Rorschach," Doc commented as they rested in the shade of a willow grove just below Hazlettville. "Everyone sees this brave new world of ours through the lens of their perceptions, of fear, anger, desire. Casting the world in their own image . . ."

"More a Thematic Aperception Test, if you want to be precise," Goldie corrected him, tightrope-walking over a log balanced across the creek. "And, sorry to break it to you, they always did." He was back in his expansive, talkative phase, no longer dressed down but instead tricked out in what he had taken to calling his Fall Collection—the electric-blue vest emblazoned with buttons, the Hawaiian shirts that never seemed to lose their brightness no matter how long they went unlaundered.

Colleen repeated more than once, and always with cause, that she really couldn't tell which she preferred less, Goldie muted or Goldie loud.

In the quiet times down the long highways, Cal, intent on formulating some plan of attack, would question Tina and Goldie as to what they might sense or see of the force waiting for them at the end of their road. But on this subject Goldie had no premonitions, could summon no image nor inkling. And as for Tina, though its call grew more insistent every day, the darkness that pulled her relentlessly remained shrouded in its own secret.

Often, after they pitched camp, Cal practiced defensive moves with Doc and Colleen, Doc sharing what he had learned in Soviet basic training and Afghanistan, Colleen what she had gleaned from her father, and the streets, and the woods. They squared off bare-handed or with sheathed knives, or wielded sword or bow. Tina would hover near, watching absently, or drift off into the shadows, while Goldie sat cross-legged, humming to himself, voraciously poring over whatever stray volume he had picked up along the way, be it Marcel Proust, Stephen Hawking or Danielle Steel.

In the glow of a campfire against the chill of twilight, Colleen wrapped her arms around her knees and smiled, all the tension shaken out of her for once. She seemed to crackle and glow with energy, like the fire itself. Her smile changed her, gentled her, so that Cal wanted to reach over and touch her—to forget, for once, about the world that was changing, about the growing despair in Tina's eyes. About the thing that they would have to face eventually if they had the grim fortune to find it.

"Fighting isn't about hitting," Colleen said, finishing a point she had made earlier, in the midst of their sparring. "It's about distance, first and foremost. And it's about always thinking, *What do I do if this person goes for me?*"

Distance, thought Cal, and *if this person goes for me.* Looking into Colleen's eyes, he understood suddenly that this was how she regarded everything, everyone: with wariness, fear, caution. *Don't give them a weapon against you. Don't let them into striking range.* It was how Cal himself had viewed the world in what he was increasingly thinking of as The Time Between, the period from his mother's death through his thralldom to Stern, before the Change. And it was how Colleen viewed the world still.

And before he could look away, she saw the compassion and sadness under his thought.

The warmth vanished instantly from her eyes, leaving them bleak and bitter and angry: *You don't understand.*

But he did, and that was what angered her. She got to her feet and walked off into the woods. He rose to follow, to draw her back, but she was moving quickly, and he lost her in the tangle of trees.

He pressed on, searching in the fading dusk, when the glow of a shifting light drew him toward a clearing.

Tina was there, unaware of him. She turned slowly in midair, arms and legs poised in an exquisite arabesque, regarding herself in the play of light against the fallen, dried leaves that carpeted the ground. Beautiful, but so forlorn.

Cal stood a long time, not disturbing her.

And, watching unsuspected from cover, silent as a hawk, Colleen contemplated the look on his face, the fear and tenderness there, and the love that she had thought beyond the capability of any man but her father.

They continued, past Wilmington and Aberdeen and Perry Hall, swinging wide of Baltimore, ever southward, moving fitfully and uncertainly, like a band of blind men drawn by a distant sound. Or, more accurately, a sound that only one of them could hear.

But then, it wasn't like a sound, Cal reflected, lying in his sleeping bag while Doc stood guard by moonlight over the camp they had pitched at Cedar Beach, the cool waters of the Chesapeake softly lapping the shore. It was like a far-off molten core radiating mad heat. Cal studied his sister's sleeping form, shielded in a North Face tent, her glow damped down to a phosphoresence that mirrored the night-washed waves. Tina's sleep was nightly raked with dreams, from which she would wake trembling, unable or unwilling to describe what frightened her. The closer they approached the white-hot glare of whatever was summoning her, the more she seemed to be melting away, growing ever more distant and abstracted. As if she were leaving them already, in small steps, imperceptibly, until she would be gone entirely.

Seeing Cal studying his sister, Doc crouched near. "When one administers an X-ray, it always gives pause," he said, seeming to catch Cal's thought. "Will this help to relieve suffering or will it, in years to come, be the one fraction of difference that causes a cancer to form? It is the same with heart surgery, with almost any choice. The physician asks himself, Am I curing, or am I—" He stopped himself from saying *killing*. "Or am I creating harm?" He laid a hand on Cal's arm. "Take heart, my friend. She is still with us, and we are together—what do you call them?—merry men, eh? And one woman who would choose to be called anything but. We will beard that lion in his den."

If only it were just a lion, Cal thought. Even closing in on it, Tina still had no idea *what* it was. *Crazy and angry and sad* . . . like the world it had created.

What lens, Cal wondered, was *it* seeing through?

Later, while the others slept and Colleen stood watch, Tina dreamed of darkness again and gasped awake.

"Sh, it's okay," whispered Colleen, bending down to her in the mouth of the tent. She reached over and stroked Tina's back, now as unsettlingly fine-boned as a baby bird's. Beside such fragility, Colleen felt clumsy and rough.

She became aware of Tina's gaze on her, turned to the scrutiny of those intense, blue-in-blue eyes.

"Your boyfriend," said Tina softly, "Rory? He changed, too, didn't he?"

"Rory was a punk," Colleen replied, and there was a shakiness in her voice that surprised her.

Tina cocked her head, not taking her eyes off Colleen. "You wanted to love him, but you couldn't . . . so you settled for him needing you."

Colleen felt her chest clench, the breath in her go dry. She felt naked, seen by this being that had been a child, had been human once, and was increasingly becoming something other, something more.

"I thought of leaving," Colleen managed to say.

"We leave when we can . . . or when something takes us." Tina scanned the dark waters, the woods enfolding them, the open gulf of air beyond the jagged coastline.

To the south.

" 'Rory was a punk,' " Tina repeated to herself, voice nearly inaudible. "And Mr. Stern was a dragon in his heart, long before the Change. Is this," she spread her spider-fragile hands, through which the light of the campfire could almost be seen to shine, "because of what I am?"

She dropped her hands, and there was resignation and release in the gesture. "Maybe soon I'll know."

Her gaze was turned inward, and she floated silent, her soft radiance filling her like an opal, playing over the interior of the tent. Colleen peered at her, sensing her despair, knowing the feeling so well and so long in herself. The fear of abandonment, the fear of loss. Striving to be the best—whether that meant being the prettiest, the most graceful or the toughest on the block, it really boiled down to the same thing. Having value to *someone* . . . and feeling so afraid of being worth nothing at all.

Colleen ached to comfort her, to say, *Everything will be all right.* But her heart brooked no false promises, to Tina or herself.

The campfire crackled as a log fell, sending up a firefly swarm of sparks, drawing Colleen's attention. On the far side of the flame, Cal and Doc and Goldie drowsed in their sleeping bags beneath the dark velvet of the eastern sky. Colleen found her glance lingering on Cal. The amber light of the fire picked out the grave features, the long chin and straight nose, the soft light-brown curls. He looked troubled, even in sleep, saddled with the weight of the world.

"Do you love him?"

Colleen turned her head sharply at Tina's question, asked in that same small voice. She was drawing breath to say something, though she didn't know what, when Tina looked up suddenly and her eyes flared.

On the far side of the fire, a huddled form darted, snatched up a leather backpack and tore off into the brush.

"Cal! Doc!" Colleen was on the run, unslinging her crossbow, keeping the shadowy form in sight. It was a puny little cuss, about the size of a child, but it moved incredibly fleetly through the darkness over the uneven terrain.

A light rose up behind her, and Colleen heard the hubbub

of Doc and Cal following, one of them having seized a burning stick from the fire. She plunged on, unmindful of the evergreen branches whipping at her face.

The little fucker was moving like greased lightning, despite the weight of the cumbersome pack, gaining ever more of a lead. By his rough silhouette, the pointed, tufted ears that stuck out on either side of his oversized head, the baggy clothes that hung off him, it was pretty damn clear just what he was.

A nightcrawler, like the bunch that had bustled past them on the way to the hospital. That had cornered Cal in the tunnels under Manhattan.

That had once been someone she'd shared her life with.

Ahead of him through the cover of trees, Colleen could see a darkness in the rock face.

It was a cave mouth.

Oh no, you don't, thought Colleen. She raised the crossbow and fired, deliberately missing him. The bolt struck a cedar trunk ahead of him with an authoritative *thwak*. He let out a cry and ducked away. She reloaded and loosed another arrow. This one lodged in a mound of earth on the far side of him.

The thief flailed in panic, then wheeled and ran directly *at* them, shrieking like a banshee.

Colleen held her ground, readying for the impact. But before the figure reached her, its foot caught on a root and it tumbled headlong, crashing down with a solid "Oof!" The pack went flying, spinning end over end, bouncing off a thick branch and deflecting into a ravine. It struck an outcropping in the cliffside and burst open, raining tins of devilled ham and apricots and baby corn into the void.

Colleen leapt to the lip of the chasm, caught the glint of the cans as they fell and were lost. "Great, just great . . . just about every meal for the next week."

A rustle of leaves alerted her. The invader was trying to crawl away.

Colleen grabbed him, pinned him with her knee to his chest. "Where you think you're going, you rat bastard?"

"Easy, easy there," Cal said, drawing up to her. "He's just a kid."

And Colleen saw, in the darting milk-white eyes and the trembling chin, that it was true. She eased her knee off him, and the boy scooted back up against the rock face, terrified and cornered. Barefoot, he wore the tattered remnants of jeans and a Darth Maul T-shirt, and Colleen wondered if he shivered from fear or from the cold, if he could feel cold.

Cal crouched down to his level. "What's your name, son? Where are you from? It's okay, we're not gonna hurt you."

He said nothing, rocking, his arms tight around himself.

Doc pulled a hunk of bread from his pocket, held it out. "Here, boy." And then, to Colleen's accusatory glare, "The boy is *hungry.*"

The nightcrawler boy snatched it, gobbled it down. But he would say nothing to their questions.

And then a warm glow, melting green and red and blue, breached the clearing, and the boy looked up in wonder.

Tina drifted liquid to him, and it was clear from his face that he had never seen her like before. They appraised each other with their altered eyes, tilting their strange, large heads, and there was kinship on their faces, and loss.

"I'm Tina Griffin," she said, settling before him like a soap bubble, throwing dancing colors onto his face. He squinted at her, the light hurting his eyes but unable to turn them away.

"Freddy Salvo," he said finally, his words distorted by tumbled razor teeth. "From Brandywine, down the road . . ."

"Pretty weird, huh?" She nodded at her weightless arms and legs, toward his gray, leeched skin.

Tears pooled in his pale eyes. "This sucks, man. My mom freaked, threw me out on my sorry ass. . . . I try to catch stuff, you know, squirrels and shit, but it's a joke."

"Freddy," Cal kneeled beside him, spoke gently. "Do you have a feeling of someone trying to pull you somewhere?"

"*Nah.*" His eyes ducked away, furtive. Then, still not looking at them, he mumbled. "I don't listen to it. Nothin' to do with me. It's blurry, far off and shit."

"Where's it coming from?"

He considered, then motioned. To the west. The south.

Cal compressed his lips, thoughtful. So it wasn't just Stern and Tina sensing it, not just New York. It was all the changed ones, at least the three kinds they knew about.

"You not goin' there, are you?" Dread and awe mixed in Freddy's voice. "Don't do it, man."

Cal asked, "Why?"

This seemed to catch the boy up short. After a moment, he merely gestured, uneasy, vague. Then, watchful of his captors, he rose shakily to his feet. "Can I . . . go?" He eyed them, looking shamed. "Didn't mean to steal your stuff. Been better, me in that ravine."

Cal hesitated, weighing the thought before asking, "Would you like to come with us?"

The boy met this with a sharp, fearful intake of air. He shook his head.

Doc asked, "Is there anything we can do to help?"

A kind of desolation passed over Freddy's face. Again, he shook his head, then turned to leave.

Something made him pause as he passed Tina. He glanced back, her aura dancing in his great white eyes.

"Do you know," he asked her, "what's going on? Do you know if we're gonna be okay?"

His manner was intent, almost pleading. Tina searched in vain for words of comfort. She averted her eyes.

In silence, he disappeared into shadow.

In the morning, Goldie caught a white perch off Gunpowder Falls, which provided them breakfast. But it was clear, with the loss of the pack, that they needed more food. Still, Colleen cautioned against going near cities and the more populous towns.

Under flocks of red-winged blackbirds migrating south, they wound their way across the coastal plain, passing fields of tobacco and corn, along the asphalt tributaries of the 702, the 150, the 97, to the 3, just north of Bowie, near the banks of the Patuxent.

Afternoon found them on a rolling green bluff, peering through stands of sugar maple and white oak at a tiny village of one main street with three blocks of shops and a defunct traffic light. A rusty sign on its periphery, pockmarked by BBs, proclaimed, "Stansbury, pop. 72." It was so small, they would have passed it by if Goldie hadn't stopped them.

"No," he said, squinting fixedly at it. "Here."

Cal unstrapped his sword, stashed it in the pedicab. And then, with Colleen, Doc and Tina hanging back in the dappled shadows, he and Goldie strolled into town.

The only resident on the main street was a heavy-set woman in a billowy flower-print dress, her long black hair streaked with white, settled in a pine rocker before an empty coffee shop. Its sun-parched, peeling sign read, "The Buttery—Real Home Cooking."

"That open for business?" Cal asked.

"It is now," she said, rising with a smile like sunshine emerging from clouds.

There was no meat, but the corn chowder was astounding, and the vegetable stew a marvel.

"Raise 'em myself, in my garden," the woman—whose name was Lola Johnson—explained as she dished out apple pie. Cal noted that her wrists were twice as big around as his own, yet she seemed robust rather than flabby. "I've always had a knack with growing things."

"And a talent for understatement," Al Tingly chimed in. Over the course of their meal, other denizens of the town had appeared: Tingly, a lean, stoop-shouldered man who introduced himself as a "hardware merchant"; Laureen Du Costa, who ran the antiques shop three doors down; a scattering of others, none younger than fifty. Goldie eagerly sopped up remnants of stewed tomato with his corn bread. Doc had joined them, too, while Colleen remained secreted with Tina—no need to alarm the townsfolk with visitations, angelic or otherwise.

Stansbury, it emerged, had dwindled since its posted population, its younger citizens having long since fled to brighter horizons, the remnant content to look back on livelier days and be thankful for present calm.

"Used to get more fresh faces before the interstate bypassed us for New Carrollton," Laureen said. "But since all this hullabaloo, we've been grateful for a little anonymity."

"You haven't been eager for authorities to arrive, get everything running again?" asked Doc.

Tingly snorted. "Electricity always was a finicky cuss. We got used to lamps and candles. As for water, our system's gravity fed, so there's no squawk there. And if you're asking us if we'd like a lot of government stooges stompin' in here and—"

"Don't get Al started," Lola cut in, laughing, "or he'll bend your ear about what a prime SOB Harry Truman was."

After they had eaten their fill and more, Cal voiced their need to stock up on supplies, and Doc offered to trade medical services. But surprisingly, no one in town had any physical complaints to speak of, nor had anyone fallen afoul of any mysterious new ailments. In fact, since "the Big Nothing," as Al Tingly called it, even his psoriasis had cleared up.

"*Remarkable*," Doc murmured. "To what do you ascribe—"

"Go on, Lola." Tingly smiled. "Take 'em over and show 'em your potato patch."

"I could get used to this," Doc said, as the three of them rocked on the pine glider on Lola Johnson's porch and the breeze blew through rust and gold maple leaves. The bang of a screen door heralded Lola's emergence from the house, bearing a tray with pitcher and glasses.

The lemonade, like the rest, was perfection.

Lola settled into a wicker chair opposite them, her expansive frame overflowing it. "Well?" she beamed, throwing her big arms wide to take in the surging tangle of asparagus fern and morning glory that spread across the porch, along the roof line, down the steps. Beyond, in her front yard, flowers the size of hats rivaled in their lushness the corn that stood tall and ready for harvest, the potatoes, yams and carrots bursting from the soil, the trees sagging under the weight of apples, plums and pears. "Not bad for a little Maryland girl with just a spade and hoe."

"It's incredible," Cal said.

"I mean, I was always *good*, but *this*—most of it's been in just the last two weeks. Can you believe that?"

"Oh, yes," chimed Goldie.

"Were any of your neighbors equally fortunate?" asked Doc.

"Well, not at first. But then I'd pop round, putter a little here and there, and. . . ."

"The same results."

"Let's just say, I don't think we'll be hearing our stomachs growling any time soon." Her summer-radiant grin appeared and Cal was again struck by the joyfulness of this woman, and her power. Enthroned amid bounty, she seemed like the ghost of Christmas present atop the cornucopia in the Dickens tale, like some primeval spirit of nature.

Which would be cause for celebration in the general run of things, if not for the bodies they had encountered on the road, the predators that roamed free . . . and what awaited them to the south.

Cal rose from the glider, set his empty glass on the tray. "From what I've seen, ma'am, I wouldn't be counting on assistance coming any time soon. Things are getting pretty hairy out there. You might consider being concerned about folks coming 'round who might covet what you've got."

She waved it away with an airy laugh. "Oh, we're such a little flyspeck, I suspect most folks'll just sail on by, won't even know we're here . . . 'cept nice ones, like you." Her eyes came to rest on his, full of easy certainty, and somehow, despite all his fears and knowledge, Cal felt reassured.

As the afternoon sun waned, Cal attempted to settle up with Lola Johnson for the foodstuffs, but she insisted they stay the night. Ed Spadaro had been off in Omaha when "the conniption" had happened, prior to which he had entrusted her with keeping an eye on his bed and breakfast.

"It's moving into the off-season," Lola noted. "Not that we get much of an on-season, really. We're quiet folks, and our charms, what little they might be, are subtle." She added that her perquisites included fixing the rates, which, if she chose, could just damn well be gratis.

In the end, they agreed and gratefully settled into their rooms at the Priory. Under cover of darkness, they spirited Tina into one of the suites. That night, they bathed for the first time in weeks, ate hot food and slept in clean, crisp sheets.

With the exception of Tina, their dreams held no ordeals.

Cal awakened to sunlight glinting through the window and the songs of bobolinks. He stretched, well rested, feeling none of the knots and aches that had plagued him in recent days.

In the clarity of half-wakefulness, his mind drifted over the bounty of Lola Johnson's garden and how she had felt so certain that the grasping, avaricious ones would pass right on by Stansbury, not give it a second glance—as if she intended not to *witness* it but somehow to *cause* it. As she had caused the peaches and pomegranates and sweet potatoes in gardens all over town to swell and grow delectable. As she, if only unconsciously, had brought an equal vitality to her neighbors themselves.

There is a power to the west and the south that caused all this, Stern had said on that fiery rooftop in Manhattan. And everywhere that power had touched, it had sown nightmare and malaise.

Scared and angry and crazy, Tina had added, and that had fit the picture of the merciless force that had shredded the world as conscious and evil—undeniably evil.

But then, how did Lola Johnson fit into that picture? How did this town?

They didn't.

Floating dreamily, his thoughts flowing free, Cal contemplated the events of recent days, remembered the storm that had come upon New York so suddenly, when his sister had first felt the call that was drawing her, drawing them all, southward.

What if this force *were* like a storm, and nothing more? A storm might wreck a house if you opened a window and let it in. Or it might nourish a crop to feed a community.

But the storm itself was a force of nature, pure and simple; it held no awareness, no moral sense. It all lay in how it was directed, what channel it was guided through.

By others.

And, if that was the case, then the power that caused all this and the sentience that was scared, angry, crazy . . .

Might be two entirely different things.

Which allowed the possibility of Lola Johnson's channeling that storm to grow and nurture and heal, a benevolent power that worked *her* will. That might continue to heal even a wayward traveler, a lost one—

Rising with urgency and hope, Cal pulled on his clothes and hurried down the hall to his sister's room.

But she was unchanged.

Colleen was in the room with her. Cal had noticed that Colleen was growing closer to Tina, a deeper bond forming, one that might well hold anguish for them both in the days to come. Looking at the two of them now, he put on a gentle smile.

"We're moving on," he said.

He found Goldie sitting on the veranda, polishing his Springfield musket—a hopeless effort considering that its metal parts were rusted through and the stock was as dessi-cated as driftwood.

"Where's Doc?" Cal asked.

"Loading the last of the jackpot from Mama Nature, I mean, Mrs. Johnson. I hope you like plums. Me, I was hold-ing out for eggplant, but I lost the toss."

Cal settled beside him on the step. "Thanks for bringing us here."

Goldie stopped polishing and looked evenly at Cal. "I saw it for what it was. You couldn't. Mama wouldn't let you."

"Yeah, I kind of figured that out."

Goldie gave him a lopsided grin. "There's hope for you yet." He returned to his polishing, whistling a snappy rendition of "Whatever Lola Wants."

"Goldie," Cal spoke tentatively, "for some folks, what happened was a good thing."

Goldie stopped whistling, though he kept his eyes on the musket. "For some. I suppose, if pressed, I myself could offer a testimonial."

"What do you think it means?"

Goldie rubbed a spot on the barrel harder, making no change in its pitted surface, glaring at it as if his will could make it resolve into something shining and unsoiled and new.

"What it means," he answered after a long silence and would say no more.

In the first twenty-four hours of what Shango had come to think of as the Darkness, the National Guard had established a depot in Lynchburg, partly to collect stock from the horse farms in Albermarle County and mostly to render whatever aid was possible to those in the mountain country beyond. In Albermarle County, there was a stockbreeder named Cadiz (or Gadiz or Cattes, the survivors at the Angels Rest Retire-ment Community pronounced it several different ways), an ex-Reservist and survivalist who was of the opinion that everyone should have been ready for catastrophe and who wasn't about to let the National Guard confiscate his stockpiles of food and water to feed lazy and inefficient parasites who had not been as prudent as he.

As the days and weeks of darkness and hunger progressed and fewer and fewer messages came down highway 95 from Washington, this had developed into what Mrs. Close at Angels Rest called "a situation"—exacerbated by the usual local politics and personalities—culminating in the cessation a week ago of any visits to Angels Rest by the National guardsmen.

"They didn't come real often," the old lady told Shango, pausing in her laborious measuring out of thrice-used tea leaves to flavor the morning's water rations. "But that nice Captain Brady used to make sure one of his men got up here every few days with something. And as long as he and his men came around, nobody bothered us much." Beyond the shade of the gallery outside the kitchen, Shango could see the two remaining attendants at work laying out bedding— bright red-and-blue blankets, worn blue-striped sheets—on the unkempt lawn and rhododendron bushes, airing it in the absence of a regular supply of wash water. Beyond, a neat row of brown rectangles under the trees marked where those who'd been on oxygen or dialysis had been buried, the new grass like a mist of pale green velvet. Mrs. Close supported herself on the edge of the table when she got up to start the water boiling on the stove—one of the other residents had converted it from gas to wood—and Shango got quickly to his feet and fetched the heavy kettle.

"Thank you, dear." She smiled up at him. She was thin as a bundle of sticks, and her hands shook with a steady, constant tremor, as if a motor within were off balance. "Mr. Dean says he saw parties of Mr. Cadiz's men riding in the woods the day before yesterday, carrying spears and arrows, he said, and wearing those camouflage jackets the National guardsmen wore." Mr. Dean was the community's scout, seventy-seven and the only Angels Rest inmate capable of walking more than a mile.

She went on worriedly, "Mr. Dean also says they were riding horses the National guardsmen had the week before. Mr. Dean sometimes gets a little confused about people, but he's very sharp on horses, so you might want to stay away from Lynchburg. Mr. Cadiz . . ." She glanced around nervously and lowered her voice in embarrassment.

"Mr. Cadiz is very prejudiced against—well, he's said some really awful things about Negroes." She looked ashamed even to bring the matter up, and Shango was touched by her delicacy.

"And if he's taken over the National Guard post and has all their weapons, you might want to be careful. Mr. Dean told us some other things, too, about that horrible Douglas Brattle—Mr. Cadiz's neighbor—who's writing that book on torture, of all things, and has all those terrible books and pictures at his house. But I think Mr. Dean must be confused about that."

"About what?" Shango poured the hot water into the community teapot. He was still getting over his shock that the inmates of Angels Rest—a dozen trembling oldsters and the two nurses—had even let him through the gate, instead of locking it and the doors against him, not that either the honeysuckle-covered perimeter wall or the unbarred, ample windows of the old house would stand up to anything resembling a determined assault. The fact that they'd not only admitted him but had voted to share their tiny stores of food and water with him without demanding work in return, made him want to sit them all down and lecture them about the facts of life: don't trust anybody, make sure you've got enough. . . .

He'd spent yesterday afternoon felling trees in the surrounding woods and hauling them up to the kitchen and repairing the plastic rainwater catches. His arms were now sore and stiff.

"About Mr. Brattle—well—being able to *do* things. Mr. Dean says Mr. Brattle could make a horse spook just by looking at it, and when one of the men argued with Mr. Cadiz, Mr. Brattle sort of—sort of waved at him, and the man doubled over and almost fell down."

And that explained, thought Shango grimly, what probably happened to that nice Captain Brady and the National Guard.

The thought of it shivered across his skin like rat's feet.

In his widening search for United Flight 1046, he'd heard of people with unexplained powers. Whispers at first, and he'd put them aside as fear-fed rumors. Then near Spotsylvania he'd encountered a woman who could start or extinguish fires just by looking at wood. *Something* was turning people into gremlins or trogs or boogies or whatever else they were called—and apparently turning people into other things as well.

No wonder McKay had looked scared that first morning, when everyone else was just concerned because the lights were out.

Hang on, Chief, he thought. The fear that had grown inside him for weeks now tore at him like broken glass. He reached into the pocket of his shorts, touched the dog tag he'd taken from Czernas' backpack. Just hang on and keep the lid on things. I'll get you whatever Bilmer knew, whatever Bilmer had.

And then what?

He looked out the windows again, to the neat row of grass-dusted graves.

"Now, you watch out for yourself in those woods." Mrs. Close pressed into Shango's hand a block of much-recycled tinfoil enclosing bread that Shango knew the community could not spare. "I don't suppose . . ." She bit her lower lip. Tiny and fragile, she couldn't have weighed eighty-five pounds; the medication that had kept her thyroid from overburning—devouring her body at a rate faster than food could replenish it—had long since run out. "I don't suppose when you've looked at that plane wreck Mr. Dean gave you the map to, you could come back? Mr. Dean says Mr. Cadiz and his men seem to be collecting all the food and water and things and taking them back to Lynchburg for their own families and people who'll work for them. We don't have very much here to begin with, and I'm sure none of us are in any shape to work for Mr. Cadiz even if we wanted to. If he takes what we have, or if he hurts Mrs. Soniat or Mrs. Metcalf, I don't know what we'll do."

His father had brought him up not to lie. "Is it yes or is it no?" he'd say. "Don't say yes and then do no. That's being a coward, and a liar."

But he couldn't speak, knowing that when he left this place she would die. They all would die. He'd done what he could to bar the windows with two-by-fours, had helped them set up a lookout post on the roof, had given them Czernas' binoculars, and he knew these defenses would do no good at all.

In his mind he saw Czernas in the hot sunlight of the parkway, standing before that beautiful old woman in the green sweatpants: that woman who might be dead now, as Czernas was dead. Like Czernas, he could not speak.

Mrs. Close patted his arm gently and smiled her understanding. "It's all right," she said. Shango wondered how many times this woman had heard *Sorry, we can't*, since her family had put her in Angels Rest. "You just do what you can, dear, and we'll hang on here. We're a lot tougher than we look. It was sweet of you to stay and cut the wood and put those bars on the windows."

"I'm sorry," he said, meaning it, hurting inside for her courage.

"We'll be all right," she said again. "You be careful out there."

In Charlottesville they'd told him about four planes that had come down south of town, in the green woodlands that lay along the knees of the mountains. One of these had proved to be an American flight, he'd seen the fuselage of the plane and hadn't gone any nearer than that. The other had burst its belly open when it first hit the ground and had spewed passengers, seats, luggage over about a thousand yards of highway 29. Shango had searched the rotted, unburied corpses until he'd found half of a boarding pass that identified it as an Air France plane.

Old Mr. Dean, who didn't look like he could stand up to a stiff wind, had gone over Shango's map last night and marked the precise location of the third plane, as well as innumerable minor landmarks of the woods. The witnesses at Angels Rest had all seen it come down, catching a wing on the ground and pinwheeling as it sheared apart; using the map and his compass—at least *that* still worked—Shango set up a grid, doing alone and without equipment a task that usually fell to professional investigation teams with helicopters, dogs, radio communication and metal detectors at their disposal. He worked doggedly, patiently, pacing himself; rationing his energy and his concentration as he'd learned to ration water and food.

There was little chance McKay or anyone else would have recognized him as the quiet, blue-blazered agent of the White House detail he'd been a few weeks ago. He was ragged and indescribably filthy—making it more of a wonder that the folks at Angels Rest had let him through the gate—and the clothes he'd gleaned from the luggage of downed planes were stained, mismatched and torn. He kept his beard clipped short but it started high, just under his cheekbones, and above it his eyes were red-rimmed, hollow with fatigue. It was as if all the disguise he'd worn for years in the service, all the neatness and presentability that made him invisible, had worn away, leaving . . .

What?

Exhaustion had ground him down to the point of feeling very little, either of revulsion or pity—only weariness, and the growing dread he felt every time he thought of McKay, of the man he should have been protecting but wasn't.

He'll think I'm dead, Shango thought. *Or worse, that I've given up, leaving him, and by now there's no one else he can send.*

And his mind turned backward on itself, conjuring images of despair and ruin until he forced it to stop, forced himself to concentrate on the task at hand. *If she was on a plane, if her stuff was on a plane, it'll be out here somewhere.*

One chance, out of how many?

Shut up and search, he told himself. *Shut up and do your job. If it's here, I'll find it.* There was nothing else but that.

The first body he found, at the edge of a burn scar in the thin woods a few miles from Angels Rest, had a boarding pass in what had been her jeans pocket. It was hard to read—blood and fluids from three weeks of decay had badly discolored the card, and animals had mauled the body—but he made out the flight information.

United 1046 from Houston.

Shango closed his eyes and thought, *Shit.* He sat down on the ground, shocked that he'd actually found the flight. That it had, in fact, come down here, instead of clear the hell on the other side of the Appalachians. For a moment he felt disoriented, like a dog who'd chased a Cadillac and then actually caught it.

Then, hearing his mother's admonishing voice in his mind, he added, *Thank you, God.*

And opening his eyes again, he viewed the scene of the wreck.

Coming down without instruments, the big 747 had caught wind shear off the Allegheny Plateau, had veered over on its side, caught its wing and bounced. At least that's what Shango guessed from what little he knew about flight dynamics, coupled with Mrs. Close's description. The thing must have been burning after the first bounce. Bodies, seats, luggage, debris would be scattered all over the back half of Albermarle County. Shango could see twisted hunks of metal on the ground among the charred trees, a couple of corkscrewed seats, a smashed and gutted suitcase, a shattered stroller. Close by, the stink of decay and a humming column of flies marked another body.

He gritted his teeth and walked to the second body, scanning the ground as he went.

For two days, he searched.

He found about a hundred and fifty suitcases, most of which had been torn open or burst on impact: suits, dresses, belts, scarves, cosmetics exploding among the light ferns and creepers. A Bally loafer had survived by falling into a puddle. A woman's mauve-and-pale-green scarf incorporated into a squirrel's nest. An old man's cane embedded in an elm tree as if it had been fired from a gun.

Some of the bodies had fared the same, torn to pieces on impact. This wasn't the first wreck Shango had checked out, nor the first time he'd moved aside a bush expecting to see a body at the end of a protruding leg that turned out not to have one. He didn't know whether the matter-of-factness he felt was because of exhaustion or because, after three weeks of heat and flies and animals, what he found didn't look particularly human anymore. It was just meat.

What he didn't feel by day, he felt in his nightmares at night—but in his nightmares, the bodies all had faces: his mother, his brother, his father. Mrs. Close. The guy in the tower with the sling on his arm. Czernas. McKay. And he'd wake sweating in the dark, in whatever burrow he'd found for himself, hearing the foxes fighting over a severed hand.

The second day he found the tail section, eighteen people still more or less seat-belted into the twisted wreckage. There was a beverage service cart and most of a flight attendant nearby.

Earphones half-crushed, gray worms in the fast-growing new creepers underfoot. Somebody's portable CD player with a Gregorian chant disc still in it. A slightly waterlogged copy of *The Velveteen Rabbit*: *after a long time, if you love enough and are loved, you lose all your soft plush and your stitching gets a little loose and you get a little faded and a little saggy and you become Real.*

And Real is the best that you can be.

Voices rang behind him in the woods.

Shango shoved the book into his backpack and slithered into the nearest cover, a thicket of sugarberry brambles near the broken impact crater of a seat section, keeping his head down and balling his body small. He heard the soft whuffle of horses and the creak of leather, not too near but near enough they'd have seen him; a man's voice said, "—live off the country till we get that first crop in. Then we'll be able to increase their rations. Till then they're lucky they're getting anything. Bastards couldn't be bothered to lay up provisions, who the hell'd they think was going to feed them?"

Shango waited till the noises faded utterly, then crept from the thicket. It was late afternoon, and he had two hours or so of daylight left. But instead of returning at once to his search, he made his way back to a stream cut he'd marked earlier in the day as a place to hole up for the night. Spring runs had undercut the bank and wild honeysuckle grew down over it, leaving a hidey hole behind. Shango dipped up water in one hand, the other hand ready on his knife, listening, always listening, to the birdsong and the soft rustlings of beasts in the woods.

The last body he'd found had been a boy of six or seven, burned, dismembered by foxes. Why that child's body affected him he didn't know. Maybe because a section of seat had covered the face, so that when he'd tipped it clear to look for flight bags or purses, the flesh had still been in place, recognizable to those who'd loved this boy.

But they were probably dead, too.

And he thought, *Those who kept the Source in existence—those who organized it, funded it, lied about it to McKay—are the people who're going to end up with the food and the water and the protection that everyone else is dying without.*

Whoever they are, they, too, knew what it meant when the lights went out.

Anger flamed within him. Anger beyond anything he'd thought himself capable of feeling, a volcano, a cataclysm: hatred for the men who had killed that child.

Hatred followed by an exhaustion so intense that it made him dizzy and sick.

He crawled behind the honeysuckle, sat with the damp cool clay of the bank against his back.

McKay was a part of it, he thought. *YOU were a part of it. All this time, being a cog in their wheel, being good at your job and proud to be good at your job. And your job was to protect the men who secretly, quietly, were working on this.*

He remembered how good it had felt, to hear Cox or McKay say, *He's good at his job. He's the best.* How good it had felt to have a scorepad that said, "Ninety-nine out of a hundred rounds in the target zone"; to spot some questionable yo-yo in a crowd and remove him, or to establish a perimeter or make a transfer from door to car without slip-ups. That sense of accomplishment. Something apart from, beyond, the chaos in which he'd grown up, the chaos of watching his father and mother giving their time and money and attention to a thousand things besides their children: buying one too many rounds of beers for friends, being gone with the church ladies one too many nights. No time, gotta go . . . Not this week, honey, next week . . .

And it had all been betrayal, in the end. It had all been to protect the people who thought that the risk of this—this horror, this catastrophe—coming to pass was less important than getting power.

He thought, *I will find Bilmer. I will get her notes, her evidence, back to McKay. And then I will protect McKay from these people, because whoever they are, they will destroy him before they'll admit that they were wrong.*

Shango closed his eyes. He'd be able to go over about another square mile of woods before it got too dark to see. He'd been marking them off on Mr. Dean's map: oak tree to pond, covered. Pond to birches, covered. Birches to the second burn scar, covered.

But what if he'd missed something? What if a fox had dragged Bilmer's body, or purse, or luggage away to its hole? The next section to search, beyond the second burn scar, might contain something, but what if the papers themselves had become exposed?

What would he do then? How would he know?

When you've gone over the whole area, he told himself, and haven't found what you're looking for, then it'll be time to go back and look again. You can't do it any other way.

Someone was singing.

Humming, whispering; Shango knew almost before he opened his eyes, before he shifted his weight forward to peer through the honeysuckle, that it was a crazy. He'd learned the sound of crazies over the years.

So in a way, the sight of the man kneeling beside the stream didn't surprise him. Only that he had made it this far from civilization unharmed.

Traveling with someone, Shango deduced at once, studying the wild black hair curling from beneath that straw cowboy hat, the jangly fruit-salad Hawaiian shirts. Father or brother or pal, he was someone they couldn't leave behind.

His back still to Shango, the man rose and sauntered along the bank with a loose-limbed casualness, a here/not-here quality that set him apart.

Every now and then, the man found some bauble in the wet earth—a water-polished stone, a sprig of greenery—and stooped to claim it, the tangle of buttons pinned to his vest clattering as he bent. Shango saw now that the fellow had a pitifully old musket, all rusted and cracked, slung over his back. What possible good might that do, even as a bluff?

Hell, thought Shango, starting to rise, *it's only an hour or so till dark, I couldn't cover the whole of that burn scar anyway. Might as well see if I can find his family, get him back to them if he isn't going to end up carrying nightsoil for Cadiz's private garden patch.*

"Stay where you are," snapped a voice from the top of the bank.

The man raised his head. *Crazy*, thought Shango, *and something more.*

It was Cadiz and his men, at the top of the bank.

Shango recognized them from the descriptions: No National guardsmen would have added all those leather jackets and extra weapons belts to their cammies. The burly dude with the Air Cav patch displayed so prominently on his shoulder would be Cadiz; the sour-faced, freckled, curiously wizened man riding at his side was probably the odd and offensive Mr. Brattle. Two of the dozen or so foot soldiers who surrounded the two riders were already making their way down the stream-bank toward the brightly garbed man, who was by this time backing away.

"Sorry," he said, in a pleasant voice, "got to go. Wish I could stay."

"I said stay put!" snapped Brattle, in a thin harsh voice like a cough. "Where'd you come from? Nobody comes through here without us checking them out."

And Cadiz said, "Grab him."

That was a mistake. The man flung up his hand and shouted, fireballs flashing in the air. Shango's breath caught in his throat. *Another of them*, like the firestarter he'd met near Spotsylvania, the others he'd heard of.

At the top of the bank, Brattle said in his tight cold voice, "None of that!" and stretched out his hand toward the man.

The man cried out, clutched his head, doubled over in pain. The fireballs frizzled and died, the smell of smoke thick in the air. The man fell to his knees in the stream, raised his hand as if he feared he would be struck. Brattle said, "Bring him. We'll need one like that."

The foot soldiers seized the man by the arms.

And at that point, one of the group around Cadiz and Brattle shifted, and Shango saw what was slung on the cruppers of their horses. Sacks of food, big plastic bottles of water such as the National Guard had handed out, a bundle of bright red-and-blue blankets lashed together. Tools—a small hatchet, a saw and some screwdrivers—bulging from faded blue-and-white-striped sheets.

You bastards, thought Shango, recognizing the few piti-

ful objects that had stood between the Angels Rest oldsters
and starvation. *You fucking bastards.*

Anger rose up in him, at all those faces, from that of the
woman by the parkway to that child's he had uncovered only
an hour ago—rage at what men had done out of power and
hunger and greed.

You have no right, he thought, *to do what you are doing*—
and his hammer sprang as if of itself into his hand. Chill iron
centered in him, terrible and hard, and no, this wasn't his job,
he thought, moving already, striding from the dusky vines and
golden flowers, and no, he knew the way to take care of this
problem was not to get himself killed by taking on twelve
armed guys *and* a wizard who had the advantage of high
ground and crossbows. But sometimes, thought Shango, perfectly cold, perfectly calm, sometimes your starry-eyed
bleeding-heart Band-Aid-plastering liberals had a point.

And he struck like the hammer of Thor, like John Henry
driving down the steel that killed him, and knocked the
brains out of one man like mac'n'cheese from a broken
dish and snapped the other thug's spine on the backhand
swing. He grabbed the Hawaiian-shirted man's arm and
pulled him clear as one of the men on top of the bank fired
a crossbow.

And then fear hit him. Crippling, staggering terror that
iced his stomach and dropped him to his knees.

Panic flooded him, screamed at him to drop everything
and RUN—

And looking up at the top of the bank, he saw the sour,
freckled face of Douglas Brattle smile.

That was his power, Shango understood.

He could throw Fear.

Shango raised his hammer in his hand.

Bellowing like thunder, he charged straight up the bank,
swinging the weapon around his head. A man leveled a
crossbow at him, and he scrambled up anyway, not ceasing
to shout, not ceasing the gush of rage that the shout summoned from his pounding heart.

Anger poured out of him, hot as blood from a wound, the anger a weapon like the hammer, that nothing could disable or fuck up.

And then something gleaming flashed across the bowman's weapon, and he heard the fiberglass crossbow snap and the *sprang!* of the breaking string, the scream of the bowman as the arrow leaped wildly back into his face. The man ran shrieking into the woods, spraying blood.

The gleaming thing had been a sword.

And amid the chaos and the screams and the blood rage pounding within him, Shango realized others had entered the fray alongside him.

Brattle's horse reared, and Cadiz drove his mount forward, spear leveled. Shango smote the spear aside with his hammer, smote aside the sword the man drew.

He grabbed Cadiz's wrist and hauled him from the horse and into the tangle of fern underfoot, drove his boot into the side of his ribs, felt bone break, as this man must have broken the bones of Mrs. Close and Mr. Dean and the others who had taken Shango in.

There was a cry behind him, and he spied another militiaman falling as a lean, muscular young woman smashed him down with a blow from her crossbow, arcing it wide like a club. Then, with a speed and agility he found impressive, the woman wheeled, loading the crossbow as a third rider drove down on her. She fired, falling back, her arrow lodging in the rider's shoulder, flinging him backward off the horse to smash on the rocks.

And now all was confusion, a blur of bodies and blades, of crushing movement. Something slashed along his cheek, he drove the attacker back with his boot. Others tried to take him around the waist, bring him down, but he threw them off, battered them away.

Beyond this, as if lit by lightning, he glimpsed the young swordsman, forcing back two of the militiamen, who parried with big hunting knives, eager to gut him. The young man was no professional, that was clear. But he fought with a fire, a determination, that brought to Shango's mind his own crazy-ass self as he'd gone screaming up the creek bank.

And there was another man, too, an older man, wielding a length of pipe against the bastards, shouting a torrent of curses in something that sounded like Russian.

Shango sought again for Cadiz, couldn't find him. A man with three gold teeth lunged at him with a bayonet. Shango sidestepped it, drove the head of his hammer into the man's solar plexus, sending him staggering back to collapse amid the rushes, choking.

Shango straightened, saw the girl with the crossbow firing off a shot into the thigh of one of the Russian's adversaries, unaware that a spearman was running at her own undefended back.

"*No*!" The word rang out over the clearing and—though it was high and musical—it took Shango an instant to realize it wasn't his own thought.

Then in the green dusk, there was a brightness like a second sun.

He saw to his astonishment a glowing, beautiful child skimming in the air like a stone skipped over water. The creature overtook the spearman and settled near the woman, the light extending out to canopy her.

The spearman cried out in terror, but his momentum was carrying him, and his spear struck the glowing canopy, its wood fracturing as though the light were solid, sending the barbed metal tip of the spear shooting back and upward into the man's own throat.

He made a gurgling, surprised sound and fell, gasping out his life.

The fear-caster wheeled his horse and pelted away into the trees.

Shango swung around, to find the surviving men gone. He was panting, trembling, the rush of anger that had lighted his whole body ebbing, leaving ash and shock and dizziness in its wake.

The ghostly, glimmering girl hovered over the dead man,

staring down at her handiwork, and she looked sickened. She appeared to be twelve or thirteen years old, Shango's niece Kitta's age, and smaller than she should have been, were she human.

"How'd you do that?" the muscular young woman asked her quietly, and it was clear to Shango that she both knew this girl and knew nothing of her power.

"I—I don't know," the girl stammered, settling like a dragonfly, ready to rise and flee. Her white hair floated weightless around a thin, haunted face. "I was just mad and scared, and I wanted him to *stop*."

Shango had heard of such creatures in his travels, had even perhaps glimpsed one far in the distance over Arlington, a light moving quickly through the midnight sky, in this world where he had thought lights no longer moved in the heavens. Fireflies, he'd heard them called, or feys, or little bright fuckers.

The man in the Hawaiian shirts was clambering up the bank, panting, helped by the curly-haired young swordsman. "You okay, Goldie?"

"I'm fine," said Goldie, looking around him with those hectic brown eyes, "though there *are* mental health professionals in several metropolitan areas who might beg to differ."

The glowing girl-angel regarded Shango with her blue-in-blue eyes and whispered, "Are *you* all right?"

"Yes. Thank you, miss." He inclined his head and, looking around him, saw that he'd killed one of Cadiz's men on top of the stream bank, though he had no conscious memory of it.

Kneeling, he cleaned the head of his hammer in the stream, the blood trailing away, his hands shaking as they'd never shaken on night bombings raids in the Gulf.

"Thank you for helping him," the young man said, sheathing his sword and approaching Shango and, in the way he held himself, his easy air of authority, left no doubt as to who was leader of the group. "I'm Cal Griffin," he added, and introduced the others.

Shango regarded them as they stood together, and, though it was obvious they were travelers, they seemed neither refugees nor brigands. Perhaps, he reflected, they were pilgrims. Like himself.

"My name's Larry Shango," he said, sliding the weapon back into the straps of his backpack, standing up again. "And I'd suggest we make tracks out of here, before more company comes."

TWENTY-SIX

With the young man called Cal Griffin, with Colleen Brooks and Dr. Lysenko and Goldie and Tina, Shango returned to Angels Rest. As he expected he found the house looted, the old men and women who had sheltered there dead. They had been clubbed like cattle, presumably a fate Cadiz considered more merciful than being left to starve.

In the potting shed behind the shady, silent house, under the dispassionate moon, they found a broken-handled shovel Cadiz had left and began digging a mass grave. Through all of this, Shango said little of himself and nothing of the business that had brought him here.

"The guy's military or security services, I know the vibe from my dad," Colleen told Cal, as the others spelled them on the digging. "Maybe AWOL."

"No," said Cal. "He doesn't strike me as a man to walk away." He glanced over at the big man working the shovel, shirtless now, the lantern light showing the dark sheen of him in the night air. His eyes were mirror mazes that reflected back the viewer, that gave up nothing. But in his actions by the creek, in his watchfulness and in the quiet, deep tenor of his voice, Cal read compassion.

As they laid the bodies in the pit, Goldie murmured some words from the Bhagavad Gita, and Doc said a blessing. Then they filled in the hole, and Shango found them a camp-site that was shielded and secure.

Huddled beside the fire, Cal told Shango of the events in New York, of the man who'd changed into a dragon, and of what he'd seen in the tunnels. He spoke of the miracles they had encountered, cruel and otherwise, along the road, and of the Plant Lady in the little town off the Patuxent. And he told him of the place they sought called Wish Heart.

To all of this, Shango listened attentively, and nodded, and observed, "Staying off the beaten path, sounds like you've had an easier ride of it." But he didn't tell them of the Source Project, or of D.C. And looking across the fire at Cal, seeing the lines of weariness on the face that was so youth-ful, and the way those hazel eyes followed the flare-girl Tina with such worry and such grief, Shango thought of the ties of obligation and affection and relation, thought of his fam-ily in New Orleans, and of Czernas and McKay.

A log broke and fell in the sheltered fire. A flake of light fell across Colleen Brooks, nearly invisible in the trees, lis-tening, standing guard; Shango saw her eyes, and they were on Cal, with a look in them that told him things that Cal had probably never seen. And Cal was watching Goldie, worried about the man but believing, caring for him. And Doc's gaze moved among them, concerned and at rest.

People holding each other's hands in the night.

"What about you?" Cal asked Shango. "Where are you bound?"

"Here," said Shango, the word speaking double to him. Where are you going, and to what place are you tied?

Here.

"I came to find a woman who was on the plane that crashed here. I don't think she survived," he added, seeing the way Cal's eyes shifted, "but she had something, was car-rying something, that I was sent to find. And I see now it's going to be a long search, especially if I've got a pissed-off

gang of skinheads runnin' around the woods lookin' for me."
He thought of those cold mad coal-black eyes in the fear-
caster Brattle's pale face, and of what Cadiz and his band
would do to him if they caught him again.

"What you're looking for . . . is it bigger than a breadbox," asked Goldie softly, "and smaller than the Empire
State Building?"

Shango glanced up and met the man's wild brown eyes.
A crazy, he thought, but he had seen the fireballs leap and
blaze from his hands.

To his own surprise he heard his voice saying, "No. It's
just a couple of sheets of paper, folded up small. She probably glued it in her purse lining. That's what she usually did."

"Did you know her?"

"I met her once or twice."

"What was her name?"

"Jerri Bilmer. Geraldine."

Goldie chewed meditatively on his corn chowder. "You
have anything she owned, or touched, or wore?"

"No."

Goldie sighed and set his bowl aside, rising. "You're
gonna make me break a sweat, aren't you?"

They insisted on going with him to the plane, despite his
protests. In the end, his pragmatism won out. With Cadiz
and Brattle in the woods somewhere, Shango needed whatever help he could get—even if his common sense told him
magic tricks were ridiculous, that this was insanity.

These were insane times.

Still, as morning had broken and they'd set off, he had de-
manded that the glowing girl and the Russian and the
Brooks woman stay behind in camp, sheltered, protected.
No need to draw them all into the crosshairs.

So now Shango stood beside the blackened, sheared metal
of United 1046 out of Houston, Griffin beside him, alert, his
sword unsheathed, while Goldman bent beside a crumpled

piece of fuselage and scooped a handful of fine gray ash that might once have been part of a seat cushion, or a backpack, or a dress. Standing, he sifted it slowly in his hand. There was no mirth to him now, no hint of the Woodstock Nation clown.

"What would she have been thinking about at the end?" Goldie asked Shango. "Her family, loved ones?"

"No . . . about the mission, and failing." And Shango realized he was speaking too of himself.

As Goldman concentrated, his color drained, and he looked wounded. He took a couple of hesitant steps to his left and then turned back and strode between two willows.

He led them to the sad, crumpled object that had been Jerri Bilmer.

She had been flung out of the dissolving plane and decapitated by flying debris. Shango soon found her purse under a shattered wing section that had protected it. Delicately, he peeled back the lining and revealed the folded sheets of paper that had cost Bilmer her life and might yet cost him his. Carefully, he unfolded them, drew them apart. Water had soaked most of the sheets, but the inner one was readable. A list of personnel, of home addresses. A last-minute marginal note concerning buffalo and wolves and blue lightning that crawled from the ground.

And that was all.

Shango turned them over in his hands, fighting the urge to laugh. All this, he thought, remembering the chaos of Dulles and the horror of plane after wrecked plane that he'd patiently searched, pawing through the corpses of people he didn't know, rifling the burned, soaked luggage that was all that remained of thousands of ended lives, and in the end getting only this.

"That what you were looking for?"

Shango looked to Cal. The young man was watching him, concern in his dark eyes, as if he saw how close Shango was to ripping the papers into white flakes of nothingness, releasing them to the winds that would carry off his soul and his life as well.

"Yes," he said.

"Is it what you need?"

"I don't know."

Shango drew a deep breath, reminding himself that his job was not yet done. It wasn't his to judge, just to find. McKay might be able to make something of this, might match up a name, or a town. If it were what he needed, if it might save the day. If the Source Project was even the cause of all this.

Shango had already done the near impossible. It was time to go.

To McKay, who had trusted him, whom he had left to the care of less-watchful souls.

On sudden impulse, Shango fished the steel dog tag from his pocket, laid it in Goldman's hand. "Can you see the man who gave me this? See if he's all right?"

The wild-haired man cocked his head questioningly. Then he took the slip of steel, pressed it between his palms, then to his lips. In the cool morning light, his eyes seemed both focused and distant, seeing beyond the hunks of metal that littered the ground, the stinks of decay. Though the morning was silent, he seemed to hear something, for his face changed, fell a little, the pale brown eyes sad. He made as if to speak, then hesitated.

"What is it, Goldie?" Cal asked.

"I'm sorry," Goldman said to Shango, handing back the dog tag. "The man you work for, the one you like . . . is dead."

Shango said nothing. Just folded the steel back into his huge palm.

"Goldie's visions aren't always accurate," Cal offered.

"Oh, geez, no," Goldie agreed quickly, as if the thought that people would take his visions as gospel appalled him. "Sometimes what I see is just 'cause I'm . . ." Suddenly, the jangly quality, the wildness ebbed out of him, and he was calm and sure. "If, when you go back, he's not there to greet you, go to a fountain near the roses." He peered worriedly from beneath his straw hat brim at Shango's motionless, expressionless face. "Just wanted to save you the trip," he said.

"I appreciate it." The words came out like the dry stir of ash. "I still have to go back."

Shango slid the metal tag back into his pocket and glanced at the retrieved sheets of wilted paper he still held in his other hand.

Time to go now.

And as he folded the sheets, his eyes tumbled down the list of names.

Wish Heart, Griffin had told him. Shango's heart was a stone in him, as he kept his silence. And he thought of his duty and of the void that lay there if it were set aside. A void to be looked into and then drawn back from.

And everyone who had drifted through his wandering life floated ghostlike before him now, the ones who had trusted him and stood for him, and whom he had failed. Czernas, and Mrs. Close and Mr. Dean, and all the other guiltless souls at Angels Rest. And perhaps McKay, too, almost certainly so.

He contemplated the men standing beside him, who had brought him here and risked themselves. They were, he knew, going into even greater danger, all innocent, like calves to a slaughterhouse.

What would *they* be thinking in their last moments?

Of their loved ones, who would be with them.

And he knew that his duty, his oath of office, that everything he stood for, decreed that he tell them *nothing* of the knowledge he held.

But if McKay were dead, where might that duty lie?

"Wishart isn't a place," said Shango. "He's a person. Dr. Fred Wishart. And he does live in the South. South of here, anyway. A place called Boone's Gap, West Virginia—though it's unlikely he was there when all this came down." Then he told them all he knew—what precious little there was of it—about the Source Project.

Surprise showed in Cal Griffin's eyes, and he was quiet, weighing this intelligence, shuffling it into all that had unfolded in the days that had brought them here.

Goldie chuckled, but there was no humor in the sound. "You know, funniest coincidence: during the Manhattan Project, there was a serious concern that if they set off an atomic reaction, it might just keep going, blow up the whole world. What the hell, they pushed the button anyway."

"This force," Cal asked Shango in a hushed tone, "is it something the scientists *made* or something they just plugged into?"

"I don't know," said Shango. "I don't even know where it was located."

"Lay you odds it's to the west," Goldie muttered.

"I can't say how to stop it or control it," Shango continued and felt his own futility. "All I know is someone was doing something they didn't want shared, that it was about power." But then, it was always about power.

Shango tucked the sheets into his pack, looked northward. The sun was rising high into the gray, cloudless sky, but it gave no warmth. *Time to go.*

Home?

Or just *back?*

Cal put a hand on his arm, smiled into Shango's dark eyes. "If you'd care to come with us, we could sure as hell use you."

And though he had his duty, though his modus operandi had been always to be alone, to rely on no one and watch his own back, Shango felt the longing rise in him to go with them, to be with them.

Reluctantly, he shook his head. "I have to make sure."

Cal nodded. "I understand." He clasped Shango's hand. Looking into Cal's eyes, Shango was reminded, strangely, of McKay.

"Keep your head low," said Goldie, as if speaking to a man who proposed to cross a busy street, as if he had said it many, many times.

"You, too," Shango said.

❧

The dead of night was the worst time.

By day, the white house among the honeysuckle was as invisible to Wilma as it was to the rest of the people in the town—she didn't see it, didn't even think about it, except when she walked to the trailer court to help Shannon and Greg care for Tessa or down to the Senior Center, where two or three of the old people were beginning to nod and doze with that same cold constant silence. But at night it seemed to come into focus again.

That was when things came out of the darkness.

Two nights ago, skeletal wolves melted into being from the gray mists that lifted from the earth to surround the house, solidifying around burning red fire specks of eyes. Wilma had watched them from her back porch steps as they'd tried to clamber through the broken, yawning windows, through the open door. Blue lightning had sizzled and snapped from the walls, and purplish flame crept from the windows in a phosphorescent stream. The wolves howled and howled, writhing in pain as they burned, and then had melted away. But when dawn came, Wilma, looking hard, saw on the dilapidated paintwork the marks of their claws and teeth.

Last night, it had started the same, with the mist rising from the ground, rolling across the trailer court, up Applby Street. Surrounding the house in the darkness. But the thing that came striding in the mist was something Wilma had never seen before, something she could barely make out: something that shrieked in a voice that was like the wind but wasn't the wind, like a machine but not a machine, a terrible hammering that grew louder and louder and resolved itself into pounding on the walls. On the back porch in darkness Wilma had waited, listening, hearing the boards and timbers of the house groan with the strain. Hearing the zap and hiss of those blue flames, that creeping lightning, and seeing the occasional flash of it through the murk. Smelling burning, like hair and flesh and feathers singed and consumed at once.

Knowing somehow that if whatever it was broke into the house, things would be worse than they were now.

The howling stopped about two hours before dawn, and the silence that stretched until morning was almost worse than the noise. Then imperceptibly the mists slunk away, and Wilma slept.

She sat again tonight on her porch with her cats around her and wiped her hands absent-mindedly with the dampened washrags that in some curious way were calming to her heart. She watched the house and watched the darkness, with the stillness of a cat, like Imp when he was waiting for a grasshopper to forget that he was there.

He has to come sometime, she thought.

When he does, he has to speak to me.

Movement in the darkness. The reflection of milky eyes. Somehow she knew it was Hank—the smell of him, perhaps, sharp and clear as any mouse in the grass or frog beneath the porch steps—and she settled herself more still, lest she break the pattern of stillness and cause him to flee. Beside her, Imp hissed softly and lashed his tail.

Dark against dark, Hank stepped from the bramble of the overgrown back hedge. Since last she'd seen him, a day or two after the Change, he'd altered little, though she thought he was smaller yet. It was as if his flesh and bones had compacted: the same man, yet more dense, in body and also in soul.

At least he was alive.

There was a smell in him of fear, and of madness. He carried a short length of metal pipe in his hand.

She waited until he was quite near her before she spoke, and then she spoke without moving: *Hank*, she said softly, speaking as she sometimes spoke without actual words to her cats. But he heard her and froze.

"Hank."

The glinting eyes turned. Wilma rose, very slowly, and held out her hand. When he didn't move, she descended the porch steps as if she were hunting and feared to startle a prey. His hand with the club moved a little, rose, then sank again. She felt his eyes on her and felt, too, the pain, the yearning in his heart, even before he said her name.

"Wilma."

"Hank, will you walk with me?" In the dark she saw his face flinch, twist a little. Some inner pinch of pain. But he didn't move, beyond the clenching of his big hand, and she came up close to him and took his arm. Her voice was the murmur of the night. "Let's walk," she said.

TWENTY-SEVEN

"I don't—know," said Hank. His brow wrinkled, sharp and hard, at her question, as if even thinking put him in pain. "There's these . . . dreams."

They had left the houses of town behind, the stink of privies and woodsmoke. The green sweet stillness of trees lay thick on the night. Wilma had led him away from the terrible flow of those glowing energies, avoiding the hot spots, the bad places.

They passed the old Simmonds house and stood in the dirt lane there, with the trees of the mountain pressing close around them. The old two-story house was dark. A hundred feet away the mist curled, pale and enigmatic in starlight.

Hank pressed his fist to his brow, as if the physical act could push down some clamor within. "I keep to myself, mainly, but . . . they know I led the men out of the mines, they're looking to me to—" He broke off, then struggled again to speak. "There ain't too much food in the tunnels. We were okay at first, but Green Mountain's nearly trapped out of deer and rabbits. It's harder and harder to catch rats in the town, even. They're talkin' of hitting the food stores—and the houses."

Wilma almost asked, *Who are?* but stopped herself. Now was not the time to break his concentration. She only waited, in the silence that was her custom now as well as his.

In time, he went on. "So there's these dreams. And in 'em I'm hungry, and it's his fault. Wishart."

"Bob Wishart?"

He nodded.

"Is Bob alive?" she asked. "I know Arleta said, right at the beginning, that his machines hadn't gone down, but now I see that might not even have been Arleta—or she might not have been in her right senses. And I know no batteries, no machines kept working. So what *is* in that house?"

"I don't know!" Hank shook his head, and the gesture graded into a quiver, like a shudder of pain. His hand twitched where hers held it and the pressure of his fingers around hers was suddenly crushing and as suddenly released. "I know what you're saying is right. And I don't know the truth of it. But in these dreams it's—there's this voice saying, *He's pretending. He's just faking us out.* He's doing it all, with the fog and the things coming out of it."

He looked up at her, twisting his neck on his bowed shoulders, and the white eyes were deadly serious, deathly afraid. "Whether it's Bob or somethin' else in that house, in the dreams it's Bob—Bob crouching in that bedroom of his with all the food in the town and all the dead around him, Andy Hillocher and Sonny and poor old Arleta, all rotting there. Bob, fat and greasy, with that geeky grin of his . . ."

"Bob wouldn't hurt a fly," Wilma protested. "It isn't just that he was afraid of his shadow. He's a genuinely good man, harmless and friendly."

"I know all that!" Hank's face screwed with pain. "Dammit, I know! But these voices, this voice, in my head, in my dreams. In my dreams, it's Bob. And in my dreams, I kill him."

Wilma was silent, thinking about Tessa and the others.

Thinking about the glowing threads of power, the Indian women screaming with their children, their pain as sharp as it had been two and a half centuries before.

After a long time she said, "Don't do this, Hank." And yet as she spoke, she saw the sweat on his face and felt his arm shake where her hand closed around his, and she knew he wouldn't attack the house because he wanted to. Yet she could come up with nothing else to say.

"Don't do it." She pressed his hands. "Whatever is telling you this, sending you these dreams—it's lying. There's something going on here, Hank, something we don't understand, but it's using you. It has no more regard for you than an old-time miner had for the canary that he used to detect gas. A living tool that would drop over dead."

Hank shook his head, weary and beaten. "I've seen into that house in my dreams. There's a nightmare in there. It's crazy, alive and strong. And the voice in my head, saying, saying—"

He stopped abruptly, looking up sharply. Wilma heard the grunters, smelled them, before she saw them. They oozed out of the night, gliding on padded feet from around the gutted Simmonds house and its broken-down sheds, resolved from the silhouettes of pine, beech and oak trees, crawled up out of the gorges. Six, eight, ten of them, grasping ax handles, bights of chain, picks rusted with long storage in the mine. They trampled the smartweed as they came, closing in, all of them staring accusingly at Hank.

"I . . . wasn't supposed to tell," Hank said.

Then, breaking into a shriek like the offended dead, they attacked.

Hank yelled, "*No!*" and flung himself at them, iron pipe slashing through the air. "Wilma, run!"

"Hank, I . . ."

"*Run!!!*"

Three of them darted around him, snatching at her, and she had no choice but to fall back into what looked like a little band of the mist, like a projection of it.

She heard the confused shouting of Hank and the other grunters muffle and fall away, the clang of metal pipes and the wrenches they used as clubs. Then the slap of bare feet on the hard dirt came to her, and she knew the grunters—a maddened few, at least—had dared enter the fog after her.

She broke into a run but grew aware that the footfalls of her pursuers were slowing, becoming uncertain as the fog enfolded and disoriented them. They stopped, were silent a moment—and then their screams began.

Wilma plunged away, through darkness her night-sighted eyes could not pierce. She stumbled on what felt like a chunk of old machinery—something in the Simmonds yard, she thought—struggled up, clutching twisted, rusty metal that cut into her. Gasping, the sick-damp air leeching the breath from her, she pressed on.

Something blue and flickering rushed at her from among the trees, driving her deeper into the mists. The ground grew rougher, sloping under her feet. Vines and creepers grabbed at her ankles. Lights flickered among the underbrush, fireballs, she saw, rolling slowly, steadily toward her along the ground, the sight of them lifting the hair from her nape.

All behind her was stillness now. She turned, speculating about heading back the way she'd come, but knowing that whatever had silenced her pursuers still lay between her and town.

Then she heard it. Coming for her, its panting breath sawing the darkness, the crunch of its feet on last year's brown leaves. Its phosphor-green light, like a swarm of disease mold, punctured the mist, growing larger and more distinct as it approached.

It had no smell, no reek of decay, no tang of electrical discharge, *nothing,* and somehow that was the most alarming of all.

The thing reared out of the darkness, and she saw it now in all its malformed detail. Not a grunter, no, nor one of the spectral, massacred Indian women. It peered at her with burning, malign eyes like the Wishart house itself, and its flesh writhed.

Gaping up at it, Wilma forced down the cry that threatened to burst from her, channeled that frenzied energy into her legs, twisting away, bolting off blindly through the mist and dark.

She heard it tearing after her, didn't risk looking back. Deadfall branches clawed her; she stumbled again in potholes, in cold rivulets of what had to be Boone's Creek.

And, running full out with all the blessed, feral strength humming through her veins, she knew that the thing at her heels was gaining and would have her.

"Oh, man, this doesn't belong here."

Goldie had been the first to see it as they had rounded the bend of the two-lane, under the gaunt September moon. The fog stretched across the road like a prison wall, flat and gray and impenetrable.

He pulled his no-speed to a halt and clambered down as Cal, Doc and Colleen drew up alongside. Tentatively, he approached the barrier, inspecting it as wispy tendrils reached out like beckoning fingers.

The others dismounted and joined him. "What do you mean, it doesn't belong here?" Cal asked.

Goldie shook his head slowly, never taking his eyes off it.

Sparkling illumination like starlight shone from behind them, dusting the surface of the fog, and Cal realized that Tina had emerged from the pedicab. She floated to the edge of the mist, contemplating it with trembling agitation, breathing in quick gasps, keen and brittle. Cal had observed this mood rising in her over the past days as she had struggled against the growing clamor in her mind, seen it become as much a part of her as the leggings and too-large denim shirt she wore, the globe of swimming light that emanated from her.

She hovered beside Goldie, peering into the coiling vapor, both of them tantalized with dread.

"Maybe if we wait till morning, it'll melt away," Colleen said without conviction, and Cal knew that no one had to tell her it wouldn't.

Nor that on the other side of it, two miles down the road, lay Boone's Gap.

Shango had given them a name, and their maps the particulars of distance and direction. But as to what might reside there, this thing that had put the name Wishart into Tina's mind, that somehow dwelled both to the west and to the south, they knew neither its nature nor its weaknesses. Only that it called ceaselessly to her, ravenously.

They had set off along I-64 that morning, their backs to the rising sun, passing Covington, making good time. Just over the state line, east of White Sulphur Springs, they had encountered the empty husk of a Cadillac El Dorado, scorched and crumpled, with perforations like big teeth marks scoring either side of it, amid the pink flowerbeds of the median. Its license plate read, "West Virginia—Wild, Wonderful."

But beyond that, the day's journey had been uneventful. No shadow had swept over them as they headed southwest, no sound of leathery wings had assaulted them. Caldwell and Lewisburg and Smoot had blurred by like dreams. And whatever mysteries lurked in the Lost World Caverns, nothing had emerged to overwhelm and drag them within.

The land had lain like a thing insensible. The sound of a bird or sight of a rabbit had proved a rarity, and no person crossed their path. At Sandstone they had dog-legged off the interstate onto State Route 20, skimming south along the spine of a mountain and then dipping down to Hinton, an old railroad town, wheeling past white-washed churches and rotted old barns and hillsides blazing red with sumac.

In the roar and spray coming off the Sandstone Falls, they had paused to fill their canteens.

"Night'll be coming on soon," Cal had said, scanning the horizon. "Best we camp here, push on at dawn." By his reckoning, Boone's Gap was still a good twelve to fifteen miles off.

He'd begun unloading a tent from the pedicab when a touch like a whisper stayed him.

"Let's finish it," Tina had said.

So now here they stood, before this gray expanse like a slammed door.

Locking us out, Cal wondered, or something in?

Colleen caught his glance. "It's your call."

Why my call? He rebelled at the responsibility for a moment but he knew the answer. *Because I brought them here.*

Let's finish it.

But looking at his sister, at her aqua gaze held on the fog, he hesitated. With every mile they had drawn nearer, the voice—voices—had been louder in her mind, a wordless tumult that deafened her, rendered his own voice a mere whisper under it.

Back in Manhattan, he had felt so certain that their only chance lay in confronting this siren force before it grew stronger, while it was still in turmoil, fractured, to know what they were fighting. Now, as his heart battered in his chest, he wondered if he had been wrong to bring her here, if they should have fled, even though he'd been sure there was no hiding place.

Could Nijinsky have fled his God, no matter where he'd run?

No.

But how do you kill a god, even a false one?

You start by stepping through the door.

Cal fetched the Coleman lantern from the pedicab and, lighting it, led them into the fog. The light bounced off the mist, rendering it opaque.

Holding the lantern before him, Cal struggled to see the path, to stay on it, while Doc and Goldie walked the four bikes, Tina floating beside them. Colleen stowed her crossbow over her back—little use it would be in the fog—and drew out her big knife.

They advanced slowly, silence wrapping itself about them, hearing only the sounds of their breathing, their footsteps on the crackling leaves, amplified alarmingly back on them. The drifting dead grayness filled Cal's eyes, and he saw nothing, save the ghost of a tree here and there, looming up and shrinking back, seeming to move and shift with the drifting fog. The clammy mist settled on his clothes and skin, bled through, passing its cold into him. He had a sense of being invaded, absorbed by the fog, and felt momentarily as if he were held trapped by it, frozen outside time and space.

Glancing about him, Colleen and Doc and Goldie looked bleached of color, wavered insubstantially. Only Tina blazed clearly. But as Cal watched her, he discerned the fog melting in and out of her nimbus, dancing patterns on its surface like oil on water. It enveloped her, held her in its embrace, seemed to draw her more quickly forward.

She was pulling farther ahead of Cal now, growing misty with distance, like a moon receding behind clouds.

"Stay close, Tina," Cal called, but got no response. "Tina!"

Then he perceived that she had stopped. She was staring blankly ahead of her, and her voice, when she spoke, was a whisper.

"You open yourself to it, and the world falls away."

Cal heard an intake of breath beside him and saw that Goldie had gone ashen at the words.

"What is it?" Cal asked.

But before Goldie could speak, they heard the thing running at them, heard its shriek roiling up in the night.

Colleen spun as the figure lunged out of the vapor, slashed wildly at it. Cal dove at her, grabbed her arm and yanked it aside as the body plunged past, smashing into Doc, taking both of them down, the bikes falling in a clatter.

"What the hell are you doing!?" Colleen cried at Cal. But then she saw that the sprawled figure was a woman, breathing hard, crazed with fear. She flailed at Doc in her panic, then halted abruptly as she made him out in the glare of the lantern. She looked about in stunned surprise. She was a big woman, of middle years, Cal could see, tall and solid, with steel-gray hair and clothes that would have been conservatively efficient if they hadn't been bloody and torn. Rising, Doc tried to help her up, but she pulled free and sprang up with a boneless fluidity that Cal found unexpected and disconcerting.

She whipped about to face the way she had come, as a greenish phospor light exploded out of the mist and a buzzing roar assailed them.

And suddenly, Cal understood what she had been running from.

It towered over them, shambling forward. The living dead heart of it was something that had been a Confederate soldier once, an officer, that much was clear from the glowing gray uniform with the curlicues of braid at sleeve and throat, the brass buttons, the wild and flowing beard beneath burning eyes like the cores of green suns. Through his own terror, it came to Cal that West Virginia had sided with the Union, and that this walking specter might well have been one of the forgotten, unburied dead.

But the man-ghost of this creature formed only the frame, a basis upon which to heap amendment and ornamentation. Hornets swarmed over him in their thousands like a fresh skin, pulsing green as if irradiated, buzzing their rage. And playing over it all, electrical discharges of green-blue energy, snapping wildly like fallen high-tension lines in a storm.

Cal saw that Colleen was nearest to it, that soon it would trample her underfoot. He was on the move already, drawing his sword. Colleen stood her ground, whipping the crossbow off her back as the thing advanced on her. She loaded a bolt and fired. It passed clean through, sailed off into the fog.

The creature paused and regarded Colleen as if it had just grown aware of her. It raised its phantom gun and took aim.

Cal realized he wouldn't reach them in time. He cried out, just as an enormous explosion rent the air and he was dazzled by a flash of light.

"No!" he screamed. But then he saw that Colleen stood

unharmed, saw the apparition blasted away and dispersed to nothingness, the hornets scattering and vanishing into the fog.

Cal looked about him in confusion and spied Goldie standing just behind him, holding the musket he had carried here so lovingly, despite all of Colleen's jibes. Sparks were still spitting from its muzzle and a golden light played over its surface, which died out as Cal watched. The weapon crumbled away, fell from Goldie's hands.

"Okay, you win," Colleen said to Goldie, still shaking. "I'm the asshole."

"They're coming back," cried Tina, floating up out of the mist. The gray-haired woman became aware of her for the first time, and her expression was amazed and beatific. Cal noted—strangely, without surprise—that the illumination from Tina reflected off the woman's eyes, like a cat's.

Now Cal heard the angry buzzing, growing in volume, speeding toward them. *The hornets* . . .

"Tina," Cal spoke urgently. "What you did back at the creek, with that spearman—*can you do it again?*"

"I don't know. . . . I think so."

"Get close about her, everyone!" They drew in around Tina. She concentrated, and the light about her spread outward to encompass them all.

Then the hornets were upon them, hurling themselves at the swirling light, immolating themselves. Cautiously, Tina moved forward through the fog as the insects pursued them, Cal and the others huddling close, feeling her Corona tingling on their skins as the fog had done, but with none of its frigidity.

Now other things were coming out of the mist and night at them. Hard spectral fingers tore up out of the earth; glowing blue stalks snaked from the mist and were repulsed.

Cal saw Tina's aura flicker, begin to fade, read the weariness in her face. He gripped his sword, tensing for what might come.

But just as her light faded out, as she sank to the earth

with a groan, they punched through the mist into the outskirts of town. No one was in sight, just a few tumbledown
shacks, a scattering of weedy farm equipment in the moonlight.

Cal crouched beside Tina. Her hair pooled around her
shoulders, her body earthbound now, with only the faintest
twinkling playing over her skin. "You did it," he said, but
she didn't seem to hear. She lifted her head and peered into
the night, away from the fog, toward town. The tension had
all fallen away from her, and her face held only a distant,
contemplative serenity. It chilled Cal, pricked memory.
Once, as a boy, he had passed the glassworks in Hurley, seen
a frantic crowd trying to dissuade a hollow-eyed man from
shooting himself. Aaron Barnes it had been, Cal went to
school with his boy Cameron. Hanging back on the periphery, transfixed, Cal stared past dark-suited legs, the babble
of scared, pleading voices engulfing him. It had looked as
though they were swaying the man, when suddenly an expression of peace came over him, of vast relief, like an exhalation . . . and he fired.

Cal made a move to gather Tina in his arms, to lift her,
but she cut him off with an abrupt gesture, still gazing away,
and struggled to her feet. Not weightless, not yet. Give her
time to recharge and to come back to them.

Colleen, Doc and Goldie were checking out the bikes,
seeing what was still attached after their flight. Cal looked
beyond them, saw that the older woman had hurried down
the dirt road to a derelict two-story house.

He walked up to her, found that she was staring intently
at a spot on the ground where he could just make out a dark
stain. Then she straightened, shaking her head. "Not blood,"
she said with relief, and Cal wondered how she could be
sure of that.

She scrutinized the tangled yard, the heaps of discarded
washing machines, the labyrinth of trees farther on, seeing,
Cal felt certain, far more acutely than he could, but not finding what she sought.

"What are you looking for?"

"A friend who put himself in harm's way for me." She shoved back her disheveled hair, managed a smile. "As you and your friends just did." She extended a hand. "I'm Wilma Hanson."

"Cal Griffin, from New York."

"Well, Mr. Griffin, I'm afraid now that you've entered—" Her eyes grew alarmed as she glanced past him. "Stop her!"

Cal spun and saw that Tina was running hell for leather toward town. He took off after her, his legs kicking up the dirt, the cold air whipping at him. But Colleen, Doc and Goldie were ahead of him. They caught hold of her, dragged her to a staggering halt. She cried out, struggling, tearing at them, but there was no strength in her. She relapsed to stillness, her eyes on the dark, the unseen town.

We couldn't have done that if her tank wasn't on empty, Cal thought worriedly.

"Keep hold of her," Wilma Hanson said. "There's something in town that gets into them, makes them do things."

Cal looked up sharply at this, caught his own look mirrored on Colleen's face, and Goldie's, and Doc's.

Something that gets into them. Into Tina and Stern and that pitiful boy in the woods, and all the twisted, anguished ones. That beckoned them all the way from Manhattan. That blighted their waking hours, made a horror of their dreams, infected their souls.

Welcome to Boone's Gap.

"Do you know what it is?" Cal asked quietly.

"No," Wilma replied. "But I know where it is."

TWENTY-EIGHT

To Cal, the Wishart house looked like nothing so much as a pale reflection seen within dusky glass, a wavering mirage, elusive and then gone.

And yet he was staring right at it.

Peering out the window in Wilma Hanson's front room, the crackling pine in the fireplace banishing the fog chill from his bones, Cal sensed or imagined—he couldn't be sure which—*shame* emanating from that house, a shrinking from even the moon's fading light.

Behind him, Goldie sat cross-legged in the corner, welcoming Wilma Hanson's regiment of cats as they brushed against him, burnished him, while Doc and Colleen stood by the hearth with Wilma. Their voices were soft, their conversation banal. It was a breathing space, a tiny harbor in a great, unyielding storm.

Leading them to her home over rutted dirt paths, through the slumbering dark of town streets, Wilma had told of the comatose children and the old ones, the sense of their being drained like rivulets of water coursing to the sea, drawn inescapably toward the Wishart home.

"Even the power held in the land is being fed on," Wilma

had said, on the move, tensing against the pulse of the night that only she could sense, "the ghosts of this town's history. . . ."

Cal let the voices behind him blur to a comfortable drone, let himself float on the scent of woodsmoke, the taste of mountain air, the homey warmth of the room about him; all the subtle sounds and smells that brought home back to him. And he was a boy again in Hurley, his infant sister dozing in the far room, his mother a watchful presence to shield them from the chaos of the world.

Then he heard a soft shifting above him and looked toward the attic. Toward Tina.

They—*he*—had locked her there.

After her emergence from the fog, her headlong flight toward town, she was passive, seemed hardly aware of them. She allowed herself to be led to Applby Lane, not even glancing at the Wishart House as they passed it, only slowing almost imperceptibly.

But Cal noted her radiance growing ever brighter, her tread barely brushing the ground. She was regaining her strength, would soon have it all, and then none of them could hope to stop her.

So, in this brief span while she still mutely acquiesed, Cal agreed to imprison her in the one room with no windows, with a door they could bar.

While the house next door shimmered and waited.

From above, another thud, louder than before.

He turned toward the hearth, saw his companions in the Rembrandt light of the fire. His glance caught the photos on the mantel of Wilma's sisters and their families, of her students.

"Have you lost many you were close to?" he asked.

"Well, it's a very small town."

"Those men," Doc said. "The changed ones outside. Why did it kill them?"

"One of my friends, the one who—" Wilma stopped as though about to reveal more of her heart than she wished. "He said something got into his mind, was telling him to kill Bob."

Bob Wishart. Bob, whom Wilma had thought should be dead already, dead when the machines went down. But who, at least in the minds of the changed ones, was very much alive.

"And you're sure Dr. Wishart hasn't been here in months?" Cal asked.

Wilma nodded as Colleen broke in, "But why the stay-at-home brother? The handyman? Why kill Bob, if he isn't dead already? What could *he* have to do with draining the town?"

"Somehow," Wilma said, "I have a feeling that whatever's compelling those attacks doesn't care about the town, about any of us."

Cal began, "But why would the changed ones—"

"Because," Goldie broke in from his cat-contented corner, "it told them to. Because you open yourself to it, and the world falls away."

Cal stared. It was what Tina had said, in the fog.

Goldie turned to him, somber. "There's two pieces to this. Here and the big one. The real one. It's not *here* your sister's being pulled. It's *through* here. To the other. The maw."

Cal looked again at the Wishart house, as though he could see it now, even through Wilma's walls. The brothers used to speak via computer; was Bob some secret whiz kid who had something to do with the Source Project without anyone's knowing?

But Wilma had known the twins all their lives, and Bob had shown no such aptitude. Fred had been the brains of the two, Bob—with his over-keen sensitivities—the heart.

Besides, Bob had been in a coma for *months*, long before—

Another thud from above—loud, startling. Through the doorway to the dining room, Cal could see the hanging lamp shudder.

Then a crash. Tina, unseen, thrusting herself against the barred attic door.

Answers or no, they were out of time. Cal had to get into that house *now*, to *see*.

Hurriedly, he said to Wilma, "We'll need something to use for shields—and the most direct route through the house to Bob."

Wilma was shaking her head, even before he'd finished speaking. "You don't understand. You have no way to know what it can do."

Cal reached out, grasped her hands. "You had nothing but speed, no protection. And those poor dead ones out there, they had nothing at all. Besides—"

From above, another crash. Cal winced, but his voice was strong. "We have no options."

The cats' eyes, huge and yellow and haughty, followed Wilma as she rose and fetched paper to draw the floor plan.

From her station on the second-floor landing, Wilma could see Cal Griffin and his companions moving slowly toward the Wishart house. The moon hung low in the sky, its light glinting off the makeshift shields they carried, fashioned from the corrugated tin of her storage shed, the leather straps from her scrap room.

The impacts resounding from the attic just above her were coming with less frequency, less force. Wilma had volunteered to stand guard over Griffin's sister, and, at first, the child's blows against the thick oak walls and door had been so frenzied that, special powers or no, Wilma had felt certain the girl was harming herself. Now, with the sounds weakening, Wilma hoped it was a sign of resignation rather than serious injury.

Poor child, with those distant, hungering eyes. So like Wilma's students, particularly the ones who had remained in Boone's Gap, settling into the life of not-enough.

Until the Change, Wilma had told herself that she'd chosen wisely when she had returned from college to stay, embracing the safe and the familiar; told herself that withdrawing from Hank's affections all those years back had been about valuing the solid, stable life she'd worked so hard to craft.

But what had she chosen, really? What bargain had she struck?

Wilma felt a silken pressure against her leg, saw Imp brushing up against her, seeking reassurance. She spied Mortimer and Theodora and the others crouched nearby, tremulous and watchful, unnerved by the unaccustomed intrusions.

Wilma reached down to stroke Imp. As the others drew close, she brought her heightened senses once more to the struggles within her house, and without.

Cal led the way, the long weeds rustling and whispering around their knees and across the six-foot tin shields. It was only when they got within a few yards of the Wishart house that he was able, suddenly, to see the place clearly in the flare of Doc's lantern. The stink of decay, of things unidentifiable and terrifying, grew stronger as they approached.

Doc whispered, *"Ty shto ahuyel."*

And Cal could feel it. Whatever was inside screamed at them, hurling against them its power and its will: *Stay out of here! Stay out! Stay out!*

He shifted his sword in his hand, signaled them into formation. They had shaped the pieces of tin so that, when joined, they became a kind of turtle shell. A clumsy solution, but they'd been crippled by lack of tools and time.

Doc, Colleen and Goldie had just taken note of Cal's gesture, begun to move, when a sudden stench billowed from the open door of the house. Colleen said, "Watch it!" even before the glow of the lantern picked up movement inside. A grunter was getting to its feet, slowly, staggering, and no wonder: dead for a week, rotting, swollen, decayed eyes staring. . . .

With an inarticulate gluey howl, another grunter corpse

launched itself at them out of the weeds beside the porch, a rusted pair of pruning shears in one hand.

Colleen cursed, swung at it with her wrench with a blow that connected in a sodden horrible splat. But Cal knew, maneuvering the bulky shield and slashing at the creature that lumbered from the porch, killing was not the answer. They were dead already. The dispassionate precision that had taken hold during his battle with Stern returned. Cal cut, not at the head or face, but first at the hands, then at the feet.

Goldie was beside him, grappling and shoving at the attacker with makeshift pike and shield, keeping it at bay while Cal hacked. He heard Colleen curse again, and then snarl, "You dead son of a bitch, will you *lay down* already!" and turned, to see the smashed, reeling remains of the grunter trying to get up to attack again. He cut off the thing's feet, sickened and hating himself, even knowing it could neither feel nor think.

The two corpses were still trying to crawl after Cal and his friends as they sprang up the porch steps and into the dark of the house, the tin of their four-walled citadel clattering into place. A whirlwind met them. Junk and dust and the very fragments of the house pounded against the reverberating metal. Splintered wood flew with the hideous velocity of crossbow bolts, denting their shields, bruising them, staggering them sideways. Bits of wire and springs writhed beneath their jolting shell, caught and tore at their ankles, stabbed through shoes while the dust of decades billowed into an impenetrable cloud.

Choking, Cal thrust the others out behind him, Doc limping from a shard of wood driven through the muscle of his calf. Back in the blackened, gore-clotted weeds, a yard from where they'd entered, they stood together gasping.

Colleen said, "House, one. New Yorkers, zip."

Cal rasped out, "Again. Momentum." He turned to Doc, "You up to it?"

Doc nodded, gray-faced. "Into the reactor."

They braced. Cal waited a moment, gauging distance and direction. *"Now!"*

They plunged forward, the boards of the porch buckling and ripping under their feet and the joists underneath spearing up at them. Cal kicked the lock of the inner door with all his strength. It splintered inward and they pounded through as one, grouped beneath their shields.

The lantern Doc held exploded in his hand. He threw it away from him, stumbling, lost them fleetingly in blackness. Goldie cried out, and fireballs whirled into being, illuminating the onrush of missiles: cans and broken glass, iron burners from the stove and pieces of china and plastic sharp as razors. They lurched back together, shields clattering, an instant before the maelstrom. It staggered them, but this time Cal shouted, "Move!"

They battled forward, Cal squinting between the shields' joining, wavering slits. Dust-thickened moonlight and sputtering, dimming fireballs painted visions suited for a madhouse.

In the corner, the refrigerator heaved and twisted, wrenching itself like a chained bull to get loose. The very baseboards and the moldings of the ceiling undulated and jerked, popping nails, battling to free themselves, to join the killing assault.

The space of the kitchen seemed to distort, twisting under the impact of malevolent will. The walls moved, cupboards gaped. Then, with the speed of a striking snake, the wallpaper pattern hissed out from the walls in gripping loops of thorny rope, and snared Colleen's foot.

Colleen went down hard, both hands encumbered, corrugated tin slamming the floor beneath her forearm as her wrench sailed into an ebony void.

Their circle was broken. All about them, shards of broken dishes, scattered and corkscrewed silverware, smashed window glass slowly rose from their resting places and began to swirl in a large but closing ring, increasing into a howling, savage storm.

At the same moment, a dead grunter inches from Colleen heaved itself up from the floor where it had lain for weeks by the smell, oozing, bones showing through the shreds of its flesh. Cal slashed at it as Colleen wriggled free of her tangling shield, rolling away into the ruins of the kitchen table, which she immediately grasped as a weapon.

The table wheeled and thrashed in her grip. Cal handed off his sword to Doc, jerked Colleen up and back against him, and stamped on her shield's curving top to stand it upright. She seized it, their circle closed again—and the storm within the house exploded with a screech.

Through the kitchen and down the hall, Wilma had directed them. *It's the door on the left.*

Only in the darkness there seemed to be a hundred doors, all banging open and shut, with nothing behind any of them but black. The roaring tempest filled ears and minds, the house rocked on its foundation with a violence that wrung groans from the wood and brick and nails.

A voice screaming: GET OUT GET OUT GET OUT.

Screaming in terror.

It was afraid.

Mortally afraid.

Images of icy water, of screaming voices, of blue sparks swirling out of emptiness . . .

Doc yelled, "Cal!" as he went down. Cal, wrenching at the single door that hadn't slammed open and shut, turned back. A sliver of floorboard had speared Doc from below, piercing his thigh.

Colleen, shifting her shield to shelter them both, was already dragging the physician back to the outer door. Goldie, standing alone and vulnerable in the no-man's land between, looked to Cal, questioning.

The knob was in Cal's hand, held shut, it seemed, not by a lock but by an invisible *other* on the opposite side.

With a desperation, a rage beyond his own comprehension, Cal jerked back. The door gave. Only a few inches. Only for an instant.

Two faces turned toward him. Identically featured and yet so different as to chill. Moonlit phantoms in blackness.

One substantial . . . and one like a reflection in glass.

The knob leapt from Cal's hand; the door slammed shut.

Cal dove for Goldie just as a huge serving dish sliced his way, grabbed him by the back of his vest and pulled him back. Cal stumbled, parrying objects with his sword. Staggering through the onslaught of the porch, they finally burst back into the damp night outside.

Doc was gasping, sprawled amid the devil grass, holding his thigh, blood spurting between his fingers, the gouge far worse than the earlier slash on his calf. Cal ripped off his bloody, grime-black shirt, removed the cleaner T-shirt beneath and folded it swiftly into a pressure bandage. A little distance from them lay the corpses of the two grunters. Cal suspected they'd rear to life again the moment anyone took a step toward the house, but they were quiet now.

Thunder growled overhead, and the air was thick with the smell of lightning and wind. Cal, Goldie and Colleen bent over Doc, getting in each other's way trying to secure the bandage, to check him for other wounds. He waved them off impatiently.

"Don't fuss over me; I'm all right. If I were to start dying, I would tell you."

"We're lucky any of us got out of there in one piece," said Colleen, rising shakily and stepping toward the spare lantern they'd left on the curb.

"I don't think it was luck." Cal stared at the Wishart house, silent now, watchful. "It could have killed us any time it wanted."

"Then what do you think it was?"

"Mercy. It did only what it needed to drive us away. Just like with Miss Hanson."

"*Only*? Cal, *that* was the old college try."

"No." Doc said struggling to his feet, hissing through pain-clenched teeth. "I concur with Calvin. Our shields were down a dozen times. On any one of those occasions—" He tried to put weight on the bad leg, nearly fell. Goldie caught him under one arm.

"Guys, I know I'm the pessimist in the group, but what's *this*?" The sweep of Colleen's hand took in the mutilated grunter forms. "Ethnic cleansing?"

The answer came from the shadows. "Nothing short of death could have stopped them, once the voice got into their minds." Wilma Hanson came up beside them with her gliding, soundless step. Seeing them up close, she put a hand to her mouth. "Oh, my heavens."

"You should see the house," Goldie said.

"How's my sister?" Cal asked.

"Quiet." Concern etched Wilma's brow. "For quite some time now."

❦

When Wilma Hanson unlocked the door and Cal stepped within, he found his sister in a state of semiconsciousness, distressingly sallow and drawn.

But also, in some inexplicable way, more human.

The attic was a ruin. Boxes of Christmas decorations were upended, board games scattered, their pieces intermingled—the Game of Life, Candyland, Mystery Date. A tangle of quilts and outgrown clothes had erupted from careful folds to take wing and land where they might.

It was an echo of the Wishart house, as if a hurricane had burst from the center of the room, then retreated. And indeed it had, Cal reflected, threading his fingers through the silk of Tina's hair. Thunder had entered her. The storm child.

"Two faces." Doc sat slumped on an apple crate, spectral in the amber light from the lantern on the floor, its radiance casting long shadows up the walls and slanting ceiling. "You're sure?"

Cal nodded. "The one on the bed, the one that looked real, he . . . I dunno. There was this quality of, 'Oh, Jesus.' Like he was shocked. Sorry for me."

"And the other?" Doc asked.

"The other . . . it's weird, he was so much clearer, even though I could see right through him. He seemed . . . outraged. Only it wasn't, 'How *dare* you!' It was more like terror. At least, that's the vibe I got."

"You're our Lionel Hampton, man." Goldie glanced up from the battered 1964 Sears catalogue he'd been leafing through. "Our king of vibes."

"Unidentical identical twins," Colleen muttered.

Wilma crossed to one of the few cartons still intact and retrieved an old photo album. Flipping to the page, she held it open. Cal regarded the bleached color photograph. Wilma radiant with youth and youth's near-infinite possibility, Wilma with the twins.

Cal's eyes went to Fred. Even then, it could be detected: the tighter set of his mouth, the opaque quality of the eyes, the hunched, defended posture.

Cal murmured, "It's him."

"I guess it makes a kind of sense," Wilma sighed. "They were so close—"

"Close?" Colleen looked up. "Didn't you say Fred hadn't visited in all the months since the accident?"

Wilma hesitated, uncertain.

"Survivor guilt." Everyone turned to Doc. His eyes evaded, and he fought to keep his voice even. "You cannot bring them back, cannot undo the tragedy of it, so you try to avoid it, not think of it—all the while thinking of nothing else."

Wilma nodded. "When all the machines stopped, Bob should have . . . Fred must have found a way to prevent it."

Colleen said, "The Source Project."

Cal answered Wilma's questioning glance with, "What Dr. Wishart was working on."

Again, Wilma hesitated. Then she asked, "Is he draining the town?"

"Would he?" Doc asked. "The Fred you know, would he be capable of such an act?"

Wilma thought, *yes*. But how could she possibly make such an accusation against a friend? It felt like a betrayal.

Then, like nonsense. Carefully, she offered, "Arleta is— *was*—a fearful woman, and she instilled that in them. We all worried about how much the boys depended on each other once, well . . . once Arleta stopped allowing company." Then she added, oddly protective, "She just didn't want anything from the outside world coming in."

Cal gazed down at his sister, her eyes closed, the points of her ears peeking out between fine strands. It's what he'd wanted for her. A bubble of safety. A line of defense between her and what he'd increasingly come to see as an assaultive world.

"It could be about more than just keeping his brother alive." Cal's gaze lingered on Tina, on the long pale lashes of her closed eyes. "Fred could be hanging on to Bob to keep hold of himself somehow, remind himself of who he is."

"Or maybe just hold on," Goldie said, not looking up from the catalogue. "I believe Fred's a wanted man. By the Big Kahuna. The one wanting to chow down on all us tweaked ones. Source-zilla."

"This isn't getting us anywhere," Colleen snapped. "It's all goddam guesses."

Turning to Wilma, Doc asked, "The energy drain. The sickness. How bad?"

"The children are getting weaker. Some of the old people, too. A few, we can't rouse anymore." She drew in a sharp breath. "And it's spreading."

"Calvin," Doc said quietly, "whatever is sapping these people, there is a battle: Fred, clinging to Bob, and something else absolutely determined to break his grip. And soon I think, very soon, more than just those creatures will start to die, unless the deadlock is broken somehow."

Wilma drew her shoulders back. "Well, we survived company thugs. We survived cave-ins. We've even survived the damn economy." Turning to her guests, she inquired, "So what do we need to do to get these battlers the hell out?"

For a moment, no one spoke. Then Colleen said softly, "We kill it. Even though it kicked our ass. We find some way to kill it." It occurred to Cal that she was calling Fred Wishart *it* rather than *he* to distance herself.

In the dust gloom of the attic, they contemplated how precisely they might destroy something that only one of them had even been able to glimpse. But to Cal, it was not the doing of the thing but the act itself that disquieted him. For in annihilating what dwelt in that shattered house, might they possibly destroy not just the illness but the cure?

"No," he said at last to the others. "We need to know more."

"Right," said Colleen. "We'll commission a study."

"Like you said, it's all guesses," Cal replied. "Only doesn't it feel like Goldie's right, that Wishart's fighting the same fight we are, that we've got a common enemy? And even if that guess is wrong, Wishart's still our only link to— what did you call it?"

Cal's eyes were on Goldie, but it was Doc who responded, " 'The real one.' "

"Look. I want to shotgun this nightmare out of existence, too. But we've got to try another way."

He added, with the certainty of a decision already made, "What Tina felt, and what I felt from Fred Wishart once we got close, was fear. Panic. And you don't approach that with aggression, you approach it with—"

"Hold it, hold it."

"*Colleen . . .*"

"Tina also came up with 'crazy,' right? Any hands here on how we should be approaching *that*?"

"Sometimes," Goldie murmured, "you talk to a crazy like he's okay, and he can become okay."

"No, no, *no*—"

Cal cut in over Colleen. "Fred Wishart is terrified and he's alone . . . so alone is how I need to go in there."

"Cal?"

The soft voice turned them all. It was Tina, eyes barely

open. He knelt quickly beside her, taking her hand. It felt cold, but her fingers tightened about his.

"You okay?" he asked. She nodded and snuggled against him.

Wilma leaned close. "Cal, you're tired, and you're not thinking. I went in only with concern, *knowing* them, and totally unescorted."

"I know." Cal stroked silken hair. "But it's not just aggression that fuels fear, it's . . . well. Wishart wanted to scare you, and he did."

Doc asked, "Calvin, are you imagining you're going to be able to go back in there and not be afraid?"

"Hell, why would he be afraid? " Colleen answered for him. "Our boy here *likes* the idea of wearing a Frigidaire for a hat."

Cal turned his gaze back to Tina. Her exhaustion appeared to have brought her back to herself, and him, at least for now.

"Tina?" His voice was almost a whisper. "Tina?"

Her eyes fluttered open.

"We've never broken our word, have we?"

Her expression clouded.

"I need to break it now. I need to try something that may mean I won't be able to come back to you."

"That's not the deal," she said in alarm, drawing back, rousing herself. "I can help you, like in the fog with the hornets."

"Tina . . ."

"You *need* me, to talk to Dr. Wishart. To get through, beneath. *I'm* the one plugged into Mutant Central."

She had heard them, all of them, talking, he realized. But had she forgotten, was she unaware of her imprisonment in the attic?

The others were silent, empty of suggestion. Wilma drew Cal away from Tina, out of earshot.

"I can't tell you what to do. That child, though . . . she has a gift. Maybe she has it for a reason."

"If that thing gets hold of her—" Cal protested.

"Something's got hold of a lot of children in this town. They're dying of it." Wilma sighed. "I can't tell you, but I can ask: Give all those other children their chance."

Her hand in his was warm in the night air, and weightless. A dragonfly, Tina flowed beside him toward the Wishart house. The light about her had returned, its pastel mists veiling her.

At the perimeter of the gouged, ravaged front yard, Cal halted and released her hand. The scattered, butchered remains of the grunters lay cold and insensate among the weeds.

Deliberately, Cal drew his sword and stuck it point first into the damp earth. Then he unclasped his belt and scabbard, laid them alongside it. He straightened and looked at his sister, into the sapphire flame of her eyes, saw her disquiet and her resolve. He took her hand, turned back toward the house.

"Dr. Wishart, please. We need to talk with you."

He had tried for a normal tone, but his voice sounded harsh to his ears, invasive. He tensed, waiting. But all was stillness, save for the cicada hum.

We're not going to hurt you. Cal aimed the thought toward the house, made a mantra of it. He pressed away what Wishart had tried to do to *him*, locked his fear behind a door in his mind.

He took a hesitant step onto the ruined lawn.

NO. The word, forceful and blunt, came at them. Cal flinched, and he saw Tina wince with it, wondered how much louder it seemed to her.

The body pieces of what had once been the sons and husbands and fathers of the town did not stir. Warily, Cal moved past them and, with Tina, climbed the broken steps of the porch.

In the porch, the battered, bloodstained corpses of the books heaved and fluttered as if blown by a breath but did not fly at them. There was a sound, a deep creaking groan, like the whole house shifting on its timbers. A sense of watching, of waiting, rose from the walls, from the air about them.

They crossed the porch, stepped through the place where the kitchen door had been torn from its hinges, and entered the house.

Wilma had finally gotten the Russian doctor to agree to lie down, but only when she had positioned her sofa by the front window so that he could monitor the progress of Griffin and his sister toward the Wishart house. Under his guidance, Wilma had redressed his wound—the impromptu bandage was soaked through—and washed the blood from his face, the doctor all the while protesting impatiently. But now, at last, he lay quiet and watchful.

Wilma glanced out the window, saw that Griffin and his sister had crossed the Wishart porch with nothing rising to bar their way. A promising first step. She said a silent prayer as they vanished into the house.

Wilma stepped onto her own porch. Goldman and the Brooks woman stood rigid, gazing toward the Wishart house, seeing only darkness, hearing only the vague sounds of the fading night.

Pausing behind them, Wilma caught a scent on the air, or thought she did, distant and elusive, of coal and earth and blood, heard a soft rustling in the woods that might have been wind. It brought Hank to her thoughts. Since they had been attacked, since he had thrown himself at the grunters and yelled for her to run, she had heard nothing of him, seen no sign. Had they killed him? Or had he managed, through the ferocity of his attack and his fleetness, to get away?

She had seen no blood at the site, and that had heartened her. But thinking on it now, it seemed strange. Hank had been outnumbered, surrounded. Surely they would have drawn some of his blood, or he theirs. In all their previous attacks, they had proven unrelentingly murderous. If they spared him, what possibly could have been their motive?

Puzzling over it, Hank's struggled words came back to her.

They know I led the men out of the mines, they're looking to me to—

To what?

And then, with a chilling certainty she could not have explained, Wilma thought she knew.

To lead them.

Hank, with his cool head and audacious nerve, his relentlessness and grit. The voice in his head had been working on him, striving to fill him with an irresistible desire to kill Bob Wishart. What if it had overwhelmed him at last, as it had Joe Rance and Eddie Dayton and the others like him? But more than that, what if Hank—who alone had kept his wits about him even as he changed and had led his team, what remained of them, to the surface and safety—what if Hank retained his ability to strategize?

Not for him the unreasoning frontal attack doomed to failure. No, he would watch and wait for his moment, until the dark intelligence in the house was distracted, its attention focused on . . .

Other visitors.

The scent was stronger, unmistakable now, wafting from the trailer park that bordered both her home and the Wisharts. And the sound, louder and most definitely *not* the wind.

Wilma stepped in front of Goldie and Colleen, both unaware of what was urgently, oppressively clear to her.

"We've got trouble," she said.

GET OUT GET OUT. It came like a blow, and Cal stepped back. Tina's fingers closed tight around his, and he felt her trembling. In its corner, the refrigerator jerked threateningly. Cupboard doors slammed in manic rage, their contents long since smashed to nothing.

GET OUT GET OUT GET OUT.

"Can you reach him, Tina?" Cal fought not to shout over the shriek in his mind.

"I'm trying." She struggled to get the words out, a pulse twitching at the corner of her eye, her breath coming in short gasps. "But there's something else in here *pulling* at me."

He could hear the panic in her voice, and he tried to will into her what calm he retained. Whether coincidence or not, she seemed to gather strength. She closed her eyes and concentrated, her feet drifting down to graze the floor.

The scream in his mind eased back.

The refrigerator quivered and was still. The cupboards lapsed into silence. They walked forward more quickly now, into the lightless pit of the hallway, the faint illumination that radiated from Tina's flesh magnified eerily by the dust.

The door of the far bedroom on the left was shut, blue-green light leaking out along its frame.

We're not going to harm you, we're not—

From the edge of his vision, Cal caught the blur of a dark object hurtling toward them. Tina saw it, too; her aura flared up to field it.

"Don't," Cal called to her. She caught his meaning—do *nothing* that might be perceived as a threat—and faded her aura back, rendering it insubstantial. Cal blocked the object, a black Bakelite telephone, with his forearm. Pain shot up his arm as the phone rebounded, bounced off a wall and lay motionless.

There was a quaking beneath his feet, he could hear cracks splintering along the walls on either side of him, and the whole house seemed to moan.

You're safe, you're safe, you're safe, but Cal could feel fear rising to engulf the universe, and he felt his own fear in answer.

In the flickering light of Tina's glow, Cal could see the picture frames lurching and slamming against the walls to get free, the carpeting tearing itself up. Tina was shaking, her hair whipping about as in a gale. Her eyes were huge, desperate, as she strained to stay focused amid the assault of clashing wills.

"Cal—Cal—I—!"

And then it was as if something deep within the house snapped, and there was a roaring that went on and on. The dead bulb in the fixture overhead ruptured, spewing glass. Cal instinctively moved to shield his sister. Picture frames tore free, and yellow pages shuddered up and catapulted at them. He batted them aside wildly, shouting. Then he felt a tingling on his skin and his eyes were dazzled as Tina's luminescence flared out to enfold him, and relief and disappointment flooded him.

Magazines reared like hawks, struck the incandescence and were rebuffed, a side table came swinging up to shatter. Medicine bottles launched themselves, exploded against the barrier; pills and glass shrapneled against the bubble and fell back.

And over the deafening fear-rage bellow, another noise, rumbling from deep within the walls, a cracking, crashing, ripping nightmare of a sound. Chunks of plaster burst from the wall, and a thick timber shot out of the opening, piercing Tina's barrier. It caught her a glancing blow on the side of the head, like a giant flicking a finger. She cried out and crumpled, her radiance damping down to nothing, leaving them defenseless.

The very air seemed to vibrate with triumph as the onslaught intensified, a cannonade of pens and paperweights and metal trays raining down on them. Cal fell on his sister, covering her with his body, taking the brunt of it. An aluminum medicine cart crashed into him, a heavy wall clock, a radio. He cried out at the spiderweb agony of cracking ribs. Doors along each wall were flinging themselves open and shut, laboring to tear themselves from their hinges. A bookcase tumbled toward him, scattering heavy volumes and figurines, which tore and shattered yet still bounded forward to expend their fury on him.

Cal curled into a tight ball around his sister, unmoving

beneath him, and he knew it was the end and there was nothing he could do. One of the doors shrieked loose and cartwheeled through the air, smashing down on him with mad exultation, and he screamed, and in the scream was the entirety of his failure and his love and how he would give anything, *do* anything to save her, to consume himself and all the world if only, only—

Oh God oh God oh God, for God's sake, please, please, please, don't hurt her!

And in the deafening silence that followed, he couldn't say whether he had screamed it or just thought it.

But the response was immediate, as all the objects dropped lifeless to the carpet, the quivering of floor and walls and ceiling halted, and the dust hung mute in the air.

Beneath him, Tina was breathing in quick gasps, moaning softly. Cal rose, pushing the heaped debris and remnant of door aside. The motion sent white-hot needles coursing up his side, and he nearly blacked out. But he inhaled slowly, pushed the vertigo down.

Bending stiffly, hissing against the pain, Cal took his sister's hands. She was conscious, breathing more evenly now. He helped her to her feet, and she rose shakily, floated up off the floor, glimmering once more.

Slices of misty, first dawn light filtered in through the frame whose door had ripped free and the others where doors hung ajar. Only the far door on the left remained shut, the ghost light seeping along its edges. Tina opened her mouth to frame a question, but Cal motioned her to silence. She leaned in to him, and he put his arm around her as they advanced.

His feet crunching on shards of glass and plastic and ceramic, he stepped to the door, reached for the knob. But before he could grasp it, the door swung open.

Like some lost city of scrap metal amid the wild, the trailer park loomed, silent and dark. Several of the elderly residents had gone missing weeks ago, with hideous gashes in the sides of their motor homes the only indication of what had happened to them. The rest had moved in with friends and relations, where light and numbers kept the night things at bay.

Moving quickly, Goldie and Colleen at her side—Doc having been ordered to stay behind—Wilma could sense the grunters on the other side of the trailers, coming fast toward the Wishart house, could hear their low, eager exhalations.

Too late, Wilma spied the rock hurled from behind a tree, wasn't fast enough to reach Colleen. It struck the lantern she carried, shattering it, quenching its light.

Then the grunters were on them, more than Wilma would have thought possible, oozing from the brush and low branches, from beneath rusty Winnebagos and corroded Airstreams. A hard, compact form dropped on her from atop one of the dented aluminum structures, and she was rolling with it on the mossy ground as it tore hissing at her. She scratched at its eyes, drove it shrieking away. She cast about in the blur of bodies for her companions, saw them amid the surging, growling forms, flailing wrench and staff and forcing the grotesques back.

But then two more of the devils came at her, and another butted his head into her stomach, and she was dragged down gasping, their fists pummeling her, one of them grabbing her throat. She twisted, tried to claw at them, but their weight was pressing her into the earth, she couldn't catch her breath, felt herself giving way, the stink of them close on her, their laughter filling her ears.

And then the smell of blood was everywhere, and the taut, heaving grunter on top of her collapsed, hot liquid spilling over her face, and she was released, the other two squealing, running away. A hand reached down to her, and she seized it, climbed to her feet.

The sword he held was still clotted with earth from where it had been plunged into the dirt in front of the Wishart house.

"Sorry to disobey your orders," Doc said.

Wilma grinned, but there was no time for words, as beyond the press of bodies, she spied a familiar, darting form.

Hank, unmistakably. On the move with a chunk of concrete in his hand, giving low, growling orders, rallying his followers as he vaulted past the others. Rolling and regaining his footing, running as he had as a boy; no, even faster.

Toward the Wishart house.

And Wilma, bounding with her uncanny feline grace, was after him.

Bob Wishart lay immobile on the bed, his eyes closed, still connected to a maze of wires and tubes and useless, dark machinery. Beside him stood his brother, lightly resting a protective hand on Bob in much the same way, Cal realized, that he had his own hand on his sister's thin shoulders.

Dr. Fred Wishart looked as he had in the flash Cal had glimpsed earlier: pale, translucent, with little indication of the power he wielded. But Cal could see that the tiny flashes of light that made up Wishart's skin were continually flickering out and reflaring, as if he were in a constant state of disintegration and rebirth, photon by photon. The mighty effort he was expending was consuming him; it took the fuel of the entire town to keep him from being extinguished.

It *was* he, not the Source, feeding on Boone's Gap.

Dr. Wishart's gaze followed them as they entered the room, and there was that same desperate fierceness Cal had seen before, with a new, indefinable note tempering it. Power murmured and flickered in the corners of the room, blue lines of what looked like fire creeping across the floor, slow-moving greenish mists oozing from the walls.

Wishart turned to his twin, spoke in a voice surprisingly melodic and gentle. "Bob?" Cal saw that the two were breathing in unison.

Bob's eyes fluttered open. Fred nodded toward the doorway, toward him and Tina. Bob turned his head dreamily to them. Barely conscious, hardly moving, he seemed held by a whisper.

"There, you see?" Dr. Wishart said. "No harm."

Bob looked relieved, and Cal was again struck by the difference between the brothers, the difference that had been branded on them before the Change, before they were grown. The frantic, anguished moment in the hall came to Cal, his despair to save his sister, who knew him best, whom he loved above all. And he understood that it was his need that had spoken to the minds of the unseen twins, had moved Fred to relent, to spare them . . . for Bob's sake, for his gentler nature.

And how much did Bob know of the rest?

Cautiously, Cal inched farther into the room with Tina. "You haven't told him?" he asked Dr. Wishart. "He doesn't know about the others?"

Fred Wishart's gaze darkened. Bob looked at him, perplexed.

"It's nothing," Fred told him, too quickly. But his brother's eyes remained on him, inquiring. "I'm not strong enough. I'm just borrowing from some of the people here . . . to keep you alive, to keep us together."

And killing your neighbors, the people you grew up with, who never did you harm. Cal wanted to hate him, this monster who had mutilated those wretches on the lawn and in the fog, who was even now draining the life from the old and the young and the weak.

But drawing his sister closer to him, holding her there, Cal found he could not.

Cal heard Tina's soft voice. "You're killing the town, everyone in it, to keep this going."

"Fred?" Bob's voice was tender and mournful, a parched croak, long unused. "Fred, we can't . . ."

"No, Bobby. If I let go, you'll die—"

"But Fred . . ."

Fred's crystalline-bright eyes flashed on Cal and Tina, and Cal felt himself assailed by a blast of thought. YOU DON'T UNDERSTAND YOU DON'T KNOW.

Bob's troubled gaze, briefly on Cal, returned to his brother. Fred reacted as though to a caress. Damping his anger, he said, "The world—something . . . happened. More important than—"

Fred Wishart froze for a moment, buffeted by some internal war he alone was privy to. He continued, ever so gently, "I let go, I'm destroyed, too. Something bad *needs* me—to be whole. . . ."

Bob turned his head on his pillow, looked pleadingly at Cal. "Please. Tell me. What's happening here?"

Again, thought crashed into Cal, guilty, frantic, desperate, justifying, words all tumbled and overlapping, a jumbled mea culpa and defense. PURE RESEARCH CHANGED OBJECTED CHANGED DEVIL'S BARGAIN CHANGED ME CHANGED NO CHANGE LOVE BOB LOVE NO—

Cal looked at Bob, trying to steady himself, trying to focus through the screaming in his mind.

Desperation-driven, panic-driven madness, Cal could empathize with. But in the face of this howling self-justification, everything in Cal rebelled.

"You should know," Cal's low voice trembled, every word a fierce battle, "You have a choice. You have a—"

NO NO NO.

It thundered in Cal's brain, the room itself shaking, tortured, accusatory.

NO TELL NO BLOCKING DOORWAY BLOCKING HOLDING CLOSED CAN'T OPEN SWALLOW WHOLE SWALLOW ME I CEASE WHO WHAT I AM MONSTER.

Cal battled to respond, to answer in words or thoughts, but the wall against him felt as solid as stone. For Fred Wishart, the continued existence of his fellow beings had fallen to nothing in the face of this higher imperative, his need to cling to Bob.

All in Boone's Gap were to die.

Cal turned once more to the waiting Bob, clearly screened somehow from Fred's words. Sensing it might end his own life, Cal struggled to speak.

NO NO NO. It was like a hurricane. Cal staggered back, grasping the doorframe. UNDERSTAND UNDERSTAND BOB DIES IT TAKES ME.

Fred Wishart ran distracted starry fingers through fire-light hair, and his wild desolate eyes shifted—boring into Tina.

AND IT TAKES HER.

Cal couldn't move. He felt as if he were falling away from himself. TAKE HER. Tina. Into the monster's maw.

Bob's eyes were on him. Waiting. While, in an instant that would, in the future, seem to stretch on for an eternity, Cal's voice was still.

Suddenly, the far window exploded inward and a small gray body flung itself through the opening, landing with a springy lightness. It whipped its big head around and spotted Bob, hurled itself toward the bed with a chunk of concrete raised high in its hands.

Cal screamed, "No!" as Fred Wishart's head snapped up, eyes no longer human, no longer of the living earth at all, a blazing blue horror of darkness. Wishart opened his mouth, and fire poured out, light streamed from his eyes. The whole fabric of the house wrenched and twisted, crushing inward, and the grunter was hurled to the floor, swept into a corner like a bug by a broom.

Glass shattered and more grunters were pouring in, through both windows now. Wishart swung his glare around to them, and they were caught and smashed back, cracking the walls, their necks snapping as they slid limply down.

But now the first grunter was back up, launching himself toward Bob. A heavy respirator lurched from its base, flew killingly through the air at him.

"*Hank!*" Cal saw that Wilma Hanson had burst in through the hall door. She dove between Hank and the respirator. It caught her hard, driving her back into Hank, ramming them against the wall, both of them splaying unmoving on the floor.

And now Cal was aware of another, oppressive presence

tearing into existence in the room, engulfing the air and his mind, a conquering, clamorous disputation of voices.

Fred Wishart cried out, a wail of despair, hands thrashing in denial, refusal, but his concentration had been broken. Shining chaos, darkness that blazed like fire, seized him, collapsing him and capturing him and spinning him away into a whirlpool of nothingness and everything. And in the same unreal, horrific instant Cal saw Bob collapse like a marionette with its strings cut.

"Cal!" Tina tried to cling to him.

He reached frantically for her, but he was hurled back, stunned, into the wall. He saw her swept away, whirling like a glowing milkweed pod, twisting in the air, helpless in the clutch of remorseless power. He thought he screamed her name, later his voice was hoarse from shouting, but he had no recollection of any sound coming out. His whole soul screamed NO! NO! NO! and he reached for her in a nightmare.

And in a nightmare she was gone.

TWENTY-NINE

Lantern light wavered over the broken ceiling, show-ing where plaster and lathe had been blown upward, darkness gaping overhead.

Tina, thought Cal. *Oh, Tina.*

He closed his eyes.

"He's breathing," said Doc.

Of course I'm breathing. It was only then he became aware that his head was being supported, something cold pressed to the back of his neck.

"Can you hear us?" came Doc's voice, and Cal realized the physician wasn't speaking to him.

He cracked open his eyes. A dim dawnlight showed through the shattered windows and ceiling, though most of the light came from the lantern.

"He's coming around." It was Colleen's voice. It was she cradling him.

Cal turned his head slightly, saw Doc crouched by the far window, just turning toward him. Before him lay Hank's crumpled form, Wilma bent on Hank's far side, grasping his hand. To Goldie, who stood behind him, Doc said, "Bring the lantern."

Doc limped to Cal and lowered himself stiffly, scrutinizing Cal's eyes. Then he nodded toward Hank. "He's going to be all right, thanks to her." He smiled wearily. "A broken shoulder in trade for a life." Cal squinted against the glare of the lantern in Goldie's hand, saw Hank stir. Then he became aware of another figure emerging from shadows.

It was Bob Wishart.

Goldie stepped aside as Bob neared. And in a voice surprisingly strong, with no hint of disorientation or weakness, Bob said, "I'm so very sorry."

Cal's focus shifted again to the blown-out ceiling, to the memory of Tina being ripped screaming away.

"She's alive; I can feel it," Bob said. "And my brother, too." His voice turned angry. "But I can't tell where."

Cal struggled to sit up, gasped as a fist of pain struck his ribs. Doc said, "No quick movements till those are taped."

Bob looked to the floor. "Maybe that thing changed him. Or maybe he was someone I never knew." His eyes were glistening. "His hold on the town is broken. But he—it—he was willing to kill people. A piece of that poison is in me . . . keeping me alive."

Cal closed his eyes. Fred Wishart, willing to sacrifice anyone, anything to save the one he loved. And Cal had seen an identical capacity in himself.

Colleen brushed the hair from Cal's face, saw the anguish there. "We'll find her."

Unwilling, unable, to share his thoughts, Cal looked away toward the shards of glass that glinted, irreparable, across the floor.

❧

"Mr. Shango." General Christiansen rose from behind the enormous cypresswood desk in the Health Building office as Shango was shown into the room. He held out his hand; his khaki uniform was neat, but like everyone else in Washington he smelled, water being at a premium now. Cisterns stood in every courtyard, on every roof, to catch the rain;

half the trees on the Mall had already been cut, to boil it and to cook. Shango wondered what the city would do when winter came—if there would be a city, then. The screened and iron-barred windows were thrown wide, and the sounds of horses, and the jangle and creak of the few National guardsmen passing back and forth in the courtyard, sounded loud against the deathly silence.

"I apologize most sincerely that you had to wait so long," the general said as Shango shook his hand. "Since the government moved up to Camp David, there's only been a skeleton force here in town. I was in Arlington, getting records into storage. We have to work with the daylight, as I'm sure you know."

The mouth moved but the pale eyes studied him, reading his face. All the other functionaries who'd handed Shango along that day had just looked tired, incurious. Too beaten-down to care about anything except getting a loose end tied up and maybe too hungry, too.

Christiansen was wary.

Shango wondered why.

"Everyone's up at Camp David now?" he asked.

The general nodded. "Once cholera broke out, we didn't really have any choice. We did what we could, but without med support—without sewage treatment or even any viable means of securing adequate drinking water—there wasn't much we could do. Shortly after martial law was declared, all key government personnel were evacuated."

Leaving the rest to die, thought Shango. If not of cholera, of those other sewer-borne plagues like typhoid, or of the yellow fever that almost certainly hummed on the mosquito-ridden air the moment the sun went down. Walking through the silent, stinking streets, past block after block of empty apartment buildings, of cars that had even yet not been hauled away, Shango had seen the rats coming and going on steps and through the half-open doors and windows with fat, saucy impunity. He knew why they looked so well-fed. One of the secretaries who'd showed him into or out of an office earlier in the day had mentioned that in many places the living had simply abandoned the dead where they lay. Cleanup crews were still being drafted but the work was slow. There were whole neighborhoods untouched after the cholera had swept through.

They're still dyin' out there, more every day, she had told him, handing him a small cup of flat-tasting water. *Hospitals and clinics are packed, and you can't get in most of 'em. You be careful what you drink.*

"Is Mr. McKay all right?"

Christiansen glanced down and to the side, then back up to meet Shango's eyes. "He's fine."

He's dead, thought Shango, understanding that what Herman Goldman had told him in the woods of Virginia was true. When first he'd heard that psych 101 lecture about the way a liar's eyes move when he or she fishes for a lie, he had thought it bullshit. But years of watching men from behind McKay's shoulder or while on duty outside an ambassador's suite had confirmed it. Practiced liars, no. Guys in other branches of the service, who ran cover for a living, no. The slightly crazy who half-believe their own tales, no. But the general run of the untruthful look aside and down, as if seeking a concealed crib-sheet.

"He asked me to go up to Philadelphia, to bring a man named Goldman down here, a professor of some kind in particle physics," Shango lied, concentrating on keeping his own eyes steadily on the general's. "I couldn't find him; nobody'd seen him after the rioting the first night."

Christiansen nodded, "He told us you'd gone to Philly, but not why. Goldman? A professor?"

"He called him that," Shango responded evenly, "but beyond that he didn't say, not even if he lived there or was just coming in. Is Ms. Diaz still in town? Or Al Guthrie?" He named two of McKay's inner circle and wasn't surprised at all when Christiansen shook his head.

"Guthrie was one of the first victims of the cholera," he

said. "I think Nina Diaz is at Camp David; I know she was in the group that went up there."

My black ass. Shango made his brow pucker a little with false consideration as he nodded. Through the windows the stink of the city was choking. He wondered how any were still able to live there, what they were living on, how they existed once the food ran low. FEMA, and the National Guard, and all the other emergency relief organizations, were set up to quickly transfer necessaries from one area to another, not to deal with everything coming to a halt at once. Shango wondered how the coup had been undertaken, and who had ultimately come out on top. *He has enemies*, Czernas had said: the military who had considered him unwise, the corporations who had regarded him as a threat to their network of favors and support. McKay had known that, to cover up the Source, he was being betrayed at the highest level.

"See Captain Nye about putting you up in the barracks for the night." Christiansen glanced at the hot gold light slanting through the window. "We'll arrange transport for you up to Camp David in the morning. I wouldn't advise you going very far outside the compound here," he added, as Shango thanked him and turned to leave. "We've been able to keep order in the city after a fashion during the day, but between the gangs and the trogs coming up out of the Metro at night, outside is not someplace you want to be once it gets dark."

"Thank you, sir," said Shango.

A service for the grunter men and Arleta Wishart was held late that afternoon. They'd all come, everyone in Boone's Gap well enough to walk, a show of solidarity and mutual support.

Cal stood at the back of the Union Hall and wondered distantly if indeed there would be peace for those interred.

Now what? What now?

He had lost his sister, been defeated by Fred Wishart, an offshoot, a *lesser* power of the whole. And all he'd learned from the experience was that he had feet of clay. Colleen, Doc and Goldie were ready to follow him, but how could he pretend he had the ability to lead?

A touch on his arm. Colleen smiled. "Got the pedicab rigged for Doc. Damn optimist says we can leave come morning."

Cal felt himself curl inward. With a cool nod, he turned back to the proceedings.

Beside him, Colleen closed her hands tightly, one over the other, and fought not to walk away, as she had done when Rory had shut her out. Fought not to react with anger, to the hurt of knowing there was nothing she could do.

Instead, she simply stroked his back and moved off.

Cal listened to the men and women at the podium, to their remembrances of the good times before their loved ones had lost themselves. Then, able to stand it no longer, he withdrew to the outer room.

Tables laden with food stood waiting. Bob Wishart peered out the front window, a figure of solitude and sadness. He motioned Cal over to him.

"I've been trying to think what I've done wrong, where I failed, to have drawn down all these bad things." Bob smiled grimly. "What is it about self-blame that's such a comfort?"

Cal looked through the window, toward the hills, no longer mist-quilted, where dusk held sway.

"You know, I said he left a part of himself in me, to keep me going?" Bob continued. "Well, I've got power. I mean, just a little, for starters. But maybe I'll be able to protect this town a tad, make up for. . . ."

He winced and lapsed into silence, contemplating the fading day. Cal thought of Lola Johnson, who could shield her town, safeguard its bounty, and he prayed that Bob Wishart might be a safe harbor for his neighbors, where his brother had brought only the storm.

"There's something I have to tell you," Bob added. "The

reason I know Fred's alive is, when he left a part of himself, he took a part of me. I can feel myself there with him."

Bob Wishart gripped the sill, and his voice hardened. "They made a mistake, taking him back. He didn't want to go . . . and he ain't alone." He turned to Cal. "They just may have swallowed a virus."

Cal studied him and it came like a warming sun that the war had not ended. It had just begun.

He left Bob Wishart and returned to the service. A bit off to the side, in the shadows, Hank sat beside Wilma. They weren't speaking or even looking at each other but were sitting close, in the way of old friends reunited. Behind them stood Colleen, Doc and Goldie.

Cal moved up to them, placed his hand on Colleen's shoulder. It was a warm touch, and she warmed to it.

Around him, he saw the faces in the glow of candles and torches: men who'd worked the mines all their lives, women who until a few weeks ago had sewed for minimum wage in little factories to support their families. Parents whose children had awakened from their cold silent sleep, weak and hungry but well. Women whose miner husbands were being buried as grunters that day.

People Ely Stern would have dismissed with a single cutting phrase. A way of life that Cal had fled, wanting something more for himself, for Tina.

And there they still were, when New York was bleeding and rotting away. In a town whose smallness and simplicity gave it an advantage when nothing worked anymore but friendship and the bonds between person and person.

Maybe better, maybe worse, in the days to come. But as Goldie had said, *Thems on bottom will be on top now.*

THIRTY

Between the dog and the wolf, Shango's Cajun friends had called this twilight time. Circling through the dove-colored twilight of the lower end of the Mall, Shango looked back toward the Capitol Building, the stout wall of sandbags and cinderblocks and barbed wire that surrounded the National Guard complex, and saw a blue-white glow of light moving along that new-made rampart.

So the dogs of war, like the wolves down in Albermarle County, were enlisting those with "talents."

Plywood and sheet metal had been wired over the palisade around the White House, but most of the plywood was gone. There were no guards. No one moved around the knee-deep grass of the untended lawns. Someone had tried to be careful about bolting security doors and grilles over the doors and windows of the Executive Mansion itself, but the place had been broken into and looted.

Did anyone really think the Army would leave food and water there? wondered Shango, as he passed it in the blue dusk. Was this just a quest for combustibles? Or the rage and revenge at a system that had promised to protect the weak and the poor, at least a little bit?

And had then, as such systems do, simply decided to protect itself instead. To protect itself, and pretend that certain of its own members weren't responsible for the horror of what the world had become. He'd seen enough of that in the service. At the time he'd just accepted that, as in the Army, it was how things worked.

He didn't go in. Light was fading; it was dark enough that sentries on the higher ground near the Capitol wouldn't be able to see him if they looked down the Mall, but not too dark for him to see what he was doing, and he didn't want to kindle a light. He'd picked up a shovel on his way at a looted and deserted hardware store in Georgetown and concealed it in the Old Executive Building. It now hung in the straps of his backpack, while he carried the hammer in his hand.

Go to a fountain, Goldie had said. *Near the roses.*

If someone had actually killed the President, would they really have been so dumb as to bury him in the Rose Garden?

Shango had no doubt that McKay was dead. *Had* he attempted to push through some program of food distribution that impinged on the Army's stockpiles? One of those sadfaced, exhausted secretaries had told him, "All sorts of people workin' for the Army these days"; people who still held power, people who'd possessed stockpiles of food or domestic animals, people who knew people in the government, who owed or were owed favors. People with something to trade. People the military wanted, for one reason or another, to keep on its side.

If you were good buddies with senators or generals, it probably wasn't difficult to be enrolled as a "special deputy" or "consultant" in order to cadge a spot at Camp David—or in the government bunkers under the mountains in western Maryland where the center of things now undoubtedly was—and a ration book.

But the members of the bureaucracy who were still struggling to govern, still trying to sort out the mess—certainly the bulk of the enlisted men, the Reservists, the National

Guard—would have remained loyal to McKay. And McKay, for all the compromises he'd made on his way to the Presidency, had lines that he wouldn't cross.

And one of those lines had been the one that divided the good-old-boy Us from the scared and hungry and militarily worthless Them.

Between the epidemic and the evacuation, it wouldn't have been difficult to put the man himself away but keep his name. Aides and press secretaries and members of the Secret Service could be dealt with, particularly if people were dying on all sides anyway. No need to make a fuss about it: X or Y just hadn't made it onto the convoy of wagons heading for Maryland, they'll be along later.

Only later never came.

It was fairly easy to find the grave. It was in a rose bed about thirty feet from the fountain, just behind a bench. Maybe the same bench where McKay and Bilmer had sat, when McKay had asked her to go look for the Source. Shango almost laughed as he started to dig in the still-soft earth—they hadn't even replaced the uprooted rose bushes, just dumped them in a crude pile on top. Some of the blossoms, brown and withered, still had a little color in their hearts. After all that, all that had survived was a list of names of people who were at the Source, people you couldn't get to anyway.

Mosquitoes whined in a cloud around the nearly empty basin, sang in Shango's ears as his shovel bit the soil. The whole lower two-thirds of the Mall, from the Air and Space Museum to the river, was marshy with standing water and humming with insects, as Washington returned to the stagnant wetland it had been before the introduction of drainage pumps and reflecting pools. Sometimes a soldier's voice carried from the redoubts of the central command post or footfalls passed along Pennsylvania Avenue—armed bands in quest of forage or fuel—but the stillness and hush were like a leaden shroud. The shovel blade made a harsh hissing crunch in the dirt.

It wasn't quite dark when Shango found the body. He scraped and scooped at the dirt, knelt in the shallow depression—it wasn't more than a yard deep—and cracked his little fireplace striker patiently over a tuft of dry lint until a spark took. The yellow glow expanded to show his dirt-clotted fawn-and-black fur, a black leather collar.

It was Jimmy, the big German shepherd whom the newspapers had delighted to call the First Dog.

He had been clubbed to death.

With him in the grave, like isolate fragments of bone, were a pair of broken, owlish glasses—a little blood and hair still adhering to a bent-in temple piece—and a woman's pink-and-white Nike, stained black with blood. Nothing more. They were the kind of thing you'd find on the scene of a killing during clean-up, after the bodies had been taken away, particularly if the killings had taken place at night.

Shango blew out his little scrap of kindling and carefully refilled the grave.

No mistaking the dog's crushed skull, the broken ribs and back. Jimmy had been thin with scant rations, but quite clearly nobody had thought it a good idea to blow the cover story by cooking him.

He had died trying to defend McKay and Jan.

As Shango himself had promised he would do.

He sat for a long time on the grave of his canine brother, while the last traces of the time of the dog faded into the time of the wolf.

And what now? he thought, his mind relaxed and clear—aware of his anger, like an acid-bath of rage, but not really feeling it, any more than a fish feels wet. Stars made their appearance overhead, hundreds of them, thousands, beautiful with a beauty that had not been seen in this place since men had first learned to burn coal gas to chase away the night. The blue flicker of witchlight reappeared along the Capitol rampart, a cold phosphor glow, and Shango wondered how many people had what his granny had simply called *Power*.

How many people—like the fear-caster in Albermarle

County, and the firestarter in Spotsylvania and crazy Herman Goldman—who would be willing to use that power, for good or for what they conceived to be good, or at least to be good for them? Of course Christiansen, and the men behind him, would be gathering them into their service as Cadiz had gathered Brattle.

They'd be up in Maryland, too.

Shango found that the idea of going along with Christiansen, riding with the convoy to the government's new headquarters, strongly appealed to him. Finding the men who'd tossed Jan McKay's glasses and shoe so casually into the nearest hole in the ground.

Finding the men who'd ordered McKay's death.

Find them and what?

Shango's mission was over. He had done what McKay had asked of him, found what he needed to find, and it was empty, useless. A weapon that broke in his hand.

And it dawned on him that he was thinking about vengeance—even at the cost of his own life—not because of his anger, but because it was another job. And if he didn't get another job, another task to absorb him, as he'd let McKay's life and safety absorb him, as he'd let being the best in the service absorb him . . .

He'd have to get a life.

A life with people in it. People like Czernas and Griffin and the lady in the green sweatsuit. People who ran around and did what they wanted and went crazy and talked to God and couldn't get their acts together and dissipated their energies when they should have been helping their children get out of the projects.

Messy, chaotic people. People whose problems and demands frightened him because there was nothing he could do about them. Because if he made a choice, and that choice turned out to be wrong, there'd be more chaos and anger and hurt.

He felt as if he'd put his hand to his side and brought it away bloody from some ancient, seeping wound. A wound whose pain he'd forgotten because he'd lived with it daily, hourly, pretending there wasn't pain as he'd pretended there wasn't anger.

He was afraid to choose, he understood then. And he was afraid to live with choice.

It was easier to be the best, to be a weapon in someone else's hand.

He remembered the fear-caster, staring at him with cold eyes like ball bearings, filling him with terror that only his anger could quell. He had run toward the fear, howling his rage . . . and the fear had been defeated.

Shango drew in his breath and let it out. He felt dizzy and disoriented, as he had after anger had burst through both fear and the self-imposed bonds of the job; shaky, as he'd heard men were, after they've been imprisoned for years, at the sight of wall-less places and sky.

He thought, *I could get another job.* There were plenty of them around. A job such as Griffin had chosen, to find the weak point of the Source. A job like the ones McKay had done, struggling to keep help and life flowing to those that needed them, until death overtook him.

Shango shook his head. Most times, he'd learned that the windmill was bigger and tougher than the knight.

And the windmill didn't care.

The stars moved, leaving the question: What now?

South to New Orleans? The town would be underwater by now, of course, with the pumping stations dead. The local military authorities would be in charge. Mother, brother, sisters would be somewhere nearby, surviving, he was sure, probably in the middle of a giant gaggle of cousins and neighbors and church ladies, hanging together as they always hung together.

His family. His people. *You have family in town?* Czernas had asked, and he wondered, for the first time, what message Czernas had left for his own family, and whether they had ever gotten it. Shango parked his own family like baggage, years ago. Maybe it was time to go back.

West to the Source? It had been a week since he'd spoken to Griffin and his friends, since he'd sent them on toward Boone's Gap. Whatever that young man and those around him were going to try to do when they found the Source— or the fragment of it in the South—it had not altered the horrible change wrought in the world. Had they been obliterated? he wondered. Or had they only failed?

McKay had known the truth, even in that first moment. The lights were not going to come back on. And he, Larry Shango, might be the only person now who had the clue that might lead to its location.

For what that clue was worth. Evidently it hadn't gotten Griffin anything.

But there was another thing that only he knew: that McKay was dead. And almost certainly, with McKay's death, any concern for retrieving that little boy from the wilds of Maine had vanished.

Did his road lie north, then? To make sure, at least, that the child lived, in this shaky and increasingly perilous world? To do what he could to help him, if necessary, as he had been unable to help McKay and Jan?

The sense of calm he felt in his heart told him that his choice—the first real choice he'd made in a long time— was the right one for him, for now; it also told him, a little to his surprise, what a right choice felt like. *Maybe it's not so hard.*

He sat for a long while in thought, between dog and wolf, turning his fragment of paper, his memories and his choices, over in his mind: Who he was, and what he was, and what he might or could be. At last, he got to his feet and walked silently along the empty street, north past Lafayette Square and on up New York Avenue by starlight.

By dawn, he was far away.

Darkness clung to the mountains.

Again, Cal watched Tina being wrenched away from

him, vanishing into that blinding whirlwind that was neither light nor darkness, woke up crying her name. Suddenly, he wasn't certain if it was his mother's face he'd seen, or Tina's, or his own.

I'll find her, he thought, and knew it was true.

But he shivered a little at the thought of what it might be that he found.

Giving up on sleep, he rose and dressed. He found Hank sitting on Wilma's porch, where Cal had heard them talking quietly far into the night.

He drew up at the sight of cans of tuna, loaves of bread, bags of rice and assorted sundries that had been piled high.

Hank smiled. "Happy trails."

"We can't take this," Cal said, knowing Boone's Gap would need every bit.

"It's not charity; it's an investment. Where you're goin' . . . well, everyone here kinda wants to be in on the fight."

Without apparent effort, Hank lifted the entire pedicab onto the porch, and together they began to load.

"Some people say we're given what we deserve," Hank said, tying down a ration of sweet corn. "Maybe it's just what we need."

And what did Cal need, for the road ahead, for the Big Kahuna? Strength? Strength to endure whatever might come in the hard days, to endure loss and pain and not falter.

Lights moved in the house behind them, and Cal heard voices. Wilma's and Doc's. Goldie. Colleen making some disparaging comment about greedy overfed butter-stealing cats.

The question of his strength faded into nothing. Cal knew he wasn't strong enough, he didn't have to be.

He had the strength of others.

Wilma, Hank and Bob walked them to the edge of town. Cal realized that Boone's Gap was in fact exactly that: a pass through the mountains. Dawn was paling the sky, and Hank blinked and flinched.

"Here," Goldie said and handed the grunter a pair of raffish blue sunglasses.

Sunlight broke over the crests of the mountains, golden on the tips of the trees, dew transforming the grass to a silver ocean. Riding the thermals, a single hawk cried its song of challenge. Cal and his party started down the road, into the blue shadows that still lay to the west.

If you enjoyed reading
MAGIC TIME, then read the following selection from
MAGIC TIME: ANGELFIRE,
by Marc Scott Zicree and Maya Kaathryn Bohnhoff
available soon in hardcover from Eos.

GOLDIE

I have that dream every night. The day the wheels came off the world. Bye-bye physics. Natural laws, who needs 'em?

And every morning I wake, realizing it's all real.

Okay, no buildings literally melted, nor did the sidewalks and streets actually roll like ocean waves. But the whole world experienced it, this moment of cosmic mayhem, this thing most of us refer to simply as the Change. At least, we think it did. Nothing we've seen in the intervening weeks has suggested otherwise.

I have other dreams too, also terrifying, also rooted in so-called reality. One of them is about a girl named Tina Griffin. Like our world, she changed—or began to change—in that Moment of upheaval. So did a lot of other people. But Tina's in my nightmares because I know her. She is the reason we left New York, the reason we head inexorably west—because her brother Cal has the same nightmare, and because that's where the Megillah has taken her.

The Megillah is my pet name for what all evidence points to as the cause of the Change. No one else calls it that. They have their own pet names for it: Armageddon, Doomsday, Kali Yuga, the Day of Judgment, the Real Thing.

Ek velt, grandmother would've said: *the end of the world.*

Apparently in elite government circles, it was known simply as The Source. A science project of sorts. Funny, the words "science project" usually bring to mind papier-mâché volcanoes and ant farms, not something that has the power to rip the world apart and put it back together all wrong.

But it appears that the Megillah has that power.

Tina Griffin, all of twelve years old, was one of the things it reassembled. And after it warped her body, clothed her in light, and granted her the power of levitation, it sorted her from among its over various types of "makeovers" and simply took her. And others like her. Where or why, we have no idea. Sort of a perverted take on the Evangelical Christian Rapture.

Before she was wrenched, screaming, out of her brother's arms in the tiny back bedroom of a rundown house in Boone's Gap, VA, the changeling Tina spoke of *Something* in the West—a power, an entity, an Enigma. Something that came into the world with a roar and that now grows in it like a malevolent cancer.

And so, a Quest. Or a monumental game of hide and seek. We seek the Enigma and it . . . . well, it doesn't so much hide as it evades. It's that thing you're certain is behind you in the dark. But a swift about-face only nets you empty air and a dark slither out the corner of one eye.

And whispers.

Since that moment in Manhattan when buildings did not melt and sidewalks did not ripple, I've heard its whispers. Which makes (lucky) me the only one with half a clue about what part of the West the Megillah inhabits. And that's about all I have—half a clue. I listen for it; I hear its Voice and we go. Tag, I'm it. Marco Polo. Games. Rough, deadly games.

Since leaving Boone's Gap, our quest has taken us through varied terrain. Quiet pastoral countryside where cows and sheep still graze and watch our passing with little interest. Places where it seemed the earth had erupted in boils, or a giant hand had reached down, dug in, and tried to wrench the bedrock out through the grass and trees and soil. We avoid cities. Cities are places of unimaginable darkness and violence. I suppose they always were, but it's a different kind of violence now, at once more focussed and more mindless, soul-deep and brutal.

There's violence of a sort in the country, too. And its effects have been devastating. We've seen ghost towns and ghost suburbs and ghost farms. But nothing like what we saw as Manhattan unraveled like a cheap sweater.

We see other folks ever-so-often. And ever-so-often we see not-folks. Ex-people who, like Tina, had their DNA radically rearranged. "Tweaks," Colleen calls them. I prefer "twists"—it's a gentler word. Although there's nothing gentle about what the Change has done to them. People tend to avoid them, and they tend to avoid people. Something I understand, completely.

Most often, we don't see them, but merely *feel* them. Since some of them are rather unpleasant, it pays to be vigilant. You develop a sort of ESP about these things. The sense of being watched creeps over your skin and through your brain like a trickle of freezing water. When this happens, Cal's hand goes to his sword, Colleen's goes to her machete, Doc's makes the sign of the cross. Mine does nothing. At the moment, I carry neither weapons nor Gods.

We're traveling on pot-holed tarmac today as we head for the border between West Virginia and Ohio. Cal and Doc are mounted on fine steeds (Sooner and Koshka by name), Colleen drives our spiffy homebuilt wagon, while I ride shotgun. I mean that figuratively, of course. Since the Change, no one I know has yet figured out how to make a shotgun work. This is one of those good news/bad news things.

Our "wagon" is a pickup truck from which the transmission has been removed and the engine compartment gutted back to the firewall. It still has its vinyl-covered seats, but no roof, no widows, no windshield, and sawed-off doors. You can crawl from the front seat right over into the bed. It was, as they say, a find. Only cost us our bicycles and a couple of days work in the Bed 'n' Breakfast from hell.

Water barrels are ranked outboard down both sides of the truck bed, which has an awning that extends from the tail gate all the way out over the remains of the cab. We roll it down in the event of inclement weather. The whole thing looks a lot like those old World War Two troop transports; only it's a brilliant shade of Macintosh yellow. For the first time in many days, the awning is rolled all the way up to the topmost strut of the support framework.

I glance at the sky and realize that's likely to change. It's a chill, cloudy afternoon—unseasonably cold. The sky presses down on the land like a heavy, gray sponge full of rain. Somewhere, there are calendars that say it's autumn, but it feels like half-past winter, and the trees are turning rapidly, as if hurrying to catch up.

Along the road ahead, I see a strip of maples with prematurely nude branches. It's only when we get practically on top of them that I realize the leaves are merely transparent. They look like those blown glass things that once glittered in Manhattan shop windows. And as the moist breeze stirs them, I hear them, too—a fine shimmer of sound that's almost music.

Fascinating. The rocking of the wagon no longer seems so soporific. I swing out over the chopped down door and hit the ground running.

A sharp snarl snatches at me from behind. "Goldman! What the hell do you think you're doing?"

Replying to Colleen's question while galloping into the forest would waste breath, so I don't bother. I make the trees and gingerly reach up to touch the crystalline leaves. They're beautiful, but hard and cold, with sharp, biting edges. A breeze moves through the branches and stirs them to song. I imagine an entire melody is cradled in those branches, but then I imagine a lot of things.

I'm enchanted. I take off my cowboy hat and carefully dislodge several of the leaves into the crown. They fall with a sweet tinkle of sound.

"What is it?" Cal Griffin peers down at me from his horse, hazel eyes darting from me into the deeper woods. His hand is on the hilt of his sword.

I hold up one of the leaves. Steely sunlight sparks cold fire in the tracery of veins. "We may have to rename a couple of seasons," I say. "How about Spring, Summer, Shard, and Bleak?"

Cal leans down from the horse and takes the leaf from my fingers. "Ouch. You're not kidding. I'd hate to be standing under a tree when these things fall. *If* they fall." He lays the leaf carefully on the palm of my hand. "Better get back in the wagon. Colleen might slow down or even stop for you if you apologize for scaring her like that."

I carefully tuck the leaves into the pocket of my buckskin jacket and set the cowboy hat back in its rightful place. As always, my hair—too thick, too curly, and too long—puts up an admirable fight, but I cram the hat down until it submits peacefully.

"Scare Colleen," I repeat. "Isn't that an oxymoron?"

He smiles fleetingly and jerks a thumb toward the wagon, which has come to a stop down the road with Doc hovering near the tailgate. "Get."

"Maybe it's just a paradox," I say, moving away from the trees. "Or an anomaly, or a mere flight of fancy."

Cal clicks Sooner into a lope and leaves me to chug my way back to the wagon.

Colleen stays stopped to let me climb in. Then she gives me a chill glance, laces the reins through her fingers like she's done it every day of her life, and clucks the team into motion. In this nippy weather, they are rarin' to go, as they say in the Wild West. They toss their heads, paw the ground, and pull at their bits. Colleen manages them effortlessly.

"You're sure good at that horsy stuff," I tell her, chipping at the brittle silence. "I guess it's because you're a native Cornhusker, and all, huh?"

She gives me a cool green glance. "You think?"

I shrug. "Okay, I don't know why you're good at it. You just are. You've been around horses a lot, I'd guess."

She repeats the glance, then puts her eyes back on the crusty tarmac ahead. One callused hand smoothes back her hair, which is almost as spiky as her annoyance. Scissors still work, but Colleen is careless of such niceties. I think she does her hair with her pet machete.

"Yeah. I got a horse when I was thirteen. Before Dad

died. You never forget the feeling of the reins in your hands, the ripple of muscle between your knees, the smooth glide of a horse at a full gallop. To this day, whenever I get stressed out or pissed off . . ." A pointed glance. ". . . I walk myself through bridling and saddling a horse just to chill. Well . . . and to prove to myself I remember how to do it."

Her eyes go back to the road then, and she closes up tight as a clam. Conservation of intimacies, I guess. I play with my glass leaves, trying to shake music out of them.

After about five minutes of this, Colleen speaks again. "You know what, Goldman? That's damned annoying."

I wrap the leaves in a handkerchief that's made its way into my breast pocket and put them away. "You know what, Ms. Brooks? No one's called me Goldman since my sophomore baseball coach. Well . . . and my probation officer."

"Your what?"

Loose lips, the curse of an unquiet mind. "Oh, look," I say. "A road sign."

There is, indeed, a road sign. It proclaims that there is a town not far ahead. Grave Creek. Nice, ominous little name for a town.

"Eight miles," says Cal, drawing his horse up close to the wagon. "If we hustle we might make it before the sun goes down."

On a clear day, we'd have some wiggle room, but the oppressive cloud cover puts us uncomfortably close to twilight. Since the Change, out after dark is not something you want to be. If the world is peculiar when the Sun is up (and it is plenty peculiar), it is insanely scary when the Sun goes down. Colleen nods and clucks her team into a brisk trot.

Barely half an hour later, we hear a shout from Cal, who's taken the vanguard. He lopes back to us through the gloamin', waving an arm. Doc draws up along our right flank to see what all the hoo-ha is about. Pulling up, Cal points southwest.

The clouds have lifted at the horizon and a baleful red sun glares at us from beneath the edge. Against the bleed of crimson, a water tower stands in sharp silhouette. Firelight flickers atop the squashed sphere.

"Civilization ho," I say.

"A lookout?" asks Doc, his eyes on the tower.

"Or a beacon," Cal says. "Maybe it's a friendly hello to wayward travelers."

Wishful thinking. "You know, there were these pirates up Newfoundland way that used to set signal fires on the cliffs to beckon to merchant ships. After the ships piled up on the rocks, the pirates would go out in little boas and collect the booty. Survivors were offered a choice: join the jolly pirate band or die."

"Judas Priest, Goldman!" says Colleen. "Do you have to be such a friggin' fountain of helpful information?"

Doc Lysenko hides a smile in the twilight over his shoulder. "Ah, a child's daydream. Didn't you ever want to be a pirate, Colleen?"

Colleen's face goes through the most amazing set of expressions: Doc has surprised a smile, but she aborts it and stretches it into a grimace, then inverts it into a scowl, then smoothes it into a look of prim disapproval. "What I want," she says finally, "is to be somewhere other than out in the middle of nowhere when night falls."

"Then we'd better get a move on." Cal turns his horse and leads on toward the looming silhouette of the tower.

Unaccountably I shiver.

Our road descends into a shallow, triangular valley where the woods stand back from the edge of the grassland like spectators at the scene of an accident. The bottom of the triangle is a mile or two distant, and a second road runs north to south along it, merging with the one we're on. As we make the descent, my eyes are on the place where the town should be. I can just make out more flickers of light sprinkled about the base of the water tower. I do hope they're not pirates.

"We have company," murmurs Doc from our starboard bow. He's staring across the valley to the north-south road.

"Where?" asks Colleen, tensing.

"There." Doc's gesture is almost lost in the twilight.

A small group of people moves along the converging road toward Grave Creek, clearly visible against the dark woodland that hugs the road. They seem to be struggling with some sort of litter. Three of the people are very small. Children. Or munchkins, maybe. These days it could be either.

"I think they may have injured," Doc says. "They could likely use our help."

"Hold on, Doc," Colleen warns him. "Let Cal scope it out first, okay?"

Cal is already doing that, I realize, moving down into the valley at a leisurely, non-threatening trot.

"I'll light the lanterns," I say, and do, suspending them from hooks—one on each side of the driver's box. Kerosene, no less. I just *love* modern conveniences.

Cal's nearing the floor of the vale when yet another group of folks comes out of the woods to our north. This new bunch heads down across the meadow on a course that roughly parallels the north-south road. There is a flicker of fire as someone in the road troupe lights a torch. There is no answering flicker of light from the folks in the meadow. They just keep pressing through the tall, dry grasses.

The newcomers, I realize, are moving very smartly. Maybe this is because they aren't hauling someone on a litter, or maybe because they're in a bigger hurry. The new folks overtake the first party and swing wide as if to pass them by. Then they veer sharply onto an intercept course, and suddenly it's as if I'm looking at them in a funhouse mirror. They become indistinct, fluid around the edges, a school of shadows flowing across the landscape as if pulled by currents.

By the prickling of my thumbs, something wicked this way comes. Hair rises up on the back of my neck and I wish I could borrow Colleen's machete—or Doc's faith.

There is a shout up ahead as Cal digs his heels into Sooner's flanks and tears off across the meadow.

"Oh, *shit!*" Colleen voices my sentiments exactly before she brings the reins down hard on gleaming horsehide.

The horses plunge into sudden and frantic motion—hot-blooded engines snorting steam into the twilight. The wagon jerks and my cowboy hat goes flying. Liberated hair tumbles into my eyes, blinding me. I hear nothing but the agonized squeaking of the truck's springs and the labored effort of the team. The truck is heavy, awkward, and probably a bitch to pull, but Colleen steers them off the road entirely and sends us bumping straight across the meadow. We're on a path that will take us directly into collision with the others . . . if our wheels don't fall off first.

Ahead of us, where the two roads meet, the first band of travelers has gathered to make a stand. There are seven of them. Three are children; two are women—one extremely pregnant. One of the two is stretched out on the litter, brandishing a torch. The others have torches too, and baseball bats, and a wildly barking dog. Slim defense against what they face. Advancing on them are strange, dark beings that are less men than shadows of men—vaporous, nebulous, writhing.

Cal rides Sooner into the breach between the two groups. His sword is still in its sheath, but he's aiming a loaded sling. Slowing Sooner only a little, he looses a scatter of golf-ball sized rocks into the shadow troop.

Surprise! The rocks connect. The sound that results is not one I ever want to hear again. It is as if the air itself has cried out—a siren of rage that drowns out the baying of the dog and the thunder of our charging horses.

The shadows seem to melt back into the tall grass. But only for a moment. Then they're back. I try to count them and fail. The shadows uncoil and ooze forward, pressing Cal and his horse back toward the crossroads and the frightened refugees.

Colleen shoves the reins into my hands. "Take the team!" she yells, then rolls off the back of the seat into the truck bed, leaving me with a handful of fat leather noodles.